Pre
Pr

REBECCA WINTERS
RAYE MORGAN
BRENDA HARLEN

MILLS & BOON

Published in Great Britain 2013
by Mills & Boon, an imprint of Harlequin (UK) Limited,
Eton House, 18-24 Paradise Road, Richmond, Surrey TW9 1SR

The Duke's Baby, The Boss's Pregnancy Proposal and *The Marriage Solution* were first published in Great Britain by Harlequin (UK) Limited.

ISBN: 978 0 263 91036 0
ebook ISBN: 978 1 472 01616 4

05-1013

Harlequin (UK) policy is to use papers that are natural, renewable and recyclable products and made from wood grown in sustainable forests. The logging and manufacturing processes conform to the legal environmental regulations of the country of origin.

Printed and bound in Spain
by Blackprint CPI, Barcelona

THE DUKE'S BABY

BY
REBECCA WINTERS

Rebecca Winters, whose family of four children has now swelled to include five beautiful grandchildren, lives in Salt Lake City, Utah, in the land of the Rocky Mountains. With canyons and high alpine meadows full of wildflowers nearby, she never runs out of places to explore. These spaces, plus her favourite vacation spots in Europe, often end up as backgrounds for her romance novels. Writing is her passion, along with her family and church. Rebecca loves to hear from readers. If you wish to email her, please visit her website, www.cleanromances.com.

CHAPTER ONE

…LANCELOT possesses all he wants, when the queen voluntarily seeks his company and love, and when he holds her in his arms, and she holds him in hers. Their sport is so agreeable and sweet, as they kiss and fondle each other, that in truth such a marvelous joy comes over them as was never heard or known.

With an aching groan, Andrea Fallon closed the book she was reading, unable to see any more words in the fading light. It was just as well since she couldn't bear to go on reading the hauntingly beautiful story.

Maybe never again.

Though the French poet Chrétien de Troyes might have written the story of Lancelot in 1171, his description of the famous knight's love for Guinevere was as stirring now as then.

What woman wasn't envious of the queen who inspired such love in the first Knight of the Round Table?

Wouldn't any woman wish to be loved with a love so all-consuming and powerful.

Cross at herself over her preoccupation with the greatest Knight in Christendom, Andrea's thoughts returned to Richard, the husband she'd buried three months ago.

"Would you have loved me more if I'd been able to give you a child?" her heart cried.

Since the funeral she'd gone over and over their troubled marriage in her mind, wondering if her unexpected barren condition had been so painful for him, some of his feelings for her had simply turned off.

Only twenty-one to his thirty-one when they'd exchanged vows, who would have dreamed she would develop a child-bearing problem so early in their married life?

Her aunt's cousin hadn't been able to have children, but that didn't seem to have affected the love between her and her husband. They went on to adopt two children. But Richard refused to talk about adoption. He wanted a child from his own body, not someone else's.

Knowing he felt that way, Andrea hadn't pressed him about it. But from then on their relationship underwent subtle changes. He grew more distant and threw himself into his work, either unaware of Andrea's pain, or unwilling to deal with it because his own was too great.

Their lovemaking seemed to have become an afterthought for him. In the last year he'd behaved more like a friend than a lover with only an occasional coming together she'd been forced to initiate.

She'd hoped they would get past their sorrow, that it was temporary. Surely in time he would ache for a child and be willing to consider adoption.

Andrea was convinced that if they'd taken the steps to start adoption proceedings right away, the anticipation of becoming parents would have brought joy and helped the physical side of their marriage get back on track. But that time never came. Now it was too late.

Oh, Richard…

Hot tears formed rivulets down her cheeks.

Her aunt had promised her this period of mourning would pass. "One day you'll meet that special someone who will want to marry you and adopt children."

Andrea didn't believe it, not when she remembered the other things in their marriage that hadn't happened. With ten years difference between them, she suffered over the possibility that she simply hadn't measured up.

Richard's academic world had been filled with brilliant men and women. What had she been able to offer if she couldn't give him a child they both wanted?

Why had he even married her?

The second she asked the question she realized grief was causing her to lose her perspective. She'd lost her appetite weeks ago.

Thirty-seven years of age was too young for him to die. Devastated by his early passing, which cut off all hope of their making a family, Andrea got up wearily from her resting place against a tree trunk.

A good night's sleep was what she needed to restore her long enough to finish her husband's latest project on Arthurian legend. Another couple of days to capture a stag or a wild boar on film—the kind you saw woven in tapestries—and her collection of pictures would be complete. Unfortunately she would have to return to New Haven without any sightings of the damsel of the lake.

Andrea had been in Brittany close to a week. Already she'd discovered that the *Forêt de Broceliande* became an enchanted world after the sun went down. In awe of the forest's almost seven-hundred-foot high canopy, she found the place secretive and quiet except for the forest creatures ambling among birch and chestnut trees.

Any minute now she expected the characters from Camelot to steal from their hiding places in this magical setting and whisper their stories.

As Andrea put the strap of her camera case over her shoulder, she thought she heard the rustle of underbrush caused by the breeze. Or possibly it was a forest creature, but her imagination had been playing overtime for the last few hours.

A little spooked she looked around, causing her hair to swish around her face.

"Oh—" she cried out.

From behind the fir trees at the end of the pear-shaped lake, simply called *Le Lac*, a lean, solitary figure in military camouflage emerged. He almost startled her out of her skin with his raw male, twenty-first century presence.

Every inch of this modern man's rip cord strong body radiated an animal-like energy. It wouldn't surprise her if he carried a knife and a gun, but she sensed his tall body was a lethal weapon. No doubt when he slept, one eye remained open.

If he'd been tracking her, he moved with a built-in radar. Andrea shivered. His enemy wouldn't be aware of him until it was too late.

The skin stretched over his hard-boned aquiline features had been burnished to teak by an equatorial sun you didn't feel in France. In the twilight she made out burning-blue eyes. They were scrutinizing her beneath black brows and a head of short-cropped black hair.

She'd never met a more fiercely handsome man.

For an insane moment she could visualize him in shining armor as he knelt before Guinevere with the heavens shining down on him. Then he spoke in a deep, grating voice, shattering the illusion into a thousand pieces.

"You're trespassing," he said, first in French then in heavily accented English.

His underlying note of hostility caught Andrea off guard. This was no young disguised prince who'd mastered the art of chivalry. There was no "*Bonsoir,*" or "*Je m'excuse,*" or "*Je regrette,*" that he'd frightened her.

This dangerous man, probably in his mid-thirties and aggressively male, glared at her as if he had something personal against her.

Unless he'd been able to make out the title on the front of her book, she couldn't understand how he knew to speak English to her. She gripped it tighter. "Actually I have permission to be here," she explained in a low tone.

His eyes narrowed to slits before he relieved her of her camera case. The action had been too lightning quick for her to prevent it. He wound the strap around one masculine wrist with its sprinkling of dark hair, making it impossible for her to take it from him. Not that she would have tried. Instinct told her he knew moves she'd never dreamed of.

"No one has permission to be here. Whoever you are, I suggest you be on your way."

"The groundskeeper told me where I could take pictures of the wildlife."

His jaw hardened. "You can redeem your camera from the security guard at the gate in the morning. If you're lying, then I wouldn't come around here again if I were you."

He raked a brazen gaze over the mold of her face and body one more time, reminding her she was a woman, with feminine curves. But unlike other men, he seemed to find no pleasure in the fact. Indeed, quite the opposite.

"Remember you've been warned," he added before moving with stealthlike grace until he'd disappeared in the foliage.

Still trembling from the combination of his chilling tone and intimate appraisal that missed nothing, it took a minute for her to find her legs before heading back to the Château Du Lac. She shouldn't have stayed out here so long. Night was fast closing in, making it difficult to see her way through the dense undergrowth.

The groundskeeper of the château who'd provided her with a quickly drawn layout of the vast Du Lac estate, hadn't indicated he'd hired another man to patrol the area at night. In fairness to him, he probably wouldn't have imagined her staying out after sunset to take photographs.

But of course that wasn't what she'd been doing just now. There was something about reading Lancelot's story in the very forest where he'd grown up that had appealed to the fanciful side of her nature. That is until the poet's words had struck a chord, disturbing her at her deepest level where she hated to admit her marriage wasn't all it should have been.

Adrenaline from her unexpected encounter with the forbidding stranger kept her heart rate accelerated. By the time she reached the gravel driveway leading up to the front entrance of the early thirteenth century château, weakness had attacked her. She'd been forced to stop to catch her breath.

After running through the thick forest in her haste to return, the imposing three-story structure with its rounded towers came as an enchanting surprise. The lights from inside brought out the deep red of the garnets embedded in the schist rock from which it had been constructed. It was like stumbling upon a rare treasure glowing in the heart of a dark wood.

A large, well-trained staff kept the château and gardens immaculate, yet she saw no cars. If it weren't for the gleam radiating from the windows you wouldn't know anyone was about.

Tonight nothing seemed real. Maybe her head was too full of Lancelot and broken dreams. It was possible she'd only imagined her confrontation with the audacious man whose unforgettable looks had managed to jolt her body to react.

His unexpected presence had jerked her senses awake from their frozen prison where a plethora of emotions had lain dormant these past few months. Andrea didn't appreciate being forced to deal with her feelings yet. In fact she resented him for intruding on her already precarious state of mind.

Before this incident she'd been able to remain in her temporary comfort zone, carried along by the plan that had brought her back to this mystical province. Taking pictures didn't require thinking, only doing.

After letting herself inside the ornate entrance hall, she hurried up the grand staircase to her apartment on the third floor. Henri, the head of the house staff, had told her the front door would remain unlocked until 10:00 p.m. every night. Till then she could come and go as she pleased by orders of Geoffroi Malbois, the Duc Du Lac, who'd been born and raised in this château.

At present the trim, distinguished looking owner was

battling pneumonia. He'd come down with it following a nasty case of the flu, yet he'd been kind enough to insist she stay on.

Through his housekeeper Brigitte, Andrea learned he'd instructed his guest be put in the rarely used green room. The second the older woman unlocked the door, its special significance became apparent.

Against the light green background of the ceiling and walls, the life-size figures of Lancelot and Guinevere had been immortalized. A fourteenth century artist had depicted their secret trysts for each month of the year. The glorious colors were still vibrant, as if he'd just painted them.

The first night Andrea lay down on the massive round bed, she kept moving in different positions to study the two beautiful lovers. She remembered thinking no living man could match Lancelot's splendor.

But as she walked in the bedroom tonight, she carried the image of the intrusive stranger with her. It was an image she couldn't seem to get out of her head despite the epitome of manhood staring her in the face everywhere she looked.

First she would change, then go downstairs for a roll or something. The thought of a meal didn't appeal. If the Duc's condition hadn't worsened, she'd check in on him to say good-night. He'd urged her to visit him in the evenings, but she'd have done it anyway.

Andrea had never met a kinder, more accommodating person. Miserable as he felt, he exuded exceptional warmth. To an extent *that* particular quality had been missing from her marriage, but she hadn't realized it so much until she'd spent a little time in the presence of her host.

He didn't stand on ceremony and had insisted Andrea call

him Geoff. Having taken particular interest in her husband's project at Easter, he'd wanted to help her any way he could. Even though the Duc was ill right now, he'd told her to make herself at home for as long as she wanted.

From their talks she'd learned he led a busy social life and was active in civic and ecological affairs. He had a son from his first marriage who lived away. The stepdaughter from his second marriage, which had failed, lived with him when she wasn't traveling. Evidently he didn't suffer from lack of company. According to Henri there were always visitors coming and going, proof of how well he was regarded by his friends.

In return for his generosity of spirit, not to mention everything else, Andrea couldn't help but gravitate to him and was worried about his physical condition. Since her arrival at the château he'd been forced to remain in bed. The last three days his symptoms had grown worse. There'd been nurses around the clock and the doctor had come by twice.

If there was anything she could do to help, she would. After losing her husband to a blood clot in his prime, she would always take another person's illness seriously.

It felt good to get out of the clothes she'd been wearing all day, especially her jeans, which felt tight. While reading earlier, she'd undone the metal button to make herself more comfortable. Since she'd only worn them once before packing them for this trip, she decided they must have shrunk a little bit too much in the wash.

Once she'd picked out a cream colored blouse and brown wraparound skirt to wear, she grabbed fresh underwear and hurried into the modernized en-suite bathroom to shower and wash the pine needles out of her hair.

Later, on her way down to the Duc's suite on the second floor, she would find Henri and tell him what happened in the forest. He would take care of the problem and arrange for the return of her camera.

For the next few days she would confine her picture taking to the mornings in order to avoid another confrontation with the rough, unfeeling man who'd warned her off.

Lance Malbois gave his father's dog Percy a good scratch behind the ears before approaching the bed. "Papa? Are you awake?"

His father's eyelids opened, revealing dull gray eyes. This illness had drained them of their normal sparkle. As he stared at his son in disbelief, they took on life. *"Mon fils—"*

Lance's heart lurched. His father's voice was weak. Without the oxygen helping him breathe—

He fought not to show his concern in front of him. The father he loved was too young a man to be this sick. His pallor alarmed Lance.

"When did you arrive?" the older man asked with effort.

"A little while ago. You were asleep. I didn't want to disturb you, so I took a walk."

After suffering one shock that his father's flu had turned into something worse, he hadn't been prepared for another one—that of coming across anyone on their private property.

"Father?" he squeezed his hand. "Why didn't you let me know your illness was this serious? How come I had to hear it from Henri? You know I would have flown home sooner."

"The pneumonia barely came on. It took me by surprise, but I'm better than I was last night." After a coughing spell he asked, "How long will you be here this time?"

Lance sucked in his breath. "I'm home for good."

At that unexpected news, joy illuminated his father's face. "You mean it?" He tried to raise his head off the pillow, but Lance restrained him gently.

"I've left the service. It's over."

"I've hoped for this day, Lance." He struggled through another coughing spasm. "I've prayed you would return healthy in mind and body. *Le bon Dieu* heard me."

What his parent saw was a shell of the man he once was. Lance wouldn't want him to know what lay beneath.

"Now that I'm back, we're going to work on your getting well. Anything you're worrying about, I'll take care of."

His father smiled through his tears. "Am I dreaming?"

Lance had trouble clearing the lump in his throat. *"Non, mon père."*

It was long past time he started helping his remarkable father who needed Lance to shoulder more of the responsibilities. His parent had not only raised him from birth, ten years ago he'd been wise enough to give Lance his freedom without making him feel guilty. In the end, that freedom had brought Lance back home of his own free will.

The reason that had driven him away in the first place no longer mattered. Since that time life had delivered him a blow from which he would never recover whether he lived at the far ends of the earth or at home. At least here he could be of use to his father.

"The nurse is making signs you need to rest. She says you've had too many friends come by and they've worn you out, so I'm going to let you sleep now."

"Don't go."

"I just want to have a word with the staff, but I promise I'll be back to stay in here with you tonight. Percy will stand guard, won't you."

The dog moaned in response.

"Do you know he won't leave me? Henri has to force him to go out when it's necessary."

Percy's love for his master was touching. "That doesn't surprise me."

A couple of years before Lance had joined the military, his father had found a stray puppy of mixed breed near to death in the forest. Some cruel person must have dropped it off to die, but his father brought him back to the château to nurse him. They'd been inseparable ever since.

"Are you settled in your suite down the hall?"

"Oui."

"We—" He stopped long enough to cough again. "We have a visitor."

A frown marred Lance's features. "Someone's staying at the château?"

"Yes." He would have said more, but another coughing spell took over.

As far as Lance was concerned, whoever it was needed to leave. His gracious father didn't know how to say no to anyone. His second marriage was proof in point. Right now he was too ill to realize what was good for him. Lance hadn't come home any too soon to take charge.

Kissing his father on either cheek, he nodded to the nurse then left his father's suite to go in search of Henri who was devoted to his parent. He found him in the foyer closing up the château for the night.

Lance approached him from the right since the head of the staff couldn't hear out of his left ear. Years earlier Henri had been a young groomsman at the stable when a hunting accident had occurred. After being released from the hospital, Lance's father had brought him into the château to take care of him. He'd been in his household employ ever since.

"I understand there's a guest staying at the château, Henri."

The older man turned and nodded. "*Oui*. A Madame Fallon."

His shuttered gaze searched Henri's. "Someone 'special'?"

"Your father insisted I put her in *la chambre verte*."

Lance was stunned. The green room had always been off-limits to guests in order to preserve its treasures. This meant his sixty-seven-year-old father could have become romantically involved.

Even if this woman was worthy of him, which Lance knew wasn't possible, his father had gone too far. Lance had to admit to being surprised his parent hadn't mentioned her before now. But after the disaster of his second marriage, maybe he was too worried over his son's reaction to tell him anything on that score.

"Has he known her long?"

"He met her at Easter, but she's only been at the château a week."

Lance had come home for that holiday on a chance twelve-hour leave, but there'd been no mention of her then.

A week was long enough for his parent to have become infatuated. He ground his teeth. What hold did this woman have over his father? He'd buried his heart with Lance's mother and had waited until his mid-forties before marrying a second time.

That travesty of a union had lasted less than a year. Long enough to scar his father, or so Lance had thought…

A blackness swept through him. "What's *your* opinion of her, Henri?"

"She's been good for your father."

Such praise coming from Henri, the soul of discretion, was unprecedented. Evidently she'd deceived Henri, too.

"When was the last time Corinne was home?"

"Last month. She's on holiday in Australia right now."

That meant she wasn't privy to this latest information about his father's interest in another woman. He could only imagine her reaction when she found out. As for her knowing Lance had returned…

He patted Henri's shoulder. "Thanks for all your care of him. Now that I'm home on a permanent basis, bring any concerns to me."

The other man smiled. "It's good to have you back. Your father has been living for the day."

If Brigitte hadn't already gone to bed, she'd volunteer certain details about his father's relationship with this latest predator. Unlike her husband, Henri, the housekeeper had no qualms when it came to expressing her opinions.

Any feelings of guilt Lance suffered for having been away this long were overshadowed by anger that another toxic female was already sleeping under their roof, counting the seconds until his father made her his third wife.

In need of a drink, he went to the kitchen for coffee first. Much as he'd like something stronger, he would opt for pain-killers in lieu of alcohol to tamp down the pain of a recent injury. However there was no medicine, no drink to wipe out the agony of shattered dreams.

From the first day of her arrival, Andrea had been told she could help herself to anything from the modernized kitchen no matter the hour. Brigitte insisted the cook wouldn't mind.

Taking her at her word, Andrea found some fresh brioche under a glass cover and ate one over the sink so she wouldn't spill crumbs on the stone floor. Since neither coffee nor fruit juice sounded good, she ended up drinking potable water from the faucet.

As she was standing on tiptoe to put the glass back on the baker's rack, someone pushed open the kitchen door and came in. She assumed it was Brigitte about to make hot tea with honey for the Duc.

"I hope Geoff's better tonight," she called over her shoulder.

"We're all hoping for that miracle."

Andrea stilled for a moment.

That deep voice with the heavy French accent—she'd heard it before. Just a little while ago in fact.

Her heart began to thud before she spun around to face the man she'd met in the forest. The quick motion caused her golden-brown hair to float about her shoulders before settling.

His searching gaze watched her, taking in every inch of her curves before it looked into the dark velvety-brown of her eyes. Like scorching blue flames, his flared in recognition.

He needed a shave and was still dressed in fatigues. The collar couldn't hide a thin white scar that ran up the side of his bronzed neck. She hadn't noticed it in the semidark of the forest. At the mere thought of how he came by it, a shudder ran through her body.

If her instincts didn't deceive her, he was not pleased to discover that the trespasser he'd confronted earlier was inside this château, helping herself to the food.

"Who *are* you?" he asked in a grating voice that managed to disturb her already sensitized nerves.

"Andrea Fallon. It appears the groundskeeper neglected to let you know Geoff had a guest."

He poured himself a cup of coffee from the *cafetière* and drank part of it, studying her over the rim. His gaze was insolent as well as bold. He had no shame.

She averted her eyes. A man who lived a life-and-death existence as he must have done, had dispensed with civilized pretense a long time ago.

"Did you give my camera to the guard at the gate?"

"No," came the unequivocal answer. "I'll return it to you later." He swallowed the rest of his coffee and put the cup in the sink.

"Morning will be fine. Now if you'll excuse me, I want to look in on Geoff."

"Not yet," he muttered. The next thing she knew he'd placed his body between her and the door. His hand grasped her wrist so she couldn't leave.

"What on earth is wrong with you?" she cried, trying to pull away from him. But his grip was far too strong. At five foot six and only a hundred and twenty pounds, she was no match for his steel-like strength.

"My question to you exactly," he bit out, drawing her nearer until she felt the warmth from his rock-hard body. The male scent of him was as erotic as it was unexpected. "What are you? All of twenty-two compared to his almost seventy years?"

When Andrea figured out what he was implying, she couldn't prevent the incredulous laugh that escaped. "Not that it's any business of the hired help, but Geoff and I are friends!"

"No doubt you'd like it to be more." He pulled her against him until she was crushed against every line and sinew of his body, sending fire through hers. She moaned in disbelief this was happening.

"Who made you his personal watchdog?" she cried, far too aware of their breath mingling, let alone his long, sooty lashes and the lines of experience bracketing his sensual mouth. No man had a right to be this attractive, yet so utterly offensive at the same time.

"Since his second marriage never took." She thought she saw pain interspersed with anger flashing from his eyes. "If you think I'm about to let him enter into a third with someone young enough to be his granddaughter, you're deluding yourself."

He'd pushed her too far. She couldn't refrain from baiting him. "Sometimes age isn't as important as kindness and love."

His lips twisted unpleasantly. "Especially when you're looking at a fortune after he's dead."

"Is that why you stay in his employ?" She flashed him a mocking smile. "Are you hoping there'll be something in it for you?"

The minute the question was out, she regretted her lapse of control and tried to jerk away from him without success.

"Why not…if you're offering," he drawled.

A thrill of fear raced through her body. Too late for escape, she couldn't avoid the hard mouth that descended on hers.

Caught off guard, her gasp of surprise enabled him to drive deeper in a kiss so intimate and all-consuming, she was shaken to the foundations. For a dizzying moment the sensations he aroused caused her legs to lose their strength.

At the very second she found herself clinging to him so she wouldn't fall, he gripped her upper arms and propelled her away from him.

It infuriated her that while she was out of breath and disheveled, he stood there mocking her with a devilish smile, seemingly unfazed by the encounter.

When she tore herself from his grasp, the force of it almost caused her to trip on her flight from the kitchen. She dashed through the hall and up the stairs of the château, needing to reach the safety of Geoff's suite.

CHAPTER TWO

A NEW nurse had come on duty. She smiled and nodded to Andrea, indicating her patient was up to a nocturnal visitor.

Approaching his bed, Andrea could see he was doing better. His oxygen tube had been taken away. Since last night he had more color and the slight wheeze in his chest didn't seem as noticeable.

Still trembling from her experience in the kitchen, she pulled up a chair next to him and put a hand on his arm, willing her heart to stop slamming against her ribs.

Whether in the Duc's employ or not, the stranger had crossed a line tonight with his primitive behavior. To manhandle a woman the way he'd just done was grounds for dismissal and a lot worse if Andrea had anything to say about it.

Without upsetting Geoff, she would learn what she could about the other man from Henri. He would know what should be done and would be discreet in handling the situation so she wasn't bothered further.

"Geoff? It's Andrea."

His eyes opened. They had more life than before. He really was improving. Nothing could have pleased her more.

"You sound out of breath, *ma chérie*."

Under the circumstances a little white lie wouldn't hurt. "I just returned to the château and wanted to see you first."

"I'm glad you're here." He patted her hand. "I have the most wonderful news."

"The doctor must have told you you're on the mend at last!" she interjected.

"It's a fact I'm feeling better, but this is something else. My son has come home for good. I couldn't speak about him or his work before tonight because it was classified. But now I can tell you. For the last ten years he's been serving in various regions of the world as part of our military's elite force."

A slight gasp escaped her throat. With those words Andrea realized she'd already met his only offspring. No wonder he'd appeared in the kitchen as if he owned the place. It explained his presence on the grounds.

Wasn't France's elite force even more deadly than its special forces?

The moment he'd emerged so noiselessly from the pines, she'd sensed the difference about him. She had living proof he was even better trained and more dangerous than she'd first supposed.

His uncivilized behavior downstairs appeared to be the result of too much time spent doing unspeakable things for far too long.

"Earlier tonight while I was wondering when I would see him again, and hopefully in one piece, he appeared in my room and told me he'd performed his final service for the country. It's over. *Grâce à Dieu.* Now he and Corinne can be married."

"Corinne?"

"The daughter of my second wife."

Andrea blinked. She supposed some stepbrothers and sisters did marry, but she couldn't imagine it.

"Corinne's had her eye on my son from the beginning. Now that he's retired from the service, I'm going to get the grandchildren I've been waiting for. She'll be home from her latest trip any day now."

Would marriage be able to tame a man as out of control as his son? Andrea doubted it.

"I'm so happy for you," she said before getting to her feet, unable to sit there calmly while she digested all the revelations of this night. If Geoff could have seen her being thoroughly kissed against her will by his only offspring, he'd be horrified.

"I want the two of you to meet."

"We already have, Papa," sounded an irascible voice that could only have come from one man. He'd just entered the bedroom. Andrea tried to smother her cry of surprise. "I discovered her by the *lac*."

"Then you probably know how much this poor child has suffered, Lance."

Lance was his real name?

Lancelot Du Lac?

"I'm afraid we didn't do much talking," Andrea broke in, not wanting to think about what had gone on during both private confrontations. Worse, she didn't want Geoff hurt. Like any father, he had great hopes for his son's future. Andrea had no desire to do anything that could bring him sadness.

"It's obvious he's anxious to spend time with you. Since you both have so much catching up to do, I'll say good-night and visit you tomorrow."

"Do you promise?"

"Of course. Keep getting better now."

She squeezed his arm, then darted away feeling a pair of accusing blue eyes leveled on her back. As she raced to the door they seemed to say, "You can keep running from me, but I know what you're up to. Be warned I'll drive you out."

By the time Andrea reached the safety of her bedroom, she'd made up her mind that tonight would be the last time she slept in this château.

Not because of Lance Du Lac's treatment of her, which was unconscionable. Not even because of his faulty assumption that she had designs on his father. An extraordinary man like the Duc probably drew the interest of many women. One or two unscrupulous types might even be after his money and title. Naturally his son would be protective of him. But that wasn't it.

Her need to leave stemmed from guilt.

She pulled the suitcase from the wardrobe and started to pack. In the morning she would slip down to Geoff's room to thank him for everything and say goodbye. It was for the best.

To have become physically aware of his world-weary son—a cynical man scarred in both a physical and figurative sense from experiences she didn't want to know about, a man who'd chosen to live life on the edge on purpose, and had probably left a trail of willing women around the globe before coming home to marry, seemed a total betrayal of Richard's memory.

He'd barely been gone three months, yet twice this evening she'd found herself unwillingly attracted to a stranger who'd shown her nothing but primitive behavior.

She could still feel his hands on her body, could still feel his mouth devouring hers. All of it a violation, though she couldn't say he'd hurt her. It was the brazen unexpectedness of his action that had surprised her.

And of course her involuntary response to his male appeal… That was the part that was so unforgivable.

When she'd first met her dark blond husband, she'd been working at a photography studio. She'd found it flattering that a university professor would be interested in her artwork suggestions for the current book he was writing.

He'd allowed her to see into his world. She'd been a good listener, eager to assist him any way she could. Not having had a college education herself, Andrea had put him on a pedestal, admiring the poet within. Their association had led to marriage. He'd been a gentle lover.

To fill the emptiness left by his death, she'd come back to France to finish up the artwork for his latest book. Work was all she knew. So what could explain her reaction to a forbidding ex-military man, the antithesis of Richard?

Maybe it was a case of the hormone therapy regimen she was on being out of whack.

What if all the clichés about a widow's needs were true? If so, how embarrassing. How appalling!

The tip of Lance's boot caught the foot of the chair Andrea Fallon had just vacated in her haste to avoid him. Guilt at being found out had been written in every move and expression of her body.

A beautiful body and face to match he acknowledged to himself with grudging honesty.

There was nothing wrong with his father's eyesight, only

with his lack of good judgment where she or any woman was concerned. They couldn't be trusted.

He nudged the chair closer to the bed before sitting down next to his parent.

"Tell me about your guest's suffering, Papa," he asked without preamble.

His father looked at him with loving eyes. "When you came home on that quick trip at Easter, did you happen to meet the American professor who was working in my library?"

Lance's thoughts flew back to those few hours when he'd stolen home to check on his father without anyone else knowing about it. "Henri mentioned you had a visitor. I recall getting a glimpse of him, but I admit I didn't pay much attention."

After another bout of coughing, his father continued. "Dr. Fallon taught medieval literature at Yale University in Connecticut, and came to La Bretagne over the Easter break to do research. He and his wife Andrea were staying at the Hotel Excalibur."

The woman whose luscious mouth he could still taste on his lips was someone's wife? Lance hadn't seen her wearing any rings.

"Maurice rang me and asked if I wouldn't allow his hotel guests to examine some of the manuscripts in our family's collection. Dr. Fallon was already published and a reputed expert on Arthurian legend."

"So of course you said yes," Lance interjected with a smile that didn't reach his eyes. The news that his father was involved with a married woman caused his stomach to clench for a variety of unpalatable reasons.

"How could I refuse when I learned he was writing a book entitled *The Definitive Lancelot Du Lac?*"

Lance had heard it all before. Every would-be writer was attempting to pen a definitive book on the subject of the famous knight.

"About a month after they returned to the States, Andrea sent me a note telling me that following their flight home from Paris, her husband had died suddenly of a blood clot to the brain."

What?

"She thanked me for letting them come to the château to see the library. Her husband had said it was the highlight of his trip. Naturally I was grieved for her sake and sent flowers. I told her that if she ever wanted to come for a visit, she was welcome.

"To my delight she wrote back two weeks ago and asked if she could come and take pictures of the forest. She wants to include some extra photographs in the book her husband had written.

"I have to tell you, Lance, if I could have had a daughter, I would have wanted one exactly like Andrea."

A daughter—

Lance's mind had to do a complete thought reversal. Suddenly certain things seemed clear, like his father allowing her to stay in the green room. He'd never offered it to anyone else, not even Corinne.

"She has your mother's kindness," his father continued, unaware of Lance's shock. "It's a very rare trait."

So rare in fact that Lance hadn't seen any evidence of it during their fiery exchange in the kitchen before his baser instincts had taken over to punish her for something she hadn't done.

In any case he'd had no right in behaving like a brute.

"As soon as she flies back, she's going to have it published as a special tribute to him. Now that you're home, maybe you would show her some significant spots only you and I know about? Since her arrival, I've been too sick to accompany her."

Lance lowered his head, massaging the knotted muscles at the back of his neck. Considering the reprehensible way he'd treated his father's guest up to this point, he doubted she'd speak to him again, let alone be amenable to spending any time with him.

What in the hell had caused him to react so violently to Andrea Fallon? He'd met plenty of women in his life more beautiful and exotic. Bile rose in his throat when he remembered one in particular…

Mrs. Fallon had said she'd been given permission to be on the property. When she'd first looked at him with that haunted expression as if she were miles away, why hadn't he recognized it as grief and believed her?

How in the devil could he explain his behavior in the kitchen when he didn't understand it himself?

He didn't really think his father would get involved with a woman that young, so what was the underlying emotion driving Lance's cruelty toward an innocent guest? It seemed he'd completely misread Henri's comment.

Obviously he'd become so hardened with life, he was more out of touch with civilized society than he realized. Apparently he was no longer fit to rejoin the world his father inhabited.

He got up from the chair. "Papa? I've got some things to do, but I'll be back."

Lance needed to speak to Andrea before she went to bed.

It was time to pick up the pieces *if* it wasn't already too late. Something told him if he didn't, she might well be gone from the premises before morning. That was one thing he didn't want on his conscience.

"Go ahead, *mon fils*. I'll wait for you."

"Try to sleep."

"I think I can now that I know you're going to be a permanent fixture around here. Corinne will be overjoyed when she returns from her trip and realizes you're home for good."

Lance looked down at his father who was too ill to deal with anything unpleasant. But the moment he improved, the truth would have to come out.

Percy followed Lance as far as the door but no further. The dog didn't appear to have much use for him. Lance didn't blame him for preferring his father's company to Lance whose nature seemed to have been inexplicably vile in the face of innocent provocation.

After going to his suite for the camera, he took the steps two at a time to the third floor and listened outside Andrea's room for signs of life. Even if she were in bed, he couldn't let any more time go by without attempting to repair some of the damage.

He rapped on the heavy door with the back of his knuckles. "Andrea? It's Lance. I have to talk to you. If you need to get dressed first, I'll wait."

In a minute he heard, "Should I decide not to open it, will you take a battering ram to the door?"

No one deserved that remark more than he did.

"You're someone my father cares for very much. I've come to apologize."

After a long silence, "Apology accepted."

That was too easy. "Enough to open the door?"

"Surely it isn't necessary."

He folded his arms. "I presume you don't want me to see the suitcase you're packing. If your departure is too precipitous, my father will never forgive me. Since I'm already in the doghouse, as you Americans say, you wouldn't wish to add to my punishment, would you?"

"The doghouse would be too good for you."

His lips twitched. Kind as his father made her out to be, she had spirit. "You're right. I don't suppose you'd believe I'm suffering from posttraumatic shock syndrome—"

"I believe it, but you've taken it to new depths. You're more like your alter ego than I'd realized."

"You mean one day I'll join Lancelot in Hell?"

"If the armor fits."

"How do you know I haven't already been there?"

"I surmised as much. Only someone who's been in hell would treat me the way you have."

Her arrow found its mark dead center. His amusement vanished. "Is there no redemption?"

"I don't know. I'll have to think about it."

He drew in a ragged breath. "I'm leaving your camera outside this door. If you choose to stay a little longer, I swear on my mother's grave no harm will come to you from me."

After a short silence, "Since I know how much your father loved her, I'll take that into consideration."

She knew how to deliver the coup de grâce. There were many sides to Andrea Fallon. She was the most dangerous kind of female.

"I'm sorry about your husband. I didn't know."

"I thought Lancelot was given special powers."

He closed his eyes tightly for a moment. "I've done too many dark deeds and have forfeited most of them."

"How sad."

She sounded as if she meant it. It was then he realized he'd given too much away, a position he loathed to be in.

"I'm leaving now to spend the night with Papa. Don't let my uncourteous behavior prevent you from making him happy. Should you disappear without explanation, I can't promise he won't go downhill."

Much as he was hoping she'd relent enough to open the door so they could talk face-to-face, he had a gut feeling it wasn't going to happen. He'd behaved like a bastard and was reaping the consequences.

"*Dors bien*, Andrea," his voice rasped before he turned away and made a swift return to the second floor.

Disturbed by the memory of the way she'd felt in his arms when he'd kissed her, he realized it was going to be a long night…

Delighted by the morning sun that pierced the clouds and filtered down through the cathedral of trees, Andrea made her way to the opposite end of the lake from where she'd been reading the previous evening.

Maybe she would get lucky and one of the forest animals following an ancient game trail to the water's edge would enter the site where she planned to take pictures.

After a good night's sleep, which came as a surprise considering her tormented state of mind last evening, she realized the worst thing she could do was run away. Geoff wouldn't understand. Since she couldn't explain it herself, she'd decided to put yesterday's experience behind her and behave like an adult.

Lance had proved to be a man with a scarred soul. Using the most elemental of ways, he'd set out to expose her for the loose, conniving female he believed her to be.

Where his father was concerned, his protective instincts were over the top. Combined with his innate distrust of women, he must have choked on that apology for his rough treatment of her. It was probably a first for him.

But coming from a family with a title and great wealth, he no doubt had reasons for his suspicions. *Which he'd carried to the extreme.*

Still, he'd returned her camera and had promised she would have nothing more to fear from him. She believed him.

As for her reaction to his virility, that wasn't his fault. It was her own unchecked response to him Andrea feared.

She should have known there'd come a day of awakening when she'd realize she was alone again and vulnerable. Somehow she hadn't expected it to happen here, or that it would be Geoff's son who made her aware of her womanhood in a way no man had ever done.

Richard was the only man she'd ever slept with and he'd taken his time to get to know her before they'd become intimate.

Troubled by her thoughts that seemed to swirl toward one inescapable vortex, she looked for a fallen tree where she could sit while she waited for a deer or some such thing to appear.

In truth she was tired even though she'd slept well. Since eating part of an omelet earlier, she'd felt a trifle nauseous.

These were signs of pregnancy, but that wasn't possible. Since she'd had these symptoms before coming in contact with Geoff, she didn't think it was flu.

What could it be except the result of her grief?

As soon as she returned to the States, she would need to find meaningful work and get on with her life. But right now the thought of making any decisions seemed too much for her.

She looked around. A few rabbits and squirrels scurried about, but the bigger animals were nowhere in sight. Maybe they'd ventured out at first light and were resting while they digested breakfast.

A short nap sounded like a good idea to her, too. Maybe she should go back to the château and come here later in the day. Even as the thought entered her head, she happened to notice something moving in the water toward her with the speed of a torpedo. Something long and sleek.

By the time she'd jumped to her feet in alarm, a dark head had risen from a cluster of lily pads in flower.

Her hand went to her throat. Lance!

While treading water he flashed her a white smile. "Good morning," came that low voice in the heavy French accent she found so seductive.

Surrounded by the heads of pink and white water lilies, he made a picture of impossible male beauty. Appearing like this made him seem part of the enchantment of the place.

"I thought swimming across the lake would be the best way to announce I was coming. After our first meeting, the last thing I wanted to do was startle you again."

Everything about him pulled the ground out from under her, but that was her problem, not his.

"You move like an animal and swim like a fish. If I see you fly, then I'm going to know Merlin haunts these woods."

His blue eyes darkened with some emotion she didn't understand. "Why not join me? I'll show you one of the château's secrets no one else knows about. You have to swim to it, but don't worry. The lake's not deep."

Her heart lurched at the thought of being alone with him like this. "I'm afraid I didn't bring a suit."

"You have one now. Corinne, my father's stepdaughter, keeps extras around for her girlfriends." He tossed her a small plastic bag he'd been holding in his hand. It landed at her feet.

Andrea leaned over and opened it. Inside was a cherry-red bikini. She found it odd Lance hadn't referred to Corinne as the woman he planned to marry. But since his personal life was none of her business, she kept quiet about it.

"There's plenty of cover. Hurry and put it on. I'll wait for you," he said before vanishing beneath the lily pads.

However much he might not like it, she realized Lance was endeavoring to extend the olive branch. Geoff had wanted to show her around and must have put his son up to this. To refuse would be churlish of her.

If she said no, it would only prove she hadn't forgiven him. In truth, considering his scathing view of women, he might think she'd read more into that angry kiss than punishment.

Forgetting her lethargy for the moment, she moved behind a pine tree and changed into the two-piece suit. It fit, but just barely.

Lured by the sense of adventure surrounding him despite his brooding air of cynicism, Andrea removed her sneakers and put them in a pile with her things, then walked down to the water's edge. He waved to her from a short distance away.

With her heart pounding hard, she waded into the cold, still water and pushed off toward him. After a few strokes she recovered from the initial shock and discovered the temperature was invigorating.

His intent gaze beckoned her closer. "Follow me," was all he said before swimming to the middle of the lake where he did an expert somersault into the depths.

With less grace Andrea imitated him, glad for her ponytail that prevented the hair from getting in her eyes. As soon as she reached him, he pointed to an object lying on the floor of the lake. She looked down.

Partially hidden among the plants lay a knight's sword and shield. Fingers of sunlight illuminated their metallic outlines. In this underworld, anything seemed possible. Andrea wanted to stay longer and inspect them, but she was too out of shape and breath. She began to feel a little panicky.

Lance must have picked up on her alarm because he put his arms around her and they ascended to the surface together. Their swift rise made her somewhat dizzy. This time she clung to his powerful body in order to drink in air.

Unlike last time he didn't thrust her away as if she'd been the one to initiate the contact.

"Are you all right?"

She felt his husky tone resonate throughout her body.

"Yes. Just a little winded for some reason." Their bodies brushed against each other in a tangle of limbs. "Where did that sword and shield come from?"

"Years ago my father planted those to give me and my friends a thrill. We decided to leave them there."

She smiled. "That sounds like Geoff. You were lucky to have such a wonderful father."

As she'd spoken, her lips happened to graze the scar at the side of his neck. It ran from his collarbone into the black hair behind his ear. The bronze of his skin made it stand out a pinkish white.

"I hope the man who gave this to you isn't in a position to hurt anyone again," she whispered, afraid to touch it with her fingers in case it was sensitive.

His lids veiled his eyes. "What if I told you it was a woman?"

A female soldier?

The picture of Lance in mortal combat with a woman managed to disturb her in a whole slew of new and different ways. Any other thoughts went out of her head.

"It looks like a recent wound. D-does it hurt?" she stammered.

"No."

"I'm glad."

"Are you?" came the voice of skepticism.

"That you're not in pain?" she blurted in exasperation. "Of course!"

Embarrassed by the intimate exchange and proximity of their bodies, she pushed away from him and began treading water on her own.

He moved closer. "After the way I treated you last night, you have every reason to despise me."

"You're right, but that was last night, and you said you were sorry. Let's forget it, shall we? Your father is overjoyed you've come home. Some men and women don't return from war, or if they do, they've lost limbs or—"

"Or other unspeakable things?" he mocked. "That's true." His shuttered eyes continued to search hers. "Unfortunately war isn't the only place for losses to occur. How long were you married to your husband?"

"Six years."

"You're still so young."

"Almost twenty-eight. Not quite the child you assumed was ingratiating herself to your father," she reminded him.

He studied her in the dappled light. "No man would ever mistake you for a child. But I did think you were younger."

"So I gathered earlier."

"I guess you know you've made a conquest of my father."

Lance didn't believe in mincing words. He'd followed her to the *lac* for a definite reason.

Andrea decided to be blunt, too. "I take it you're not happy about it."

"No," he answered in a morose tone.

One thing she could count on with him was his brutal honesty. "Give me through to tomorrow afternoon, then you'll have him all to yourself."

He trod water opposite her. "You know as well as I do he doesn't want you to leave."

"Geoff has his son back. That's all he cares about."

"Not all," Lance muttered cryptically.

She shook her head to avoid a bee buzzing around her. "I'm aware he has great plans for you."

Maybe it was a cloud blotting out the sun that threw his features into shadow.

"Do you know, you have the softest skin I've ever felt."

The unexpected change in conversation had been spoken

with such stark candor, white-hot heat spread through her body. She started to swim away from him, but he made a lazy circle around her.

"I'm the first man to kiss you since your husband, aren't I?"

The heat of anger filled her cheeks. "Don't worry. I'm not waiting for a repeat performance."

Of course he didn't believe her, but the slight hint of mockery etched in his expression was the last straw.

"Not every recent widow is desperate to jump into bed with the next available male. Not even when he's as attractive as you are. Especially not with the emotional baggage you wear like a dark mantle."

Without hesitation she struck out for the shore where she'd left her clothes. He matched her strokes though she knew he could have reached the edge long before she did.

Scrambling out of the water, she darted for the pine tree, anxious to cover herself. His eyes and personal remarks left her feeling exposed to the bone. Though he'd done nothing wrong, he'd touched a nerve. She was much too aware of him to be comfortable and he knew it!

Andrea hadn't ever met a man like Lance. In her experience she'd only associated with her husband and his colleagues—teachers caught up in the pedantic world of legend and prose, far from the killing fields of war.

While her husband spent his life searching for stories of a famous knight's adventures in times long past, Lance had been living one dangerous adventure after another in the present.

What was it like to fight hand to hand, let alone with someone of the opposite sex? Andrea couldn't imagine it, yet

Lance had returned from the battlefield with scars to prove he'd survived its atrocities by sheer guts and an indomitable will.

A life that could be snuffed out at any second had to change a man. Though she admired the heroic service Lance had rendered his country, Andrea's instinct for self-preservation told her to keep her distance from him, even if he was Geoff's son.

Or because of it…

After changing into trousers and a cotton top, she put the wet swimsuit in the bag. Once she'd reached for the camera, she left her hiding place, determined to avoid him until she left for the airport tomorrow afternoon. Geoff had assured her one of the staff would drive her when she was ready.

But she needn't have been concerned. One glance at the lake and she realized Lance had disappeared. Now that he'd done his good deed by providing her a moment's excitement where the famed Lancelot was concerned, he had more important things to accomplish.

All the way back to the château she told herself she was glad he'd gone. Besides being tired, it saved her from having to sidestep any more discussions about her vulnerability, never mind personal remarks about her skin. Those subjects were way out of bounds.

What she craved was sleep. During those unconscious hours she would be free of certain thoughts plaguing her since last evening.

CHAPTER THREE

WITH a feeling of déjà vu, Lance knocked on Andrea's door, but there was no answer. After leaving her at the lake yesterday, he'd gone into Rennes on business and hadn't returned until late.

This morning his father felt well enough to ask if Andrea could join them for breakfast. But after trying to rouse her for the last few minutes, Lance decided she'd already left for the forest.

Andrea Fallon was one woman independent to a fault. The females of his past had shown a different tendency altogether.

He left the third floor for the kitchen, hoping one of the staff would enlighten him. After several inquiries, it turned out no one had seen her. Henri reminded him she was an early riser.

Frowning, Lance went down to his father's room and told him he'd bring her back for lunch.

Not particularly hungry, he reached for an apple and left the château under an overcast sky. The elements portended rain. Being summer it wouldn't last long, yet Andrea would be soaked if she got caught in it.

No telling where she'd wandered to this morning, but it

didn't matter. On horseback he could cover the grounds much faster in his search for her.

After reaching the stable, he climbed on Tonnerre. In case she was still waiting to spot an animal near a watering hole, he set out for the lake first.

In no time at all he'd circled it without seeing any sign of her. Perhaps she'd tried to find the fountain of youth his father had told her about, and she'd gotten lost.

Lance urged his horse on toward it.

Not finding her there, he rode swiftly to the top of a nearby hill overlooking the Val Sans Retour where his voice would carry.

It was just the place Andrea probably would have come to take pictures. Lance called to her. Again no response.

Maybe she hadn't come to the forest at all. It was possible she'd walked to the village of Lyseaux, taking the main road.

As he rode his horse down the other side of the grassy slope, one raindrop then another began to spatter him. Intent on returning to the château for his car, he didn't see a woman's body curved on its side near the base until he was almost upon her.

Turning Tonnerre aside abruptly to avoid trampling her, Lance jumped down from his gelding and rushed over to her. One of the hooves had smashed her camera. He shuddered to think what damage might have been done if it had come six inches closer.

"Andrea—" he cried in alarm, getting down on his haunches. If she'd fallen and had hurt her neck or spine, he didn't dare move her yet.

He heard moaning sounds. To his relief she turned on her

back seemingly without a struggle, but she exhibited a pallor that told him she was ill.

"Lance—" she said his name on a shaky whisper. After the way they'd parted yesterday, she wouldn't have responded like this unless she was in trouble.

His body helped shield her face from the rain, which had started to come down hard. "What happened to you?"

"During my walk I felt sick so I lay down, but it hasn't passed yet. I think I must have the flu after all."

"Then you've been ill before today?"

"Yes," she admitted in a faint voice.

When he saw the beads of perspiration beading her hairline and brows, he swallowed hard. "You must have caught father's bug. It's a nasty one."

Without hesitation he lifted her in his arms and carried her over to his horse. "I'm taking you to the doctor in Lyseaux. If you're too ill to sit up against me, I'll lay you across Tonnerre."

She shook her head. "I—I can sit—I think—"

He knew she felt like death, but she hung in there long enough for him to climb on behind her.

"Just rest against me and let me do the work." With one hand around her waist, he used the other to guide the horse.

The rhythm of the gallop molded their bodies together. After yesterday's experience when he'd felt her rich curves, he'd longed to repeat the experience.

At the moment she lay helpless against him. Though he was worried for the reason that had put her in this state, he had to confess he enjoyed her needing him like this. After the way she'd lit up for him at the lake, he hadn't expected to get this close to her again.

Once they reached the canopy of trees, they escaped the worst of the rain. Lance knew a shortcut that would bring them around the rear of the château where his car was parked.

"Am I going too fast for you?" he murmured into her fragrant hair. It smelled of apricots. She'd pulled it back like the day before.

"No," came the half-moaned word.

That was good. He wanted her examined as soon as it was humanly possible.

Before long they came out of the woods onto the gravel. He led the horse to the passenger side of the car. Luckily the downpour had turned into drizzle.

In a quick movement Lance slid off Tonnerre. Carrying Andrea in his arms, he opened the door and put her inside. After lowering her seat so she could lie back, he shut the door.

With a pat to the horse's rump, knowing it would return to the stable, Lance jumped in the driver's seat and started up the engine.

Lyseaux was only four miles away. Andrea didn't try to talk. Lance's gut clenched at the thought of her lying out there in the rain all alone.

If he hadn't been home, his father would have sent someone from the château to look for her. But under the circumstances Lance was glad he was the one who'd discovered her body lying there inert. The idea that someone unscrupulous might have come upon her didn't bear thinking about.

He pressed on the accelerator, heading straight for the clinic. If the doctor said she needed to be in a hospital, he would drive her to Rennes.

The next few minutes became a blur of activity. As soon

as the surprised receptionist saw him carrying Andrea through the main doors, she jumped up and showed him into one of the rooms down the hall. "I'll get Dr. Semplis."

"I don't want anyone but Dr. Foucher looking at Andrea."

"I'm sorry, *monsieur*, but today is Dr. Foucher's day off."

Lance muttered an imprecation. He didn't know Dr. Semplis and hated the idea of a stranger taking care of her, but it couldn't be helped. She needed immediate attention. "She's very ill."

"Dr. Semplis will be right in."

At the sound of the woman's voice, Andrea's eyes opened. Lance looked into them as he lowered her onto the examining table. "Help is coming, *chérie*." The endearment came out unsolicited from someplace deep inside, surprising the hell out of him. "We're at the doctor's office."

"Thank you," she murmured.

It sounded heartfelt, which meant she was even sicker than he realized, otherwise she wouldn't be speaking to him.

Soon after the receptionist left, a nurse entered the room. "If you'd please step out, *monsieur*."

The last thing Lance wanted to do was leave, but he had no choice. "If you need me, I'll be right outside the door, Andrea."

She gave a barely perceptible nod before her eyes closed again.

The last time he'd left a wounded buddy at the field hospital in a near unconscious condition, the poor devil had never recovered. It was the stuff that had made up part of Lance's nightmares for the last ten years.

He drew in a ragged breath and exited the room. While he waited in the hall, he drew the cell phone out of his jeans' pocket and phoned the stable.

After learning that Tonnerre had returned safely, Lance phoned his father and told him he and Andrea had decided to drive to Lyseaux before coming back to the château. They'd all have lunch together another day.

His father seemed fine with it, particularly since a good friend of his had dropped by.

Lance told him he'd see him at dinner and hung up, relieved his parent was still in the dark about Andrea. Now that he was rallying from his bout with pneumonia, Lance didn't want any setbacks.

His main concern was to find out what was wrong with Andrea and make certain she recovered. For some inexplicable reason he felt responsible for her. He grimaced to think about anything that could have put her life in jeopardy.

"Monsieur?" Lance wheeled around to see a younger doctor coming down the hall. "I'm Dr. Semplis."

"*Grâce à Dieu* someone's on duty! Andrea became ill in the forest. She couldn't sit up, let alone walk out on her own. I had to carry her in; I think it could be flu."

The other man eyed him curiously. "I won't have any idea until I examine her, but don't worry. We'll know soon enough. Why don't you take a seat out in reception."

"I'm staying here," he declared.

"Suit yourself, but it could be a long wait."

His jaw hardened. "So be it."

Andrea drifted in and out of sleep, haunted by dreams of Lancelot braving the elements to carry her to safety on his marvelous steed.

In her waking moments the doctor told her she was dehydrated. He'd ordered an IV. Soon a lab technician drew her blood.

She fell asleep again. Later she became aware of Lance's presence. He'd pulled up a chair next to the examining table.

Other than asking her if he could do anything for her, he didn't force her to talk. By his brooding silence however, she could tell something serious was on his mind.

Even if Geoff had prevailed on Lance to stay with her, she found it rather touching that such a fierce, dominant male who probably hated confinement like this more than most people, was keeping a constant vigil at her side.

It made her feel guilty that instead of being with his father who needed him, Lance had to worry about her.

She felt a little stronger and turned her head to look at him. "I should have gone home yesterday."

He leaned forward, eyeing her narrowly. "To what? An empty house full of memories?"

"A condo," she corrected him, wondering at his savage tone.

"Who would take care of you?"

"I have a friend, who's the wife of one of my husband's colleagues."

"No family?"

"When my parents were killed, my mother's sister Aunt Kathy and her husband Rob raised me along with their two daughters. They still live in New Haven, but they're very busy. I wouldn't want to bother them, not after everything they've done for me."

Lines darkened his handsome face. "Then let's be thankful you remained here. You could have collapsed on the flight over."

Since the possibility was patently true, Andrea couldn't deny it. "I'm sorry to take you away from your father."

"He's on the mend. You're the one I'm worried about." She saw that his hands had formed fists. "I can't figure out what's taking the doctor so damn long to give you a diagnosis. Dr. Foucher should have been here."

"I think you've been on the battlefield too long where everything happens fast, and decisions have to be made in a split second. Things go more slowly back in civilization."

He rubbed the back of his bronzed neck. "You're right." His probing gaze roved over her features. "There's more color in your cheeks."

"I'm feeling a little better. Must be the IV."

"Dieu merci."

"I'd like to tell you something," she whispered.

A stillness seemed to envelop him. "Go ahead."

"You redeemed yourself today."

"I thought there was no redemption," his voice grated.

"I was wrong. You rescued a damsel in distress. That's what heroes do, even if their crown has slipped."

"I never had one," he bit out in what sounded like self-abnegation. "You're imagining things."

"No. I'm awake, and I was with you when it happened. No one, and I mean no one else could have pulled off what you did unless his name was Lancelot Du Lac. I must confess I'm in awe of you."

"All right, Andrea—" The doctor swept in the room, bringing Lance to his feet. "I finally have confirmation of what's wrong with both of you."

"Both?" Andrea's anxious gaze flew to Lance's. "Are you ill and you didn't tell me?"

Dr. Semplis laughed. "You're going to have a baby, *maman*." He turned to Lance. "Congratulations, *papa*."

"A baby?"

"But that's impossible!" Andrea cried, trying to sit up. "I mean I *can't* be pregnant!"

"I'm afraid you are," the doctor interjected before she could say anything else. "Twelve weeks along in fact."

"*Twelve*—" Her cry resounded in the tiny room.

The doctor eyed both of them with amusement. "I'm surprised neither of you recognized the symptoms. Under the circumstances I'll leave you two alone for a minute, then I'll be back in to talk to you."

"Wait—"

"Thank you, Dr. Semplis," Lance said, taking charge as if he was used to dealing with her. He put his strong hands on her shoulders to ease her back. "We do need some private time."

The door clicked shut.

Overwhelmed by emotions bombarding her, Andrea broke down sobbing. Once she got started, she couldn't stop.

Lance said her name in alarm several times and handed her a box of tissues. "Andrea…tell me what's going on," her urged.

"You wouldn't understand." The words came out in another gush of tears. How could he when she could hardly comprehend it herself.

"You said it was impossible. Does that mean your husband isn't the father?"

Her breath caught. "No— Yes—I mean I've never been

with another man, so it has to be my husband's. But I was told it would take a miracle."

"Why?" he demanded softly. His hands were kneading her upper arms, but he didn't seem to be aware of it.

She raised drenched brown eyes to him. "Because I went through premature menopause several years ago, ruling out pregnancy. It happens in a certain small percentage of women. My specialist told me that in my case, the chances of ovulating were so astronomical, I should never count on conceiving a child."

Andrea wondered if a trick of light was the reason his eyes suddenly darkened.

"She's been helping me experiment with herbs and hormone therapy to keep my heart healthy. I assumed the physical changes to my body were a result of the hormones. My hands have been so swollen, I left my rings at home."

"So that's the explanation," Lance murmured.

She nodded. "Since Richard's death I've been more tired than usual, and have experienced quite a bit of nausea. But I thought the symptoms had to be the fault of depression and the hormones.

"To think I'm almost through my first trimester of pregnancy and didn't know it! I—I'm in shock."

She looked at him through blurry eyes. "Oh, Lance—Richard wanted a baby so badly. Now he's gone, and he'll never know our child or be able to help me raise it."

He remained silent while another explosion of tears poured out of her, more profuse than before. When they finally subsided she said, "In the beginning we had such plans for a family. He was an only child. We wanted two or three so they could be friends. It's wonderful when siblings have each other.

"Then we found out I couldn't have any. We were both devastated. I—I wanted to have his baby. Once we heard the awful news, he was so crushed," she said on another sob.

"When I buried him, I thought it was the end of everything. I came to France so empty, and now—"

"Now everything's different," he murmured in a thick-toned voice. She felt him rub the arm that didn't have the drip in it.

Andrea wiped her eyes. "Except that my baby will grow up without its father. I was deprived of both my parents. I—I can hardly bear to think of history repeating itself. Every child needs a daddy.

"Why did Richard have to die—" Her sorrowful wail rang in the room.

Wordlessly Lance put his arm around her back. She found herself sobbing against his broad shoulder. After a time she realized she was getting him all wet and pulled away embarrassed.

She reached for some tissues and sniffed. "I'm sorry for breaking down like this. You must think I'm insane."

"I think Richard was a damn lucky man. With you as his child's mother, his legacy will be carried on. Maybe there's a future professor growing inside you. Do those motherly instincts tell you if it's a boy or a girl?"

"What instincts?" she challenged, clearing her throat. "I didn't even know a baby was living inside me until a few minutes ago. I still can't believe I'm pregnant!"

"Thank God the diagnosis is one of joy," Lance exclaimed.

"When you were lying there in the grass so ill, too many negative thoughts ran through my mind."

"I was frightened, too." Her eyes glazed over with fresh tears. "Thank you again for helping me. I–I'm sorry the doctor assumed you were the father. When he comes back in I'll explain."

A half smile broke the corner of Lance's sensual mouth. "Hearing the news with you made me feel like *I'm* the father. It's an experience I wouldn't have missed. Do you know my heart leaped when he told us?"

She bit her lip. "So did mine."

His expression sobered. "If I'd realized you were pregnant, I wouldn't have asked you to follow me to my underwater treasure yesterday."

Andrea recalled the experience, particularly the moment when he'd clasped her body against his to take her to the surface. The baby had been pressed against his hard muscled physique.

"It was a unique experience," she admitted softly. "Someday when my child is old enough to swim on his own, I'll have to bring him to France so he can dive in the lake and discover its secrets for himself."

"So you're thinking a boy." Lance flashed her another rare half smile that transformed his features and made her heart kick.

"I guess I am."

"Wait another month and we'll find out if you're right about the gender," the doctor inserted.

Andrea hadn't heard him come in the room.

"I knocked, but you two didn't hear me. Would you like to listen to the heartbeat?"

He put on his stethoscope and found the spot on Andrea's

stomach, then let her listen. It sounded like horse's hooves galloping across the prairie.

"I don't believe it." All this time her child had been growing inside her and she hadn't been aware of it.

"Your baby's approximately three and half inches long, and is developing nicely."

Lance reached for the stethoscope so he could listen. A slow smile broke the corner of his mouth, once again accentuating his striking features. When he relinquished the instrument, his gaze still clung to hers.

"After not knowing what was wrong with her earlier, Doctor, your news has made me a very happy man."

"I'm glad to hear it."

Heat crept into Andrea's face. She looked over at the doctor. "There's something you need to know. You've misunderstood the situation. I'm a guest at the Château Du Lac. Monsieur Du Lac isn't my husband."

He wrapped her arm to take her blood pressure. "What's stopping you two from getting married?"

"You don't understand. The baby isn't his."

The doctor did a double-take. "Then the birth father should be told."

"I can't tell him." Her voice trembled. "On the morning I must have conceived this baby, my husband left for work. By evening he'd died of a brain aneurysm. That was three months ago."

"Andrea…"

The compassion in Lance's tone caused her eyes to close.

"I'm sorry for your loss," the doctor said, "however he's left you with a marvelous legacy."

Lance's exact words.

"I know, but I can hardly take it in."

"Miracles tend to affect a person that way. I'm pleased to announce you're a healthy woman. If you'll start the nausea medicine I've prescribed, you should be feeling much better before long. Take them three times a day before meals. Pick it up at the front desk.

"I've also written an order for vitamins, which you need to start taking. I want to see you in a week to make certain all is going well. We'll do another blood test in case you're still a little low on iron."

"I'll be returning to the United States in the next few days, so let me thank you now for all your help."

"In that case, be certain to get in touch with your doctor immediately."

"I will."

He paused at the door. "You can leave as soon as the nurse takes out your IV. Remember to stay hydrated, eat whatever appeals and get plenty of rest over the next couple of days."

"She'll do it," Lance proclaimed. Andrea tried to hide her smile. He couldn't help who he was, but she didn't mind.

Once the doctor had left the room the nurse came in, preventing Andrea from talking to Lance until the other woman had removed the needle and had gone.

Without being told anything, Lance opened the cupboard and pulled out the sack containing her clothes. He turned to her. "Do you need help getting dressed? I can ask her to come in again."

"No. I'm able to manage, but thank you anyway."

His gaze played over her with concern. "Then I'll see you at the front desk."

After Lance closed the door, she removed the clinic gown

and felt her stomach, which had filled out and was hard. Why hadn't she realized a baby was growing inside her?

When her jeans were too tight, she should have guessed at the reason, even if the specialist had told her getting pregnant would require a near miracle.

Over the last few years Andrea had given up all hope of having a child from her own body. The news that she was pregnant was fantastic!

At the moment she felt suspended between two worlds where nothing seemed real, yet the proof was there she was carrying Richard's baby. To her consternation however it was Lance Malbois who'd first heard the news with her. If it weren't for him, she could still be lying there in the forest too sick to move.

How would she ever forget it was *his* eyes that had flickered at the incredible news, almost as if he'd been the one to father her baby and was pleased about it. Even the doctor had thought they were a couple.

Andrea couldn't understand Lance's reaction. She meant nothing to him beyond being his father's guest. Yet that was probably the reason why. He felt responsible for her. Under the circumstances she'd be wise to leave France as soon as she felt well enough for the flight home.

Knowing she would be a mother in six short months changed the way she felt about returning to New Haven. Maybe she could work part-time for her old boss at the photography studio. If not, maybe the literature department at the university could use her services. The rest of the time she would start getting a nursery ready for her baby.

So many things needed to be bought. A crib, a playpen, one

of those adorable little swings, a stroller… All the items available for modern day mothers. Now *she* would be a mom, too!

Whether it was a boy or girl didn't matter. She loved her baby already. The knowledge she was carrying a life inside her filled that empty place in her heart.

Though she would always be grateful for her aunt and uncle who'd raised her with their children after her parents died, she'd never really belonged to them. To think she would have a child of her own to love and cherish.

After the baby came, she would make the small amount of insurance money left to her stretch so she could be a stay-at-home mom. Through her various university contacts, maybe she could arrange to do word processing at the condo to bring in some income.

A fatal car accident had deprived her of her parents, and now a blood clot had taken the life of her baby's father. Andrea was determined to be there for her child and not miss a minute of its upbringing if she could help it.

If the nausea medicine worked the way it was supposed to, she'd be feeling well enough again in a few days to fly home and get busy. With a new sense of purpose in her life, she felt able to cope with her physical state.

Once she'd finished dressing, she made a stop to the rest room, then hurried out to the reception area. Lance stood in the crowded waiting room near the door. His hard-boned face and physique drew the eye of every woman including the medical staff. In thigh molding jeans and a black pullover, he was the most spectacular looking male Andrea had ever seen.

She could feel their envy as she approached him. "Do you have the prescriptions?"

His concerned eyes intently took in her features with an intimacy that made her heart race. "Yes. Shall we go?" He opened the door for her and escorted her outside to his car.

Without saying anything, he helped her in the passenger seat, then walked around to the driver's side and took off for the pharmacy in the center of the village.

"Stay where you are," he ordered. "I'll be right back."

Long before he'd gone into the military, Andrea was in no doubt Lance Malbois had been a man meant to be in charge. His service there had only refined those instincts, protective and otherwise. Right now she wasn't complaining.

He'd come across her in the forest and—in his unorthodox way—had seen to her needs faster than she'd been able to breathe. If she had to choose one person in this world to help her survive a difficult situation, she'd choose Lance, no questions asked.

This Frenchman more than lived up to his legendary name, which had to be unique among men. In fact Andrea had a feeling the military couldn't have been happy to learn he was retiring. Not so for the woman planning to marry him.

Andrea could understand a stepdaughter who was no blood relation being infatuated by Geoff's son. As Andrea was coming to find out, there was no man to compare to him.

In a few minutes he'd rejoined her. "Here." He undid the cap and handed her a pill. "You're to take this now with water." He produced a bottle of mineral water. "The vitamins you can start tonight so they won't upset your stomach."

"Yes, Doctor," she teased before swallowing the medicine. "That water tastes good. Thank you." She put the pill vials in her purse.

His darkly lashed eyes met her gaze. Their faces were only inches apart. "Let's hope your appetite improves by tomorrow. Before we drive home, is there anything you need to buy?"

Andrea averted her eyes. "I can't think of anything."

"I can. A new camera. Tonnerre's hoof smashed yours. After I get you settled, I'll take a trip into town and purchase a new one. I'm afraid the film was ruined."

"Don't worry about it, Lance. I put in a new cartridge this morning, so no pictures are lost. As for the camera, I don't need another one right now. I'll wait till I get home and arrange to buy one through my old boss. He'll get me something wholesale."

Lance started the car and they took off for the château. Since the downpour earlier, the greenery bordering the road looked wet and fresh. He drove with an economy of movement.

"Where did you work?"

"At a photography studio."

"Did you like it?"

"As jobs go, it was fine. I started working there part-time during my high school days. After graduation I increased my hours to full-time to save money for college."

"Did you attend Yale like your husband?"

It appeared Geoff and Lance had been talking.

"Oh, no," she scoffed. "I was a mediocre student and couldn't have afforded it. I took a few night classes at a local college before meeting Richard. After that I sort of became his unofficial assistant."

"And wife," Lance interjected.

She nodded. "Yes."

"No more school?"

"No. One day I'll go for a degree in something, but now that a baby is on the way, that will have to wait until my child is in school full-time."

"In other words, you don't plan to let someone else raise it."

"There are jobs I can do at home. I'll try anything in order to be there for my son or daughter," she vowed.

"That sounds final."

"It's the way I feel."

She heard him take a deep breath. "Then your child will be lucky. Until the day she died my mother was always there for me."

"Geoff told me she passed away while you were at the university."

He slowed down to negotiate the turn into the Du Lac estate. "That's right. Looking back I had an idyllic upbringing." His head suddenly turned toward her. "How early did you lose your parents?"

"At four years of age. Pictures are the only things I have to remember them. Knowing I'm going to be a mother makes that my first priority, no matter what it takes."

"At the moment it requires bed rest." He brought the car to a halt and levered his long legs from the front seat to help her.

She could have managed on her own, but he cupped her elbow to assist her inside. The minute they reached the foyer, she found herself in his arms once more. Her ponytail swung back and forth.

"You don't have to do this," she protested, but he ignored her cry and carried her up the two flights of stairs as if she were light as air.

CHAPTER FOUR

LANCE opened the door of her suite, not releasing her until he'd laid her on the bed. To her relief she didn't think any of the staff had seen them.

His eyes bored into hers. "Don't you dare lift a finger. I'll be back in a little while and bring you a dinner tray. You can take your vitamins then." He acted more worried than a mother hen with her chick. After their stormy beginning, she would never have guessed Lance had this side to him.

"I don't need waiting on."

"I beg to differ." His mouth was so close she could feel his breath on her lips before he stood up. "Defy me at your own peril."

Lance was a force she had no desire to contend with at the moment. She spread her hands apart. "All right. But please don't say anything to Geoff. He shouldn't have any worries."

"Agreed," Lance murmured before disappearing from the room.

The moment the door closed she got up and hurried into the bathroom. After getting caught in the rain, and then being examined at the clinic, she needed to shower and wash her hair.

Once that was accomplished, she toweled herself and left her hair loose so it would dry faster. She put on a clean yellow nightgown and matching fleece robe. When she climbed back into bed, it felt good.

She'd barely nestled under the covers when the door opened and she saw Lance walk in carrying a tray in one hand, and a bunch of magazines in the other.

Through narrowed lids she noticed he'd showered, too. He wore a silk shirt in a dark coffee shade and tan trousers. Whether he donned formal clothes or military khaki, he was so attractive she found she couldn't take her eyes off him.

As he crossed the distance and started to lower the tray to the bedside table, she glimpsed one of the life-size wall paintings of Lancelot directly behind him. The handsome knight was leaning over the queen in their bedchamber, as if he'd just come in from hunting and was eager to taste her mouth before joining her.

The gorgeous man waiting on Andrea was in much the same position. In that instant she couldn't separate the two pictures in her mind. The pulse at her throat began to throb a wild crescendo.

Lance must have noticed her reaction because his wandering eyes focused on that telling spot for a breathless moment before they continued their slow, intimate journey to her face.

Heat swept through her body to her cheeks. Their gazes fused.

"How are you feeling now?" His voice resonated deep inside her.

She inhaled unsteadily. "I—I'm fine."

"Fine enough to try and eat something?"

Andrea looked over at the magazines and tray he'd put next

to her pills. He'd brought hot tea, broth, apple slices, grape juice, water and a roll. She had an idea he'd picked everything out himself. Though she wasn't hungry, she didn't want him to think she was ungrateful, so she reached for an apple slice and began munching.

The gesture seemed to please him. He moved away. She thought he intended to leave. Instead he reached for an upholstered chair and brought it over to her bedside before sitting down to drink a cup of the steaming brew.

Lounging back with one long leg crossed over the other at the ankles, he looked the epitome of the French aristocrat relaxing at home in luxurious surroundings. A far cry from the man in camouflage who'd moved through the forest with the stealth of a savage cat. Yet both made up part of the same fascinating man standing attendance on her.

"Good? Bad?" he asked, reminding her of the fruit she'd just swallowed.

"Good actually. I'm surprised." She reached for another slice. "You make an excellent nurse." He was a man of many talents. "I'm sorry you returned home from war to discover you have two patients to wait on."

He stared at her over the rim of the cup. "Since both are improving, I have no complaints."

She reached for the glass of grape juice and took a sip. "Have you talked to your father since we got back from the clinic?"

"Yes. Because he had a visitor today, I told him I thought he should have a quiet evening. Tomorrow will be soon enough for you to join him for lunch. He agreed with one stipulation."

"What was that?"

"He expects me to keep you entertained." Her heart raced for no good reason. "I told him it wasn't a hardship."

"Your father's a wonder."

"I'll keep him," Lance said in a thick-toned voice.

She nodded. "I would, too. I've never met anyone as warm and kind. He said your mother was the same way."

He put his empty cup on the tray. Lines darkened his face. "At this point you're wondering how they could have produced a defect like me."

Her breath caught. "Defect?"

"You don't need to pretend. I saw the shock on your face when you discovered I was his son."

She sat up in the bed. "If I registered that emotion, it was because I realized your experiences in the military had to account for your treating me like I was the enemy."

"I'm afraid certain experiences in my life have caused me to distrust women. In that regard Papa and I are at opposite ends of the spectrum."

"I have proof of that." Andrea studied him for a moment. "What did you think I was doing in the forest the other night?"

His eyes flickered. "To be honest, I forgot I wasn't on a mission. My automatic response was to render you helpless and either kill you or send you on your way depending on my gut feeling."

She shivered. "What did your instincts tell you?"

A frown marred his features. "When you stood your ground, I realized I'd turned into some kind of monster."

"Ten years in the elite force would change anyone, especially since you suspected me of ulterior motives where your father was concerned."

After a strange silence, "Are you afraid of me, Andrea?" he drawled silkily.

Wishing she hadn't spoken her mind, she reached for the roll and took a bite. "How could you ask me that when you were the one who rescued me today?

"If I didn't make myself clear, let me do it now. I'm very grateful for your help, but you won't have to worry about me much longer. After tomorrow I should be feeling well enough to fly home."

His expression remained inscrutable. "Even if that's true, my father wouldn't hear of it. He's been sick the whole time you've been at the château. I'm afraid you'll have to stay on for a while.

"As soon as he's well enough to walk around again, Papa plans to delight you with a special tour of the grounds. The experience will give you the opportunity to take more pictures to add to your husband's book. That *is* why you came, *n'est-ce pas?*"

She lowered her eyes. "Yes, but—"

"No buts. The matter's settled. While you recover your appetite, the doctor told you to get plenty of bed rest and drink fluids. I'm here to see that you do."

In one lithe movement he got to his feet. "If you need anything, all you have to do is pick up the phone and press two. I'll answer." He continued looking at her. "Let's hope the little you've eaten makes you feel better. I'll be in later to say good-night."

She sensed his disinclination to leave. "I'll be fine. Thank you for everything."

He pursed his lips. "I don't want to come back and find you lying on the floor."

"If I feel that weak, I promise to let you know."

"See that you do," came the grim rejoinder before he left.

Feeling oddly bereft after his departure, she reached for one of the magazines to keep her mind occupied. It was full of articles on European architecture. Though printed in French, she didn't require a translation to digest the fabulous photographs.

However nothing she saw equaled the magnificence of the Château Du Lac. Or Lance himself…

Her thoughts wandered back to his comments at the clinic. *Hearing the news with you made me feel like I'm the father. It's an experience I wouldn't have missed.*

He'd sounded like he'd really meant it. What an incredible man…

After putting the magazine back on the table, her gaze traveled to the wall paintings. Guinevere seemed exactly the same as before. But this time when she studied Lancelot, it was Lance Malbois's face and body she saw everywhere she looked. The way his eyes adored the queen filled Andrea with a strange envy.

For the first time she found herself curious about Lance's stepsister. Did she elicit that same kind of worship from him?

The Galerie Bouffard in Rennes stayed open until nine-thirty on Thursday nights. Lance made his way through the crowded store from the book section to the camera department.

After explaining what he needed to the employee, the man showed him several upgrades of the camera Andrea had been using. It didn't take Lance long to choose something state-of-the-art to replace the one his horse had smashed to pieces.

He included a pack of film with his purchase, then asked for directions to the infant department. He'd never shopped for baby clothes in his life, but learning Andrea was expecting made him want to do something to help her celebrate. Since he didn't know if she was carrying a boy or girl, he decided to stick with white and yellow, both safe colors, the assistant had assured him.

By the time the young female employee had shown him everything, he left the store with half a dozen little outfits and two baby blankets in those colors, a baby book and a Fifi the poodle-in-the-box that played a French tune, all gift wrapped. Among the ribbons the clerk tied three rattles he'd picked out.

As she handed him the bag of packages, she winked at him. "Your new baby's lucky to have a father like you."

She'd made a wrong assumption, but he liked the sound of it. "I'm the one who's lucky."

"Don't be a stranger now. Babies grow."

They did indeed. Lance found himself looking forward to watching Andrea blossom. During that moment in the lake when he'd helped her to the surface, he'd felt a quickening as the rich contours of her body pressed against him. Her imprint still lingered, causing him to think thoughts he hadn't entertained for a long time.

"Merci, mademoiselle."

After emerging from the *ascenseur*, he made his way to the main doors of the store.

"*Eh bien*, if it isn't Lance Malbois, you handsome devil. Geoff didn't tell anyone you were home on leave."

He looked back over his shoulder to discover Helene Dupuis,

the wife of his father's best friend. She was a good person, but a gossip. Lance had hoped to keep his homecoming a secret for a while, but bumping into her had dashed that idea.

"Bonsoir, Helene. Comment ça va?"

"I'm very well, and I have to tell you I'm thrilled to see you are, too. Geoff worries about you. It's no wonder he's been so sick even Yves and I have been barred from dropping in," she chided.

Henri knew what he was doing. Though she meant well, a visit from Helene would have been too exhausting. "He's getting better now. By next week he'll want to see both of you."

"Yves will be delighted to hear it. How long can we expect you to remain this time?"

Lance decided to tell the truth since it would come out anyway. "I've retired from the service."

"You're home for good?"

"Oui."

Her eyes lit up. "Oh—I must give a party!"

He shook his head. "That's very nice of you, but no parties. I have too much work ahead. Now if you'll excuse me. Papa's waiting."

"But of course. You go to him, and we'll see you soon."

"À bientôt, Helene."

"I know someone else who's going to be ecstatic at the news you're home," she called after him. But he pretended not to hear as he strode around the corner to his car. Corinne was like all unpleasant things one had to deal with on occasion.

As he was putting his packages on the passenger seat, the streetlight reflected in one of the baby rattles. It drew his thoughts back to Andrea who might or might not be asleep when he returned. He hoped she was still awake since he was eager to see her reaction when she opened her presents.

He couldn't get back to the château soon enough, and raced up the stairs to the third floor two at a time.

When the housekeeper came in at eight to take away the dinner tray, she brought a small, battery operated radio for Andrea.

"Lance said you were tired. Since this room hasn't been wired for television, he thought you might like to listen to some music from his transistor," she explained before setting it on the bedside table.

Lance thought of everything. Had he told the staff she was pregnant? If so, Brigitte was being discreet. She was also amazing. Andrea would give anything to speak French the way the older woman spoke English.

"That was very thoughtful of both of you. By the way, how is Geoff tonight?"

"Doing better than yesterday."

"I'm relieved to hear it."

"If you need me, call me on four."

"I will. *Merci*." It was one of the basic words Andrea had picked up so far.

After a few minutes of playing around with the radio, she found a music station and lay back against the pillow to listen. It was fun to hear songs sung in French, even if she didn't understand the words.

While she studied the paintings on the walls, she smiled to herself, remembering Lance's tenderness at the doctor's.

Deep in thought over the revelations of this day, she lost track of time. When she heard a knock on the door, she was surprised to see that her watch said nine forty-five. The idea that it might be Lance on the other side caused her pulse to speed up.

"Come in."

Her breath caught the second their eyes met for an intense moment.

"How are you feeling?"

"Good."

"The truth," he commanded.

"I honestly feel better. If you want proof, ask Brigitte. She came for my tray and will tell you I ate all my roll and drank half the juice. So far I've kept it down."

"I'm glad to hear it."

After shutting the door, he walked toward her carrying several shopping bags and handed her the smaller one.

"Go ahead and look inside. If it isn't what you want, I'll return it."

Intrigued, Andrea sat up against the carved headboard and reached inside to discover a new camera and film. He'd already been to town for one! She couldn't believe it.

"You didn't need to do this," she said, pulling it out of its box. There were instructions in four languages including English. She examined all the features. "This is perfect, but it's much more expensive than mine."

"As long as it works for you, that's all Tonnerre cares about."

She laughed gently. "That was very generous of him. Please thank your horse for me, Lance."

His compelling mouth lifted at one corner. "I'll be sure to do that."

"What does his name mean in English? I'm curious."

"Thunder."

She smiled. "How apropos."

He sat down in the chair he'd pulled up earlier and handed her the bigger bag. "This is from me."

Andrea shook her head. "I can't accept any more gifts."

"These aren't for you. Not exactly."

Just as he spoke, she saw a rattle entwined in ribbon peeking at her. Letting out a small cry of delight she lifted her head. "What have you done?"

"What any excited father-to-be would do upon hearing the news he'd made his wife pregnant."

Lance's words shouldn't have caused her to tremble, but they did…

To cover her emotions, she reached inside and pulled out box after box wrapped in white paper dotted with adorable little baby faces. Before long she'd opened everything and sat half buried in cuddly newborn outfits and soft blankets.

Beads of tears glistened on her lashes while she looked through the baby book. He'd brought several books in English about becoming a parent. She was so overcome by the gifts, tears spilled from her eyes. Within seconds she was convulsed.

"What's the matter, Andrea?" his voice rasped. "Have I done something to upset you?"

"Oh, no, Lance—" She lifted her moisture-drenched face to see the deep concern in his eyes. "Anything but. It just hurts to realize Richard won't be here to do these kinds of things for the baby. He'll have missed the whole experience, and our child will never know him.

"I can't believe the timing of everything—" she cried out. "He should be here to help me! It doesn't seem possible he's not going to be around to be a father to our baby. How unfair that he was taken before he could experience the joy of even knowing he was going to be a dad.

"I know how I felt when I realized my parents had died and I would grow up never knowing them. It's so cruel to an innocent child. I don't want my son or daughter to grow up without their father."

The tears kept coming. She felt like a bottomless geyser. "Forgive me, Lance. I didn't mean to fall apart like this in front of you. You've been so good to me and have made this day so special.

"Look at all these darling clothes you took the time to purchase. And yet how sad it is that Richard couldn't have been the one to do it. It's what he would have wanted to do." She shook her head. "Why is life so hard?"

Andrea tried to undo the other package he'd put on the bed, but she was having trouble. Lance must have become impatient because he reached over and finished opening the toy he'd bought for her. Out of the box bounced a French poodle. It played a tune but she couldn't hear it for the radio, so she leaned over to shut it off.

He pushed the button again and the cute white dog jumped out, accompanied by the tune *"Alouette."*

She smiled sadly as tears dripped off her chin. "I know that song. It's probably the only thing I can sing in French."

"Prove it," he challenged her in that deep voice of his. She knew he'd said it to try to cheer her up. After all the trouble he'd gone to, she didn't want to disappoint him.

Andrea shut the lid, then pushed the button once more and sang along. "My accent's horrible," she said when she'd finished.

His gaze had narrowed on her mouth. "I found it charming."

Her heart was pounding too fast. "Lance— You've overwhelmed me with these gifts."

"That was my intention." He got to his feet. "Now do my father a favor and stay at the château for as long as you like. I understand you want to honor Richard's memory with this book. I'd like to do all I can to help in order to atone for my sins."

"You've already done that," she whispered.

His body stiffened. "I'm aware how much you loved your husband. No matter how you deny it, I said and did things to hurt you, unaware of your grief. Let me try to make it up to you."

For Lance to plead had to be a rare occurrence. Yet the longer she stayed here, the more she would be around Geoff's arresting son. She didn't need that complication in her life, especially when she was expecting Richard's baby.

"Have you told your father I'm pregnant?"

"That's not my place." After a tension filled moment he said, "The doctor said you needed rest. Be honest. Nothing pressing requires you to get back to Connecticut right away."

"No," she murmured.

"Then the matter's settled." Before she could take her next breath he put the gifts he'd bought back in the bags and set them at the end of the bed. Then he handed her the pills and glass of water left on the table.

After she'd taken one he said, "What else can I get for you?"

"Nothing. You've done far too much already. I need to thank you for the radio. It has kept me company."

He nodded. "When I need a distraction, I prefer it to television even now that I'm out of the service. However I could have you moved to the second floor if you're missing TV."

"Oh, no. I wouldn't understand it anyway. I much prefer being in this room where I can study all the paintings."

He flashed her a glance she couldn't decipher. "Can you guess which of them is my favorite?"

She knew which one *she* loved the most. It was the painting of Lancelot leaning over the queen in the bedchamber, a look of love and desire burning in his eyes. Her gaze went back to it again and again.

"Since you rode your horse as if it were a part of you, I presume you like the one where Guinevere is riding through the forest with Lancelot." The queen lay in the crook of his arm and stroked his chin while her eyes devoured him.

Lance cocked his dark, handsome head. "You're close. I'd rate that second. Think about it some more and tell me later."

She wished he hadn't put the thought in her mind. Now she'd spend the rest of the night trying to imagine which scene spoke to him at his deepest level.

It was probably the one where Lancelot lay on his back in a flowering meadow. He'd removed his armor. Guinevere was leaning over him, tickling him with a long pheasant feather from her cap. They were both smiling at each other, as if they didn't have a care in the world.

Lance Malbois had so many cares he kept to himself, Andrea assumed he would love that painting best. It represented a moment out of time where Lancelot could forget the world and love this woman of his heart without strife or fear of being caught out by the other knights.

Aware he was still standing there she said, "Before you go, let me thank you again for the presents. They're so lovely, I'll never forget."

"I'm glad you like them."

"One day you'll make a wonderful father for some lucky child."

"No." He shook his head.

"Don't be ridiculous, Lance."

When she looked up at him, she glimpsed a bleakness in his eyes. After a tension-filled moment she heard him say, "Would it help if I told you life hasn't been fair to me, either?"

Her gaze flew to his scar. "If you're referring to your injury, in my opinion it adds to your attraction and makes you more interesting. Ask any woman and she'll tell you the same thing."

"That's always nice to hear," he said dryly, "but I'm referring to another one."

She bit her lip. "You have more than the scar?" her voice shook.

"Sometimes the wounds on the inside do the most damage."

He'd caught her attention. "What's wrong with you?"

There was an unnatural quiet in the room before he said, "I can't father a child, Andrea, I'm impotent."

The impact of his words was so painful, her heart plunged to her feet. She pressed a hand to her mouth to stifle her cry, but it escaped anyway.

They stared at each other while streams of unspoken words flowed between them.

"You're the one person I know who understands how it feels to learn you'll never be able to create a life from your own body. In fact you're the only person in my life I've told," he admitted soberly.

She groaned remembering Geoff's excitement that Lance

had come home for good. His expectations of grandchildren had put a new light in his eyes.

Those ever ready tears stung hers once more. "Oh, Lance—How did it happen? When?"

After a sharp intake of breath he said, "During one of my assignments in the Middle East, I was exposed to a chemical agent that put me in the hospital for a while. That was seven years ago. After I recovered, I was told I'd never be able to have children."

To be told that was like being given a death sentence of sorts. She understood. Oh how she understood.

He would never know the joy of seeing himself in one of his own children. There'd be no flesh and blood baby who would grow up to look like the Malbois family.

"If you hadn't gone in the military…"

"But I did." His barely leashed anger revealed his pain. "Unlike you however, there's no miracle that can change my condition."

Andrea had nothing to say to that. There weren't any words to give him the smallest hope. She'd never felt so helpless.

"Suffice it to say, not many women of childbearing age want to marry a man who can't give them a child."

Right now wasn't the time to assure Lance there were plenty of women out there who'd give anything to be his wife if he were in love with them. They'd agree to adoption. In any case, the woman who wanted to be his wife wouldn't make children the issue.

Yet with hindsight she could see that her being infertile *had* mattered to Richard. He hadn't even wanted to discuss adoption. If she'd heard she couldn't have a baby before she'd married him, he would have lost interest in her and walked away. He liked a well ordered life, everything in its place. Anything less than perfect didn't suit.

Andrea had turned out to be less than perfect. Maybe that was why their sex life had suffered in their marriage. It could explain why he'd ended up burying himself in his books.

When she looked back, she realized she'd been the one to reach out to him on the day he'd died, hoping to ignite that missing spark.

She buried her face in her hands. "Your father's going to feel terrible for you. You're his *raison d'être*."

"He'll deal with it."

"But what about you, Lance? Honestly..." With her heart aching for him, she lifted her head to look at him.

"For a few moments in the clinic today when Dr. Semplis congratulated us, I felt as if you and I had made your baby together. I liked the feeling. So much in fact that I'd like to be its father on a permanent basis."

She sat up straighter. What was he saying?

"You've asked for an honest response from me, so let me ask you a question. How would you like to marry me?"

For the second time in one day, her world stood still. It took her a minute before she could speak.

"You're talking a marriage of convenience?" she asked in wonder.

"I guess that's one way of putting it," he drawled. "From the outset it's been clear you and your husband enjoyed a great marriage. I realize a love like that only comes once in a lifetime.

"Life has dealt us both a great blow to our dreams, so I'm not going to ask for the impossible. But if you'd let me, I'd like to give you my name. Then I can be there to help you through your pregnancy, and after. I'll provide for you and the baby for the rest of my life. Everything I have will be yours.

"I can promise you it won't be hard to say it's mine. After listening to its heartbeat, I already feel a bond. What are the chances of that happening again? This will be the closest I'll ever come to playing the role of father right from the cradle.

"Think about it, and we'll talk more tomorrow after I've come back from Rennes. If you're feeling up to it, we'll take a drive into the country for dinner.

"In the meantime, do me a favor and mind the doctor. I'll instruct the kitchen to send up your meals tomorrow. That way you can give those pills a chance to do their job while you rest.

"*Bonne nuit,* Andrea."

Still in shock, she watched him leave, knowing there'd be no rest for her from now on. Not when the future Duc Du Lac had just asked her to marry him so he could have a baby.

Richard's baby.

But Richard wasn't alive, and Lance, who was very much alive, yet could never get a woman pregnant, was prepared to step in and father her baby.

It meant she'd never have a financial worry. She could be the total stay-at-home mother she'd dreamed of being, and her baby would have a daddy who would raise him and love him.

Andrea had no doubts about Lance's devotion to her child. His reaction at the clinic, the excitement in his eyes when he'd gone out to buy her the gifts, let her know he'd be a natural when it came to fatherhood. After all, he was Geoff's son. What better role model could any man have.

Her baby would inherit a grandfather who would lavish his love on his grandchild.

Three people who'd known loss would dote on her baby. What a lucky boy or girl to be the recipient of so much love.

The only way the decision to marry Lance wouldn't be convenient was if he eventually met a woman and fell madly in love.

Andrea had no doubts he would always be there for their child, but he would feel trapped in the marriage he'd entered into with Andrea. *That* would be the risk she'd be taking if she said yes to him now, and then further down the road he wanted out.

For the rest of the night she tossed and turned, wishing she couldn't feel or understand his pain that he couldn't procreate.

She should never have listened to him—never have given him the chance to broach the subject with her. Something had told her there'd be a price to pay if she did.

There was a price all right.

He'd stripped her of her of peace of mind. Lance knew she'd become emotionally involved and had purposely left her to writhe while she considered the pros and cons of his outrageous marriage proposal.

It was a desperate measure on the part of a very desperate man. If she agreed to it, what did that make her?

Every kind of a fool for even entertaining something that could bring untold pain and anguish down the road.

CHAPTER FIVE

"THIS is a lovely old inn, Lance. What does the name of it mean in English?"

He studied Andrea's oval face in the candlelight. She had the classic features of a true beauty. He doubted she wore anything but lipstick.

"It's called the Gold Chestnut Tree. If you hadn't become ill the other day, I would have shown you the real one."

She blinked. "Real one?"

"In 1990 there was a fire here in the Valley of No Return. It burned for five days. Afterward thousands of donations poured in from around the world to help save the mythical heritage that abounds here. Papa was one of the people instrumental in spearheading it."

"Five days—"

"It was devastating. You may have heard of the Parisian sculptor, François Davin. He created a huge golden chestnut tree with pure gold leaves to pay tribute to international cooperation. The tree symbolizes the immortality of the dreams of men of goodwill."

"I believe Richard did mention something about it. The branches are supposed to resemble a stag's antlers."

"That's right. It's to commemorate the wild animals who led the knights through the enchanted forests, and to remind us of the power of man's love of Mother Nature."

"How lovely," she mused.

The personification of loveliness was seated across from him. "How was your crêpe?"

"As you can see, I ate most of it. Combined with the cider, everything tasted delicious."

"No nausea spells this afternoon?"

She shook her head. The golden-brown strands glistened against her shoulders. With eyes dark as poppy throats, she had an enchanting color scheme.

"I spent part of the afternoon with your father in the garden and kept waiting to be sick, but it didn't happen. The medicine has worked wonders."

That was good news.

Since driving away from the château with her, Lance had purposely kept up desultory conversation to put her at ease. To his chagrin she'd seemed so comfortable with him throughout dinner, he had the premonition she'd made up her mind to turn him down hours before. As a result, she was enjoying their evening out without any accompanying nervousness.

Lance on the other hand found his appetite had left him. Once having asked her to consider his proposal, the idea that she might turn him down was getting harder and harder to accept. In fact it was quite unthinkable.

Baby or no baby, he discovered he wanted to be with her

all the time. His physical attraction to her had been immediate. Knowing she was pregnant made her even more desirable.

Tonight she looked lit up inside. In the simple black dress and strand of pearls, her curvaceous body moved with a femininity that made him ache to touch her. He was charmed by her soft laughter. She was a person who enjoyed the small moments.

Andrea wanted nothing from him. As a consequence, he was prepared to give her his name. So far no other woman had meant enough to him that he wanted to live with her on a constant basis, let alone be responsible for her.

No longer able to enjoy the evening when he didn't know her decision, he announced they were leaving the restaurant. She went along without demur, which probably meant she was tired and wanted to go home.

On the way back to the château, he drove her past Paimpont abbey to the pool nestled in the foothills his father wanted her to see. He shut off the engine and glanced at her profile.

"One night after your baby's born and you're able, I'll bring you here for a swim. Merlin fell madly in love with Viviane in this spot. They used to make love here. When the moon is full, it reflects off the water like the silver chalice Perceval sought."

She put down her window, allowing the sultry summer night air to filter through the car. "This place could be right out of a fantasy. Ever since I've been in Brittany, I feel as if I've been caught in a spell."

Lance liked the sound of that. "It's because you've entered the sanctuary of the wicked fairy Morgan-le-Fay, Arthur's half sister. Remember those red rocks we passed earlier where the waters are turbulent? She would lure fickle knights here, then imprison them.

"Motivated by his love for the queen, Lancelot braved untold dangers to break those poor souls from Morgan's evil spell. In the process he found the way out through this enchanted pool."

"You're part of that same enchantment," Andrea spoke up. "Like a shapeshifter you take on a different form depending on the moment. I never know who's going to appear next.

"Will it be the loving, devoted son? The battle scarred military man? The impeccable host? The knight in modern armor still rescuing damsels in distress? The wounded soldier who believes he's lost his manhood? The boy-man yearning for his idyllic childhood? The Duc-elect of Du Lac fame? The unofficial fiancé of his stepsister?"

Mon Dieu.

Except for her not knowing about his history with Corinne, she had him figured out better than any psychiatrist.

"If I'd wanted to marry her, I would never have joined the military. Enough said?"

She was staring out her window. "Then it was always her fantasy?"

"Always."

"What about your father's?"

"Naturally he wants me to settle down and be happy. But just so you know, the choice of bride has always been up to me."

His hand resting on the seat behind her dug into the leather upholstery. Any hope he'd held out that Andrea might go along with his plan was fading fast.

"How about viewing me as a simple man who would love to be a father, and can see a way to helping himself and you at the same time?"

"There's nothing simple about you."

He leaned closer to her. "Is that the overwhelmed mother-to-be talking? The widow who's still in mourning for the husband she'll always love? The girl-woman who never felt she belonged? The student of the world wishing she had her degree? The grieving daughter who never knew her parents? The woman who's on her own for the first time in her life and is afraid she likes it?"

A minute must have passed before she turned her head to look at him. "*Touché*."

"Would you be willing to take the plunge with me into unknown waters and see what happens? With my money, you'll never have to worry about going to work. Your child will always have my name and protection. Best of all, you'll be able to be a full-time mother to your baby, and I'll be there to give support."

A troubled sigh escaped her lips.

"What else is on your mind?" he prodded. "Now is the time to unearth it."

"I didn't say anything."

"Yes, you did," he whispered. "Let me ask you a question. Do you trust me?"

She lowered her head. "If I didn't, I wouldn't have come out to dinner with you, and we wouldn't be having this conversation."

The tight band constricting his chest burst, allowing him to go on breathing. "Then let it be your answer. Promises are only just that anyway. You and I will be going where neither of us has gone before.

"Your sense of adventure is as great as mine, or you wouldn't have come to Brittany a second time. For the sake of the baby, let's agree to make the most of every second of it."

He felt in his suit jacket pocket. "Give me your hand." When she didn't react fast enough, he reached for it. She trembled as he slid the engagement ring on her finger without problem.

"I bought it this afternoon. The minute I saw the pear shape of the stone, it reminded me of the lake where we met. What do you think?"

She spread her fingers in front of her eyes. "I think it's the most exquisite diamond I've ever seen. I can't imagine how you got the fit right."

"After telling the clerk your height and weight, I added that you were pregnant. He figured out the rest."

In spite of the tense moment, her mouth curved in a seductive smile if she'd but known it.

"After the baby's born, you can get it resized so you don't lose it," he added.

"The stone's so large, it would be impossible to miss." New energy hovered around them like a livewire. "But I can't accept it."

The breath froze in his lungs. "So your forgiveness of my sins stops short of matrimony, even if it's for the baby's sake."

"No, Lance. That isn't what I meant."

His guts clenched. "Then explain it to me."

"This is the kind of ring you give the woman you love. I'd prefer something more modest."

A shudder of relief passed through his taut body. "If that's the only thing bothering you, do me a favor and wear it until I can get you another one."

Afraid she'd take it off and break the enchantment of the moment, sending him back to the black hole where he'd been living for so long, he started to turn on the engine. That's when he saw something move at the edge of the pond.

"Andrea—" he murmured. "Don't make a sound. Just turn your head slowly toward the water."

She did his bidding.

One of the things he enjoyed most about her was her acceptance of the unexpected. She had an inner calm, no matter her shock or fear. Not many people possessed that enviable trait.

He had trouble tearing his eyes from her long enough to watch the stag who'd come to the pool to drink. The woman at his side drew in her breath, letting him know how much the scene delighted her.

They watched for a few minutes. Then Lance heard the sudden hoot of a nearby owl. It startled the stag who threw back his head and pranced off into the foliage.

"I've never seen a deer with such a huge rack, and yet he was so graceful. Majestic…"

"That one's been around a long time."

"To think I've been trying to get a picture of the animals, and tonight I'm without my camera."

"We'll come tomorrow night about this same time and wait for him."

"He was beautiful."

So was she…

If he stayed here with her any longer and did what he felt like doing, he could frighten her off.

"Let's go home. If my father's still up, we'll tell him our plans. Otherwise it will have to be tomorrow."

"I think it would be better to wait until he's had a good night's sleep."

"Then that's what we'll do." Now that she'd agreed to marry him, he wasn't about to argue a minor point.

Once they were headed back to the château he turned to her. "While I was in Rennes the other evening, I bumped into Helene Dupuis who often plays hostess for Papa. She wants to give me a homecoming party. I'll tell her to go all out since we're already engaged and want it to be our wedding reception.

"I'd like to schedule it soon. To wait any later in your pregnancy might not be wise. I wouldn't want to endanger your health. Two to three weeks ought to give your aunt and uncle time to come."

"Oh, I don't know about that. I'm afraid they wouldn't be able to afford the plane fare."

"I don't expect them to pay for anything. That's my privilege. I want your friends to come, too. Anyone on the faculty you feel close to."

"Lance—"

"This will be my one and only wedding. I'd like to meet the people in your life. So will my father. Your family did an outstanding job of raising you. If your parents were alive, there'd be no question of their coming.

"Don't be concerned about other social engagements. Because of your pregnancy, we'll limit the number of parties to our wedding day and the christening. When you and I get better acquainted, you'll learn I'm not a social animal like my father."

"I already know that about you."

"Do you mind?"

"No. Richard and I had to attend a lot of functions, but I must admit that most of the time I would have preferred to do something alone with him."

"I'm a homebody myself. Once the baby comes, we'll have our hands full."

They'd reached the château. He pulled around the side and shut off the engine.

"My uncle liked to be home. He was a family man."

"I'm looking forward to it myself." Lance undid his seat belt. "During my downtime in the military, some of my married buddies would receive letters and pictures of their children through e-mail.

"I envied them having a family to go home to. After my hospitalization, I envied them for being able to give their wives a child. Under the circumstances it made sense to stay in the service and let those poor devils go home to the people who needed them."

She released her seat belt.

"I can relate. In fact I've lived for so long without hope, I'm still in shock I'm pregnant."

"Our baby will be here within six months. Maybe by then we'll both believe it."

After being burned by his past, Lance was astounded that he was putting himself in a position where he had to be willing to trust a woman again. Upon leaving the service, he never wanted or intended for this to happen. He was still in shock that he'd returned home to a situation where a woman had the power to make him vulnerable again.

But he couldn't deny the emotions building inside him where Andrea was concerned. The attraction to her was too strong to ignore or deny, even if she was still in love with Richard.

When she'd broken down in Lance's arms while she gave into her pent-up grief, it should have doused any fire building in him whether physical or emotional.

Instead the opposite had happened, and therein lay the problem. The one thing he feared was intruding on her grief. How to deal with this woman who was still mourning her husband?

That was the burning question Lance wrestled with at the moment. The only way to respect her feelings and keep his needs from growing out of control was to concentrate on the baby.

With that decision firmly in place he kissed her cheek before levering himself from the driver's seat to help her out.

When he looked up, he noticed the light in his father's room had been turned off.

"Papa's gone to bed," he said as he ushered Andrea into the foyer and up the stairs. "We'll tell him over lunch. That'll give both of you time to sleep in. How does that sound?"

When they reached her door she raised tremulous eyes to him. "That'll give you time in case you have a change of mind during the night."

He drew in a harsh breath. "Not a chance in hell."

When morning came Andrea didn't experience any nausea, yet her stomach felt fluttery. What if Geoff had reservations? She'd see it in his eyes immediately.

Without time to lose she hurriedly took another pill and her vitamins before getting dressed for the day. Andrea didn't want anyone waiting on her. No one should have to climb all those stairs to bring her something to eat.

She put on fresh coral lipstick and brushed out her hair. It swished against the shoulders of her khaki blouse. Since all her pants were too tight to be comfortable, she donned the same wraparound skirt she'd worn a few days earlier. It accommodated her thickening belly.

The next time she went to town she'd buy some new clothes. She still had to pinch herself that she'd joined the ranks of those fortunate women who needed to visit a maternity shop.

As she descended the stairs, her whole world felt different. Because she was going to be a mother, and Lance would be the baby's father, the knowledge colored her thinking. She had a new reason to live.

Lance happened to be on his way up to her floor wearing charcoal trousers and a claret toned sport shirt. Her breath caught at the sight of such potent masculinity. If she hadn't cried his name in time, they would have collided.

As it was, his hand fell on her shoulder. She felt its warmth all the way to her bones. His eyes roved over her features in male admiration. "You look like a different person this morning. Motherhood becomes you."

Everything he said sounded intimate and personal. "It must be *that* and the medicine. I'm much improved even since yesterday."

She noticed the visible rise and fall of his well-defined chest. "I'm glad to hear it. I told Papa we wanted to have lunch with him. He's looking forward to it."

"How does he seem physically?"

"He's getting back to his old self in a hurry." Lance's eyes scrutinized her. "Where were you going so fast?"

"To the library to do some research before lunch."

His hand slid away from her arm with seeming reluctance. "While you do that I'll be in the study doing some business."

By tacit agreement they went down to the main floor together. She'd never been more aware of his height. He smelled so good—looked so good— If Lancelot had this same effect on Guinevere, Andrea could understand why Arthur's dream failed and Camelot ceased to exist.

Lance accompanied her to the double doors of the library. His close proximity created havoc with her senses.

"I'll look in on you later and remind you to take another pill," he whispered.

Inhaling an unsteady breath she said, "There's no chance of my forgetting."

"I'm not so sure. With all those drawings to look at, you'll be riveted. I spent a lot of my boyhood in there and know their fascination."

"I don't doubt it."

Afraid to look at him she hurried inside, needing to put distance between them as a safeguard against her growing attraction to him.

The château's library contained priceless books pertaining to the Du Lac family as well as thousands of titles dealing with all aspects of Arthurian legend. Some had been written in Breton, an old Brittany language resembling Cornish and Welsh.

Andrea found its history intriguing. She could understand how Richard had gotten caught up in the lore of the region.

The various versions of the Knights of the Round Table could keep you engrossed indefinitely.

Two hours later, after she'd settled down to read an interesting piece in English on Perceval's search for the Holy Grail, she heard female voices outside the door. It was probably a conversation between the maids. She continued her study of the text, unaware someone had entered the library until a woman spoke to her.

"Mrs. Fallon?"

"Yes?" Andrea got to her feet. A tall, striking blonde in an expensive three peach colored suit had entered the room. She appeared to be Andrea's age, or maybe a little older.

"I'm Corinne Du Lac."

Du Lac?

That meant she must have taken Geoff's name when her mother married him.

"How do you do."

The woman Lance planned to marry emitted amazing self-possession. And why not? Geoff would have welcomed her like a beloved daughter because it was the way he was made.

She drew closer until Andrea could see her light blue eyes. "Brigitte explained why you're here. I understand you lost your husband recently. May I extend my condolences."

"Thank you."

"Have you accomplished everything needful for his book yet?"

"For the most part, yes. I'm still hoping to get a picture of a stag or a wild boar."

"They're very elusive creatures. I've never seen a boar in

the forest. It could take a long time. If you'd like, I'll ask the groundskeeper to keep a watch and get some pictures. I'd be happy to send them to you."

She spoke excellent English. Andrea could only marvel. "That would be very nice of you. Geoff has been wonderful to let me stay here."

"Everyone adores him, but no one more than I. He's the only father I've ever known. Mine abandoned me and my mother."

"I'm sorry," Andrea commiserated. "My parents died before I turned four, so I understand how it leaves a big hole in your heart."

"Geoff filled mine. When he and mother divorced, he didn't let it make any difference to our relationship."

So far Lance's name hadn't been mentioned. An intentional omission?

"He wouldn't. He's too genuine for that."

"We love each other."

Andrea didn't doubt it.

"Since he's resting, would you like to drive to Lyseaux for lunch? I just got back from a long trip to Australia and am yearning to taste French food again."

Evidently she hadn't caught up with Lance yet.

"I'd enjoy that, but I need to finish up my work here this morning."

The other woman's brows knit together. "Why is that? I thought the book was your husband's project."

"It was, but I was also his assistant and am looking for something special on Lancelot to turn in to the publisher with his manuscript."

She folded her arms, resting her slender hip on the edge of the table. "There must be thousands of books on him."

"There are. I'm sure my husband read them all. He was steeped in legends surrounding King Arthur's court. But being a professor, he was determined to add his own fresh outlook. The Château Du Lac captured his imagination and mine."

After a brief silence, "I suppose you were told you can't take pictures of the room where you've been sleeping."

"I would never do that without permission."

"Geoff doesn't want anything about the room to get in print."

"I don't blame him. In my opinion those paintings constitute some of France's greatest art treasures. If the public knew about them, he'd be hounded to death."

"It's good you understand."

"Of course. I feel privileged to be allowed to stay in there."

"You have no idea how fortunate you are."

Uh-oh. The other woman's comment had a territorial sound to it.

"How long before you return to the States?"

The burning question was finally out.

"I'm not sure."

"You don't need to get back to your job?"

"If by that you mean do I work at Yale University? The answer is no. After teaching classes, my husband would come home and I'd help him do his research on the computer."

"What will you do now?"

"Andrea's going to have her hands full from here on out."

The deep masculine voice could only belong to one person. She hadn't heard Lance enter the library.

Corinne swung around. *"Chéri—"* she cried with uninhibited longing. "I heard you were back!"

"Bonjour, Corinne." He shut the doors behind him, but made no advance toward her. "I'm glad to see you two have already met. It saves me having to find you in order to make introductions."

"Mrs. Fallon and I were just getting acquainted." She hurried toward him, and grasped his arm. "Now that you're here, let's go somewhere private. It's been forever since I last saw you, and we have so much to catch up on."

"We can do that later. Right now I have something important to tell you."

"Not in front of your father's guest surely," she pleaded in a hushed tone, but Andrea heard her.

"This involves Andrea. It can't wait."

At this point Corinne's head jerked around. Her eyes stared at Andrea as if she were some kind of alien. "What could she possibly have to do with us?"

"Since you became my stepsister ten years ago, and we're family so to speak, I would say quite a lot."

Andrea was coming to know Lance's moods. Right now his features had taken on a faintly chiseled cast. She was reminded of that night in the forest when he'd ordered her off the property. It sent a shiver down her spine.

The other woman looked less sure of herself. "Lance—I don't understand you."

"Then let me enlighten you."

He removed Corinne's hand from his arm and crossed the expanse to reach Andrea. "I told you I'd be in to remind you to take your pill," he said to her sotto voice.

"I would have taken it when we went into lunch."

To her surprise he put his arm around her shoulders and pulled her close against his hard physique.

"Corinne?" he addressed the woman standing there like a piece of petrified wood. "You might as well hear our news now."

"What news?"

"I'm in love and have found the woman I'm going to marry."

It was a good thing Lance was holding on to Andrea, otherwise she would have collapsed in a heap.

"If Papa continues to improve, we're hoping to be married within three weeks time."

Corinne's face lost color. *"Married—"*

Lance hugged Andrea tighter. Looking down at her he said, "It happened so fast we can hardly believe it either can we, *mon amour*. I never believed in the *coup de foudre*. Not until I met you. It was love at first sight."

He lowered his head and kissed her hard on her astonished mouth before turning to Corinne. "I know you'll be happy for us, but I have to ask you a favor. Papa doesn't know yet. We're going to tell him at lunch."

His smooth shaven jaw brushed against Andrea's cheek. Despite the chaos of her emotions, the feel of his skin sent a curling warmth through her body.

"I'd like the two of you to become good friends. In the meantime I hope you'll forgive me for interrupting, but something has come up. I need to talk to Andrea alone."

He grasped her hand and started walking toward the door. Corinne stared at Lance in anguish before leaving the room ahead of them. She disappeared down the hall with her suit jacket flapping.

Lance headed for the staircase. He tightened his grip, letting Andrea know he had no intention of allowing her to break free until they'd reached the third floor.

CHAPTER SIX

ANDREA walked in her room ahead of Lance. After shutting the door, he leaned against it while she went over to the bedside table and took another pill with a glass of water.

"You deserve an explanation for what happened just now, and you'll get it. Just hear me out before you consign me to hell for a second time."

She rubbed her forehead where she could feel a headache coming on. "I'm listening."

He began pacing, then stopped. "I had no idea Corinne had arrived. Thank God Henri told me he saw her head for the library. I had to get you out of there fast. There was only one way to do it. For once I was able to strike the death blow before she could see it coming."

Andrea swung around. "It *was* a death blow to her," her voice throbbed. "I've never seen anyone so crushed in my life. By now she has probably run to your father and told him everything."

A cruel smile broke out on his lips. Only moments ago she'd felt them on hers and was still weaving from the effect.

"She would like to, but she won't dare because she's unsure of her ground at the moment."

Andrea's temper flared. "Perhaps you've forgotten I'm a guest in your father's home. He has allowed me to sleep in this incredible room and use his library. Even if I've agreed to marry you, for you to draw me into some kind of intrigue that involves your stepsister is hardly the way to repay him."

"Have no fear. He knows you're the innocent here. My issue with her goes back years."

Their eyes met. His had darkened until there was no more blue left to be seen.

"Lance—"

"Do me a favor and sit down while I talk to you?" he said emotionally. "After your emergency visit to the clinic the other day, this is all you need to suffer a relapse. If anything happened to the baby because of me—"

The fear in his eyes and voice drove her to obey his suggestion. In truth, since the ugly confrontation with Corinne, she felt drained.

After she sat back against the pillows, he leaned over to ease her legs onto the bed. Every touch increased her awareness of him.

Like before, he drew the chair close to the bed and sat down. She watched him run a hand through his hair in a gesture that could have meant resignation or defeat. Andrea had the impression he was tired, as if he'd been wrestling with the same nightmare for years.

It brought out her compassion, a reaction she fought against, yet she doubted he was aware of its effect on her.

His head reared. "Where to begin," he muttered.

She moistened her dry lips. "Try the beginning."

A nerve hammered at the corner of his mouth. "In the beginning, there was a happy family of three. I was halfway through my engineering studies at the University in Rennes where I was living in an apartment when mother came down with the flu. She had a low immune system, and it took its toll on her.

"Rennes is only a forty minute drive from here, so I moved back home temporarily. Papa and I watched her like a hawk, but we couldn't prevent her from catching the pneumonia that took her life."

"How awful," Andrea whispered. A tight band squeezed her lungs to think Lance had come home from the military to discover his father suffering from the same condition.

"It was a hellish time." His eyes had a wintry look. "Life wasn't the same for either of us after that. I went on to finish up my degree, but Papa fell into a decline. When I graduated, his closest friends Helene and Yves Dupuis gave a party for me.

"It was there my father met an attractive divorcée named Odette de la Grange. She was from Paris. According to Helene, Odette's husband had divorced her, but left her well enough off.

"Her daughter Corinne was reputed to have suffered from the divorce and had been in and out of several unsatisfactory relationships. A strong hand was what she needed. She was twenty-two at the time, two years younger than myself.

"Papa was lonely. In his vulnerable state both needy women brought out his protective instincts. So he married Odette who it turned out had no money left. Papa didn't worry about that. He was much more concerned about taking care of them and being a good father to Corinne."

"Your father's a sweetheart."

Lance grimaced. "Unfortunately he had no idea how much more his ambitious stepdaughter wanted from life."

"You mean she wanted *you*."

There was a sustained pause before she heard him say, "Yes."

Andrea took a fortifying breath. "She's a beautiful woman."

A strange sound came from his throat.

She locked her arms around her knees. "What did Corinne do?"

"What *didn't* she do—" he bit out. "Everywhere I turned, there she was. To please Papa, I made an effort to be her friend, but she had something else in mind. She was like my shadow. I couldn't shake her. Before long she became repugnant to me, but of course I didn't want to tell him.

"It had taken him so long to consider remarrying, the last thing he needed was to find out Odette's daughter had problems only a psychiatrist could help her solve, mainly abandonment issues."

Andrea nodded. "While we were downstairs, she mentioned that her father had left her early in life."

Lance used the heel of his hand to rub his eyes. "About a week before my father's wedding I was invited to spend a few days at Mont Saint Michel with a girlfriend whose parents ran a restaurant there. I needed the break and told Papa where I'd be if he needed me.

"The next thing I knew, Corinne showed up alone with her usual sob story of feeling left out. Could she hang around with us?

"To say I was shocked is putting it mildly. She was totally out of line, Andrea. A normal mother would have taken her daughter in hand, but Odette wasn't normal, either."

"Obviously."

"My girlfriend couldn't believe it, but she was great about

it. She made Corinne feel welcome, which prevented the trip from turning into a complete disaster. But my aversion to Corinne reached a new low. I could scarcely abide her presence and avoided her whenever possible.

"After the wedding I assumed she would go back to Paris where she'd been living with her mother. But as my father was leaving for the South of France on his honeymoon he said, "Odette couldn't afford to keep up her apartment, so I've told Corinne she can live with her mother and me for the time being.

"The news twisted my gut. I'd just graduated from college and had arranged to live in Rennes while I worked at a hydraulics plant there. But knowing Corinne would track me down and never leave me alone meant that idea was out.

"After the reception I went to my room in a complete funk. That's where I found Corinne naked in my bed waiting for me."

Andrea groaned.

"I was repulsed. When I told her to go to her own suite, she refused. The horror story had begun in earnest."

She stared at Lance. No one could make up something so awful.

"There was only one thing to do. I packed my things and left the château. She chased after me all the way to my car wearing *my* robe. Do you know what she said to me?"

"I can't imagine."

"If you walk away from me, Lance Malbois, I'll tell our parents you tried to rape me."

Andrea was aghast.

"I told her to go to hell, then I drove away and stayed at Giles's house. He's my best friend. We talked everything over and came to the conclusion that the only thing I could do was leave the country for an indefinite period. That way Corinne couldn't have access to me on any level, and she'd give up."

"That's why you joined the military?" Andrea cried.

He eyed her solemnly. "It was the only solution."

"What a brilliant move on your part," Andrea murmured. "You had a legitimate excuse for being gone where she couldn't come after you. But it had to be the last thing you ever thought of doing in your life."

"I was young, I needed to leave and it seemed like an exciting option," his voice grated.

"Your father must have suffered terrible pain when he found out."

"Except for the fact that he had a new wife and stepdaughter to keep him occupied. By the time their marriage ended he was used to my being gone.

"I must say that from the beginning he hid it well. Once he got back from his honeymoon, I phoned to tell him I'd decided to go into the service as a classified officer where I could use my engineering training. I half expected to hear that Corinne had carried out her threat, and he wanted an accounting. When he answered, I was prepared for the worst.

"To my astonishment, he said he was proud of me for choosing to serve our country. Then he confided what he'd learned from Corinne.

"Apparently she told him the two of us had gotten physically involved and were so attracted, I thought it best to leave for a discreet amount of time. On my next leave, we'd explore our emotional feelings and see if they led to marriage."

"You're right," Andrea murmured. "She's incredibly clever."

"Clever like a psychotic vixen. I decided to let Papa go on believing her lie for the sake of peace in his new marriage. I hoped that in time Corinne would give up her impossible fantasy and move out.

"After my father's second divorce she ended up in the hospital following a failed suicide attempt."

Sickened by what she'd just heard, Andrea couldn't lie there any longer and slid off the bed. "Did she really mean it?"

His hands curled into fists. "I doubt she intended to go through with it, but you never know. Her talent for manipulation is unexcelled. She'd claimed Papa for her new father and wasn't about to let that relationship go.

"He felt sorry for her and brought her home. Slowly she began wrapping her tentacles around him. I'm afraid he allowed it because of the guilt he felt over his second marriage not working."

"I can understand that. Guilt has a lot to answer for."

"Indeed."

"Yet while he suffered, her true intent was to lie in wait for you."

"Afraid so. Father set up Odette in a new apartment in Paris, but Corinne stayed on with him, and never left the château except to travel.

"After I learned about my condition, I saw no point to my life except to stay in the service. I worked my leaves around her absences to visit Papa, but there were times when I couldn't avoid her."

"Ten years in exile is too high a price to pay."

This time it was Lance who groaned. "When you don't give a damn about anything, you don't notice time passing. Not until I received a phone call from Henri telling me about Papa's illness. It made me realize he needed me. That's when I decided to come home for good."

She took a fortifying breath. "Are you sure Corinne isn't the real reason you asked me to marry you?"

His eyes turned to flint.

"If you can ask me that question, then you don't know me at all and a marriage between us would never work."

"Don't go, Lance—" she cried as he started to leave the room. "I'm trying to understand. When you kissed me in front of her—"

"I did what came naturally," he cut her off. "We're going to be married soon. We're having a baby. In private I'll never ask you to do anything you don't want to do, but in public I plan to treat you like my wife. If you have a problem with that, tell me now."

She swallowed hard. "No, of course not."

"Then let's go downstairs."

As they left her room, Andrea felt Lance's fingers twine through hers in a tight grasp. When they reached the doors leading to the terrace, he turned and put his hands on her shoulders. His eyes held a fierce glint.

"You don't have to do this if Corinne makes you uncomfortable. I'll talk to Papa in private."

"No, Lance. She's part of your family. If not now, when?" Only a sick woman would hold him and his father captive with her lies all these years.

"Andrea—" his voice grated. She had the curious feeling he was about to kiss her again when Corinne opened the doors. She must have been standing there waiting for them.

The other woman flashed Lance an odd smile. "Geoff's been counting the minutes."

"So have we."

He ushered Andrea past Corinne. They moved out to the patio where lunch had been served.

Geoff's gaze fastened on Andrea. "Excellent. We're all together. Where did Lance take you to dinner last night?"

"A little inn called *Le Marronier d'Or*. The bacon crêpe was out of this world."

"That means he took you to Merlin's trysting place as well."

Andrea nodded. "We saw a magnificent stag."

He smiled. "Were you able to get a picture?"

"No." She let out a soft laugh. "Isn't that the way it always goes?"

Lance put a hand on her thigh beneath the table. She felt the heat curl through her sensitized body. "I'll take her another night when we're more prepared."

Corinne had seated herself next to Geoff. "I told him you had news of vital importance, Lance."

"But I couldn't pry it out of her," Geoff admitted.

"I can always count on Corinne." Lance sounded so sincere, Andrea wouldn't have understood the double entendre if she hadn't known all the facts. "In truth you've been such a good stepsister to keep my secret, I give you permission to tell Papa right now."

It was obvious Corinne hadn't been prepared for that sally, but she recovered with remarkable aplomb. She turned to Lance's father with her fingers woven together around her wineglass.

"Would you believe Lance and *Mrs*. Fallon have fallen in

love and are planning to be married right away? What has it been? All of three or four days since Lance came home?"

"I believe it." Geoff smiled. "I watched it happen."

Andrea decided Geoff was a great actor himself. His comment seemed to throw Corinne. She turned to Andrea.

"How long has it been since you buried your husband? Did I understand two months?"

"Three," Andrea corrected her.

Her gaze flew to Andrea's left hand. "It sounds like the fastest courtship in history. Is that the ring your deceased husband gave you?"

"It's the one I bought for her," Lance spoke up. He looked at his father. "Last night I asked Andrea to marry me, and she said yes."

Andrea knew Geoff would always behave like the great gentleman he was, but she didn't expect to see the illuminating smile that lit up his eyes. He studied both of them for the longest time.

"Except for Lance coming home in one piece, that's the best news I've ever heard. Congratulations you two." He stood up and walked around to Andrea. "Let me welcome you to the family."

Lance squeezed her arm before she got to her feet to hug his father. He kissed her on both cheeks. She felt his happiness. It couldn't all be pretense. The knowledge filled her with relief.

When he reached for Lance, the two men embraced with the kind of warmth between a father and son who loved each other without reservation.

Corinne held back. "You don't honestly expect people to believe you're in love this fast—"

"Why not?" Geoff took his place once more. "There's no accounting for matters of the heart. Lance has asked Andrea to be his wife. We've got a wedding to plan."

"But he can't marry her—" Corinne blurted.

Geoff studied his stepdaughter for a moment. "Whatever do you mean, *ma chérie?*"

"They haven't waited a decent interval. Her husband's barely dead. What will people say?"

"Corinne?" Andrea addressed her. "Since you and I are going to be related through marriage, there's something you should know."

Her jaw hardened. "What else is there?"

"I'm sure you're familiar with the old expression about a door closing and another one opening. It's true my husband only passed away recently, but he left me a precious legacy."

"I haven't the faintest idea what you're talking about."

"I'm pregnant."

The news must have stunned Corinne because she went perfectly still.

"For the sake of my health and the baby's, Lance and I have decided to marry as soon as possible."

"Did you know about this?" Corinne demanded of Geoff.

A little smile broke the corner of his mouth. "When Dr. Foucher came to see me yesterday morning, he told me Andrea had been to see Dr. Semplis at the clinic the other day. Naturally I was sworn to secrecy. But under the circumstances I can shout it to the world!"

"You're going to get the grandchild you've always wanted, Papa."

There was an undercurrent of excitement in Lance's voice that let Andrea know she'd done the right thing to accept his proposal.

"Except that it won't be a Du Lac."

Andrea heard his sharp intake of breath. "It will once we say I do at the altar," Lance informed her. "In fact it will be exactly like the way you became a Du Lac when your mother married my father."

The strange expression in Corinne's eyes sent a shudder through Andrea's body.

"When did you first suspect you were pregnant?" Geoff wanted to know.

"I didn't have a clue. The doctor had to tell me. No one could have been more surprised than I was."

In the next breath she told him about her premature menopausal condition and the subsequent chain of events that had happened after Lance found her sick in the forest.

"Your son lived up to his name. He was a true knight who didn't need anything but Tonnerre for his great deed."

Geoff laughed. "Now I understand why Brigitte was so worried about you. She said you haven't eaten anything while you've been here. My wife was like that in the beginning. She couldn't keep anything down."

"Obviously all that suffering was worth it," Andrea said.

"Indeed it was." He stared at Lance. "She gave me a most wonderful son."

"I agree. You and Lance are blessed to have each other. I can't wait till my baby's born."

"Have you thought of names yet?"

"Give her time, Papa," Lance broke in. "She barely learned she's *enceinte*."

"Actually I've had names picked out for years," Andrea interjected. "If you can believe, Richard's great-grandfather was a French-Canadian named Geoffroi Fallon."

"Incroyable!" Geoff exclaimed.

"I always planned to name a boy after him. When I first met you and learned your name, it took on even deeper meaning for me. Of course if I have a girl, I'll name her Germaine. That was the middle name of Richard's great-grandmother."

The older man's smile widened. "This calls for a celebration!"

"Not until after the *bébé* arrives," Lance declared. "No alcohol for Andrea."

Always the protector… She had to admit she liked being looked after by him. How did he know so much about a pregnant woman's needs? It was a luxury totally foreign to her.

She put a hand on Geoff's arm. "It's a celebration just to be a guest in your fabulous home. To be honest, ever since I came to Brittany I've felt like I was in a beautiful dream."

Lance's lips twitched. "Except for the nausea."

Andrea chuckled. "I suppose you have to accept a little bitter when you've been given something so sweet. A miracle has happened to me. I was reading in one of the parenting books Lance bought me. Do you realize that in three months my baby is already fully formed with its little finger and toenails and eyelids."

A happy laugh broke from Geoff. "You must get a nursery ready."

"Everything in order, Papa. First thing tomorrow I'm going to drive Andrea to Rennes. I want her to see *Maman*'s family home. I've decided to open it up and we'll live there."

Corinne didn't move a muscle.

Geoff gave a happy nod of approval. "If your mother were alive she'd be overjoyed."

"Once Andrea has seen the place, we'll get going on the nursery."

"While you do that, Corinne and I will get together with Helene and start planning the wedding reception won't we."

"Of course."

Andrea didn't trust the other woman. Nothing about her behavior was natural or normal.

"In case it rains, let's do it inside, Papa."

"I was going to say the same thing. We'll open up all the rooms on the main floor. What date shall I tell Helene?"

"Andrea and I were thinking three weeks from now. Shall we say June 30? It's a Saturday. For her sake I want it kept fairly small so she doesn't have to be on her feet a long time greeting guests."

"Excellent idea, *mon fils*."

"I'll phone Père Loucent at the St. Vierge Church in Lyseaux. I think a morning ceremony followed by the reception would be best."

"So do I."

"Don't you have a voice in any of this, Andrea?" Corinne had finally ventured a question.

"Lance and I discussed everything in detail at dinner."

Geoff burst into laughter. "You two remind me of my marriage to Lance's mother. She got her way in private, but she let me direct traffic in public. I was the envy of my friends."

"I wish I could have met her."

"So do I, Andrea. So do I."

Maybe it was the melancholy note in Geoff's voice that prompted Lance to stand, bringing their lunch to a close.

"Andrea and I are going to run into the village for our marriage license. We'll see you two at dinner. I'd like to hear about your trip to Australia, Corinne."

"So would I," Andrea echoed him. "I've never vacationed outside the States except to come here. According to Geoff you're the world traveler. You're so fortunate to be able to do that, I envy you."

When there was no response Lance helped her to her feet, keeping a possessive grip on her waist.

His father smiled up at them. "You've made me an extremely happy man. Another daughter joining the family, and a grandchild on the way—what more can we say, eh, Corinne?"

Andrea admired Geoff. For his stepdaughter's sake he pretended nothing was wrong. Yet they all knew their announcement had shattered her world.

Corinne pushed her chair back and stood up. She'd leveled her gaze on Lance. "Could I talk to you for a moment before you go?"

Andrea put a hand on his arm. "I'll get my purse and meet you at the car."

Lance pressed a brief and reassuring kiss to her lips. "I'll see you in a minute." After she disappeared through the French doors he turned to Corinne. "Why don't you walk out with me."

With a nod to his father he headed for the foyer with Corinne in pursuit. By the time he'd reached his car, she'd caught up to him.

"After what you've done, I'm going to have to tell him the truth."

Lance opened the driver's door and got in behind the wheel. "Which version of the truth, Corinne? That you and I got too close while he was on his honeymoon? Or that you offered yourself to me ten years ago and I said no thank you."

"Lance—" She moved closer. "I'm prepared to be generous and forget everything if you'll call off your wedding to *her* and marry me."

It was chilling to come face-to-face with someone who wasn't in her right mind. "You're delusional, Corinne. You need help."

"What I need is you." There was a fanatical gleam in her eyes. "I've won the right."

"Won the right?" he growled the question.

"While I've been waiting for you all these years, I've taken care of Geoff like a daughter."

"Then you've already received your reward. You've earned his affection."

"He expected us to get married."

"No. That's a piece of fiction you invented so long ago, you actually believe it."

"I told him I'd give him a grandchild."

"Then you need to find a man who wants to marry you."

"I found the man I wanted a long time ago."

"Those wants have to be mutual, Corinne." Lance added gently, "I never wanted you."

"You've never given us a chance, yet in four days you've decided you're going to marry a perfect stranger."

"That's right."

Her cheeks looked blotched. "I could have turned Geoff against you, but I never did."

"Your cry of rape is a figment of your mind. Don't lie, Corinne."

She gave him a strange smile. "It's your word against mine. Are you sure you want to risk his revulsion of you?"

He'd had enough of this conversation and started the car. She put her hands on the door.

"I suggest you listen to what I have to say, Lance. If you insist on going through with this travesty of a marriage, then I'll have to go through with my plan for you."

He shook his head. "I must admit I'm disappointed you've wasted all these years thinking up your revenge against me when you could have worked on becoming a decent human being.

"Going after me will earn you Papa's loathing. Then where will you be? What will you have accomplished?"

Her question coincided with Andrea's appearance outside the château. His pulse raced just looking at her.

"You'd be surprised," Corinne muttered.

Without waiting to hear anything else he got out to open the door for his future wife. She was carrying precious cargo. He'd do whatever it took to see her safely through this pregnancy.

CHAPTER SEVEN

EIGHT hours later Andrea was finally alone with Lance in her bedroom. The solemn look on his handsome face set off alarm bells.

"You know your father better than anyone in the world. He wasn't putting on an act at dinner tonight, was he?"

"No. In fact I would go so far as to say he had to hold back most of his joy in order not to hurt Corinne."

"Then what's wrong besides the obvious?"

"It's Corinne."

Andrea nodded. "I know that."

"I thought I knew, too…"

A strange nuance in his voice sent a chill down her spine. "What did she say to you before I came down to the car with my purse this afternoon?"

He slid his hands up and down her arms. "Corinne made a threat."

"What kind?"

"I didn't give her the chance to tell me."

"But you can't dismiss it? Why didn't you say something to me while we were in the village. I thought we were in this together."

His eyes roved over her upturned features. "Because I didn't want to worry you unnecessarily."

"I already am worried. Her behavior is irrational, Lance. One minute she's hysterical. The next she's like the calm before a storm."

"She's mentally ill. I'm sure my father believes it, too. He chose his words very carefully tonight."

"I have to know what you're thinking!"

His hands circled her upper arms. "Last night I asked if you trusted me, and you said yes."

"I do."

"Then let me deal with this in my own way first. I've already taken some precautions. If the need arises to talk to you about it, I swear I will. In the meantime we'll do everything together. I'm not leaving you alone."

For him to say that could only mean one thing. "You think she could be physically dangerous?"

Lines marred his face. "At this point I believe Corinne is capable of almost anything."

Andrea groaned. "When your father gave us his blessing, she saw her dreams smashed. There's a violence in her, Lance."

"It's always been there."

"At the lake you told me it was a woman who gave you that scar. Women commit crimes against men on a regular basis. When I think Corinne once came to your room uninvited—there's nothing to prevent her from doing it again to make certain you don't get married."

He kissed her forehead. "Nothing's going to happen to anyone, Andrea. Until our wedding I'll be sleeping with you in this room."

"But, Lance—"

"Don't worry about the servants talking," he cut in on her. "That's exactly what I want to happen. The gossip will reach Corinne's ears. Knowing you and I are together will act as a natural deterrent."

"I was thinking of your father."

The trace of a smile formed on his lips. "Since it only took me four days to propose to you, he would wonder about me if I continued to spend my nights apart from you."

He relinquished his hold of her and reached for the phone at her bedside. "I'll let the staff know about my new arrangements, then we'll call your family with our news."

His eyes swept over her. "You look tired. Why don't you get ready for bed first? It was designed so half a dozen people can gaze at the paintings comfortably. You won't even know I'm in there with you."

Andrea's thudding heart accompanied her into the bathroom where she clung to the sink until she could get herself under control.

The brilliance of the diamond ring he'd given her drew her gaze.

It's in the shape of the lake, he'd said.

The lake hidden in a mystical forest was where this whole thing had started—where she'd met Lancelot Du Lac come to life. Only he was *bigger* than life.

The myth wasn't a myth after all.

He'd put Andrea under his spell. How else would she have agreed to enter into this marriage with Lance?

He was waiting for her when she emerged from the bathroom wearing her nightgown and robe. In the short time she'd been occupied, he'd changed into a pair of sweats and a T-shirt. No matter what he wore, she was aware of his incredible male physique made hard by his life in the military.

His slumberous eyes followed her progress, taking in every inch of her, starting at her bare feet.

"Ready to make that phone call? Afterward I want to hear which painting you think is my favorite."

Andrea sank down at the side of the bed and put a phone call through to her aunt. The whole time they talked, Lance lay stretched out on the other side of the bed with his hands propping his dark head. He proved to be such a distraction, she had trouble concentrating on the conversation.

"If you're so attracted to him this soon, why don't you stay on in France and get to know him better before you commit yourself to another marriage?"

It was a good question. One Andrea would have asked her aunt if their positions had been reversed.

"Lance has been in the military a long time, Aunt Kathy. He wants to settle down."

"That's fine for him, but what about you? Even though you're free, you're still grieving. I should think you'd want to take a couple of deep breaths first."

Her aunt didn't understand Andrea's problem. Andrea had been grieving in her marriage for years. And now, just thinking of Lance made her so breathless she could hardly function. The realization that they'd be sleeping in the same bed had made her feel more desire than she had felt in years. Shame coursed through her.

"I probably should."

"Well, it sounds like you've made up your mind. Rob and

I just want you to be happy. Does your invitation include the girls and their husbands?"

Her hand tightened on the receiver. "You *know* it does. I want all of you there."

"We're stretched for money, as always. Are you sure your fiancé's willing to pay for everything?"

"Yes. He wants you to stay at his parents' home while you're here."

"What a generous man. That's a big change from Richard."

She lowered her head. "I know."

"Sorry. I had no right to say that."

"Yes, you did, because it's true." In a way it was a relief to know her aunt hadn't been blind to certain problems in Andrea's marriage.

Lance was a different man from a different world.

Andrea hadn't told her aunt anything except that she'd met a Frenchman named Lance Malbois who'd just retired from France's elite force.

When the family arrived in Brittany, they'd see and understand everything for themselves. At that point she'd take her aunt aside and tell her she was expecting a baby. It didn't seem right to tell her over the phone.

"Lance and I will make all the airline arrangements. You'll be getting your tickets and the invitation some time next week by express mail."

"Andrea?"

"Yes?"

"I know I haven't said it often enough, but I love you. I want only the best for you."

Her eyes smarted. "I know. I love you, too. Being away

has made me realize how lucky I was to be raised by you. It must have been so hard at first." When she thought of Geoff and the way he'd reached out to his troubled stepdaughter, it was humbling.

"If it was hard, it was because I was afraid I could never be the mother my sister would have been to you. Rob says I'm anal, but he loves me anyway. Your mother was more calm and laid-back. You have that same quality. It's one I envy."

"Then we're even because I envy your courage in taking on another woman's child."

"Your sweet disposition made it easy to love you."

Where had all this come from? Tears dripped down Andrea's cheeks. "Thank you for saying that. I'll call you next week to make certain you received everything."

"I'm getting excited. I've never been to Europe."

"It's a whole other world, Aunt Kathy. Talk to you soon."

She hung up the receiver, using her arm to brush the moisture away. In her mind's eye she could imagine their surprise as they read the invitation with the Du Lac family crest engraved at the top…

> Geoffroi Malbois, Le Duc Du Lac, requests the pleasure of your company at the marriage of his son Lancelot Malbois Du Lac to Andrea Gresham Fallon on the Thirtieth of June. Eleven a.m. at the Church of the St. Vierge, Lyseaux. A reception will follow at the Château on the Du Lac Estate, La Bretagne, France.

"What did your aunt say to make you so emotional?"

Andrea looked over at him. "A lot of wonderful things.

If you hadn't urged me to phone her, I might never have heard them."

Lance rolled on his side to face her, all six feet three inches of lean, strong male. "Even with darkness at work, are you saying I'm good for you?" His voice sounded husky.

The time for honesty had come. "I guess I am."

"Then humor me and get into bed. Our baby needs rest, too."

Our baby. Oh, Lance—

"Don't turn out the light yet. I'll take care of it after you've answered the question I asked you the last time we were in here."

Oh. He was talking about the paintings.

She slid beneath covers. Several feet separated them. His body still lay on top while he studied her.

"Have you decided which of the twelve months appeals to me the most?"

"Yes." She should have known from the beginning, but it hadn't come to her until tonight when they'd left a scary acting Corinne sitting with Geoff.

"How long do you plan to torture me? In case you hadn't realized it yet, I'm not a patient man."

"I'm aware of that," she murmured. "You also thrive on danger, which leads me to think June is your favorite."

He raised up on one elbow. "You know me well. In June Lancelot's love was in full flower. He'd held back his feelings for Guinevere too long. Now he was on fire for her. No bars could keep him out. He would risk death for one taste of her mouth."

"I thought that sounded like you."

He flashed her a white smile so seductive, she had to look away. "Admit June's your favorite month, too. Who else but Guinevere, queen among women, was brave enough to enter into a tryst with Lancelot and welcome him into her bed knowing evil was afoot in every corner of Camelot."

Somehow the conversation had become a case of art imitating life. It was all too personal. Her eyes slid to the painting in question.

"The artist did an exceptional job of conveying their emotions. I think a woman did it."

"I don't know about that. A man can paint with the same amount of feeling. When I was young and hadn't yet understood a female's magic, I thought they were an embarrassing oddity. Several years had to go by before I let my best friend have a look."

"By then you'd both discovered the lusty month of May had taken on new meaning. When June followed, your passion ripened."

Rich, deep laughter poured out of him. "You're one in a million, Andrea. I wonder which painting our child will like best."

The conversation was getting out of hand.

"If we have a romantic daughter, she'll tell us right away. If it's a boy, we'll probably be old and tired before he admits his preference."

"Even then he'll tell us there was no such thing as Camelot." Lance was reading her mind.

"That's when we'll tell him it was only a beautiful dream."

"I think I'm beginning to know how Arthur felt when everything fell apart. We haven't even said our vows, yet you're talking about us sitting around in our rocking chairs. I don't envision us like that."

"That's because you grew up in the land of dreams. The

truth is, Guinevere and Lancelot lost their heads. If we haven't learned from their mistakes, then heaven help us."

He moved closer, putting his chin on his bronzed arm. "You think their love was a mistake?"

She struggled not to be affected by his proximity. "Don't you?"

"And miss out on the greatest love the world has ever known?" he drawled.

Her hand plucked at the covers. "They had to pay too great a price."

"But while it was good, they knew indescribable rapture. I noticed you reading Chrétien de Troyes when I found you in the forest."

Nothing got past Lance.

"The bedroom scene is one of the most famous passages in all literature," he reminded her. "Wasn't there a line about their sport being so agreeable and sweet while they kissed and fondled each other, that in truth such a marvelous joy came over them as was never heard or known?"

Andrea's face went hot. "Chrétien got a little carried away portraying Lancelot's feelings. Since he wasn't a woman, he didn't understand Guinevere. She was married to Arthur, and was always plagued by guilt."

Lance sent her a seductive smile. "I think that's the widow in you talking. Take another look at the painting," he told her. "Do you see any guilt in her eyes or her body straining against him?

"She's so eager for him, her eyes are alive. You can feel them burning for each other. All the months he's been at court they've dreamed of this moment. By suppressing their passion, it has only grown into a conflagration.

"You can tell she's completely forgotten anyone else is in the room with them. She's begging him to touch her. Lancelot is out of his mind with desire.

"He's been eaten alive by images of her that won't give him rest. He burns for her in his sleep, yet now he's awake and he's come to her, and there's no power on earth to stop their sweet pleasure in each other."

Stop it, Lance.

"I've looked enough for one night, and now I'm tired. I should think you would be, too." She leaned over to flick off the bedside lamp. "Good night."

"Do you mind if I talk to you until we fall asleep?"

"As long as it's not about fairy tales." She turned her back on him and wished he'd plant himself in another area of the bed several feet away.

"The university is only five minutes from the house in Rennes. If you're interested, you could take a couple of morning classes while you're waiting for the baby to come. The term starts in August and will be over before you deliver at the end of December. I could drive you on my way to work, and pick you up at lunch."

He'd anticipated everything. It would give her something worthwhile to do until she went back to the States to live.

"Where will you be working?"

"At the hydraulics company I told you about. Since being home I've made inquiries. They're in need of an engineer with my qualifications."

"How soon will you start?"

"Right after the wedding."

She was glad he hadn't mentioned a honeymoon.

"I'd be very interested."

"Do you have any idea what kind of classes you'd like to take?"

"French, and maybe a survey of early French literature."

"Sounds like you're planning to follow in Richard's footsteps," came the flat response.

"I have no desire to be a teacher. I was thinking I'd better know something about your language and culture since the men planning to be father and grandfather in my child's life are Frenchmen."

"That's a fact."

Andrea couldn't tell what he thought of her choices.

"Someday I'll decide on a career and go after it. Right now I can't think beyond being a mother."

"To be honest, I'm glad Papa wants to be in charge of the wedding festivities. With Helene's help, they don't need anyone else. That leaves us time to get the house ready and plan a nursery."

"Is it vacant?"

"Yes, except for the caretakers Jean and his wife, Louise, who live there on the ground floor. Anything you want and they'll take care of it."

"What's your mother's home like?"

"It's a cottage with a plaster exterior called a *bastide*. Two floors, four bedrooms. One full bath, and two half baths. There's a terrace and a garden. Inside and out it's perfect for a child."

"I think it sounds charming."

"When my grandparents were alive, I loved to stay there where I could run around and make messes."

"You mean you were a normal little boy?"

"Afraid so. Papa didn't take too kindly to my building model rockets on the grand hall dining table. The cement glue spilled on the surface and ruined it. They had to have it redone. If you got me started on the damage I did, it would take weeks."

"Sounds like you made up for several siblings."

He chuckled. "I wish I had a brother or sister. *Maman* suffered through three miscarriages. Each for a different reason."

"She was lucky to get you. I'm living testimony of that."

"Amen. Tell me about your cousins."

"Julie's twenty-nine. Sharon's twenty-six."

"Les Trois Mousquetaires."

"I wish it had been like that. If I'd been adopted at birth, it might have been different."

"What did they do? Remind you that you weren't one of them in order to dampen your sails when you got something they didn't?"

"How did you know?"

"Corinne pulled her 'poor me' stunt the first night I met her in the hope I'd feel guilty for having been born a Du Lac."

Lance's problems had been so much worse, Andrea didn't have room to complain. "Now that the girls are married, things have been better."

"I wish I could say the same where Corinne's concerned."

Andrea shivered. "Wouldn't it be wonderful if she just gave up and went home to her mother."

A strange sound came from his throat. "I thought you were the one who said no more fairy tales."

"I'm sorry. What do you suppose she's doing right now?"

"Let's not worry about it. Go to sleep. You're safe with me."

Safe.

If there was anyone in the world who could protect her, she knew it was Lance. The knowledge helped her to relax. At some point oblivion took over.

When she awoke, she couldn't believe it was midmorning already. Lance had already gone. Knowing he'd been with her all night must have been the reason she'd slept longer than usual.

The absence of nausea prompted her to take her pills. She wanted this feeling of well-being to continue.

As she started across the room there was a rap on the door. "Andrea?" Lance's deep voice permeated to her insides. "Are you awake?"

"Yes."

"I brought you breakfast."

He shouldn't have. "I don't need waiting on."

"What if I like doing it?"

"Then I'm very grateful, but I need to shower first."

"Go ahead. I'll bring the tray in and wait for you."

"Okay. I'll hurry."

Excitement welled up in her that he was going to show her his mother's house today. It would be her baby's home. Her home with Lance.

Three weeks from now and she wouldn't have to see Corinne again except on the chance meeting at the château. In the meantime she and Lance would be occupied getting ready to be parents.

She grabbed a blouse to wear with her skirt before scurrying into the bathroom to shower and dress. He was going to get tired of seeing her in the same outfit. When they went to Rennes today, she would ask him to take her to a store where she could buy some loose fitting outfits.

After brushing her hair, she let it hang free from a side part. After applying lotion she was ready.

He'd put the tray on the bed. Cold cereal and grapefruit. "This looks good."

"So do you," he murmured, eyeing her thoroughly.

He did, too, but she refrained from telling him and started to eat.

This morning he'd donned a light blue suit with a darker blue shirt. No tie. With that burnished skin and blue eyes hot enough to cut steel, she wouldn't be surprised if the women in town formed lines just to get a look at him.

"Thanks to your presence throughout the night, I slept well."

"Your body next to mine had the same effect on me. It must be comforting for the baby to be all snug inside you."

A section of grapefruit caught in her throat before going down. "The problem is, one of these days soon I'm afraid *I* won't be able to say the same thing. But I'm not complaining."

"I'll give you back rubs. Maybe that will help."

No. All that would do was arouse certain longings better kept at bay. After their conversation last night, she was a mass of feelings and emotions spiraling out of control.

"Are you the kind of woman who wants to have the baby the natural way?"

She shook her head. "No. I'm a coward and plan to avail myself of the latest epidural."

"That means no Lamaze class for me?"

"Would you want to do that?"

He studied her over the rim of his coffee cup. "I want to do anything that helps me feel closer to the baby."

"You can come to all my doctor appointments. I'll be getting the ultrasound next month."

"I was already planning on it. Needless to say I'll be driving you to the hospital when your time comes. I've never seen a baby born. Giles and his wife had a little girl last year. He said it was the greatest experience of his life. I've envied him that."

Her heart told her this wasn't an act on Lance's part. Having been denied the possibility of creating a child from his own body, he was willing to do whatever it took to be a part of her pregnancy. Andrea was one person who understood that need.

With the last bite of cereal gone, she went over to the dresser where she kept her purse. Reaching for her lipstick she said, "Did you happen to see Corinne while you were downstairs?"

"No. Papa said she had breakfast with him before going for a horseback ride."

"Does she do a lot of riding?"

"From what I understand."

"How's your father this morning?"

"Euphoric. I left him on the phone with Helene."

"Did he say anything about Corinne?"

"No."

Her anxious eyes flicked to his. "It's like waiting for a time bomb we didn't set to go off."

Lance nodded grimly. "Papa would like to drive to the house with us, but the doctor says he has to stay in for a couple of more days."

"There'll be time enough for that when he's all better."

"That's what I told him. Shall we go?"

He opened the door for her, then followed with the tray. They'd almost reached the foyer when she heard his cell phone ring. She noticed him check the caller ID before he clicked on.

She might not be able to understand French, but the violence of his expression needed no translation.

"What's happened?" she asked the second he rang off.

There was a white ring around his mouth. "That was the groomsman. Corinne took Tonnerre without permission. He went after her on another horse.

"It seems she tried to jump the fountain, but didn't succeed. She took a nasty fall and appears concussed, but Tonnerre's front legs are broken. He's in agony."

That meant his beautiful horse would have to be put down.

"Go, Lance—" she cried. "I'll phone for an ambulance."

He handed her the tray and his cell phone. "Dial 112. Tell them to come to the Fountain of Youth in the forest. They'll understand."

Her heart went with him as he disappeared down the hall toward the kitchen. Poor Tonnerre. He'd carried both her and Lance when she'd been ill. It was going to kill him to have to put his animal out of its misery, but he had no other choice.

In the next instant she set the tray on the nearest credenza and called the emergency number. After getting the details, they said they were on their way.

"Andrea?"

She looked up to discover Geoff standing on the first landing.

"Henri told me Corinne had an accident on one of the horses. Is she all right?"

"The groomsman said he thought she'd be fine. Lance went to see about her." Andrea hurried up the stairs and walked him back to his suite. They sat down opposite each other in the sitting room.

"I'm relieved he's with her."

"He'll take care of everything. It's good we hadn't left for town yet."

"She's an excellent rider. I can't imagine what happened."

"We'll find out soon enough. Shall I ask Brigitte to bring you some tea while we wait to hear?"

Andrea didn't dare tell him the truth. She'd let his son explain. Thanks to Henri's discretion, Geoff didn't appear too upset.

"No, no. As long as we're alone for a minute, I want to tell you something."

"What is it?"

For the first time since she'd known him, Geoff seemed hesitant.

"When you've been a mother for a number of years, you'll understand better what I'm about to say to you."

"Go on," she urged gently.

"Our children mean everything to us. We know their joys and their fears. We know what makes them happy. We know what brings them pain.

"Choosing you for his wife has made Lance happy, and that makes me happy. But Corinne is devastated. She fell in love with him when she first met him. There's been no one else for her."

"He told me he suspected as much," she admitted.

"That's good. There should be no secrets between the two of you. Corinne has always felt rejected. I've tried everything to help her feel secure, but nothing can completely make up for a bad mother and an absentee father."

"You're right."

He lifted his hands. "It's no one's fault, and I'm not trying to hurt you. Heaven knows it's been difficult for Lance who didn't ask for any of this."

He looked at her with a hint of pleading. She sensed he was going to beg them to postpone the wedding for an indefinite period.

Once again Corinne had manipulated Geoff, but this time Lance wouldn't fall for it. By driving his horse to its death she'd done such an unforgivable thing.

"Would it be too much to ask if you and Lance got married in private right away?"

Andrea was so surprised, she almost fell off the chair. "You mean just forego the wedding trappings?"

He nodded sadly. "It would be the kindest thing you could do for Corinne. She's told everyone we know that Lance was going to marry her when he returned from the service.

"Hearing you plan your wedding and the talk about the baby last evening was too much for her. If you get married quietly, it will save her the extra humiliation. I know my son. He wants to give you the wedding of your dreams, but more than that, he wants *you*.

"I realize I'm asking a great sacrifice of you. The two of you deserve to be feted. There's nothing I'd love more, but—"

"You don't need to say another word, Geoff. I already had a big wedding when I married Richard. I don't need another one."

"You mean it?" his voice trembled.

"With all my heart. Why deepen that hurt? When I see Lance later, I'll convince him it's the only thing to do."

"If anyone can get to him, you can."

Except Lance wouldn't need convincing. If he were in love

with Andrea, it would be different. But what he wanted was a son. He would be glad they didn't have to wait three more weeks to go through a ceremony to make everything legal.

It would mean they could move into his mother's house in the next few days. After this accident Andrea had no desire to be around Corinne.

"Geoff? Why don't I go to the kitchen and bring us back some tea? I know I could use some."

"That sounds good to me, too."

"While I'm gone, why not call Helene back and tell her Lance and I have decided to get married now. Explain it's because of the baby coming. The doctor wants me to take things easy. Something like that. I'm sure you'll find the words so she doesn't question the change in plans."

"Bless you, *ma chérie*."

Andrea hurried downstairs to the kitchen and started fixing the tea. While she was adding the honey, she heard footsteps along the back passage. Suddenly Lance emerged.

"Thank God you're in here. We had to put Tonnerre down."

"I knew it," she whispered.

Without conscious thought she gravitated to his arms. He crushed her against him. For the next few minutes he rocked her. She felt the shudders that racked his proud body.

"Just remember he's gone to horse heaven where he's happy."

A heavy sigh escaped. "How did you know I needed to hear that?" Lance cupped the sides of her head and pressed kisses all over her face.

"Because my uncle had to put our family dog out of its agony. We gave him a funeral."

He buried his face in her hair. "How much does Papa know?"

"Henri told him Corinne had an accident out riding, but that she'd be all right." Andrea pulled away enough so she could look at him. "Will she?"

His pain filled eyes darkened. "I think so, but she hit her head pretty hard. The ambulance has taken her to the village. From there she'll be flown by helicopter to the hospital in Rennes as a precaution. I asked Henri to get hold of her mother.

"In the meantime one of the maids volunteered to stay at the hospital with Corinne so she won't be alone."

"That was a kind thing to do."

Lance kissed her cheek. "I thought so, too."

For a moment he sounded far away. She eased out of his arms. "I've got tea ready for your father. It only needs honey."

"I could use some, too. I'll get it."

While he went to the cupboard for it she said, "Lance? There's something I have to tell you."

He brought the jar to her. "What is it?"

Without preamble she repeated the conversation she'd had with Geoff. When she'd finished, silence reigned while he added some macaroons to the tray. She couldn't tell what he was really thinking.

They joined his father who was on the phone. At the sight of the two of them, he waved Lance over. "It's Odette. She heard about Corinne's accident. How bad was it?"

Andrea watched Lance put the tray on the table. "Henri already told her Corinne has a concussion. She's been taken to Holy Cross hospital in Rennes. One of the staff is with her. Tell Odette to call there and speak to the doctor in the E.R."

Geoff relayed the message, then covered the mouthpiece. "She wants to speak to you."

Lines of anger bracketed Lance's mouth. He reached for the receiver. "Odette? I don't know anything more than you've been told. The person you need to talk to is your daughter.

"Right now I have my father to worry about. He's still recovering from pneumonia. I hope we understand each other. I'll make certain Henri keeps you informed of anything we learn. *Au revoir.*"

Andrea sank down on the love seat next to Geoff and handed him some tea. His lids hooded his eyes, making him look older than his sixty-seven years.

He took it from her and sipped a little of it. "Merci, *ma chérie.*"

"Papa— Corinne took a jump on Tonnerre that cost him his life."

A lone tear rolled down Geoff's cheek. "Under the circumstances I don't know how you found the strength to even speak to Odette."

Lance got down on his haunches in front of his father. "As Andrea reminded me, my horse has gone to a better place. She also told me what you two talked about before I came in.

"If I'd thought I could get away with it, I would have asked her to run away with me and get married last night."

Though she knew he'd said that to please his father, Andrea's heart skipped several beats.

"Since Corinne's needs have to be our primary concern, I'll phone the priest and ask him to marry us right here in your sitting room. Henri and Brigitte will be our witnesses. After the baby's born and Andrea has recovered, we'll give a big reception and invite everyone."

His father wept. "You're a wonderful son."

"This is no sacrifice to me, Papa. Corinne needs medical attention in a number of ways. I used the phone at the stable and took the liberty of calling the psychiatrist who treated her before. He's going to meet with Odette and set up some sessions with both of them.

"Let's give them a few days. By then you'll be feeling even better and we'll pay her a visit *en famille*."

"*En famille*," Geoff repeated, smiling at both of them. "That has a beautiful ring to it."

Lance flashed Andrea an intimate regard. "I agree."

Needing to cover her emotions, she handed him his tea, which he drank in one go.

"Papa— One more thing. When Corinne phones and asks for you, the doctor suggests you let Henri handle those calls. Just until the situation improves."

Geoff nodded. "It's a good plan. Now if you don't mind, I'd like to be the one to talk to Père Loucent."

"Go ahead. Andrea and I are leaving for Lyseaux right now. We won't be long."

CHAPTER EIGHT

"I NOW pronounce you husband and wife. In the name of the Father, the Son and the Holy Spirit. Amen."

Andrea heard Brigitte sniff before her brand-new husband's mouth descended on hers. A few days ago he'd kissed her hard in front of Corinne. This time he was kissing her as if he meant it for his father's sake.

She let him coax her lips apart, but she wanted Lance to get the message that she wasn't reading more into this than he intended.

When she thought it had gone on long enough, she eased herself out of his arms without looking at him, and turned to thank the priest for officiating.

"It was my pleasure, Madame Du Lac. *Félicitations* on your nuptials. May you and Lance live a long happy life together."

"Thank you, Father."

Lance shook the older priest's hand. "It won't be long before you'll be christening our baby."

He nodded his balding head. "Geoff told me you were expecting. I'll look forward to the event. May I inquire where you're going on your honeymoon?"

"We're not taking one," Andrea spoke before Lance could. "We don't want to leave Geoff while he's still recovering from pneumonia."

Lance's arm tightened around her waist. "I'll be taking her away after the baby's born and she's well enough to travel. Then we'll let *grand-père* baby-sit for us."

Geoff got to his feet with ease. Yesterday Andrea feared the news about Corinne's accident and the horse would set him back, but that wasn't the case. This afternoon he seemed more like the Geoff she'd met at Easter.

"You don't know how long I've been waiting for Lance to give me a daughter." He walked up to Andrea and gave her a kiss on both cheeks. "And what a daughter. You're a blessing to this family."

Andrea couldn't hold back from hugging him. "I couldn't love you more if you were my own father," she confessed for his ears alone.

"I told Lance the same thing about you the first day he arrived home," he whispered back.

Once they'd let go of each other, she thanked Henri and Brigitte for standing up for them. They were all smiles as they wished them well before leaving the room. Père Loucent followed them out.

The three of them were finally alone. Geoff eyed his son. "What are your plans?"

"I'm taking Andrea to the house. We'll spend the night and be back in the morning. If you need us for anything, all you have to do is call."

Andrea put a hand on his arm. "Will you be all right?"

"Don't you worry about me. Yves and Helen are coming over for dinner."

"I'm glad. You shouldn't be alone."

"Have you forgotten I'm no longer an invalid? Go on—forget everything and everyone except each other. There'll never be another night like this again in your lives."

"Thank you, Geoff." Andrea couldn't refrain from hugging him one more time.

She felt Lance tug on her arm. He acted anxious to leave, but they weren't in any hurry now. With the marriage behind them and the baby on the way, everything could settle down.

Certainly Andrea should have been relieved. Yet she felt a strange letdown that made her angry at herself.

Lance hadn't married her because he was in love. Therefore she shouldn't be having any feelings at all except to be glad that the formalities were over.

He helped her into the car. Showing great care, he moved the hem of her new dress out of the way so the door wouldn't close on it. It was a sleeveless silk jersey in a cream and café-au-lait color that fell from the shoulders. She'd be able to wear it to the end of her pregnancy.

She'd bought it and several casual outfits yesterday when they'd gone into Lyseaux. The shopping had taken longer than she'd supposed, so Lance had only driven her by the house to give her a glimpse of it.

After getting dressed for the wedding, Lance had come to her room and surprised her with a garland of orange blossoms for her hair, which she'd decided to leave loose.

"Wear this for me?"

The perfume from the petals made her feel bridal.

"I had it specially made up. You'll notice in the May painting that Guinevere is wearing the one Lancelot made for her. There's something utterly feminine about a woman with fresh flowers in her hair."

So saying, he lowered it over Andrea's head, then studied her for a moment. Maybe she just imagined the sudden darkening of desire in his eyes.

"I'll be in Papa's sitting room waiting for you."

Her heart refused to quiet down after that. It was still galloping as they drove away from the château.

"A *centime* for your thoughts, *ma femme*."

She really was Lance's wife. Her gaze fastened on the new gold wedding band adjoining her diamond ring.

"I think I've been waiting for Corinne to appear out of nowhere and interrupt the ceremony."

"No talk of Corinne today." He reached over and grasped the hand closest to him. "We've become a family. You, me and our baby-to-be. That's all that matters."

"No, it isn't, Lance. When you phoned the hospital earlier, what did the doctor say about Corinne's condition?"

He kneaded her fingers. "The attending physician says she can be released tomorrow. Her psychiatrist would like to transfer her to the psychiatric unit to begin treatment, but he can't do anything without Odette's approval, or Corinne's birth father.

"So far Odette is in denial about her daughter, and Odette's ex-husband washed his hands of both of them a long time ago. I doubt he's even in the country."

"What about Geoff?"

"He's not her legal guardian."

Andrea's head served around. "But Corinne said she was a Du Lac."

"Father certainly made her feel that way, but he never adopted her. She has no legal claim on our family.

"In any case Odette is outraged that Papa would think Corinne has mental health problems. My guess is she doesn't want any interference from him, not if it means she has to be under a psychiatrist's scrutiny, too."

"No wonder Corinne's been currying your father's favor over the years. If she couldn't have you…"

"There's only one woman who has me." He squeezed her fingers before letting them go so he could make a turn into a lane lined with old graceful oak trees.

They'd come to the outskirts of Rennes already? She'd been so involved with Lance, she hadn't noticed anything else.

At the end of the street she spied the rose colored bastide with sky-blue shutters she'd seen yesterday. They flanked tall windows with their small windowpanes, all symmetrical and set off by an imposing entry at the center of the house. Talk about enchanting…

"Why don't we take Papa's advice and concentrate on each other for tonight. We can eat dinner in or out. Whatever pleases you."

The minute he drove around the side and she saw the terrace, she knew what she wanted. "I'd love to eat out here." It overlooked an overgrown garden filled with roses. There was a stone bench and a little fountain. "I can't believe how beautiful this is."

"I was hoping you'd say that. Louise will have made one

of her delicious *galettes au veau* with fresh peas from her vegetable plot."

Before they even went inside, Andrea insisted on exploring the exterior. "I've never seen walkways like this."

"These are river pebbles chosen for their colors. Water runs off them easily. They're placed next to each other in a kind of mosaic that's been popular since the 1600s."

Her gaze flew everywhere, landing briefly on the wrought-iron furniture, then flicking to urns of potted ranunculus and poppies.

The Château Du Lac was a small castle built for an aristocrat. But this French house draped in wisteria and bougainvillea was the embodiment of her dream of the perfect home.

A half hour later Lance had given her the grand tour. The smaller bedroom upstairs across the hall from the master bedroom would make a perfect nursery.

The main floor's common rooms were full of light and so delightful she couldn't find the right words. She loved everything so much it frightened her. Already her heart had taken root here.

In the alcove leading to the doors bordering the terrace, Lance gripped her waist and pulled her back against him. "Welcome to your new home, Madame Du Lac. I swear I'll do everything in my power to make you and our baby comfortable and happy."

Trembling, she turned in his arms and looked up at him. "You already have. A person would have to be made of stone not to be affected by all this beauty. I swear I'm walking in some kind of dream."

His hands slid to her shoulders. He pulled her closer. "I feel the same way."

Blood sang in her ears.

"You're very beautiful, Andrea. I want to kiss you."

He probably did. There was definite chemistry between them. But she had the feeling that whatever moves she made from here on out, she would end up paying the consequences for down the road.

More than anything in the world she would love to know his kiss. Not the angry one he'd given her in the kitchen that first night, but the one a new husband would like to give her out of normal male desire.

Yet to succumb to her own burning needs would be her first false step. His regard for her could diminish if he thought she had more feelings for him than her husband.

Though guilt ridden because it was true, she was terrified Lance might think less of her for responding to him when she was still mourning her marriage. Andrea simply couldn't take the risk of him thinking less of her.

"C-could you give me time, Lance?" she stammered.

He didn't so much as move a muscle, but she felt his tension.

"Are you remembering your honeymoon with Richard?" His voice sounded like it had come from an underground cavern.

The heat of guilt rose from her neck to fill her cheeks.

No. It was this man holding her who commanded her thoughts.

"No. I think it's a combination of everything that's happened since his death. Meeting you brought me out of the cocoon I was living in. I'm still trying to assimilate the fact that I'm your new wife, yet I'm carrying his child. I'm not sure what I'm feeling. Can you understand that?"

Slowly his hands fell away from her shoulders. "Better than you can imagine. Let's go out on the terrace. Jean and Louise are anxious to be introduced."

Oh, Lance—it would be so easy to give in to her attraction for him. But she didn't dare.

Losing Richard had changed her life, yet somehow she'd been able to move on.

Instinct told her that if she were to lose Lance, she'd mourn for the whole of her life, baby or no baby.

Lance stood in the doorway off the terrace. The house had grown quiet. By now Andrea ought to be in bed. He'd given her enough time to get ready.

In his gut he knew she wasn't indifferent to him.

The way she'd hugged him in the kitchen when he'd come in from the stable—her reaction in the bedroom while they were talking about Lancelot and Guinevere—the throbbing in her throat whenever he got too close to her— All that telling behavior indicated there was a fire burning beneath the surface.

She'd agreed to marry him so she wasn't going away. He just needed to be patient. Not his strong suit.

Even Lancelot had been forced to bide his time until the stars were aligned in his favor.

Lance looked up at the sky. There were none out tonight. A wind had come up which meant a storm was brewing. The elements matched his mood.

Five more minutes and he locked the French doors. Making certain the rest of the doors and windows were secure, he walked through the alcove to the staircase in the front hall. No sooner had he taken his first step than his cell phone rang.

He'd been expecting a call from the undercover agent before now, and clicked on. "Oui?"

"I'm sorry, *monsieur*, but Mademoiselle de la Grange has disappeared."

That came as no surprise.

"Tell me what happened."

"A technician took her for another X-ray, but she never came back to the room."

"That means she had help. Probably her mother."

"What do you want me to do?"

"You've done everything you could. Go back to the château and we'll wait to see what happens."

"Very good."

He rang off and phoned Henri to alert him to the situation. "You'd better tell Papa in case Odette and Corinne show up tonight. The agent should be there within the hour."

"Brigitte will watch for her."

"Thank you, Henri."

Lance wouldn't put it past Corinne to come to the house looking for him in order to cover all her bases. The hospital was only ten minutes away.

Grabbing one of Jean's beers from the fridge, he went outside and planted himself on the bench in front where he could see anyone driving down the lane.

A long night stretched ahead of him. He decided to phone Giles and let him know he was a married man with a baby on the way. His friend would be dumbstruck.

As it turned out, Lance was the one *boulverse* when Andrea came out of the darkness toward him like a beautiful apparition. The wind whipped her new nightgown and robe around her body. She looked anxious.

"What are you doing out here?"

She sounded upset, like she'd been waiting for him. That was music to his ears.

When he told her, she sat down. In the process she accidentally disturbed the empty beer can that toppled to the stones. She leaned over to pick it up.

"I can feel rain. Go back to bed, Andrea."

"Why don't we go in the living room. We'll watch out the window together."

"You need your sleep."

"So do you."

"I'm not the one pregnant with your husband's baby." He felt reckless and couldn't prevent the sarcasm from escaping in time.

"You're going to be its father," she came back. "Or have you changed your mind?"

Lance leaped to his feet, rubbing the back of his neck. He wheeled around. "You *know* I haven't. Forgive me for taking my frustration out on you."

"You have every right to be upset. We're in the middle of a complicated, dangerous situation."

"One you never asked for," he reminded her.

"No one held a gun to my head, Lance. I'm in this with you all the way of my own free will. Does that clear up some of the gray areas for you?"

Their eyes held. "A lot of them. Come on, or you're going to be soaking wet."

He drew her inside and shut the door. They went into the living room. Reaching for the throw on the back of one of the chairs, he wrapped it around her and pulled her down on the couch next to him. He could still see the road from the window.

She nestled against him. His wedding night was starting to look up.

"What will you do if she comes here? Honestly?"

"I'll detain her and call the police. She's become a threat to herself and to others. Something should have been done about her a long time ago. I should have come home years sooner and dealt with it."

"I don't know. I've a feeling you enjoyed your career."

"I did. Parts of it, anyway."

She lifted her head a little to gaze up at him. "Do you mind if I ask you a personal question?"

"You're my wife, Andrea. You can ask me anything."

All of a sudden he felt her trace the scar above the polo shirt he'd changed into after they'd come to the house. "Did Corinne do this to you?"

He breathed in deeply. "She's certainly capable of it. But the truth is, I became involved with a woman while I was on an assignment in the Middle East. We got together every so often.

"She knew my life in the service didn't permit me to put down roots. There came a point in the relationship when I realized she was getting too emotionally involved."

"In other words she wanted to get married and have children."

"Yes. I told her I wasn't the marrying kind. Any more togetherness would only bring her pain, so I got up to leave. I couldn't admit I was impotent, I was too proud. I just wanted to shut her out.

"Since it would be our last time together, she begged me to stay with her another hour or two. Against my better judgment I gave in. At one point I fell asleep.

"The next thing I knew, she was leaning over me and had

carved a line down my neck with a dagger. She put her bloody fingers in front of my eyes. "This is so you'll never forget me."

Andrea cupped his chin so she could look into his eyes. Hers were flooded with tears. "You mean to tell me she purposely maimed you for life because you turned her down?"

"I was lucky, Andrea. She could have done much worse."

"I can't comprehend such evil. All this time I thought you must have been injured in combat by a female soldier."

"She *was* a soldier. Our personal combat happened in a supposedly neutral zone."

A moan came out of her. "Between her and Corinne, I don't know how you could trust any woman."

"I swore I never would again. When I returned home, I hadn't spent one night at the château before I discovered a new woman in residence. She'd been given the honor of sleeping in a room no one else has slept in while I've been alive.

"Papa trusted her with a treasure that's irreplaceable. The staff lit up at the mention of her name. I was convinced that behind her beauty lay treachery. Convinced she was up to no good, I determined to expose her true face for everyone to see. But once I kissed her, I got snared in my own trap."

"Given your past history, it all makes sense," Andrea murmured. Once again she rested her golden-brown head against his shoulder.

His chin grazed her soft hair. "Did Papa ever tell you the background story on our château?"

"No. I want to hear. I can't get enough."

He couldn't get enough of her.

"When it was built, my original Du Lac ancestor named it

Joyous Gard. It means the 'happy keep,' after Lancelot's castle which is somewhere in Northern England.

"Legend has it that before he broke the spell of a sinister enchantment, it was called Dolorous Gard, which means 'painful keep.'

"When Lancelot explored the castle, he came upon a tomb with his own name upon it. He knew at once it was destined to be his home and eventual resting place. After Arthur and Guinevere visited there as his guests, the name of the castle was changed to Joyous Gard. But the strife that ensued caused the name to revert back to Dolorous Gard. Ultimately Lancelot's body was taken there for burial.

"I wanted to explain all this so you'll understand that when Corinne came into our lives, our happy home turned into Dolorous Gard. That's the way I thought of it. I'm sure my father did, too.

"But no longer, and that's because of you."

"What a beautiful thing to say, Lance." She turned in his arms and kissed his lips. Not with passion, but a sublime sweetness. "Let's go up to bed. Whether she comes or not, we shouldn't give Corinne any more power over us."

Lance knew it wasn't an invitation to make love. But they'd become friends, and that was a start.

He picked up his bride in his arms and carried her to their bedroom. When he laid her down, the picture of Lancelot leaning over the queen assailed him.

One day Andrea would welcome him with love and trembling. One day he would know the heat of her embrace. He was dying for it.

* * *

Andrea came awake suddenly. The storm had passed over. It must have been her bad dream, but she couldn't remember it. Her watch said five-fifteen.

She turned on her other side. In the semidark she could see Lance's outline, but not his scar. He slept on his stomach with one arm outstretched, as if he'd been reaching for her.

Such a beautiful man.

So much pain in the last ten years.

He wanted to be a father and had married her to that end. It made her want to be the kind of wife he deserved. She would make their marriage work for as long as Lance wanted it.

She slid off the side of the bed and padded into the en suite bathroom. Her trips were becoming more frequent. When she came back in the room, she was wide-awake.

Lance was sleeping so soundly, she decided to go downstairs to the study and phone her aunt. With the time difference to the States it would be a good time to reach her. She should have called before now to tell her about the baby and the change of wedding date, but too much had been going on. Finally Andrea felt ready to explain everything.

Once her aunt got over the happy shock that Andrea was expecting, they talked about Corinne.

"You're dealing with someone who's unstable, Andrea."

"We know."

"You need to be careful."

"Don't worry. Lance won't let anything happen."

"He must really be something."

"He is."

"I'm sorry we won't be getting to meet him for a while."

Andrea bit her lip. It was better this way. "Maybe one day after the baby's born."

"A miracle happened to you. I couldn't be happier for you. Send pictures over the Internet."

"I will. Talk to you again soon."

As she put down the receiver, her diamond sparkled in the light. She took her rings off to examine them and noticed an inscription on the wedding band.

She held it closer. Her breath caught when she read the words. *Joyous Gard*.

CHAPTER NINE

DR. SEMPLIS stared at Lance. "The receptionist told me you two are now officially Monsieur et Madame Du Lac. That was fast work. Congratulations."

"After our first visit here last month, I decided I liked the idea of being Andrea's husband. Fortunately I was able to talk her into it."

The doctor looked down at Andrea who was lying on the examining table. "Marriage becomes you. I would hardly know you're the same dehydrated woman your husband carried into the clinic before."

"The medicine did the trick, along with a lot of pampering."

Over the last month Lance had done everything to make her comfortable. When he came home from work at the end of each day, he was so attentive to her she could almost believe he was excited to see her.

Sometimes they ate out, or went for walks. They'd entertained his friend Giles and his wife. Geoff and Percy were constant visitors now that he'd recovered from his pneumonia and could drive to Rennes.

Her days were full of doing light gardening. Louise had

been teaching her how to cook some French foods Lance would like. All in all Andrea knew her life to be idyllic. On the surface…

But since their wedding night when she'd asked Lance to be patient with her, he'd honored her wishes to a fault! She feared she might have turned him off for good and couldn't bear it.

What if he never reached out to her again? What if the time came when he turned to another woman for the intimacy Andrea had denied them? If she tried to initiate something tonight, would it do more damage? She wanted Lance's love, was aching for it, but he'd given her no sign to indicate he was aching for it, too.

In all fairness to him, she knew he had other things on his mind. Since the night Corinne had disappeared from the hospital, there'd been no word of her. She hadn't made contact with Geoff. As long as her whereabouts remained a mystery, Andrea couldn't totally relax and knew her husband couldn't, either.

He never talked about Corinne. That in itself made Andrea suspicious. His brooding moods when he thought she was asleep didn't fool her.

"I'll start the ultrasound now. If we're lucky, we'll find out if you've got a boy or a girl in there. Sometimes the baby won't cooperate."

Lance had pulled up a stool next to her. Smiling into her eyes, he grasped her hand. "This is it, *ma belle*."

She nodded.

It was the first endearment Lance had used with her since their marriage. No doubt he wanted to impress the doctor that he was the loving husband.

Lance played the part so well there were times when she was in danger of forgetting their marriage was on paper only.

He lifted her hand to kiss the palm. A feeling of delight trickled through her body making her feel weightless.

"Are you excited, *chérie?*"

"I've been living for it," she confessed.

"So have I."

As the doctor undraped her to get a reading, she felt Lance's intense gaze fasten on her belly.

How odd was it that he should see her like this when they'd never been intimate or anything close to it. In the last two weeks she'd noticed herself beginning to blossom. She'd already put on a few pounds, and was hardly a fetching sight for a man who could have any beautiful woman he wanted.

The doctor moved the instrument around, intent on the task. In the semidark of the examining room, the baby's fast heartbeat reverberated, drowning out other sound. Andrea wanted to ask him if everything was all right.

"What's the verdict, Doctor?" Lance demanded.

Andrea had come to find her husband's impatience rather endearing. He was a man of action. For him the shortest distance between two points was a straight line no matter the obstacle.

"So far everything looks fine. The baby's the right size. It's growing in the right location. The heart sounds strong and perfect."

"Oh thank goodness," she cried softly.

Lance squeezed her fingers. She sensed his emotions were too involved to realize how much pressure he was asserting, but she didn't mind. This was one of those unforgettable moments in life.

The doctor made a satisfied noise in his throat. "What did you say you were going to call your child?"

Andrea told him her choice of names.

"Take a look at the screen right here and say hello to Geoff."

"A boy!"

She wasn't quite sure what she was looking at, but it didn't matter. Tears filled her eyes. "Oh Lance— We're having a little boy."

He leaned over and kissed her warmly on the mouth. "A son. We'll christen him Geoffroi-Richard Fallon Malbois Du Lac."

Moved by his deliberate mention of her husband, she cupped the side of his arresting face. "He'll be the luckiest little boy in the world to have you for his father."

While he kissed her fingertips, the doctor covered her with the sheet. "When you two are ready, here are the printouts of your baby. Keep up what you're doing to stay healthy. See you next month."

He put the pictures on her tummy. After turning on the light he left the room.

She blinked to get used to it again. By this time Lance had gotten to his feet. He walked around studying the photos with a look of happiness on his face she'd never seen before.

"I can see his profile, and hands and legs. Do you know how incredible this is?"

Incredible was right. Earthshaking events had happened to her since arriving in Brittany.

Andrea sat up and swung her legs over the side. The gown rode higher, exposing her limbs. Having captured his attention, his gaze wandered over them and continued until it reached her face. She hurried to cover them and could hardly catch her breath for the physical sensations attacking her body.

He came closer. "Here. See for yourself."

With one arm around her shoulders, he used his other hand to give her the pictures. Together they examined them in detail.

"I've been working on the baby book you gave me. There's a special page for these."

"This calls for a celebration. After you get dressed, we'll drive back to Rennes and pick out baby furniture for our son."

"I can't wait. But first let's stop by the château and show these to your father."

He caressed her arm. "I knew you would say that. He'll be delighted."

"I hope so," she lamented. "Geoff needs cheering up. He puts on a happy face, but I know he's worried about Corinne. Frankly I am, too. She could be up to anything."

Lance helped her to get down. "Let's make a pact and not think about her. This is our day. I'd rather concentrate on the baby."

That was easier said than done. "So would I."

"I'll go out to the reception room and wait for you."

She nodded. "I'll hurry."

"Take your time." He pocketed the pictures before disappearing out the door. Today he was wearing a pastel green sport shirt and jeans that molded his powerful thighs. Her knees went weak just looking at him.

A half hour later they were sitting on Geoff's veranda eating lunch with him.

"When Lance was born, there wasn't such a thing as an ultrasound. We had to be patient and wait to see what God sent us."

"I'm glad I didn't have to do that. With this news we can get the nursery outfitted for a boy right now and be ready. There are so many darling things for babies."

"My wife had Lance's christening gown and cap preserved. I'd like to give it to you for Geoff's."

"How sweet of you!"

Lance eyed his father in surprise. "I didn't know that."

"The box is on the shelf in my closet. I've kept it all these years in the hope that it would be used again."

As Andrea got up to give Geoff a kiss, Henri appeared. He walked over to Lance.

"There's a man at the door here to see you."

"Who is it?"

"He's from the court to deliver you some papers."

Lance didn't act surprised, but something unpleasant was going on inside of him. She could tell by the way the hand resting on his thigh curled into a fist beneath the table.

Alarmed, she asked, "What's going on?"

His eyes darted to hers. "Just business concerning some litigation over a property. Excuse me for a minute. I won't be long."

He was lying, but she didn't want to say anything in front of Geoff.

"While my son is busy, let me find that box for you."

Being deserted by both men gave her too much time to get worked up. She'd lived with Lance long enough to recognize certain signs. Whoever was at the door had brought bad news. Andrea could feel it. When she was alone again with her husband, she would learn the truth.

"What do you think, Andrea? Shall we go with the natural wood, or the Provence green?"

The salesman was waiting for her answer.

They'd narrowed down their choices until only two were

left. She'd been watching Lance as they looked at all the baby furniture. His eyes kept going to the set the clerk called *Goupil*.

It included a crib, a dresser with gold knobs, a child's table and a little rocking chair. The sides of it were in the shape of a very cunning looking fox handpainted in vivid colors. Andrea didn't need to ask which set had grabbed her husband's attention.

"We'll take the one with the fox."

"A wonderful choice, *madame*."

Despite what was on Lance's mind that had made him so serious since leaving the château, he flashed her a gratified glance. "Are you sure?"

"I love it."

Lance gave the man a nod. "We'd like it delivered right away." He walked over to the counter to pay for it, then suggested they go to the Galerie Bouffard to get the rest of the baby things.

Andrea remembered seeing the name of the store on the bags when he'd brought her some gifts a month ago. It appeared the attractive woman in the infant department remembered Lance. In fact she couldn't take her eyes off him! She didn't seem to care that Andrea was married to him.

Though Lance did nothing to invite the saleswoman's attention, Andrea experienced a stab of jealousy. She couldn't believe she'd just had that reaction.

"How can I help you this time?"

As far as Andrea was concerned, the flirtatious woman was doing her best to make a conquest. It brought out Andrea's possessive streak—another surprise since she wasn't the possessive type. Or at least she hadn't thought so until now.

"We'd like a crib cover, a liner and a quilt. Do you happen to have something with a fox motif?"

"There's a Renard the Fox collection from the animated cartoon version of Robin Hood. It has a mobile with all the forest animals."

"May we see it please?"

"Bien sûr." Her eyes slid to Lance, appraising him. *"Un moment."*

The woman wore a dress that clung to her tall, willowy figure. Andrea felt like a vanilla pudding in comparison. She looked away sharply.

"Andrea? What's wrong?"

"Nothing."

"I'm your husband, remember? I know your moods."

Her head flew back. "If you must know, I'm surprised how brazen some women can be."

A broad smile transformed him into someone so gorgeous, she felt her bones dissolve. "Ignore her."

"If I can't take my eyes off her electric hips, I don't see how *you* can."

He burst into rich male laughter. Then he sobered. "Today my eyes beheld a wondrous sight in the examination room that blinded me to everything else. I wish we didn't have to wait so long for the baby to come."

Lance wanted a child. No doubt he'd hoped for a son. Now that he was getting his wish, he didn't want or need anything else. Or anyone…? Like the first winter blizzard after a glorious warm autumn, the thought sent a pang to her heart.

"Here we are." The piranha had returned.

Andrea thought the collection adorable, especially the

quilt. It portrayed a castle and a wood and all the animals including the fox in wonderful colors of green, gold and red against a creamy background.

"We'll take it."

The woman eyed Lance with a seductive smile. "Can I interest you in anything else?"

"No," Andrea spoke for him. "We have everything we need." She reached in her purse and put enough Eurodollars on the counter to cover the cost.

Lance didn't interfere with the transaction for which she was grateful.

Once the woman had bagged everything, Andrea reached for the handles. "Thank you for your help."

"A votre service. Come again."

Not on your life, Andrea muttered to herself. Lance must have heard her. Once the elevator doors closed she heard his chuckle all the way down to the main floor.

He ushered her out of the doors. "I'd like to make one more purchase. The book department is to our right."

Curious to know what he was looking for, Andrea followed him up one aisle of books and down another until they came to the children's section. His keen eyes searched authors names.

"Ah… Samivel. This is what I was after." She watched him pull a substantial nine by twelve book from the shelf. "When we get home, I'll translate this for you." He sounded excited. "You're in for a very special treat." She could sense his eagerness.

Once he'd paid for it, they left the store. With his arm possessively gripping her waist, he accompanied her to the car parked around the corner.

She eyed him furtively. "Thank you for a wonderful day."

He put his hand over hers and pressed gently. "It's not over yet."

Though he often did that, lately her body felt his touch like a jolt of electricity. Andrea couldn't talk. She had all she could do to tamp down her emotions that were running away with her.

Lance drove her past Rennes's famous timbered houses, part of the city's colorful history. Near the end of the Motte de Madame avenue they ate dinner at a quaint restaurant. It bordered on the parc of the old orangerie. She cherished the time spent with him.

"There's a lot to explore here. After the baby's born we'll be able to push him in the stroller all we want."

As long as the three of them did everything together, she couldn't possibly complain.

They drove across the river to the outskirts. Once they'd reached their house and turned in the driveway he said, "It's time for you to be off your feet and in bed. It's been a big day."

He came around to open her door, then followed her inside with the packages. "Shall we go up?" With each step on the stairs her heart pounded faster.

Like clockwork she made a visit to the bathroom and changed into one of her new nightgowns and robe. When she came out into the bedroom she noticed Lance had put the packages on one of the upholstered chairs.

Andrea found him still dressed, propped against his pillow with the book in his hands. He lay there with his shoes off. It might be her nightly ritual to climb into bed with him, but each time she did lately, she found his nearness almost too much to handle.

Since the night he'd asked if he could kiss her and she'd turned him down, he'd treated her like he might a cherished sister. Andrea couldn't fault him for anything, yet her frustration level was over the top.

His glance swerved to hers. "Are you ready for a bedtime story, Madame Du Lac?"

"I'm all ears." She arranged the pillow to support her head, then turned on her side to face him. The combination of the heat of the day and his fit body made her awareness of him that much more potent.

"This was my favorite book as a child. My copy is somewhere at the château, but I'd like our son to have his own."

Andrea made an impatient sound. "You've intrigued me to the point that I'm going to burst if you don't tell me what it's about."

He turned it so she could see the cover.

Goupil by Samivel.

The drawing of the fox was so marvelous, Andrea reached for it and found herself devouring every page of pictures in the book.

"Oh—look at the giant trees and the toadstools—"

All the little forest creatures set in medieval times had been drawn with such energy and originality, she was awestruck.

"No wonder that little chair caught your attention. This is fantastic. The author has created a mood that pulls you in, even if you don't understand the story."

"I used to study these drawings for hours. I still get lost in them," he murmured.

"I can see why."

"*Goupil* is a funny word."

"It was the original French word for fox. The story of Goupil Renard appeared in the late twelfth century. Do you know he became so popular, a thirteenth-century abbot complained that the priests in the monastery preferred to decorate the chapels walls with the animals in Goupil's world rather than with images of the Virgin?"

"What?" Andrea burst out laughing.

Lance broke down, too. "It's true," he said, wiping his beautiful blue eyes. "Goupil was meant to mock our perception of the heroic knight and courtly tradition. I developed an affection for him because of his cleverness and charm.

"He's always battling the stupid greedy wolf, Ysengrin, and his unfaithful wife Hersent. But he also pulls pranks to humiliate the other animals in the forest. In spite of his somewhat malicious intent at times, Goupil always manages to capture your sympathy.

"The story's a balancing act between animal and human attributes. Our son will have to be older to appreciate it, but he'll love the drawings."

"He'll love his chair." She looked up at him. "Will you read it to me now?"

For the next half hour she lay there entranced, not only by the story, but by Lance's voice. He was a natural narrator who knew the tale so well he would emphasize certain parts making the story come alive. She never wanted him to stop.

"Did I put you to sleep?" he whispered.

"No. Don't let my closed eyes fool you. You're the best storyteller in the world."

"Is that so."

"Yes."

"No one's ever told me that before."

She opened one eye. "Have you ever read to anyone?"

"Not that I can remember."

"You're going to have a full-time job after Geoff arrives on the scene. I could never compete with you and that accent."

"What does the accent have to do with anything?"

"You'd be surprised." He wouldn't believe her if she told him how seductive he sounded just being French.

He changed positions. It brought him closer to her. "Would you like to be left alone now so you can sleep?"

She'd thought he was going to ask her something much more personal, and felt fierce disappointment that he hadn't.

"No. Actually I'm wide-awake and would like to know what that interruption at the château today was really about? You didn't fool me or your father. It had to do with Corinne didn't it? Were you afraid to tell me in case it would upset me?"

His fingers played with a lock of errand curls pooled against her neck. It spread fire through her veins.

"We weren't going to think about her today. Remember?"

"You're avoiding answering my question. I'll be a lot more anxious if you don't tell me what's going on."

"Andrea—"

"Please don't ask me again if I trust you. You *know* I do. Now that we're married, you don't have to shoulder this alone. Confide in me. Use me for a sounding board.

"A month has gone by while we've waited for her to make her next move. Now that she has, I have to know. I'm not a fragile creature."

Shadows darkened his features. "If I thought that, I would never have involved you in anything this precarious. Unfortunately the situation has gotten uglier. I'm considering sending you back to the States right away as a precaution."

"Against what?" she cried. In the next instant she'd gotten up on her elbow to face him.

His eyes held a glint of pain she couldn't mistake for anything else. "If I tell you, I risk losing your trust in me."

She shook her head. "That could never happen."

"You have no comprehension of what it is I have to tell you. It's my word against somebody else's."

"If you're talking about Corinne, we've already been down this road before."

"It's not Corinne."

"Then who?"

His eyes grew veiled. "Remember the woman who gave me this scar?"

"How could I forget?" she asked with a pounding heart, fearing what she was about to hear. "Please go on," she implored him.

"After I left for good, she had a charge of rape brought up against me, and got two of her buddies to testify that they saw it happen. I was taken before a military tribunal.

"After a month of brutal interrogation, I was sent back to active duty for lack of evidence because one of the officers under my command was able to prove that he was with one of her friends that night. She couldn't possibly have seen what supposedly transpired.

"That evidence made the other bogus witness's testimony less credible. Also, the judge advocate defending me brought in a surgeon who testified that the cut she made to my neck was too precise to have been inflicted by a woman struggling against a rapist.

"When I left the service, I didn't receive a commendatory medal because I'll always be under suspicion. In my country, you're assumed guilty until you're proven innocent."

Her eyes filled with tears.

Without conscious thought she threw her arms around him. "I'm so sorry," she whispered into his hair, getting him wet. Wanting to stop the pain, she couldn't hold back from kissing his face and neck.

"You've been through too much," she cried against his eyes and cheeks. "It isn't fair. Not for you of all people."

She'd found his mouth.

In wanting to prove that she believed him, she kissed him over and over again. Short kisses, long kisses. "I know you're innocent, Lance. I know it."

At first she didn't think she was getting through to him. Then there was a gradual change in him until he began returning her kisses. Suddenly she was the one being engulfed.

"Do you have any idea what those words mean to me?" his voice shook. He crushed her to him, revealing a deep seated hunger that spelled so many things.

She found herself caught up in the thrill of desire overtaking both of them. For a little while she lost her head. The exquisite feel of his mouth tasting hers had become a permanent craving.

He drank deeper until they seemed to be devouring each other. She wanted this ecstasy to go on and never stop.

That was because she realized she'd fallen irrevocably in

love with him. But she wasn't naïve enough to think the desire on his part translated to her level of feeling.

Lance had kissed her out of sheer male need, but she'd been the one to initiate it. He felt gratitude that someone believed in him. More, she was carrying the child he planned to father.

Mix all those feelings and emotions together, but they didn't necessarily add up to love. He'd never said the words. In fact when he'd proposed marriage, he'd been careful for her to understand love hadn't motivated him.

The few flawed women from the past he'd been unlucky enough to tangle with had made the terrible mistake of pretending he was in love with them. When faced with the truth, they hadn't been able to handle it and were still attempting to crucify him.

Andrea wasn't anything like them. Most women weren't.

She would prove she could be trusted to honor her commitment to him and never change on him.

When he allowed her to take a breath, she eased away from his body. The expression on his handsome face changed to one of alarm. "What's wrong, Andrea? Did I hurt you by accident?"

He was referring to the baby of course.

"Heavens no," she assured him. Out of self-preservation she got to her feet before she changed her mind and threw herself at him again. "I'm afraid I need to go to the bathroom." It was the perfect excuse that wouldn't hurt him.

When she came back in the room he was standing at the window overlooking the garden. He jerked his dark head toward her. His mouth had formed a grimace.

"You were with me all the way just now," his voice rasped.

"Then something happened. Is there still someone else sleeping in our bed?"

If he only knew, Richard hadn't been there for some time.

"No, Lance," she answered honestly. "I'm afraid my mind is on that horrible woman who scarred you." She moistened her lips nervously. "What does she have to do with Corinne? I know there's a connection."

Across the width of the bed he stood there facing her like an adversary. She could feel his struggle to tell her.

"What goes on in those tribunals is supposed to be top secret," he began. "Yet somehow through a military contact of Odette's, Corinne found out what happened. She's using that information in the rape case she has brought against me."

"She's already built a case?" Andrea was incredulous.

"Corinne always covers her options. The first hearing is next week."

Rage consumed Andrea. "She'll never win."

"That isn't her purpose." He folded his arms across his chest. "She's doing this for the negative publicity to ruin me and my father socially."

"I can't comprehend any of it. Does Geoff know about that tribunal?"

"No. I'd hoped to God he would never find out. Thanks to Corinne, it's going to be all over the news the moment the prosecuting attorney levels the charge against me. As my wife, you'll be hounded by the media. You can't stay in France, Andrea.

"If the attorney I've hired can perform a miracle and prevent this case from going to court, then Papa won't ever have to know. But it means I've got a lot of work to do in Paris. That's why I want you to go back to New Haven."

"You're serious!"

"Deadly."

She weaved in place.

"I'm sending Louise with you so you won't be alone. She's grown very fond of you in the last month."

Oh, Lance.

"After she's helped you get settled, then I'll pay for someone to take over for her so she can come back. If you lost our baby, I wouldn't be able to handle it."

There was no way under heaven she would leave Lance now, but while he was insistent on protecting her, she wouldn't argue with him.

"How soon do you want me to go?"

Andrea must have surprised him because he was silent for a moment. She watched him brush his bottom lip with the pad of his thumb as if he'd expected an argument. That dark, remote look had crept into his face.

"Tomorrow. There's a noon flight leaving Rennes for New Haven. I'll put you on board, then head for Paris. When I think it's safe, I'll fly over and bring you back. If worse comes to worse and you have to stay there until the baby's born, then I'll visit you when I'm able."

He had it all planned out.

Well, she'd come up with a plan of her own. One she had no intention of telling him about.

"In that case I'm going to go to sleep now and get as much rest as I can in preparation for the trip home. I'm afraid I'm one air traveler who stays awake the whole time."

She watched his hands make those telltale movements into fists. Did she dare read into it that he wasn't happy at the prospect of her leaving? Or was he simply worried for her health? Most likely the latter.

"While you do that, I'll have a talk with Louise and Jean. *Bonne nuit,* Andrea." With those words, it meant he wouldn't be coming to bed for a long time.

"Let me thank you again for a memorable day." If she could hear the throb in her voice, surely he could. "*Bonne nuit,* Lance."

CHAPTER TEN

ONCE Andrea was seated in first class next to Louise, Lance leaned over and pressed a hard kiss to her mouth.

"Don't let anything happen to you. I bought you that satellite phone so you can call me day or night from wherever you are. You know my cell number. I want a call the moment you've landed."

"I promise. When are you going to tell your father I decided to fly home to surprise my family with a visit?"

"I'll phone him from Paris tonight."

Good. She still had time.

Andrea lifted her eyes to his. "*Bonne chance*, Lance." Louise had been teaching her a few phrases.

"I'm going to need it." He lingered long enough to press his lips against the side of her neck. "Now I have to go. My plane's ready to board."

Passengers were still boarding hers.

"Please be safe."

He'd spent all morning helping her get ready. They'd talked about everything she was going to do when she got back to her condo. She felt sorry for every woman who didn't know what it was like to be taken care of by him.

"À bientôt, mon amour." He squeezed her shoulder, then he was gone.

What she'd give if those gruffly said words hadn't been for Louise's benefit, but for hers and she *really* was his love…

After he'd been gone five minutes she turned to the housekeeper. "Do you think we've given him enough time?"

"I hope so. Otherwise if he sees you, *oh-la-la*—I dread to think what his reaction will be."

Louise and Jean were in on her plan. They'd emptied the things she needed most from her suitcase before putting it in Lance's car.

"I guess I'll just have to take the risk."

She got out of her seat and headed for the doorway of the first class compartment. Louise followed. After explaining to the flight attendant she wasn't feeling well and would book another flight, they left the concourse and went outside where Jean was waiting for them in his car.

Another forty minutes and they arrived at the château. She gave them both a kiss before hurrying inside with an overnight bag Louise had packed for her.

Henri met her in the foyer. He told her Geoff was out on the lawn giving Percy some exercise. Perfect.

She raced out the west entrance as fast as she could go in her pregnant condition. Geoff saw her coming. "Over here, Andrea—" Percy romped up to her and rubbed his head against her legs. "How nice for this unexpected visit."

She kissed his cheeks. "Do you have time for a talk?"

He studied her for a moment. "Daughter to father?"

"Yes."

"There's nothing I'd love more. Shall we sit down?"

Andrea had been ready to suggest it. They walked over to the bench bordering the flower garden. Once they were seated, she leaned forward. "I'm not going to beat about the bush, Geoff. I have something very serious to discuss with you."

"I already sensed that. Otherwise you'd be home with Lance on a lovely Saturday like this."

She nodded. "I'm going to tell you some ugly things Lance confided to me that he's never told anyone else. Some of it's old news, some of it much more recent. You have to know it's because he loves you so much that he's tried to spare you. But he's in terrible pain, and only you and I can help him."

"Go on."

For the next twenty minutes Andrea unburdened herself about Lance's demons. Geoff's eyes glazed over. She left nothing out. By the time she'd finished, he clung to her and wept. It wrenched her heart.

She finally sat back and wiped her eyes. "I felt an attraction to your son from the moment we met. Over the last month I've learned to love him with every fiber of my being. He's guilty of nothing!

"You and I both know that, but this trial is going to slander the name of the Du Lac family. That's what is killing him. For myself I don't care."

"Nor I—" Geoff suddenly blurted and got to his feet. It was the first time she'd ever seen him angry.

She looked up at him. "In that case, I have a plan to end his misery."

"I'd love to hear it."

After she'd explained, he said, "It's so simple."

"I know. But by telling you this, he's going to feel betrayed again."

"Non, ma fille. You leave Lance to me."

He reached in his pocket for his cell phone. "Henri? Will you phone my son and tell him he needs to come to the château immediately? That's all you need to say."

Damn if Lance's flight to Paris hadn't been delayed due to engine trouble.

At least Andrea was on her way to Connecticut out of harm's way. That is if her plane got there safely, but he couldn't deal with that kind of nightmarish possibility right now.

Growing impatient, he pulled out his phone to call another carrier. Maybe he could make another flight leaving in the next ten or fifteen minutes. As he started to ask for information, a call came through from the château.

He clicked on. "*Salut*, Henri."

Without preamble the older man said, "Your father asked me to call you and tell you to come home immediately."

Since Andrea was gone, there could only be a few reasons for such a gut-wrenching request. His hand tightened on the phone. "Is he ill?"

"He wouldn't tell me. He just said for you to hurry. I gathered from him that it was critical."

Maybe Corinne had paid him an unexpected visit. No one knew her exact whereabouts. A cold sweat broke out on his body.

"By some stroke of fate I'm still in Rennes. I'll be there as soon as I can."

His meeting with the attorney forgotten, he dashed out to the car park. Breaking all the speed limits, he made it to the château in a half hour.

To his shock and relief, his father came out the front entrance and hurried over to the car looking perfectly well.

He searched his father's eyes. They searched his with such pain and pleading he was floored. "Papa? What's going on? Why did you send for me?"

"There's someone inside who will explain. Please hear her out first, then you'll understand."

A shudder passed through him because he knew who it was…

The blackness he'd lived with for the last ten years caused something to snap inside Lance. In a white-hot fury, he got out of the car and raced inside the château.

"Corinne?"

Andrea, who'd changed into a robe and was resting while she waited, felt her husband's deep voice. It shook the very beams of the green room.

"No, Lance—" She could hear Geoff's panic all the way down the hall to the staircase.

She raised up from her pillow. He was here so soon? How could he have gotten back from Paris this fast?

"You can try to hide, Corinne, but it won't do you any good."

If Andrea had been Geoff's stepdaughter, she would have fled for her life. Instead she got up and stood inside the open doorway with fear and trembling in case Lance couldn't forgive her.

The second she saw him coming down the hall, she could tell by his body language he'd slipped into military mode. Seek and destroy.

I'm not your enemy, darling.

His hands started to reach for her when he realized he'd caught hold of the wrong woman.

"Andrea—" came his strangled cry. He looked like he was seeing a ghost. His sudden pallor was testimony of his shock.

"What in God's name are you doing here? Not two hours ago I put you on the plane."

"I couldn't leave you, Lance. You've carried your burdens too long by yourself. It's time you let your father and me help you."

"Your wife's right." Geoff walked up to them with Percy at his side.

Lance shot her a wounded glance that made her reel before he addressed his father. "My wife had no right—"

"If the woman who loves you with all her heart and soul doesn't, then who does, *mon fils*? Do you think Andrea or I care if Corinne wants to blacken our name forever? The three of us know the truth. So does God. He's the only judge who matters. Forget the tribunal.

"I've phoned our attorney and asked him to give Corinne her inheritance now. It'll be more money than she would win in a judgment, therefore there'll be no case and no media frenzy."

Lance's eyes closed tightly for a moment, reflecting his pain. "That's like making a plea bargain with the devil."

"As Andrea said, it's only money, and I *had* planned to will it to her. She can never hurt us where it really counts. If she ever comes near anyone in the family again, she'll be arrested.

"Your wife has not only saved you a needless trip to Paris, she's put this family back together. Today it feels like *Joyous Gard* around here. *Que Dieu te benisse, ma chérie.*" He kissed her on both cheeks.

"Now I don't know about you two, but I have other plans for the rest of the day. Come on, Percy."

Andrea moved back in the room and waited on the bed for Lance. At first she was afraid he wouldn't follow her.

An eternity had to pass before she felt him stare down at her through his dark lashes. She could only see little slits of blue.

"If all the sins of omission and commission were supposedly exposed through you today, why did you leave my father with the impression that you're in love with me?"

The air caught in her lungs. "Because I am."

His hand went to the back of his neck in a gesture she'd come to understand helped prevent him from doing damage. Lance was going to need some convincing.

"That night in the forest, love happened to me, Lance. I heard your tread. At first I thought it was the sound of an animal carried by the night breeze. Then I saw your face. When you took my camera, I felt your touch for the first time and was never the same again.

"On that warm summer night I'd gone there a widow who'd long since done her grieving, yet found herself in mourning for something she couldn't put a name to.

"In one chance encounter you transformed me into a trembling woman who recognized she'd met the man who would change the tenor of her life forever.

"Lie down with me, Lancelot Du Lac. I want to feel that marvelous joy come over us as was never heard or known."

The hand at his neck slowly fell to his side, as if dropping an invisible sword that had become too heavy to wield. "For how long?" came the husky question. "A night and day?"

"For as long as you want me. Have no fear I'll ask for more."

He leaned over her until their breath mingled. "What if I want more?" His eyes had ignited into blue flames.

She took his hand and pressed it against her heart. "Feel that?" His breath stilled. "It's yours."

He sank down beside her.

Growing more emboldened, she moved his hand lower, giving him permission to explore her burgeoning body. "One day soon you'll feel our baby move inside me. I've pledged him to you. Not for a night and a day, but a lifetime and beyond if you'll have us," she whispered against his lips.

The sweet, liberating calm of a woman who knew she was loved washed over Andrea. It was the trembling of her beloved's body that fed the wildfire running through her veins.

Filled with desire, she wrapped her arms around his neck and drew his head down to her heart. To her delight his hair had grown longer over the last month. As her fingers made furrows through the black curls, he buried his face in the warmth of her ripening body.

Yearning toward him, she cried out in joy.

Lance came out of sleep hungry for his wife. He wanted nothing but her. He needed her and reached for her beautiful body the way he'd done over and over again in the night.

To his shock, the place where she'd lain beside him was empty.

The green room had no windows. In panic he felt all around him in the darkness. Nothing.

Had he been dreaming?

Grabbing her pillow, he pressed it to his face. The scent of her still lingered.

He jackknifed into a sitting position. "Andrea?" he cried, fearing Merlin had tricked him with one night of fantasy, and now he was left with nothing but memories so fantastic, he would never recover.

"I'm right here."

The vision of her body outlined against the hallway light started his heart beating frantically again. She held a tray in her hand. "It's almost noon, *mon amour*. I'm quite sure my knight needs to feed his other appetite. Turn on the bedside lamp."

Feeling like he was under some hypnotic spell, he did her bidding. She closed the door before coming to him all glowing and fresh from the shower.

The soft light picked out the gold in her flowing brown hair. Above the neckline of her creamy nightgown, a flush tinted her high cheekbones. Combined with those dark velvety-brown eyes and that mouth made for him, her beauty transcended any image of Guinevere.

She put the tray on the bed, then knelt next to him to serve him. He caught her hand and kissed the palm.

"I think I'm going to commission an artist to fill a room in our home with full-size pictures of you."

Her mouth covered his. "You don't need to do that. I plan to be by your side and in your arms from here on out.

"And after the baby comes, I plan for the three of us to go to the Galerie Bouffard so that predatory female with the swivel hips will eat her heart out!" She bit into her toast.

He grinned before consuming several strips of bacon at the same time. "When we bought those things for the crib, I decided maybe there was hope for you loving me after all."

"Liar," she whispered. "You knew how I felt about you from the beginning."

After finishing off his eggs he said, "You gave me some bad moments when you wouldn't open your door. That decided me on a campaign to win you over no matter how long it took."

"All of an embarrassingly short four days as I recall."

He trapped her gaze. "We had a marriage on paper. But it requires more than that to make it real. I rushed you into something you weren't ready for."

"Lance…" She put down her juice glass. "Just a minute. There's something I want to show you."

She slid off the bed and went over to the chair where she'd put her overnight bag. After drawing something out of it, she came back to the bed and handed it to him.

It was the baby book he'd given her. Surprised she'd brought it with her, he glanced up at her.

"Go on, darling. Open it."

Sensing her urgency, he turned the cover to the first page. At the top he read, *My name is Geoffroi-Richard Fallon Malbois Du Lac.*

Below the writing she'd left a blank place for his picture.

"Keep going."

The second page said, *In memory of my father, Richard Fallon, the brilliant professor and scholar who gave me life. He descends from a long line of French-Canadians.*

Andrea had inserted six pictures of her deceased husband in various settings and poses with her.

Lance had never seen him before. He was a nice looking dark blond man. They made an attractive couple, yet Lance couldn't relate to the woman in the picture. These had been taken at a different stage in her life when he hadn't known of her existence.

"Look on the next page."

He did her bidding. The second he saw what was there, his throat swelled with emotion. She'd put in an eight by ten photograph of Lance in uniform. It was an enlargement of a snap he'd sent his father soon after he'd been commissioned in the elite force.

This is my father, Lancelot Malbois Du Lac, son of Geoffroi Malbois, the current Duc Du Lac. His ancestry goes back to Clovis. The greatness of a king flows through my father's veins. He served with honor in France's elite force.

"Andrea…"

He felt her arm slip around his shoulders. "There's more."

After he turned the page, Lance found himself having to blink back the moisture.

Staring at him was an eight by ten photo Henri must have taken at their wedding ceremony. It showed the two of them staring into each other's eyes while they were repeating their vows.

His eyes went to the top of the page.

My father married my mother, Andrea Gresham Fallon, on June the seventh. My mother told me it was a marriage of the heart."

EPILOGUE

"AFTER he's taken two ounces, don't forget to burp him each time."

Geoff looked up at his son in consternation. It made Andrea laugh. "You'd think I'd never been around a baby before. With Brigitte and Henri here to help me, my little grandson and I will get along just fine.

"Why don't you leave so he and I can finally get acquainted! We have a lot to discuss. One day he'll be Duc. It's not too soon to let him know about his responsibilities."

In six weeks their bald baby still hadn't grown any hair. Lance seemed worried about it until she told him it might be months before it started coming in.

He had the cutest little face and sturdy body in the world. He was half Richard, half Andrea. She'd thought she might feel pain to see Richard's resemblance. She knew Lance had been secretly worried about it, too. But the reverse happened. All they felt was joy in this new life who'd come to live with them.

Lance took great pride in his son's strength. When he put out a finger, the baby grabbed hold and wouldn't let go even when Lance started to pull him up. He loved to diaper him and take care of him. It was a revelation to watch.

"If you need to reach us, we'll be at the Chez Juliette in Lyseaux."

Geoff waved him off. "I won't need you!"

"We'll be back by eleven so Andrea can nurse him. He doesn't like the formula that much, so don't be surprised if you have to coax him a little bit. He likes the back of his head rubbed, but do it gently."

"Sacré bleu, mon fils—assez!"

After being in France over a half a year, Andrea understood her father-in-law's French very well. Geoff had been living for this moment, and her husband was ruining it. If she couldn't drag him away, there were going to be fireworks.

"Come on, darling. They won't hold our table forever." Andrea was so excited to be going out with her husband. She thought he was anxious to get her alone, too. That's why she was surprised how much trouble she was having to tear him away from his little *raison d'être*.

Fatherhood agreed with him. In fact he'd embraced it so wholeheartedly, she understood a certain scene in her favorite old film a lot better than she did in her teens. The one where the father brings home a gift for the baby and the mother is lying there in bed ignored.

"Hey— Remember me? I'm your wife. I don't suppose you thought to bring me a gift, too?" the woman had said.

Andrea didn't want or need gifts, but she did want Lance's complete and undivided attention for a change.

"Lance?"

He kissed the baby before striding toward her. "I'm all yours."

Her eyes widened. "Promise?"

"Do you trust me?"

Uh-oh. "Always."

"Good," he said as he helped her out to the car.

Her premonition that he was up to something grew stronger the minute he made a turn that led to the woods. "Where exactly are you taking us?"

"Tonight there's going to be a full moon. I thought you'd enjoy a swim in the enchanted pool."

"In January?" her voice rose several decibels.

"Just a dip. I'll warm you up after."

"Lance Malbois—you stop the car right now and turn around."

He let out a devilish chuckle. "Not on your life, *mon amour*. The last time we went swimming together, you were *enceinte*. That's not your problem anymore."

"You wouldn't really make me go swimming with you tonight, would you?"

"I want to prove it's my face you see in the water."

"How much more proof do you need that I love you?"

While her question reverberated, he pulled the car off the road beneath a huge oak and turned off the engine.

In the next instant he'd crushed her to him. "I don't need proof. I simply wanted an excuse to get you alone so I could tell you I'm so in love, I'm frightened. *Tu compris?*"

Yes, she understood.

Several things had happened to liberate him. It was discovered Corinne had suffered a complete psychotic breakdown, forcing Odette to get her the professional treatment she'd needed for so many years.

Learning this, Geoff decided on another course of action and cut her out of his will. But he agreed to pay all her hospital expenses and provide for her comfort on the condition she told the truth about Lance. Geoff would love her but not at the expense of his son's future.

To Andrea's and Lance's joy, she eventually did admit her lies, wiping the slate clean.

As for the tribunal, Lance's father hired the best attorney in France to get at the truth. It didn't take long for the woman who'd scarred him to confess to her lie.

When the highest medal of honor was awarded to Lance for his invaluable service to France, the whole country read about it in the newspapers. He'd become one of Brittany's most famous celebrities.

He hated the publicity, but Andrea reminded him their son would love it.

She loved it.

She loved *him.*

Wrapping her arms around his neck she began showing him just how much. She had an idea they wouldn't be getting home to their baby before morning…

THE BOSS'S PREGNANCY PROPOSAL

BY
RAYE MORGAN

Raye Morgan has been writing romances for years and has been fostering romance in her own family at the same time (current score: two boys married, two more to go). Raye has published over seventy romances, and claims to have many more waiting in the wings. She still lives in Southern California with her husband and whichever son happens to be staying at home at the moment. When not writing, she can be found feverishly working on family genealogy and scrapbooking. So many pictures, so little time!

To Patience—
for her compassion, perseverance,
and…well, patience!
Thanks so much.

CHAPTER ONE

EMPTY offices were dark and spooky at night.

Callie Stevens took the stairs. She didn't want to use the elevator. Too noisy, and the last thing she wanted was to draw any attention from the night watchman.

By the time she'd climbed to the fifth floor of ACW Properties, she was beginning to rethink that position. But she had to be careful. After all, she'd just been fired by Harry Carver, the elderly CEO. She wasn't supposed to be here at all.

Reaching the sixth-floor landing, she stopped to catch her breath and listen for signs of life. Glass sconces lined the hallways giving off a dim light, but nothing was stirring. A sigh of relief and she made her way toward the area where her little cubicle stood among all the rest.

The light from the hallway cast an eerie spell over the room, lengthening shadows and making hiding places where they weren't meant to be. She stopped for a moment, orienting herself and feeling a sharp pang of regret. She'd liked this job. She was going to miss it—and the money that went with it.

Looking around quickly, she finally saw the object of her quest—her treasured orchid plant. She'd left it behind during the hectic ten minutes they'd given her to clean out her desk before escorting her off the premises. She'd been afraid someone might have thrown it in the trash, but there it was up on the high corner of a metal bookcase.

She glanced around quickly for something to climb on. There was no stepladder, so she pushed a chair over and hopped up, stretching high. Her fingers could barely reach. She'd just made contact with the ceramic pot that held her floral darling when the lights of the room snapped on and a deep male voice sent a shock wave slicing through her.

"Looking for something, Ms. Stevens?"

She screamed.

It wasn't a very loud scream, more of a yelp, really. But it was enough to cause her to lose her balance. She grabbed at the edge of the shelf, but it was too late. She was falling and so was the ceramic pot with the orchid she'd come back to rescue.

She hit bottom with a thud, but not the sharp, painful smack she'd expected. It took a couple of seconds for her adrenaline to fade and her mind to register that the man who'd startled her had stepped forward and tried to break her fall, and that she'd smashed him to the floor for his trouble—and now they were locked together in an embarrassing tangle of hair and limbs.

This was not good.

"Oh!"

She scrambled to her feet and looked down at him. It was Grant Carver—her ex-supervisor—nephew of the CEO who'd fired her and just about the last person she wanted to see.

He looked a bit dazed. She could probably make a run for it and get away. She drew in a sharp breath, wondering….

But then she saw the ooze of blood at the corner of his mouth and she gasped. The back of her head must have hit him in the face.

"Oh!" she cried again, dropping to her knees beside him. "Are you all right? Oh my God, you're hurt."

His deep blue eyes opened and regarded her coolly from beneath thick, dark lashes. "Ya think?" he murmured. Grimacing, he reached up to touch his lip and drew back a bloody hand.

"Oh, I'm so sorry," she said. "What can I do?"

"Here's what you can do," he said, his voice husky. "You can walk over to that desk." He gestured toward the supervisor's desk.

She jumped up and did as he suggested, looking back at him questioningly. "This one?"

"Yes." He nodded, and winced in a way that made her bite her lip in regret. "Now you can pick up that phone."

She did so, still watching him for directions.

"And you can dial 9 for building security. Tell them to call the police. We've got an intruder who needs arresting."

"Oh!" She slammed the phone back down.

She should have known. All her compassion drained away. She'd worked with Grant Carver quite a few times in the year and a half she'd been here and she had yet to figure him out. Though he was cool and somewhat sardonic on the surface, she'd often sensed an underlying current in him that disturbed her. The man had secret demons.

Most of her female co-workers tended to swoon as he passed, but she'd never been one to fall for wide shoulders and crystal-blue eyes. She knew from experience that male beauty could hide a shriveled soul.

Still, did it matter? She didn't really believe he would have her arrested. Tongue-lashed, certainly. But arrested? No.

"Sorry to disappoint you," she said, walking slowly back to stand with hands on her hips over where he'd pulled himself up into a sitting position on the floor.

He was rubbing the back of his dark head as though he'd hit it hard enough to get a lump. He was still dressed in suit pants and a white shirt, though that was open at the neck and his tie and suit coat were missing. She couldn't ignore the fact that he was a very large, very handsome man. But that hadn't mattered when she'd worked for him. Why should it matter now?

"You're not going to have me arrested," she told him firmly, watching as he pulled a handkerchief from his pocket and held it to his cut lip.

He looked skeptical. "I'm not?"

She shook her head. "No, you're not."

"I don't know," he said doubtfully, looking up at her. He began counting off the charges on his fingers. "Trespassing. Possibly breaking and entering. Definitely assault and battery. Assault with a deadly…" He frowned. "What is that thing?"

She picked the remnants up off the floor. The purple glazed pot was in pieces, but the inner plastic container looked unharmed. It held a couple of leathery leaves and a long stalk with a full violet blossom wobbling giddily at the end of it.

"It *was* an orchid pot."

"Okay. Assault with an orchid pot."

He considered that for a moment, frowned slightly, then shook his head. "On second thought, maybe we ought to skip the phone call," he said, rising effortlessly to his feet and towering over her. "I can exact my own brand of punishment."

That gave her a momentary shiver, but she would rather eat dirt than let him see her squirm. She tried to tell herself that his height was partly exaggerated by the finely tooled cowboy boots he wore, but she knew the truth. He was tall.

"I hardly think that will be necessary," she said, holding his gaze with her own, no shivers showing.

"And I hardly think you're in the position to make these decisions," he shot back.

"Look, the only reason I fell was because you startled me." A thought occurred to her and she frowned. "What are you doing here, anyway?"

He stared at her. "What am *I* doing here? It's my family's company."

She shrugged. She wasn't going to give up any ground if she could help it. "I thought you were off in West Texas somewhere for the week."

"I'm back."

So it seemed. Just more of her bad luck. "It's after hours. This building is supposed to be empty."

He looked at her as though he'd decided she had a screw loose after all. "Oh, I see. So *I'm* the one not following rules."

Ridiculous. She knew that. But what the heck—the best defense was a good offense. She'd heard that many times. And she certainly had no intention of begging for mercy. So what else could she do?

"Exactly," she said, holding his gaze. "You're certainly the one who caused all the trouble."

He stared at her and suddenly, he grinned. And then he laughed.

She stepped back, startled again. Who knew he even had a sense of humor? She felt hesitant, thrown off guard. She was perfectly comfortable defending herself against a strong man, but she wasn't sure what to do with a man who laughed.

"Oh, I don't know," he drawled at last, eyes sparkling. "I say we blame it on the orchid. That makes about as much sense."

She looked down at what she'd gathered in her hands. Watching her, he held back a chuckle. She seemed to be taking him so seriously. And that reminded him of what he'd always liked about her. She wasn't a flirt.

He'd had his fill of flirts. Women sometimes seemed to respond to him like flowers opened to the sun. There'd been a time when he'd reveled in it. But that time had long since passed. Now it just got in the way.

Not that he was dead to physical appeal. With her thick blond hair and her large dark eyes, Callie Stevens was a looker and he had the same involuntary attraction to her any normal man would have. Still, he was experienced enough to know it didn't mean a thing. It would never touch him where he lived. Nothing much did anymore. Life was more tolerable that way.

"Orchids are plants," Callie was saying, looking at him with a crease between her brows that told him she knew he'd been teasing her, but wanted to challenge him anyway.

"Agreed. So what?"

She looked triumphant. "No free will. You can't assign blame to them. They have no choice in how they're flung about."

He had the grace to pretend chagrin. "I'll have to admit, you've got a point there," he said.

She hesitated only briefly. If he was admitting things, it was definitely time for her to make a grand departure. "Of course I do," she said regally. "Now if you'll excuse me…"

She turned to go, but his hand on her arm brought her to a halt before she'd made a convincing attempt at a getaway. She looked up at him, wishing she could read the intentions in those clear blue eyes.

"Hold it," he was saying. "We're not finished here."

For the first time, she really did feel uneasy. She was alone in a darkened building with a man she really didn't know all that well. She'd been one with six others in the research group under Grant Carver, but they were only one of four groups he supervised. She had worked closely with him on a couple of projects, but there'd been a natural reserve between them and it hadn't only come from her end of the relationship.

She'd had a strange encounter with him once, months ago, where he'd made a proposal that was so off-the-wall, she sometimes wondered if she'd dreamed it. She'd turned him down and he hadn't seemed to hold it against her. But it had made her wonder about him. She knew there was tragedy in his life. If she hadn't known it from the office buzz, she would have recognized it in the depths of his eyes.

But that was all he'd ever revealed. In fact, she'd probably seen more honest emotion from him tonight than she'd seen in over a year of working for him.

For some reason, her attention dropped to his open shirt and stuck there for a beat too long. It wasn't as though she could actually see anything. The lighting cast dark shadows on his chest. But the fact that the crisp white fabric that was usually closed behind a tie now lay open, exposing something mysterious, was somehow intimate and exciting in a way she hadn't expected. Her pulse stuttered in surprise and began to race.

But she couldn't let him know.

"I'm finished," she responded, looking back up quickly. "I came for my orchid and I've got it."

"There must have been an easier way," he noted dryly.

"Probably," she said. "But I never seem to do things the easy way."

He nodded. "You do things in a pretty good way, from what I've seen. As I remember it, you worked on the Ames Ranch project last year, didn't you?"

Work. Yes, if he kept this on a professional level, she could handle it. If only he weren't touching her. His fingers had curled around her arm in a casual grip, but when she tried to pull away, he didn't budge. For all intents and purposes, he had her trapped.

"Yes, sir, I did," she said stoutly.

"And quite handily, too." His handsome head tilted as he studied her from narrowed eyes. "You were the only one on the staff who seemed to understand what the hell was going on most of the time."

You actually noticed? She didn't really say it, but it was on the tip of her tongue. But she would have followed that up with, *Why didn't you give me any credit for that at the time?*

He was gazing at her speculatively. "I think we could do some good work together. I've got a new project coming up..."

Her eyes widened. Tossing her thick blond hair back, she stared right into his deep eyes.

"Too late. Your uncle fired me today. Didn't you know?"

She'd expected him to react with surprise. Maybe even shock. After all, he'd just admitted she was one of the best employees he had. When he realized what had happened surely he would do something to straighten things out. Surely he would tell her he'd reprimand whomever it was that put her on the list for layoffs. Maybe he would invite her to come back and even give her a nice fat raise to make up for…

Her head jerked as she came out of her dream and heard how he actually responded to her announcement of her firing.

"Yes, I know."

"You know?" she echoed stupidly.

He knew. He'd probably put her on the list on purpose. *Hey, fire the blond chick—she's good but she gets on my nerves. Smart is one thing, smart aleck is another. Get rid of her.*

Suddenly she was furious—as angry as she'd been when she'd first heard she was a goner. Pulling away from his grip on her arm, she turned on him fiercely.

"But you think you know everything, don't you? Did you also know I just lost my second job, the one I use to help get out of a mountain of debt that's about to eat me alive? Did you also know that I'm about to be evicted from my apartment because I can't pay the rent?

Do you ever think about things like that when you casually toss people overboard? Or are we just like chess pieces in a big, careless game that doesn't mean a thing to you?"

His handsome face could have been cut from stone. "Are you finished?"

"No! There are others just like me. Everyone in the research department, in fact. We were all living by the skin of our teeth, paycheck to paycheck…because you don't exactly pay a lot to your lower-level employees, do you? And now every one of us is out on her ear, wondering where the next meal is coming from…."

"Okay, enough," he demanded, stopping the words in her throat. "Can the outrage, Norma Rae. We don't encourage peasant rebellions around here." He'd pulled out another handkerchief and was wiping at the blood on his face and dabbing at the mess it had made on the front of his shirt.

"Imagine the damage you could have done with a pitchfork," he muttered.

A sharp retort sprang to her lips, but before she could get the words out, she noticed that the bleeding was worse than she'd thought. She had to bite her lip to hold back a small cry. Every instinct in her wanted to leap forward and do something about the wound. Heal him. Maybe even comfort him. After all, it was pretty much her fault, no matter what she said to him.

The funny thing was he'd never looked more attractive to her. His dark hair was mussed, some of it falling down over his forehead. And there was a sort of vulnerability to him because of the cut and the blood and all. He usually looked so invincible. It was a refreshing change in a way.

And then he ruined it all by looking up with his mouth twisted in the usual sardonic style.

"Come along, my little attempted murderess," he said, turning toward the corridor. "You're going to have to fix what you've broken."

She followed willingly enough as he led the way to his office. Guilt was making her pliable for the moment.

She hadn't been in his office very often. She knew women who looked for any excuse to make a visit here, but she wasn't one of them. As the best-looking unattached male—and the CEO's nephew—he was considered quite a catch.

She'd never found him all that attractive herself. Too much arrogance there. That take-charge attitude did nothing but put her off. It reminded her too much of her short but miserable marriage. Not that Grant was anything like Ralph, really. At least Grant's arrogance was based on a certain level of competence. Ralph's had been mostly bluster.

Still, she'd vowed she would never again let a man rule her life the way her husband had tried to rule hers all those years and she tended to stay clear of men like Grant.

His office was a lot like him—handsome and well-maintained. Plush carpeting muffled sound; leather, wood and black glass provided a rich atmosphere. One framed photograph, set high at the back of the office, immediately drew the eye. The beautiful dark-haired woman holding an even more beautiful dark-eyed toddler had to be the wife and child she knew had died in a horrible car accident a few years ago.

The tragedy of losing a child—she could hardly bear to think of it. They said he'd changed after the accident. That he became a completely different person. She had no way of knowing what he'd been like before, but she found it hard to believe he'd been full of joy and laughter and the milk of human kindness in his earlier incarnation. The man she knew was totally focused on business and success and not much else.

So…just as she was a widow, he was a widower. She'd never put those two identities together like that before. Just the thought made her jump back mentally, as though she'd put her hand on a hot stove. No, she didn't want to go there.

"So, where is your first-aid kit?" she asked. She put the pieces of her orchid pot on the desk and turned, noting there was a door leading to a private bathroom.

"I'll take care of the cut," he said, beginning to shrug out of his shirt. "You take care of the bloodstains on this."

He held out the shirt to her but she had a hard time noticing. Her attention was caught and held by the incredible sight of his beautiful torso.

Men his age weren't supposed to look this good. He had to be in his thirties. By then, most males she knew had started to let lust for potato chips and beer overcome the desire to work out at the gym. Somebody had forgotten to clue Grant in to the routine. He was as gorgeous as a Greek statue.

And just as cold, she reminded herself quickly, working hard to keep her breathing steady.

She felt numb as she took the shirt and started toward the sink in the bathroom. Had she stared too long? Had he noticed? *Oh please, don't let him have noticed!* She turned the faucet up high and began scrubbing at the shirt with all her might.

"I don't know," he was saying, and there he was right behind her again, looking into the mirror over her head and dabbing at the wound. "What do you think? Iodine? Mercurochrome?"

She turned to look at his cut, but he was standing much too close and all she could look at was the golden skin, the stunning muscles. Could she actually feel the heat from his body? He smelled so good, like soap and fresh-cut grass. For just a moment, she was overwhelmed by the need to touch him. It swept over her in a choking wave and she felt herself yearning toward him. Every part of her wanted to feel that beautiful flesh.

It had been far too long since a man had held her in his arms.

"Oh!" she cried, turning back. "Go out," she ordered, staring down at the white shirt still in the sink and pointing toward the door.

"What's the matter?"

"You're like…naked!"

"I'm not naked. I just don't have a shirt on."

She closed her eyes and took a deep breath. "You're naked. Either you go out or I will."

He was about to say something. She could feel him revving up for it. He was either going to blast her for being ridiculous or tease her for being a ninny. She gritted her teeth, getting ready for it.

But to her relief, he resisted the temptation and quietly left the room. She sighed, knowing she'd given the game away. But there had been nothing else she could have done, except maybe to run screaming from the room herself.

It wasn't really him, she told herself a bit hysterically. It was just…well, she was a woman, after all. And he was the most gorgeous man she'd been this close to in a long, long time. Still, she wished she hadn't revealed herself that way.

She finished washing his shirt and when she came out into the office, she found him pulling on a T-shirt he'd found somewhere. It hugged his bulges and emphasized his assets, but it was better than his being naked.

"I hung your shirt on a hook in the bathroom to dry," she told him without meeting his gaze.

He turned to look at her, reminded immediately of what he liked about her. She was efficient and to the point. Her smile didn't drip with saccharin and she didn't bat her eyes. He'd been surprised at the way she'd reacted a few minutes before. Usually she was almost as careful and controlled as he was.

And that was why he'd thought she might be interested in a business proposition he'd put to her a few months before. She'd responded as though he'd asked her to sign over her soul to him and he thought she'd overreacted. Still, he hadn't been able to get the possibility out of his mind ever since.

"Am I allowed this close to you?" he teased.

"As long as you're dressed," she said calmly, flashing a sharp look his way. "Naked men make me nervous."

"Me, too," he said. "Naked women, on the other hand…"

"Should obviously be kept out of your reach."

He laughed. "Don't get the wrong idea. I'm just a tame family man." Reality flashed into his mind and his smile faded. He had no family anymore.

"Or at least I used to be," he murmured softly, staring into space.

Funny. It had been almost two years since Jan had died. There were now times when he could go a few days without the wave of nausea, the sharp pain in his heart and the cramping of his stomach muscles at the thought of her and what he'd lost. And then it would come again, slapping him in the face when he least expected it. Like now.

She was the only woman he'd ever loved or ever could love. And because of that, he almost welcomed the pain. Anything that would bring her closer for a moment. He would never get over it. He didn't want to get over it. Jan was still his wife, now and forever.

On the other hand, he ached for a child. His little Lisa had been as beloved as a baby could be and he missed her almost as much as he missed Jan. But over the last year or so, the need for another child had been growing in him. He wanted a son. A baby to fill up the hole in his heart. A child to give him a future.

"Are you thinking this way because of Granddad?" his sister, Gena, had asked him just the other day when he'd hinted at his longing. "I know he's on all the time about wanting you to marry again so you can have a son to carry on the name."

"'Grant Carver, the name of Texas heroes'," he quoted his grandfather in a voice very like his, and they both laughed. "No, this has nothing to do with getting married."

"Children usually come with mothers attached," she'd warned him.

She meant a wife, of course. She thought he ought to look for someone to marry.

"I'll find a way around that," he'd told his sister artlessly.

"You can't have a baby without getting married," she'd insisted.

"Oh, yeah? Watch me."

But he wasn't as confident as he pretended. He'd looked into the various options open to him and had found it wasn't as easy as you might think. You couldn't just order up a new kid the way he'd bought his new Lamborghini. Not if you wanted the child to actually carry your genes.

And that was what he wanted—deeply, passionately, with all his heart. He just wasn't sure how he was going to be able to make it happen.

"Do you have any family around you?" he asked Callie curiously. He knew she was a widow, but he didn't know much else about her circumstances. "Any parents or aunts and uncles?"

She had the look of someone who was thinking of edging toward the door.

"Family?" she repeated. "Uh…no, not really. I'm pretty much alone."

Leaning against his desk, he dabbed at the blood on his lip again. "Everybody needs some sort of family," he advised her. "I just spent the last few days at a friend's family reunion in San Antonio. Watching all those people enjoy each other and care about each other and depend on each other really brought it home to me. We all need other people in our lives."

And I need a son.

He didn't say it aloud, but somehow he almost felt she heard his thoughts. Watching her eyes change, he knew she was thinking of the same thing he was—of that rainy fall day about six months before when he'd nipped into his cousin's medical clinic and found Callie Stevens sitting in the waiting room.

Babies—that was his cousin's business. Ted ran an infertility clinic that specialized in in vitro fertilization. Tortured by his longing for a child to love, Grant had stopped in to see if he could get some information from his cousin about surrogate mothering—without actually planning to come clean on why he was asking about it.

And there was Callie, flipping nervously through a food magazine. He'd nodded in recognition. She'd turned beet-red and nodded back, then pretended fascination in tofu recipes. And he'd left without the information he'd come for, but with a new curiosity in just what a woman like Callie had been doing in his cousin's waiting room.

As a widow, could it be that she, like him, longed for a baby but didn't want the complications of another relationship? The thought was tantalizing and he'd spun a whole scenario around it, getting more and more enthusiastic. His cousin's office wasn't the first place he'd gone to find out about surrogates. He'd gone as far as to interview candidates at two other clinics. And he hadn't been impressed. But if he could interest a woman like Callie Stevens…

He knew instinctively she would never have a baby for mere money. So what could he do to provide an incentive? He'd mulled it over for days and thought he'd come up with a plan that would be mutually advantageous. She obviously wanted a baby. He could provide the support for her if she had a child for him—and then stayed on to basically be the child's nanny. That way they both could get what they wanted.

It sounded good to him.

The next day he called her into his office and ran it past her. She'd acted like he was setting up a baby smuggling ring and wanted her to provide the baby. She couldn't get out of his office fast enough. He was actually afraid she might quit her job or file some kind of harassment suit.

She hadn't done that, but she had acted very wary around him for a while. He hadn't brought it up again. But the possibilities were provocative, and he'd done his share of wondering—what if?

CHAPTER TWO

"YOU'RE bleeding again," Callie said, jerking Grant's attention back to the present situation. "We really need to do something about it. You need a doctor."

"Oh, no," he said, dabbing at the wound. "I can do this myself."

"No, you can't." She shook her head in exasperation. "I know you're a control freak, but you can't control everything yourself. There's a time to admit when you need help."

His blue eyes rose and held her gaze. There was nothing warm there, no teasing, no humor.

"What makes you think you know me, Ms. Callie Stevens?"

"I don't really know you, Mr. Grant Carver, but I know your type." She was on a roll. Things seemed to work much better when she took the initiative. He was scary in his way, but he could be tamed. At least, she hoped so.

"My type? Please, enlighten me. What is my type?"

She tried to glare at him but it didn't come off. He looked strangely vulnerable in the T-shirt with his mouth still bleeding. Like a fighter after a fight. All his hard edges were blurring a bit.

"Go on," he pressed. "I want to know what you think 'my type' is."

"Okay." She raised her chin. "Type A for arrogant. Type C for controlling. Type T for tyrant. Should I go on?"

"I get the picture. You don't like me very much, do you?"

She blinked at him and words stuck in her throat. Like him? What did that have to do with it? She didn't really know him, just as he'd said. What right did she have to be name-calling? Suddenly she regretted that she'd let herself tumble down this blind alley.

His handkerchief was soaked with blood and he was fishing in his desk for another one. The cut seemed to be getting worse the more he fooled with it.

She frowned. "I think you should sit down while we figure out what to do about your face," she said.

He looked up at her with a spark of humor in his eyes. "You don't like my face, either?" he said, managing to make it sound pathetic in a way guaranteed to touch her heartstrings.

She bit her lip to keep from smiling at him.

"Sit down," she said.

"I don't need to sit down, I..."

Reaching out, she flattened her hand against his chest and gave him a shove into the large leather desk chair behind him. He let her do it and didn't resist, sinking down into the leather and watching her curiously, as though he was interested in what she thought she was going to do with him next.

"Now pick up the phone and call a doctor," she ordered.

He gave her a skeptical look. "Be serious."

"I'm serious as a heart attack. You need help. I'm not leaving you here to bleed to death in the night. Pick up that phone."

"At the rate my blood is flowing, it'll take a week to bleed to death," he scoffed. But he did glance at the soaked handkerchief. Still, he hesitated. "Listen, my sister's a general practitioner. She can take care of it—if I decide that's necessary."

She motioned toward the telephone. "Call her."

"What are you talking about? It's after ten o'clock. I can't call her."

"Call her. She won't mind."

His dark eyebrows rose. "Do you know her?"

She gave him a tight smile. "I know sisters."

He stared at her for a long moment, and then something changed in his face.

"All right."

He picked up his cell and punched in a code, then put it to his ear. "Hi, Gena. It's Grant. Sorry to call so late, hon. No, nothing's wrong. I just wanted to say 'hi' and..."

It must have been because he didn't see the move coming that she was able to get the phone away from him so easily. It obviously hadn't occurred to him that anyone would do such a thing. But she could tell his conversation with his sister was going nowhere, so she turned, zeroed in on her target and snatched the receiver right out of his unsuspecting hand, then quickly moved out of his reach while she pressed it to her ear.

"Hi, Gena. This is Callie Stevens."

"What the…?" he growled.

She waved away his rude expletive.

"You don't know me. I work…er, I used to work for your brother. I just wanted to let you know that he's just had an accident…."

Grant swore again, but she ignored it.

"No, no, he's fine. But he is…damaged, so to speak." She made a face at him. "He's got a cut lip and it looks like it needs stitches to me. It keeps bleeding, and… Oh, great. Yes, we're at the office. Thanks."

She handed him back his telephone and gave him a superior smile. "She's coming right over."

"What?"

"She said she's only minutes away."

"Wait one dang-burned second here," he said, his blue eyes frosty. "I'm getting confused. Who got fired today, you or me?"

The superior smile was working, so she kept it up. "You'll be taken care of. So I figure we're even now. And I'm leaving."

His expression hardened. "Not yet. The key, please." He held out his hand.

She bit her lip and tried to look innocent. "What key?"

"The one you must have used to get into the building tonight."

Oh, that key.

It was one she'd had for opening the office early a few months before and she'd found it with her things when she'd gone through the boxes of stuff from her desk. Reaching into her pocket, she pulled it out and handed it to him.

"Wait a minute," he said. "I need to talk to you."

She turned toward the door. "Write me a letter."

He rose and followed her. "I'm quite serious. I've got something I need to discuss with you. I've got some ideas on ways we could use you here at ACW. How would you like your job back?"

There was a certain sense of satisfaction in hearing his words. This was almost an apology, wasn't it? At any rate, it was an admission that she shouldn't have been fired.

Yeah. That and a quarter will get you a ride on a pony. Big deal.

She turned back and studied his eyes. "You could do that?"

"Of course. I wouldn't have let my uncle fire you in the first place if I'd known his plans. I've been out of the office all week, as you know, and I only found out that he'd scuttled the entire research department when I got back this afternoon."

She hesitated, considering. "What makes you think I would want to come back to a place that's treated me so shabbily?"

He looked pained. "Please, no more self-righteous speeches. I thought you desperately needed this job. What happened to all your tales of woe?"

She started to speak, then thought better of it and shook her head. But she turned back, because she'd forgotten her orchid again. It would be completely ridiculous to leave it behind after all the trouble she'd taken to get it.

"You weren't really lobbying to get your job back, were you?" he said, eyes narrowing. "You were just trying to make me feel bad. Is that it?"

She looked up at him and didn't answer. What could she say? He was only partly right.

For some reason, this seemed to anger him. His hand gripped her arm, fingers curling around it.

"Just between you and me, Ms. Stevens," he said coolly, staring down into her eyes in a way that made her heart pound, "I *don't* feel bad. I never do."

Her breath caught in her throat. She prepared to yank her arm away from his grip, but he released her before she had the chance.

"Just be here first thing in the morning," he said. He glanced at the open calendar on his desk. "Oh, wait. Damn. I've got a couple of important meetings in the morning. It'll have to be after lunch." He looked up at her. "How about two o'clock? Right here in my office."

She couldn't muster any more of the superior smile shtick. Her lips were beginning to ache. So she made do with a superior shrug. "I'll think about it."

He saw right through her facade. "I'm sure you will,"

he said, his voice tinged with just a touch of sarcasm. "And while you're at it, think about this." He gathered her pot shards and the still-perky orchid plant and stuffed them into a drawer in his desk. "You don't get your orchid unless you show up."

She sprang toward him, as though to rescue her plant, but he was ready for her this time and she stopped herself at the last second to avoid another close contact with his large, hard body.

"You can't do that," she cried in outrage. "That's my property!"

It was his turn to try the superior smile.

"And you are here after breaking into *my* property. So I guess we're even again."

She felt like pouting. Jaw rigid, she held out her hand. "May I have my orchid, please?" she said.

"You know, I don't think I'm going to let you take it."

She glared at him. "That's despicable."

A half smile was curving his full lips. "I think I'm going to hang on to it to make sure you come back tomorrow."

"That's…that's like blackmail."

He considered her charge. "No, more like bribery."

"Whatever. It's illegal."

He smiled. "So sue me."

"I just might do that," she said, though they both knew there wasn't a chance in the world of that happening. "And you know what? If I'd had the chance, I'm sure I *would* have fired you."

And with that nonsensical statement of defiance, she turned and stormed off, taking the stairs again because she needed to work out her anger on something physical in order to keep from killing the man.

It was long past midnight. Grant still sat behind his desk, staring moodily at the dark window. His sister, Gena, had come and gone, working her medical magic, and now half of his face felt numb. But that wasn't what had him brooding. His encounter with Callie was nagging at him like a burr under a saddle. He'd mulled it over and he'd come to a decision.

Callie Stevens was the perfect woman to have his baby.

He remembered when he'd brought it up to her before. Her reaction had been extreme in his opinion. She was so calm and logical about most things. Why wasn't she logical about this? The entire plan the way he'd presented it to her would be to her benefit—that was just so obvious. And yet he knew if he came at her from that perspective again, she would react just as irrationally as she had before.

There was only one thing for it: he had to figure out how to appeal to her better nature and get her to see things his way. What was he going to do if she didn't show up tomorrow at two o'clock? What if she decided that she didn't really want to work for him and her orchid wasn't worth another run-in?

He couldn't wait for that. He would have to go to her before she had a chance to develop a real program of opposition. He didn't know where she lived but there must be a record of that in the files.

That was what he would do. He looked at his couch and grimaced. He would catch a few hours' sleep, take a shower in the washroom and take her orchid plant to her. That would make a good excuse. He shouldn't have kept it anyway. That was a foolish thing to do and he regretted it. He would stop off and pick up some doughnuts to take along as a peace offering. Just a friendly visit. That way he could get the lay of the land, see how things were with her where she lived. Maybe get an idea from her situation. Become friends with the woman.

He shrugged. It was worth a try.

"So, is he incredibly sexy?"

Tina Ramos was keeping a straight face, but the mischievous light in her dark eyes gave her away. She sat on the well-worn couch, her legs folded in around her, a cup of steaming coffee in her hands.

Callie stared at the friend who shared her apartment with her. They were sitting in the living room, watching Tina's thirteen-month-old daughter play with a round plastic toy on the floor in front of them. Callie had just finished telling Tina about what had happened the night before when she'd gone in search of her abandoned plant.

"Sexy? What? Who?" Despite her words, she knew she sounded artificially dismissive. She wasn't fooling anyone.

"Grant Carver, of course," Tina said with affected nonchalance. "We already know he's incredibly handsome."

Callie was astonished. "Oh, really? And just how do 'we' know that? I've never said a thing about his looks."

"And never noticed either, I suppose."

"Well…"

"Oh, come on, Callie." Tina was laughing. "You should see the way you look when you talk about him."

"That's crazy!" Blood was rushing to her cheeks. She could feel it. It had to be because this line of conversation was so darn annoying. Had to be. "I've never thought twice about the man."

Tina's eyes sparkled. "Oh, is that it? I guess I mistook the look."

"I guess you did." She threw up her hands and wailed, "Tina…!"

"Oh, I'm just teasing." Tina raised an eyebrow. "Are you going to the meeting?"

"Of course not."

"Why not?"

Callie hesitated, unwilling to admit aloud that it was exactly because he was sexy and he was handsome that she didn't relish going. There was something strangely compelling about the man and that made her uncomfortable. She'd built herself a little island and she fended men off with a virtual firehose. But he was the sort of man who might walk right through the blast, damp but undaunted. And mostly, she was afraid that she might let him.

"I have other things to do," she said, knowing it sounded lame, but that it had the advantage of actually being true. "I have to go out to Shady Meadows Rest

Home and see my mother-in-law. I'm hoping I can talk them into keeping her where she is for just one more month while I try to scrape up enough money to transfer her to full nursing care."

"Scraping together money isn't going to be easy now that you've lost both jobs," Tina said, her eyes losing their sparkle quickly.

Callie sighed. "I will go out and see him later," she said, knowing it was childish to go late, just because he wanted her to come at two. But when you came right down to it, she did need the job. She had to go.

Tina hesitated, then reached out and took her friend's hand. "Callie, I called the agency last night and told them to double my assignments. If I can make a bit more…"

Callie winced. Tina was trained as an elementary teacher, but after a cancer scare, she'd taken up cleaning houses for a living, working for an agency part-time and making just enough to get by on.

"No, Tina. You need to be home with your baby while you can be."

Tina pressed a finger to her lips. "I'm taking her with me," she whispered.

Callie groaned. "You're not allowed to do that and you know it."

Tina shrugged. "No one's turned me in yet. Everyone loves having Molly around."

Callie glanced down at the beautiful child. Of course everyone loved Molly. What was there not to love? With her head of shining chocolate-colored curls and her huge dark eyes, so alive and so interested in everything, she was as fresh and pure as a snowflake.

The little darling had certainly turned Callie's life around. Tina and Molly had come to live with her just before Christmas and nothing had been the same since. There was joy in her life now. Joy, and a beautiful baby.

It wasn't her baby, and it was only temporary—like everything else in her life. But that didn't really matter right now. A life that had been cold and lonely for years had become warm again. She'd been searching for something to live for. She'd even looked into having a baby on her own. The hunger for a child was deep and raw inside her. But no matter which way she turned, she couldn't seem to manage to find a way to do it that made sense. Now, with her own little rag-tag family, she had something. At least for the moment.

Rising, she started toward the kitchen but the sound of the doorbell startled them all.

"I'll get it," Tina said, heading for the door.

Callie frowned, wondering who it could be and smoothing back her hair. She'd thrown on a big purple sweatshirt and an old pair of baggy jeans when she'd rolled out of bed. She thought she remembered brushing her thick hair, but it felt a little wild at the moment. She wasn't really ready for company, especially not…

Grant Carver.

"I hope I'm not intruding," he was saying as Tina let him in.

And then there he was, handsome and sexy, just as

Tina had surmised—if a bit wounded. His lip was swollen and that side of his face was slightly discolored. Callie winced, looking at him. And then she wondered once again why the injury made him look so much more appealing. Did she feel a natural attraction to damaged men?

Carrying a large Stetson, he was dressed for the office, very sharp and very elegant—while she knew she must look like a refugee from the hill country.

Was he intruding? Oh, yes, very definitely.

"Oh, no, not at all," Tina said quickly when Callie didn't answer him right away. She threw him a bright smile that spoke volumes as to her opinion of the way he presented himself. "I'm Tina, the roommate. We've been up for hours. Just talking, you know. About…" She stopped and bit her lip, looking guilty as sin.

"About?" he asked, waiting.

"About things," Tina said with a sigh and a quick look of apology toward Callie. They all knew that he knew he'd been the object of their conversation.

"'Shoes and ships and sealing wax'?" he quoted helpfully.

"Oh, yes. Those things, too." She smiled at him. "Cabbages and kings. All that stuff."

"Wonderful." He held out one of two bags he carried with him. "I brought doughnuts, just in case."

"Lovely," Tina cried, taking it from him. "How do you take your coffee?"

"Black, thanks."

"I'll be just a moment."

"Take your time," he said, turning slowly to look at the room and wondering what the hell he was doing here.

Well...bringing Callie back her orchid plant. That was the official objective. And to take the first steps toward becoming friends. But now that he was here, he realized he might be walking into a trap of his own making.

And then he looked at Callie and he was sure of it.

Crazy. That was the only word for it. He was crazy. Just being here went against every rule and every plan he'd made for himself.

He hadn't been able to get her out of his mind. He told himself it was because she represented such possibilities. Looking at her, he knew it was more than that. And now he knew something else.

The efficient, no-nonsense Callie he was used to at work fascinated and intrigued him. But there was another Callie. This one had sleepy eyes and a thoroughly kissable mouth and hair that glowed like a wild, golden cloud around her pretty face. No makeup. Bare feet. Lovely breasts that were emphasized by the way the cloth of her sweatshirt draped across them.

And suddenly he felt something he hadn't felt for a long, long time. Deep, hungry, carnal desire.

He looked away quickly. Wow. This was no good. He didn't want to feel sexually attracted, not like this. He needed distance so as to keep control.

"Hey," he said, nodding to her and looking stormy on purpose. "I had a hell of a time finding you."

"Really?" She shrugged nonchalantly. "And here I didn't even know I was lost."

"Oh, you were lost all right. At least to me. The employee card I used had your old address."

She looked incredulous. "So you went to Buckaroo Court, looking for me?"

"Yeah." He made a face. "Not exactly the garden spot of Dallas, is it?"

She sighed. "Not exactly. Which is why I moved over here as soon as I could."

He nodded, and she frowned.

"And someone told you my new address?"

"Yes." One dark eyebrow rose. "A semidelightful gentleman named Butch. He was throwing soapy water on his motorcycle in the driveway but kindly took a break to give me your whereabouts."

"The so-called manager." She shuddered. "More like the game warden." Giving him a wise look, she added, "How much did he stick you for?"

"A cool twenty got me the information. I thought it was a bargain."

She winced, eyes sparkling. "Yikes. I guess I'm going cheap these days."

He shrugged. "I got a discount after I roughed him up a little."

She gasped, then didn't know whether to take him seriously or not. "You didn't!"

He gave her a half smile, not ready to satisfy her curiosity. "Enough about Butch. He's not very interesting anyway. I brought you your orchid." He held up a brown paper bag and peeled back enough to show her a flower peeking from inside.

"So I see," she said, looking at it warily, then shifting to look up into his eyes. "What do you want for it?"

He gave her a pained look. "See, that's exactly why I brought it to you. I decided you were right. It wasn't fair to hold your orchid as bait to draw you back. I ought to have enough faith in you to assume you'll do the right thing without having to be coerced."

"Thank you." She snatched up her plant, hugged it to her chest, then looked at him gingerly. "But you see, that's where you make your big mistake. Now that I've got my plant…"

"You'll be so grateful, you'll probably come early and camp on my doorstep," he said, but his expression was cynical.

And she suppressed a smile. "Dream on."

She peeked inside the bag. The orchid looked as though it enjoyed car trips. That was a relief. Her orchid was no longer held hostage.

Setting it down on the tiled window ledge alongside two others, she turned back to Grant. His lower lip looked even more swollen from this side and she could see evidence of stitches, though they were just about invisible. At least he'd let his sister take care of his injury.

"What happened to your important meetings?" she asked.

"I'll make them. I only stopped by for a moment."

Tina brought out coffee and doughnuts on a plate, prattling with small talk all the while. Callie and Grant sat cautiously on the couch, eyeing each other like two gunslingers meeting at the corral, each waiting for the other to move toward the doughnuts first.

Watching them, Tina grinned, then scooped up her baby, who was sucking on a red lollipop, and turned back to say goodbye.

"We're going to the park," she explained.

"Oh, don't go!" Callie cried fervently.

But Tina merely gave her a wink. "We'll be back soon."

Callie hardly noticed the wink, because she was caught up in watching Grant's reaction to Molly. He took one look at her and recoiled as though something had stung him. It was quickly apparent that he wanted to be as far away from the baby as he could get.

Tina didn't seem to notice, and neither did Molly. The little girl gazed at him intently, then her chubby arms shot out as though asking him to take her from her mom.

"Da Da!" she cried, her eyes lighting up.

"No, honey," Tina said, laughing. "That's not your da da."

Turning, she looked back over her shoulder at Callie.

"More's the pity," she muttered with a significant look. And then the two of them were out the door.

Grant reached out and took a piece of doughnut in his hand, then popped it into his mouth.

"So you live here with Tina," he noted, reaching for his coffee next.

"And Molly," Callie said. "Our little angel."

He winced and avoided her gaze. At a glance, the little girl had looked just like Lisa. And thinking about Lisa was the one thing that rendered him helpless. He didn't want to hear about Molly, or anything else that reminded him of his own baby.

"What does Tina do?"

She gave him a suspicious sideways look. "Why do you want to know?"

"I'm interested in you and your life."

She turned to frown at him. "Why?"

He shrugged in exasperation. "Weren't you the one telling me that you and your fellow workers were real human beings with real lives and not chess pieces? I'm trying to learn to be a better boss. I'm empathizing."

For a moment, he thought she was going to laugh in his face.

"Right," she said skeptically. "Okay, Mr. Sensitive, empathize this. Tina is a wonderful person. My best friend. She's had some bad luck and hard knocks, and right now she's in and out of remission of her cancer and trying to raise her baby on her own."

"That's insane," he interjected coolly. "A woman with that sort of health danger has no business having a child."

Her eyes widened and she looked at him as though he were a freak. "Sometimes these things are beyond our control."

"Nothing's ever beyond control."

"Oh brother." She rose from the couch and picked up her coffee cup. "You're so wrong. I've been on a runaway roller coaster for years and I still haven't found the brakes on the darn thing."

"Maybe I can help you with that," he said softly.

She stared at him and he stared right back. She tried so hard to keep a mask of quiet competence in place, but he was beginning to see through it. She wasn't as good at hiding as she thought.

She went into the kitchen to refill her cup and he followed her.

She turned, startled. "Did you want more coffee?" she asked.

"No, thanks," he said. "I've got to get going."

She looked up at him and his gaze went to her mouth, then veered quickly away.

"I'll be expecting you at two," he said, picking up his hat.

"Why?" she asked simply.

He turned back and looked at her. "Because I want to talk over some possibilities with you. I told you I wanted to find a way to get you back at work at ACW."

She frowned, obviously suspicious. "Why do you care whether it's me or someone else?"

He stopped dead, staring at her. "Callie, why don't you trust me?"

"I trust you."

"No, you don't. You're suspicious of everything I say and do."

"That's not really true."

"What have I done to make you so wary? Or has someone else hurt you?"

Bingo. He saw it in her eyes. But she wasn't going to admit it.

"This is ridiculous," she said, turning away. "I like you better as a boss than a therapist."

"Then we agree," he said, turning to follow her.

She passed so close he thought he caught the scent of her hair. She was very real, very flesh and blood. She put up a lot of barricades and hid behind defenses, but there was nothing coy or artificial about her.

He liked her. He liked the way she looked and the way she walked and the way she held her head when she talked to him so seriously. He actually liked that she was wary of him. He wouldn't have respected her if she'd jumped at the things he said too eagerly. She was pretty and smart and classy.

Yes. He had to have her as the mother of his child. She was perfect. She was the one.

"Will you come?" he asked, resisting the impulse to grab her and sling her over his shoulder.

She looked at him. "I'll think about it."

"Two o'clock sharp."

"I know. I got that."

He went to the door. "If you don't show up…"

"You'll come back and torture my orchid?" she suggested lightly.

"No." He favored her with a slow grin. "But I will be back."

He left whistling. She would come. For curiosity's sake if nothing else.

CHAPTER THREE

IT FELT odd walking down the corridors where Callie had been an employee only one day before. People glanced up and did a double-take when they saw her. She smiled and held her head high. A few smiled back but she hadn't made many friends outside of her own department—and they were all gone.

Lynnette, Grant Carver's administrative assistant, didn't smile. She rose from her desk and ushered Callie into Grant's office immediately, but she didn't look happy to do it.

The woman thinks I'm some sort of gold digger, Callie guessed perceptively. Oh well. She was protective of her boss and Callie supposed that was a good thing.

Grant rose in a courtly manner and shook hands with her, establishing the businesslike mood right away. He wore beautiful wool slacks and a crisp white shirt with a sky-blue tie—the picture of the ideal entrepreneur.

"Please have a seat, Ms. Stevens," he said, gesturing

toward the chair he'd pulled up before the desk. "I'm glad you decided to come."

"Thank you." She sat down feeling nervous and wondering why she'd let herself wear such a short skirt. No wonder Lynnette was leery.

"Well, let's get right to it," he said, barely glancing at her shapely legs before shuffling papers on his desk. "Looking over your record, I see you've had a few prelaw courses in college. Were you planning to go to law school?"

She hesitated. Her past was tangled with twists and turns she didn't want to get into. "At one point, I had hopes along those lines," she admitted.

He nodded, his gaze cool and reserved. Looking at him, she could hardly believe this was the same man she'd fallen on the night before, the same man who'd thrown her for a loop by taking his shirt off, the same man who'd appeared on her doorstep with doughnuts.

"ACW Properties has a couple of openings, but the one I would think best for you would be a position in the paralegal section of our law department," he was saying. "Perhaps you'd be interested."

"I don't have any paralegal training," she said quickly. "Don't they usually want a certificate for that?"

He nodded, his wide mouth twitching at the corners. "They might. But I think I can get a waiver on that. Even personnel tends to do what I tell them to."

"Oh. Of course." He was the boss, after all. She just wasn't used to getting favored treatment from anyone.

"You would start out as an assistant to our paralegal staff," he said. "We would expect you to develop quickly into a fully qualified paralegal. Here's the projected salary."

He wrote the number on a piece of paper and passed it to her. Her eyes widened as she noted the sum.

"It's a nice raise," he said.

She looked across the desk, trying to read something in his eyes. It *was* a nice raise. Too nice. What did he really want?

"This is more than I expected," she said mistrustfully. "What are you going to want me to do for it?"

His eyes glittered and she realized what she'd at first taken for irritation was actually humor.

"So young and yet so cynical," he said. "I expect you to do a good job for ACW. A very good job."

She frowned, searching his eyes. She was usually pretty good at reading people, but for some reason she couldn't get a handle on his moods and motives today.

"I don't get it," she challenged. "This is too much money for a job that's actually an assistant to an assistant."

He shrugged. "Why don't you turn it down, then?" he said softly, watching her like a cat watching a mouse.

"Heck no," she said, tossing her hair back and looking him straight in the eye. "I need the money badly. I just want to make sure I know what the money is actually buying before I agree to take it."

"I expect top-notch work and I'm willing to pay for quality."

Funny, but she was still uneasy, feeling there was something behind what he was saying, something he was holding back. His comment about being willing to pay for quality seemed to have an added significance she just wasn't getting.

"I won't disappoint you," she said.

He nodded slowly, but his eyes seemed to be seeing right through her. She waited a moment, then added a question.

"Well then, shall I start tomorrow?"

"Tomorrow?"

She frowned. What was the matter with him? He was gazing at her blankly as though his mind was a million miles away.

"Hello," she said, waving a hand before his eyes.

"Oh, sure," he said quickly, realizing he'd been drifting away from the conversation. "Tomorrow would be fine."

He ran a hand through his thick hair, staring at her. His mind hadn't been a million miles away at all. It had been right here, trying to figure out how he was going to bring up the baby thing as he'd planned to. Why couldn't he seem to get together the right words to ask her? It had to be done. It needed to be done. And here he was, at a loss as to how he was going to do it.

This wasn't like him. He never lacked ideas, never shrank from difficult subjects. He went after what he wanted with a singular confidence some even labeled as arrogance. It hadn't even occurred to him that he would have trouble putting what he wanted into words. But here he was, struggling—and running through different options with no clue.

What should he say? How should he approach it? With humor? Seriousness? Casual unconcern?

Uh...Ms. Stevens? One more thing. You can qualify for a big bonus if you agree to have my baby.

Oh, yeah. That would work.

Ms. Stevens, in looking over your records, I see that you would be the perfect person to have my baby. What do you say?

He winced, knowing very well what she would say to that and not wanting to hear it aloud.

Ms. Stevens, I'm sure you know that the Carver family looms large in the history of Texas. We weren't at the Alamo, but we were just about everywhere else. The tragedy is, I am the last in the Grant Carver line, and I need to have a son to carry on the name and the legacy. You seem to be uniquely qualified and have been selected for this honor... If you would like to contribute to the cause of Texas history...

Oh hell, that wouldn't work, either. Why couldn't he think of anything workable?

But maybe it was just as well. He was probably rushing things. Maybe it would be better to give it a few weeks, to let her get comfortable with him, maybe even start to trust him a little. Maybe...

"Is there something else?" She was looking at him curiously.

He sighed. “No. Not yet.”

“Not yet?”

“I mean… No. Thank you for coming in. I’ll make sure personnel has your paperwork ready in the morning.”

“Fine. I’ll see you later, then.” She rose. “And thank you, Mr. Carver. I appreciate this.”

Rising as well, he shook hands with her and said, “Till tomorrow, then.”

She threw him a last puzzled look and turned to go. It was pure fancy, he knew, but some of the light seemed to dim as she left the room.

“Hey, Mr. Carver.”

He looked up to find Darren Evans, a bright young lawyer who had recently been hired, entering his office but looking back at where Callie was disappearing into the elevator.

“Pretty lady,” he noted, one eyebrow raised as he gestured toward her.

“Yes.” Grant frowned as Darren dumped a stack of contracts on his desk. He seemed to be a pretty good lawyer, but his reputation as a ladies’ man was beginning to loom larger than his talent.

“I heard she’s a widow. Is that right?”

“That’s right.” Grant’s frown deepened. “Why do you ask?”

“I just wanted to make sure.” Darren had a young man’s casual confidence in his own irresistibility. “I was thinking about asking her out.”

“I’m afraid you’re a little late for that,” Grant said

without a second of hesitation. Every male instinct in him rose up in a makeshift defensive posture.

"Oh, yeah?"

"Yes. She's not available."

"Really? Who…?"

"Darren, that's really none of your business."

"Oh. Okay." He sighed. "That's a shame. Early bird gets the worm, huh?"

Grant scowled at him. Darren finally seemed to notice that his boss wasn't pleased with his company and bowed out quickly, but Grant's mind was churning. What Darren said had opened his eyes a bit. He was beginning to realize he couldn't fool around waiting for the right moment with Callie. If he didn't get a commitment from her soon, she might just fall prey to some playboy like Darren Evans. He had to think of a way to approach her with it. Very soon.

But he wasn't going to think of anything just sitting here. Rising, he shoved his hands deep into his pockets and began pacing the floor. Going to the window, he looked down. And there she was. Callie had stopped at the courtyard fountain and was gazing down into the water.

Now. He had to go now before he lost this chance. Turning on his heel, he raced out of the office, past a startled Lynnette, past the elevator, straight for the stairs. Taking them two at a time, he sailed down six floors like a downhill skier on powder, bursting out into the courtyard at full tilt and coming to a quick stop. She was still there. He was going to do it and he was going to do it now.

As he walked up behind her, he took in her trim form, her slender neck, the way her hair tumbled down her back. This was the woman he wanted as the mother of his child. And suddenly he knew that, once again, where Callie was concerned, all his plans were sailing out the window.

Had he really contemplated asking a woman like this to have his child without offering her marriage? Was he nuts? He couldn't insult her that way. Maybe that was what had been inhibiting him—knowing it wouldn't work no matter how gracefully he tried to put it. If he was going to do this thing, he was going to have to go all the way.

"Callie," he said, and she turned, startled, and stared up at him, her mouth slightly open.

"Callie Stevens…" He took her hand in his and gazed down earnestly into her dark eyes. "Will you marry me?"

Tina was sitting in the middle of the living room rug, rolling a ball to Molly.

"You're home already?" Callie said as Molly ran to greet her with little baby kisses. "I thought you were taking two jobs today."

Tina was smiling, but her face was strained. "I got so tired, I just couldn't go to the second one. I… I'm sorry, Callie. I know I promised you."

"Oh, Tina, please! If you feel the least bit tired, you are to come home immediately! Don't think twice. We don't want you getting really sick. Molly needs you. Don't you, pumpkin?"

Molly squealed as Callie tickled her tummy.

"But we need the money," Tina was saying.

"No problem," Callie said briskly, depositing the wriggling youngster in her mother's lap. "I've got an armload of newspapers. I'm going to scour the ads and get my résumé pulled together tonight, then head out onto the pavement first thing in the morning. I'll get something right away. You'll see." She smiled at her friend. "Don't you worry."

"Callie, I do worry. Things were already tight before you got laid off."

Molly was beginning to fuss and Tina whipped out a red lollipop to tempt her with.

Callie frowned. "Should you really be giving those to her? Won't they rot her teeth?"

"What teeth?" But Tina was joking. They both knew Molly was developing quite a set. "Don't worry. I usually only let her have one a day and I brush her teeth right after she finishes. And also, you'll note the stick is rubbery, so it's not dangerous." She sounded defensive as if she'd had to explain this to others before. Her smile was a bit watery. "They're her favorites. She just loves them. And I feel like she got the short end of the stick in so many ways…."

Her voice trailed off and Callie regretted having said anything. Tina had enough to worry about without her best friend criticizing the way she was raising her baby.

"How did the meeting go?" Tina said, changing the subject.

Callie hesitated, wondering how much she wanted to tell. "He offered me a job. As an assistant in paralegal."

"Great!"

Callie shook her head, feeling frazzled. Life was spinning out of control and she had to stop it somehow.

"It's no use. I can't take the job. The man is a raving lunatic."

She raised a hand to stop Tina's inevitable questions. She had to think this through before she could analyze it with her friend.

"Sorry, Tina. I really can't talk about it right now. Maybe later."

"Oh. Okay." Tina's puzzled look turned tragic. "Oh. The home called. They said they couldn't hold your mother-in-law's room any longer. Unless they get the extra fee by Friday, they are going to transfer her to the county facility."

Callie felt as though she'd been slugged in the stomach. She had to struggle not to show her dismay to Tina. Instead she took a deep-cleansing breath and tried to smile.

"Oh, Callie, if it weren't for you, she would have been there over a year ago. You're so good to her. But I've got to say, I don't understand why you've taken on such a big responsibility. Why do you feel she's your burden?"

Callie thought for a moment, wondering how she could explain. "She's my husband's mother. She was good to me."

"Your husband wasn't."

"No. But that's not really her fault." She shook her

head. "I'm the only family she has left, and she's the only family I've ever had."

Tina sighed, looking at her own little girl as she played on the floor.

"Not many daughters would be as generous as you, not to mention daughters-in-law." Tina shook her head. "Callie, you've got to look out for yourself sometimes."

"I look after myself just fine. Don't worry about me. I'm okay."

She went to the kitchen and began wiping down the counters, more because she needed to be doing something than because they needed it. Her mind was still reeling from Grant Carver's proposal. She felt as though she'd passed into an alternate universe. What he'd suggested was insane. Impossible. Outrageous.

"Will you marry me?" he'd said, and she almost fell into the fountain.

At first she'd thought he must be joking. Or playing some sort of wicked game. But he'd been so sincere and spoken so earnestly, she quickly realized he meant it. He wanted to marry her—and more. He wanted her to have a baby for him.

She supposed that shouldn't be so shocking. After all, he'd brought it up before. She'd been trying to forget that offer ever since. He'd thought she could have a baby for him and then be the baby's nanny. Fat chance! That had been just a little too cold-blooded for her and she'd told him so.

But now he'd upped the ante. He'd brought marriage into it.

And yet, what difference did that make? He was still basically proposing to pay her to have a baby for him. People didn't do things like that.

Well, they did, but…

He brought up that day he'd seen her in the fertility clinic, and she had to admit she'd been looking into the feasibility of having a baby with artificial insemination—that she wanted a baby just as badly as he did. That she, like him, didn't want to marry again. And that she hadn't been able to go through with it.

But that didn't mean she was ready to marry Grant Carver, no matter how hard he argued that it would be more a business proposition than a real marriage. That would be crazy.

She pulled open the refrigerator and took out an onion and some carrots. Taking them to the cutting board, she began to cut them up into small pieces, chopping hard, and at the same time, she tried to think about something else. Anything else.

But her mind had blotted everything else out. All she could think about was this insane issue.

What right did Grant have to come into her life and turn it upside down? She'd been perfectly happy… Well, maybe not perfectly happy. In fact, maybe a bit stressed. But still. He'd brought up things she didn't want to think about. Like what did she actually plan to do with her life?

Not get married. That was for sure. After all, it wasn't

as though she expected to meet her prince charming in the next few years. It had been six long years since Ralph had died and she hadn't met one man whom she would remotely consider marrying.

Okay, maybe just one. But that one was Grant Carver. So why wasn't she considering him?

Because he doesn't love you, stupid!

At least he was honest about it.

And yet, a little tiny part of her brain was whispering, "What if…?"

No!

Better a life of lonely misery than marrying a man who didn't love her.

She stopped for a moment, frowning. Was she really thinking this through? Or just spouting slogans?

Her thoughts were still swirling when a really startling epiphany popped into her head. If she did what Grant wanted, she would be making life better for four other people. And that wasn't even counting herself.

No! Impossible. There had to be another way.

She rinsed the washcloth she'd used on the counter and started toward the refrigerator, but noticed that Tina had put the mail on the kitchen table. She leafed through the envelopes. Nothing but bills. A gnawing ache had settled in the pit of her stomach.

And then she came to a note at the bottom of the stack. It was from Karen, the apartment building manager.

"Callie, I'm sorry, but I'm going to have to have this month's rent check by Friday or…"

The ache became a sharp pain and she gasped, clutching her midsection. Tears filled her eyes. She'd been close to the edge before, but this time she was hanging on by her fingernails. What was she going to do? Even if she took the job Grant had offered with its new salary, it wouldn't come close to covering all the expenses she was drowning in.

"Ca-ee."

Callie looked down. There was Molly, tugging on her skirt. She smiled at the adorable child. Grant had lost a little girl very much like this one. For just a moment, she could catch a hint of how horrible that must be for him.

Molly reached up with her chubby arms and Callie leaned down to lift her. The baby stared at the tears in Callie's eyes, then reached out and touched one on her cheek with the end of a tiny finger. Her mouth opened in surprise when her finger came back wet.

Callie laughed and let Molly wipe away the rest of her tears, one by one. Hugging her close, she dropped a kiss on the top of her curly head, marveling at how the sweetness of the child helped to wash away a lot of the fear.

She so longed for a baby of her own and holding Molly just brought that ache front and center. A baby was something real and permanent.

Everything in her life had always been so temporary. She'd never known her father. Her mother had been the sort of woman who needed a man in her life, yet couldn't keep one for more than a few months. After her mother died, she'd lived in foster homes. Nothing real, solid, enduring. Her life was always in flux with nothing to hold on to.

When she'd married Ralph, she'd thought that would be it. She would have something lasting. It hadn't taken her long to realize that hope was just as big a failure as all the others. Ralph as a suitor was very different from the man she ended up married to. Once again she was on her own.

She knew that was one reason she was so drawn to having a child. A child wasn't temporary. A child was forever. A child was tenderness and trust and a stake in destiny.

A baby filled your arms with more than soft, clean-smelling flesh. A baby filled your arms with love and happiness and hope for the future. She wanted that. She needed it.

And if she was honest, she would admit that Grant could make all that possible. And at the same time, she could make it possible for him.

She could give that to Grant.

She had the power to do it.

She could give that to herself.

Did she have the nerve to do it?

CHAPTER FOUR

NEGOTIATIONS had begun.

The setting was a trendy café with reflective surfaces and hard edges. The mood was wary and exploratory. The outcome was uncertain.

"So how would this work exactly?" Callie asked, trying very hard to be cool, calm and collected while her stomach was manufacturing butterflies in herds. "I think we should be very clear on all the details from the start, so we both know where we stand."

Grant nodded. "To start with, what we're talking about here is a business deal, not a love match," he said, gazing at her levelly across a tile-covered table.

He'd said that before. She had no doubt he was going to say it again. Many times.

"Yes. I understand that."

At least, she thought she did. When you came right down to it, she wasn't sure she knew what a "love match" was. She wasn't sure she even believed in them. When she'd married Ralph, she'd done it out of gratitude, not passion. She'd known right from the beginning that love had very little to do with it.

She didn't even think there'd been much love on Ralph's part. There had been an obsession—but it was an obsession with control. They'd gone very quickly from being good friends to wary adversaries and she wasn't sure how or why it had happened that way. She only knew she didn't want that to happen here—if she decided to do this crazy thing.

"In fact," Grant was saying, his hands curled around a large mug of coffee, "when I first started thinking about it, as you know, marriage wasn't really a part of the plan."

"Well, it is now," she said quickly. "In fact, it's a deal breaker."

He nodded. "I know. Don't worry." He smiled at her in a reassuring way. "I feel the same way, now that I've thought it through."

"Good."

She was trying hard to seem composed, but he could sense her unease and he hesitated, wanting to get this right. He'd deliberately chosen a rather noisy, modish restaurant for this meeting. He hadn't wanted white linen tablecloths and roses, with violins in the background. Techno music and hard surfaces made a better match for their purposes. It would be best to hammer out the future guidelines for their relationship in a cool, neutral atmosphere. No emotions allowed.

Yesterday had been a day from hell. He'd been so clumsy, practically assaulting her with his appeal that she marry him. He'd tried to explain, tried to tell her about his family heritage, and his own overwhelming need for a child. She thought at first that he was joking. Then she thought he was crazy. She'd placed a few well-aimed barbs in his hide and taken off, flinging a demand that he not ever, ever contact her again behind her as she left.

And who could blame her? He'd done a lousy job of making his case. So he'd spent the night pacing the floor of his penthouse apartment, trying to think of a better way to approach her. He was usually good at this sort of thing. There were some who said he could charm the socks off a cat, but his natural abilities seemed to fade away when his emotions were involved so strongly.

And that was why emotions had to be controlled, tamped down—blotted out if possible.

When she didn't show up for work in the morning, he knew he'd really made a mess of it. By noon, he'd been about to go out to her apartment and break down her door if he had to. And then Lynnette had looked into his office with news.

"There's someone here to see you," she'd said, seeming disapproving.

When Callie appeared in his doorway, his heart had been thumping so loud, he was afraid they could hear it in the lunchroom.

"I've calmed down," she said, looking at him warily. "And I'd like to talk things over."

So here they were in The ZigZag Café, surrounded by young twenty-somethings, meeting and greeting and listening to electronic music that made his teeth hurt. But they were keeping emotions out of it. Sort of.

"I think we ought to pin down just what exactly you would expect out of this," she said, putting down her café latte and looking like a lawyer ready to take a statement from the witness.

"Sure. I expect—" He stopped himself, then purposely relaxed. "No, let's put it this way. I hope for a child. With his mother attached. I hope for a warm family group. I'd like to end up with some basic emotional support, and I expect to give the same to you."

She nodded, biting her lip. "Like good friends?" she asked, looking skeptical.

"Like good friends," he agreed.

She frowned thoughtfully. That worried her. It sounded too familiar. But she didn't see an alternative.

"If I agree to do this, what happens if…" She swallowed hard and avoided his bright gaze. "What happens if it doesn't pan out?"

He had to work hard to keep from grinning at her. He could tell she was getting closer and closer to saying "yes." He drummed his fingers on the tile table to keep from showing what he was thinking, how excitement was growing in him, deep down.

"We'll negotiate an agreement to include things like that."

She managed to smile and tried to make a joke. "If

that happens, I suppose, like Henry the Eighth, you'll move on and find your Anne Boleyn somewhere."

He smiled back. "So you're channeling Catherine of Aragon now?"

She shrugged. "Better a divorce than losing my head."

He winced. "I'm having my lawyer draw up a contract," he said. "It will cover all contingencies."

"Fine. If we end up doing this, I'll have my lawyer look it over." As if she had one. Well, she would have one before things were finalized. "I'll get back to you on what changes we'll want."

He shook his head, studying her through narrowed eyes. "Why do you assume there will need to be changes?"

Her smile was brittle. "Because I'm sure this would be made from your point of view. That's only natural. But I'm bound to have my own concerns. Equal time."

He nodded slowly, reminding himself that he was going to have to take her thoughts into account. This wasn't like hiring an employee, really. It was going to be more like a partnership. That gave him a momentary qualm. He did like to be in control. But then he relaxed and congratulated himself on being so perceptive—and magnanimous.

A partnership. Of course.

Callie seemed to be reading his mind.

"You do understand that I couldn't have a baby and then just hand him over to you," she said, looking him straight in the eye. "I won't be a surrogate mother. I'd be in this for parenthood as much as you are."

"Absolutely." He frowned, trying to make out what was hidden in her eyes. "So tell me, Callie. I want to know why you're considering this. What is it that *you* expect?"

She took a deep breath. "A good father for my child. A protected situation to raise my child in."

"Exactly what I plan to provide." He was having a hard time containing himself. "Callie, we can do this thing. We can have a child together. Are you starting to feel how possible this is?"

"Maybe." She hesitated and steeled herself. Now came the hard part. "But I've got to admit, there's more. I've got to be totally honest with you. I really, really want a baby. It's a desire that almost consumes me at times. But there's another factor going into this." Taking a deep breath, she went on. "I'm in major financial difficulties right now."

There. The words were out. And she felt horrible about it. She glanced quickly at his eyes. Was he radiating contempt? Was he sneering? To her surprise, it didn't seem to be that way.

"No problem," he was saying, waving it away as though money was no object. "Just let me know what you need."

"No!" She said that a bit too loud and looked around quickly. Luckily the music had hidden her cry, but she leaned in closer. "No, really. It's not like that. What I would want to do is to keep working as long as I possibly can."

"Why would you do that?" he broke in. "You don't need to."

"Yes, I do. I can't just…"

"Callie, we'll play it by ear. Whatever feels most comfortable for you, that's what we'll do."

She closed her eyes for a moment. He was being almost too nice about this. She didn't deserve it. But then, he did want something from her.

Looking at him earnestly, she quickly tried to explain her dilemma, how she desperately needed to pay for her mother-in-law's nursing care, how she wanted to be in the position to get the best medical help possible for Tina—how she was so far in debt both goals were completely out of reach at the moment.

"So you see, all my motives are not so pure," she told him, chin high but bright spots in her cheeks. "If I do this with you, I have to know if you will be willing to help me financially. Purely as a loan," she added quickly. "Believe me, I'll pay back every penny. But if this is going to be a problem, even just a nagging thing with the potential to build…"

Watching her, he could see how hard this was for her to ask. Didn't she understand how laughably easy it would be for him to do this for her? No. In a flash of perception, he knew she *did* understand that. Still, she felt this would look like she was offering herself up for sale and she hated that.

Hey. No problem. He could take care of something so simple, so why not do it? There would be plenty of difficult things down the road. Get rid of the small stuff.

"Callie…" Reaching out across the table, he took her

hand in his and held it. "It's done. I'll have my accountant call you and arrange for what you need."

She flushed and tried to pull away, but he wouldn't let her.

"Listen to me. It's done. I won't even be personally involved." His gaze darkened. "And it's not contingent on our plans. You can walk away and think it over and decide against marrying me, and it's still done. Consider the matter closed." He smiled at her doubtful look. "Now let's get back to baby talk. What'll we name him?"

Her eyes stung and there was a sudden large lump in her throat. To think he could so casually wave a magic wand and take a weight off her shoulders that had been threatening to crush her. She wanted to thank him, but she couldn't speak. And now it was she who was holding tightly to his hand.

"Why, Grant Carver, you handsome man, you!"

They both jumped and Grant jerked away from Callie's hand as though it had suddenly turned white-hot. He looked up at the tall, beautiful woman who'd stopped by their table, then rose to his feet to greet her.

"Amy. How nice to see you."

"Oh, Grant!"

The woman came in for a hug and clung to him so long, he had to peel her off his chest.

"This is Callie Stevens," he said, looking a little grumpy and stepping back so she couldn't do that again. "Callie, this is Amy Barnes, an old friend."

Amy nodded to Callie but it was obvious she only

had eyes for Grant. As slender and sleek as a high fashion model, she was wearing a tight designer suit that had probably cost about as much as Callie's car.

"I'm here with the girls," she said, gesturing toward where three other women who could have been her clones waited, giggling and looking coy. "We're having lunch. Isn't this the most adorable place? I love the music. It just makes me want to dance." She did a little two-step to demonstrate, looking as provocative as possible. "Listen, honey, why don't you come over and say hi to the girls? They'd love it if you did."

Grant looked as though he'd been asked to eat a bug. "Uh...well, you see, Ms. Stevens and I are in a kind of a meeting about something important right now. And I'm afraid—"

"Oh." She flashed a false smile Callie's way. "Well, okay then. But you call me, ya hear? We need to get together and talk over old times. You know..." She moved closer and spoke in a hushed voice. "It's Jan's birthday next week. I think we really should—"

"I'll give you a call," he said hastily. "Give my best to the girls."

He dropped back down into his seat as she sashayed her way across the room.

"My wife's best friend," he said by way of explanation.

She nodded, glancing surreptitiously toward the women and wondering if his wife had been one of that type as well. If so, was he going to be satisfied with a complete change of pace? He was in for a major culture shock.

But she pushed that thought away, because adding it to her other doubts would put her brain on overload. She just didn't have room for more. She had a big decision to make. Whatever she decided, it was going to change her life for good.

She took a good long, penetrating look at the man sitting opposite her. Could she marry him? Could she live with him? How well did she really know him?

Well enough, she decided. Yes, she knew a lot about him when you came right down to it. And the fact that he was impossibly attractive didn't hurt. If he'd been a small, cramped, ugly man who had an annoying voice, would she have been able to marry him?

Luckily she didn't have to answer that, because no one was going to ask her.

"Okay," he was saying, glancing at his watch. "I've got to get back to the office. You go home and think it over."

"How much time do I have?"

He thought for a moment, looking at her warmly. "How about twenty-four hours?" he said. "I'll pick you up for dinner tomorrow at five. We'll talk it out then. Okay?"

She nodded slowly, then frowned. "I don't suppose you'd be up for making a list of your bad points, just so I'd have something to mull over?" she asked.

He threw back his head and laughed. "Not on your life. It's all good, Callie. It's all going to be good."

It's all going to be good.

She wished she could believe that. A lifetime of bad

outcomes had trained her to expect the worst. That was why she called Grant the next morning and told him she couldn't do it.

"I'll be right over," he said.

"No," she countered quickly. "It's no use. I'm going out. You can't change my mind."

"Why, Callie?"

She drew in a deep breath and sighed. "There is one big fat obstacle we didn't cover, and the more I think about it, the more I think it will doom our plans, no matter how careful we are."

"And that is…?"

"Love."

"Love?" His voice was hoarse. "I thought we'd settled that. We're against it."

"It's all very well to say this is totally a business deal, based on mutual benefits and ruled by facts and logic. But once we're married, we'll be together a lot. What if one of us loses our objectivity and…" She searched for the right words. "How are we going to guarantee we can keep this on a business level?"

He was silent for a moment. "That's a tricky one, I'll admit. In order to do this at all we have to have a certain affection for each other. We have to like each other."

"And I think we do," she said almost reluctantly.

"Absolutely. But neither of us wants any emotional entanglement. You don't want a reprise of your marriage, do you?"

"Heaven forbid." She sighed. If only he knew how

bad that had been. "But, Grant, there's still the danger of—well, one of us starting to care too much."

"I can tell you right now that this is not going to be a real problem for me," he said.

He paused and she could almost hear him weighing what he could tell her with what was just too much to reveal.

"I don't know how much you know about my marriage. Jan was the love of my life. The moment I met her I knew that she was the woman for me—and that was going to be forever." His voice lowered a bit, as though he was fighting off emotion. "I'm a forever kind of guy. We had our ups and downs, but she was my heartbeat." His voice sounded choked and he paused, steadying himself. "When I lost her and my little girl, I lost my life."

Callie closed her eyes for a few seconds. His pain was hard to bear.

"But my grandfather needed me," he said, going on after a pause to center himself. "I couldn't hurt him, he'd had enough grief in his life. And little by little, I pulled myself back out of the darkness."

His voice was gruff. This was obviously difficult for him to talk about. "I don't usually spill my guts this way, but I feel like we have to be honest. This is a big decision. I don't want to fall in love again. I've done that once. I just want to move on."

She nodded, though she knew he couldn't see her. She could hear the sincerity in his voice and she believed him.

"At the same time, I have this deep, hungry need for a child. I can't really explain it. It's partly that my grandfather would so love to see an heir in the pipeline. That would make up for a lot with him. But there's more to it. Maybe it's something embedded in my DNA. I don't know. But I need to have a child."

"I know," she whispered. "I feel the same way."

He was silent for a long moment, letting their agreement on the most important aspect sink in.

"Callie," he said at last. "Please give this more thought. I'm begging you."

She didn't answer him and he paused for a moment, then added, "I'll see you tomorrow night. Okay?"

"Okay," she said softly. And listened as he hung up.

Callie did give it more thought. The morning sun brought back her optimism and things didn't look so black and white. The entire project looked possible again.

And more thought brought up another issue. For all she knew, this might be her only chance. After all, she was almost thirty. There were no other prospective husbands on the horizon. Maybe this was just what she needed. All she had to do was throw caution to the wind.

Well, if that was all!

She was going to do it. She was going to marry Grant Carver and try to have a baby with him.

"It's a business arrangement," she told Tina, who took the news with openmouthed surprise. "It's not a love match."

Tina had the audacity to laugh at her for that pathetic proclamation.

"Right. There's no way in the world you could fall for a man like that. No way." She nodded wisely, then collapsed in giggles.

But Callie was determined to stand firm. After all, she'd been married before. She knew the ropes. Sort of.

Grant picked her up right on time and they cruised to the Cattlemen's Club for dinner. He didn't ask for her decision until they were seated at a round booth on a platform high enough to see out over the Dallas lights. They sat very close together this time, instead of across a table from each other. A sommelier poured out ruby-red wine in their crystal glasses, and Grant made a toast.

"To wedding bells and the pitter-patter of little feet," he said, smiling at her. "Will you drink to that, Callie Stevens?"

She knew exactly what he was asking. She met his gaze and felt a tingle. Here it was. Taking a deep breath, she nodded and held up her glass.

"Yes, Grant Carver," she said. "I'll drink to that, and what's more—I'll marry you."

The joy that leaped in his eyes made her breath catch in her throat and her heart start to thump. It was nice to be wanted—even if it was just a business deal. For just a moment, she thought he was going to toss aside his glass and take her in his arms and kiss her. She was ready to say no and to push him away, but her heart was beating even harder and she knew, no matter how hard she tried, she was not going to be able to avoid feeling a certain excitement when it came to being near this man.

She didn't have to do any jujitsu to keep him away. He controlled himself, but his smile wrapped around her almost as warmly as his arms would have.

"Brilliant," he said softly, his blue eyes shining. "You've made the right choice. Callie, we're going to make a great couple, you and I."

That would be lovely. She only hoped it was true. They sat very close and their heads got closer and they talked together almost like lovers, lost in a world of their own. Salads were served, and then the entrées, grilled duck for her, grilled steak for him. The food was delicious, the music from a string quartet romantic, the clinking of crystal and sterling silver a fine backdrop to the murmur of voices all around. Callie felt as though she'd stepped into a charmed land, a parallel universe, where good things just might happen after all.

"Well," she said at last. "When are we going to do it?"

"Tie the proverbial knot?" He smiled at her. "I've arranged for a marriage to be performed by a justice of the peace I know at his chambers next Wednesday. Subject to your approval, of course. That will give us time to clear up all the paperwork. We should bring along two witnesses. I'll bring my sister, Gena."

She nodded. "I'll bring Tina."

He paused and a shadow passed over his face, surprising her.

"Are you two really that close?" he asked.

"Oh, yes. We've known each other forever." She hesitated, then decided he might as well know the truth. "You see, we both had single mothers who died when we were teenagers, and no other family to go to. So we met when Social Services moved us into a group home with about ten other kids."

He stared at her, astounded. "Callie, I had no idea. My God, what you've been through!"

She meant to give him a reassuring smile, but she could tell it was coming off a bit tremulous.

"It was pretty ghastly at first. But once Tina and I found each other, it was like we formed a little family of our own. It made the whole experience bearable."

"So Tina is about as close to you as my sister is to me," he said, looking resigned.

She nodded. "I would do just about anything for her."

He looked troubled for a moment, and she wasn't sure why that should be. But he shook it off quickly enough as dessert arrived. Bananas Foster for them to share—set on fire by the waiter to caramelize the brown sugar.

"Oh, this is heavenly," Callie said. "I could live on this."

Grant didn't answer and she looked up to see why. He was watching her eat with a strange look on his face. Feeling slightly uncomfortable, she quickly brought up a new subject.

"I guess we ought to get some of the details settled," she said.

"Right," he said, nodding slowly. "I'm assuming my penthouse apartment will do until the baby comes. Of course, if you'd like to come over and see it so you can plan to move in right after the wedding…"

She stared at him, surprised. "Oh, do I really need to do that? I thought I would just stay where I am now until…"

"Callie, we're going to be married. Married people live together."

He was right, of course. She felt a little silly. She hadn't thought that through. Naturally they had to make this look as much as possible like a real marriage. What was she thinking?

"I guess you're right. But I'll have my own room."

He frowned. "If that's the way you want it," he said grudgingly.

She was surprised it was even an issue. "I think that would be best."

He shrugged, then thought of something that lifted his spirits.

"I've got a gift for you," he said, reaching into his pocket. "Close your eyes."

"What is it?"

"A surprise. Close your eyes."

She did so and felt him putting something on her finger.

"And now, we're officially engaged," he said.

Opening her eyes, she gasped at the beautiful ring he'd put on her hand. "Oh my goodness! Oh, it's beautiful!"

The diamond had to be over a carat, surrounded by smaller diamonds that sparkled with cool, crisp fire.

"Oh, Grant!"

"It was my mother's."

She froze, then turned slowly to face him.

"I can't take your mother's ring. Not for a business deal."

His eyes seemed to glow in the candlelight.

"Don't worry," he said with a twisted smile. "I've got a clause in the contract. If we divorce, you'll have to give it back."

"But Grant…."

"My mother passed away almost a year ago. She would have liked you. I'm sure she would approve."

She didn't know what to say. Somehow, this just wasn't right. His mother's ring—what if she lost it? But she could see that he wasn't going to listen to argument tonight. She would save that talk for later.

"It's wonderful, Grant. Thank you so much."

He smiled. He was so close, she could feel him as well as see him. He was going to kiss her now. She could sense it. And this time, she thought she might just let him. She smiled and looked at his beautiful mouth and waited, heart beating. But he didn't come any closer. And suddenly he was talking about garage parking places and getting her a key to his apartment and all the other details of everyday life they were going to have to adjust to.

She hardly heard him. She'd been so sure he was going to kiss her. It wouldn't have been much of a kiss, of course. This wasn't the place for passion—and anyway, passion wasn't supposed to be a part of their relationship, she added to herself hastily. But a soft kiss to seal the deal would have been appropriate. Wouldn't it? She'd been so ready. Surely he'd seen how she'd tilted her face to accept him. And yet, he'd held back.

She would have liked to blame it on his mouth still being sore from the stitches. Maybe that was it. But somehow, she doubted it.

Bottom line, did he feel anything for her at all?

Hold on there, Callie, she told herself briskly. He wasn't supposed to feel anything. Remember?

This is not a love match. This is pure business.

Okay. Then that was the way she was going to treat it. Even if she fell in love with him.

Deep inside, she groaned. Where had that thought come from? From her darkest fears, no doubt. She'd been telling herself for years that she didn't have the knack for falling in love. She'd come in contact with a lot of attractive men and felt nothing. She didn't expect to fall for Grant. But what if she did? Was she crazy to risk it this way?

Maybe. But she'd made her decision and she was going to stand by it. A lot was riding on success here.

"Should we decide on a doctor?" she asked when he'd stopped talking for a moment.

He looked surprised. "Don't you have an ob/gyn?"

"Of course, for the pregnancy. But who are we going to use for the… You know." She gave a small shrug, surprised to find herself embarrassed.

But he frowned, looking at her as though he couldn't believe what he was hearing.

"No, I don't know. What are you talking about?"

She couldn't imagine why he was being so obtuse. What had he been talking about all this time, anyway? He was the one who'd wanted to do this first.

"Well, we're going to need to be tested," she reminded him, trying to be as delicate as she could. But it wasn't easy with a subject like this. "And you're going to need to…make a deposit and…"

"Wait a minute." He stared at her, thunderstruck. "You thought we were still going to use artificial insemination?"

She blinked at him. "Why yes. I thought…"

"Callie!" He laughed a big, booming laugh that rolled across the room and turned heads. "I think we're perfectly capable of doing this on our own. Don't you?"

She wanted to put a hand over his mouth and quiet him down. The whole room was listening. And here was Grant, saying…

"On our own?" She gazed at him, puzzled. "Oh, you mean…"

"Of course. That's what I mean. You and me. Together."

He stared at her, suddenly realizing she was serious. It hadn't occurred to him that she would still be thinking along those lines. He was going to have to step lightly here.

"It's up to you, of course. But I think we can manage something a little bit more personal, don't you?"

She bit her lip. Her heart was thumping. She hadn't realized… But of course he was right. One of the things that had turned her away from artificial insemination had been the cold, clinical nature of the process—not to mention the prospect of all those doctor's visits.

"After all," he was saying, "we've both been married before. We're both sexually experienced. Aren't we?"

"Actually..." She looked down at where her hands were curved around a coffee cup and turned beet-red.

"You're kidding." He didn't know what to say. "You were married, right?"

"Yes, but..." She looked up at him, her dark eyes filled with a confusion that touched him in a way he hadn't expected at all. "He couldn't... He didn't..."

How could she explain her marriage to a man who seemed to think of her as a sort of doll, a prized possession rather than a flesh and blood woman? His lack of interest in marital relations had confused her from the beginning and she still didn't really understand it herself.

"You poor kid." He wanted to pull her into his arms and hold her tightly, but this was too public a place for that. Instead he touched her cheek lightly. "Callie, don't worry. We won't do anything until you're ready."

Her smile seemed a bit tremulous at first, then she appeared to regain her equilibrium and it broadened.

"Same here," she told him, a mischievous light in her eyes. "I won't push you into anything you're not ready for, either."

He grinned. "Don't worry about me. I'm ready right now."

She laughed, but he wasn't joking. Watching her, with her beautiful face and her silken skin, and that hair that fell around her shoulders like a symphony come to life, he knew he was more than ready. He wanted her in a deep, aching way that was going to be a problem if he didn't watch out. But something told him it would be a problem he could live with.

CHAPTER FIVE

WHITE lace and promises.

What a picture those words conjured up—every girl's dream. Callie had always loved weddings, the more white lace the better. But she hadn't loved her first wedding much. Stark and quick, it had been kind of strange. She was beginning to worry that her second wedding wasn't going to be any better. She was going to have two weddings under her belt and neither one of them traditional. Oh well, maybe she just wasn't meant to be a traditional girl.

Grant had made the arrangements and from what he'd told her, the prospects were good this one was going to be as spare and unromantic as the first one had been—a utilitarian ceremony in a government office somewhere with just two witnesses. It sounded a lot like getting a driver's license. She'd been dreading it the way she dreaded a trip to the dentist—something unpleasant that had to be done in order to get on with life. Nothing to look forward to at all.

She'd been working at the office all week and she liked her new job. She even liked seeing Grant across the room every now and then. The people she worked with had oohed and aahed over her engagement ring, but she'd managed to keep the name of the groom mysterious. It was going to be an awkward moment when she finally revealed that she was marrying the boss. Oh well. Just another of life's little bumps in the road.

Grant had taken her to dinner a few nights into the week, and his sister had joined them. Gena was tall and slender and just as attractive as her brother was. They both had the look of Texas aristocracy—people whose ancestors had ridden through the purple sage and fought off attackers and run cattle across the land and built this state into what it was today.

And here she was marrying into that legacy and expected to produce an heir with those bloodlines. When you thought about it that way, it was quite a responsibility. Maybe she should feel honored. Somehow, she didn't.

"Will your grandfather be at the wedding?" she'd asked Grant. She knew that both his parents had died, but that his grandfather was still very much a part of his life and active in Texas affairs.

"No. His mind is still sharp as a tack, but he can't get around very well any longer and it would be too hard on him to cart him over for the wedding. We'll pay him a visit instead."

He took her to meet the older man the next day. Grant

Carver IV lived about half an hour out of town on the Lazy Drifter Ranch that had been in Carver hands for about a hundred and fifty years. A dignified, elegantly aging man, he terrified her at first, looking her over narrowly and peppering her with questions. But after a few minutes, he warmed to her and by the time they excused themselves so that Grant could give Callie a tour of the ranch, he'd given her a hug and given both of them his blessing.

"I like him," she said as they walked through the huge foyer of the ranch house. "Do you suppose you'll look just like that when you're in your eighties?" She gave him a teasing smile. "After all, you're the sixth edition of the Grant Carver icon." Her smile faded as she remembered what that meant. "And I'm supposed to produce the seventh, aren't I?"

"That's the plan," he admitted. "Having second thoughts?"

She looked around at the beautiful house, the spacious vistas out across the huge ranch, the modern equipment juxtaposed with working cowboys on horses, and finally, at the man himself.

Second thoughts? Sure. Plans to back out? No. After all, she'd bought into a life most women could only dream of. Whether it would turn out to be her dream—or her nightmare—only time would tell. But the old saying came to mind, nothing ventured, nothing gained. She was taking chances, but she was ready for them.

She smiled at Grant. "Ready or not," she said in answer to his question, "I'm here for the party."

"Good."

She liked the way he looked here in his family home. She'd worn white slacks and a soft blue shirt with a white scarf at her neck and she'd thought that would look country.

But Grant was the real deal. His boots looked like they'd been worn at the Alamo, his jeans were scuffed almost threadbare in places and held up by a wide leather belt sporting a huge brass belt buckle with a big rattlesnake worked into the metal. His cotton shirt was open at the neck, displaying some gorgeous flesh. The sleeves were pushed back, revealing muscular forearms. All in all, he was the picture of what a fantasy cowboy would look like. It made her gasp a little every time she looked at him.

She met Misty, the family dog, a golden retriever with a permanent grin and a mischievous glint in her eyes. Then Grant introduced her to Rosa Cortez, the woman who had been housekeeper at the ranch, "since time began," as he put it. A plump, chatty woman, she promised to fix them a nice lunch for later in the day. Taking Misty along with them, they made their way outside and he led her to the barn and then to the stables, where Callie touched a horse for the first time in her life.

"They are so big!" she cried, awed and a little nervous at the same time. "They don't seem that big in the movies."

"I can't believe you've never been riding," Grant said, shaking his head. "We'll have to remedy that real soon. We'll get you up on ol' Bessie there. She's gentle as a kitten. You'll love it."

Callie stroked Bessie's nose and looked into her deep, soft eyes. She liked Bessie just fine, but she didn't think she was going to relish riding her. "I've always liked having both feet on the ground," she said. "I don't really see any reason to give that up."

He laughed. "You just wait. Once you get used to horses and we let you go, you'll feel like you're flying."

She didn't bother to quibble aloud, but she had no intention of ever getting up on a horse. Still, she had to admit they were beautiful and she loved their eyelashes. Following Grant through to the opposite doorway, she stopped and spoke to each horse she found. Some snickered back, some ignored her. But she didn't want anyone to feel left out.

Out behind the stables was a corral where a number of cowboys had gathered. As she and Grant approached, Callie could see that they were working with large calves and from the smell of burned hair, she realized they were probably branding them. She wrinkled her nose, not sure she was going to enjoy this much. She glanced at Grant, thinking to suggest going on back to the house, but then she noticed the look on his face and she turned quickly to see who he was looking at.

A tall, handsome cowboy wearing leather chaps detached from the others and came toward them. The two men stopped in a squared-off fashion and grinned at each other.

"Hey," said Grant, touching the brim of his hat.

"Hey," said the cowboy, touching his as well.

That was it, but she could tell these two men were old, close friends. In California, they would have hugged. In France, they would have been kissing cheeks. But this was Texas—old Texas. And she liked it.

"Callie, meet Will Jamison."

She smiled and he touched his hat again and said, "Nice to meet you, Callie."

"Will's the ranch foreman. Just like his daddy was before him." Grant nodded. "He and I go way back."

"Back so far," Will agreed, "I sometimes wonder if we weren't switched at birth. Maybe *I* should be the one riding around in that fancy car and you should be the one working here, eatin' dirt all day."

"Pay him no mind, Callie," Grant advised her. "He's just aiming to play on your sympathies." He grinned. "Just try to get this man into a suit and tie for even one day. He'd come running back to the ranch so fast."

"We were raised together," Will told her in a friendly manner, bending down to scratch Misty behind the ears. "Two peas in a pod. Until he had to ruin everything by going off to become a city slicker."

"Hey, man's gotta work for a livin'."

Will snorted. "You call that sissy stuff you do in the city working? I'll show you working." He reached for a coil of rope he had slung over his shoulder. "Here, let's see if you've still got the touch."

Grant took the rope, looking at it almost lovingly.

"Let's see you bring in one of those young ones," Will said, gesturing toward where the work was going on. "And lay our brand right on his backside."

Grant tried his hand with the rope, twisting it and twirling it a bit. "Man, I haven't done this for years and years," he said, pulling up one end and starting a slipknot.

"Well, never mind then," Will teased. "I wouldn't want to mess up those soft, lily-white hands of yours with some real man's work."

"Stand back, cowboy," Grant drawled, his lasso in his hand. "I got me some ropin' to do."

He set off toward where the calves were being released with a Western swagger that was only partly facetious.

Will grinned and winked at Callie. "Come on over here, Callie," he said, leading the way to a good vantage point against the railings. "You don't want to miss this."

Grant did pretty well, actually. Will kept up a running commentary, mostly for Callie's sake, but also to poke fun at Grant occasionally. Watching Grant hog-tie a big, rough-looking calf made Callie wince and bite her lip, and when he reached for the red-hot branding iron, she had to close her eyes and groan a little.

Will looked at her curiously. "You from Texas?" he asked skeptically.

"Yes, I'm from Texas." She tossed her hair back and raised her chin proudly. "Born and raised."

"In Dallas, I'm thinkin'," he said, shaking his head as though it were a darn shame.

"That's true. I'm city raised." And then she added something she'd never told anyone before. "But I'm told my daddy was a rodeo champion. A bronc buster."

Will's face changed. "No kidding. What was his name?"

She shrugged. "He didn't stick around long enough to give me his name. My mother told me once and I wrote it down somewhere. I suppose I could find it if a real need arose."

"I see." Will's gaze darkened a bit. "One of those drive-by parenting situations, huh?"

"You got it."

They were quiet for a moment, watching Grant. He was working hard and doing quite a bit of shouting, it seemed to Callie. Misty was bouncing around, trying to help, and barking whenever Grant shouted, as though to back him up. But he looked to be in his element. Who would have thought she'd be marrying a cowboy? That made her smile.

As the newly branded calf ran off to get away from these crazy ranchers, Will turned to her again.

"So I hear you and Grant are fixin' to get hitched," he said, giving her a searching look.

She nodded. "You heard right."

"You couldn't get a better man. He'll do you proud. Don't you doubt it."

She heard the sincerity in his voice and saw it in his

eyes. "You know," she said softly, "I think you just may be right."

He nodded. "But we're going to have to teach you how to ride and how to be a ranch wife."

She tried to smile but couldn't quite make it. "Do I have to?"

"Sure. You're going to be a Carver. You gotta know your way around ranching."

Hold it just a minute there.

This wasn't what she'd signed on for. She gazed at him, a little worried.

"Did Jan do it?" she asked, and the moment the words left her lips she wished she could pull them back. This was none of her business. Why was Jan on her mind so often?

But Will didn't seem bothered by the question.

"No, as a matter of fact, she did not. And believe me, that was a problem now and then." He looked as though he was about to launch into a fuller explanation, but he caught himself and stopped, staring at her.

"To me, you look like a smarter gal," he said instead. "I think you probably understand that compromises must be made in all parts of life, even when wrasslin' cattle. One person can't always be the one to win. You got to develop an instinct for where to give in and where to stand firm. Just like Grant's been doing out there right now."

Grant called to him and he responded in kind, but Callie stayed where she was, thinking over what he'd said. One thing she hadn't expected was a lesson in life from a cowboy. But she had to admit, Will had a few home truths to convey. She was glad he seemed to take to her. He might be an important ally in the future.

Grant came back to her looking a bit worse for wear, but very pleased with himself.

"I can still hold my own," he proclaimed proudly. "Hell, I could come back here and take over running this ranch and have it doing twice as good as it's doing now."

That last was for Will's benefit, and they argued good-naturedly for a moment or two. Grant slung an arm around Callie's shoulders and began to lead her back to the house, still ragging on his friend. But when Callie glanced back, she caught Will giving Grant a thumbs-up that was obviously meant to convey approval of his marriage choice. That gave her a glow that matched the one Grant was riding on.

Back in the house, Grant washed up while Callie wandered around, admiring the rustic but strangely elegant furnishings. He came out looking freshly scrubbed.

"Rosa says she'll lay lunch out in half an hour," he told her.

"What will we do until then?"

He thought for a moment, then had an idea.

"Come on," he said with a lascivious wink that was pure mockery. "I'll take you up to my bedroom."

CHAPTER SIX

FEIGNED suspicion filled Callie's dark eyes and she dug in her heels.

"Why?" she demanded to know.

Grant grinned and tugged on her hand. "Just to show you."

She frowned. "Show me what?"

"I don't know. All my trophies. How's that?" He laughed. "Come on. Follow me."

She wasn't seriously reluctant, so she did follow him and they ended up in a large room overlooking the back garden. A huge bed took up most of the middle of the room.

"Wow. This bed looks big enough to have a party in," she said.

She colored when he laughed and she realized how that could be taken.

"Too bad I was such a shy guy I never thought of that myself," he said sadly.

She threw him a skeptical look. "Shy guy" just

didn't fit with the man she was getting to know. "Right."

Lowering herself to sit on the edge of the bed, she looked around at the furnishings. Basketballs, baseball gloves, a snowboard, a racing bike, trophies and banners. There was no doubt this room had belonged to a male child. She had a quick vision of all the friends and fantasies that must have passed through this room over the years.

"You know, this is just crazy," she said softly, looking up at him. "How can I marry you? I don't really know you. I don't know what sort of person you really are." She studied him, frowning. "I don't know if you've been a solid citizen or a womanizer. I don't know if you cheat on your taxes or…or rescue little donkeys from the snow. Who are you?"

He stared at her for a moment. "It doesn't usually snow in this part of Texas," he said at last. "At least not when the donkeys are out."

She bit her lip. She refused to laugh. Instead she rose and began wandering about the room, looking at the artifacts of his growing up years.

"Tell me something I don't know," she said, picking up an endearing picture of a young Grant in a soccer uniform. He was trying to look tough and fierce for the camera. "Tell me what you were like as a child," she said, setting it down.

"As a child?" His shrug was nonchalant. "I was a boy genius, of course."

"Really." She perused the titles in his bookcase—mostly old textbooks. "Tell me more."

"Well, let's see." He struck a pose as though harkening back in time. "Naturally I was a Boy Scout. Helped my share of old ladies across the street. Won all my badges."

"What else?" she asked, assuming he was only half-serious. There was a mocking tone to his attitude that let her know he wasn't going to reveal any more than he had to.

"There's not much more."

She gave him a look. "Come on. Make an effort. I need to know."

He shrugged and his voice took on the timbre of a radio announcer.

"I was a studious lad right from the start. Top honors in recitation. Walked miles through the snow to get to school."

"I thought you just said it didn't snow around here."

"Snow in the metaphorical sense, of course."

She sighed, losing hope of getting anything honest out of him now. "I should have known."

He went on. "When I wasn't studying, I was collecting things. Coins, stamps, butterflies."

"Girlfriends?" she suggested casually, finding a stack of annuals and taking one up to flip through.

He scowled at her. "Never."

"No kidding." She raised an eyebrow as she found a page in his annual signed by lots of girlish sounding names.

"Of course. I was the model student. Summers I spent at science camp. I wrote journals and was president of the entomology club. Advisor to Student Scholars. Champion at one-hour chess. I had no time for frivolous things like girls and parties and…"

"Hmm. Then I guess this yearbook must belong to some other guy named Grant. Here's a note from someone named Snookie. 'My dearest Grant,'" she read from the page, glancing up to see how he was taking it. "'Thanks so much for giving me your picture. I keep it under my pillow so I can kiss you good-night every night. I pretend I'm your one and only girl, even though you explained to me how you don't believe in going steady…'" She looked up at him, aghast. "You cad!" she cried.

He shrugged and tried to look innocent. "Snookie? Never heard of her."

"Here's another one. 'Grant, you hottie! I saved you a seat in assembly but you didn't show up. I'm looking forward to Friday night. You are so hot! Love, Mimi.'"

Grant's innocent act was beginning to fray around the edges and he was looking a little shifty-eyed.

"I don't remember any Mimi, either," he said before she had a chance to make a comment.

"I'll bet she remembers you."

He frowned, shoved his hands down deep into his pockets and looked at her sideways, trying a new direction. "You know, I really think this is a sad case of mistaken identity."

"Really?"

He nodded hopefully. "It's like you said. She must have meant some other Grant."

"Right." She nodded, eyes dancing. "I'll bet your school was just brimming with guys named Grant Carver."

He grimaced. "Brimming with Grant Carver wannabes, maybe," he muttered.

She grinned. "Okay, let's see if we can pin this down," she said, turning to the index. "This Grant Carver was captain of the swim team. King of Junior Prom. Senior class president. Does that ring a bell?"

He blinked blankly and shrugged. "Who remembers high school?"

"Oh, wait! This Grant Carver was voted 'Most Likely To Be Shot By A Jealous Husband.'" She looked up, her eyes dancing at his discomfort. "Grant, I don't see anything about the chess club here."

"They must have left that out." He grimaced. "Never mind. Let's go down and see if lunch is ready."

She shook her head. "Let's read more of those letters."

"Let's not." He made a halfhearted pass at grabbing the book from her but she kicked off her shoes and jumped up on the bed, out of reach.

"'Dear Grant,'" she read. "'You are so cool, but your kiss is so hot.'" She laughed. "All these references to heat. A theme seems to be coming through, don't you think? Hot, hot, hot." She made a face at him.

His eyes were smiling but he was pretending to frown and tried to grab the book again. "Give me that."

"No!" she cried, bouncing away from his reach. "We

must read all the letters. The truth must come out! Your wild past can't be suppressed forever." She frowned down at him. "Was this really your attitude toward girls in those days? Sexist pig."

"I told you. That isn't me."

"Then who is it, your evil twin?"

"Could be. I won't know until you hand over the book."

"Hah!"

He held out his hand. "Give me the book."

She taunted him with a grin. "Make me."

He didn't hesitate. In one bound, he was up on the bed with her. Laughing, she tried to get away, and when that didn't work, she clung to the yearbook, trying to keep him from taking it. That didn't last long. He had the book, and then she was falling onto the soft surface of the bed and he was falling with her.

They landed together, face-to-face, her hands flattened on his chest. She was still laughing, but when she looked into his eyes, she saw something darker and more disturbed there.

"Hi," she said softly.

He couldn't answer her. He was too busy trying not to want her.

His hands were clutched in fists to keep from touching her. And because this was so hard, he had to ask himself—could he do this? Could he marry another woman? He stared down into Callie's dark eyes and searched for an answer.

Callie's face had a look of impatience, as though

she'd waited for something that hadn't happened and she was getting darn tired of this. With a flash of quick irritation, she threw her arms around his neck.

"If you can't even kiss me, how are we ever going to make love?" she whispered.

He stared down at her. She didn't understand. Sex was just sex. He could do that anytime, anywhere. But kissing—that was opening up and letting someone in—a connection between heart and soul. Once he'd kissed her…

She was giving up. Her hands slid down from his neck and a hurt look filled her eyes. He couldn't stand that, and without letting himself think, he lowered his mouth to hers.

Hot buttered rum. That was what she tasted like. Smooth and creamy and slightly intoxicating. And addictive. Once the kiss started, he wasn't sure he was going to be able to stop it. She was so soft, so sweet… Desire rose in him like a sort of madness, threatening to take away his ability to reason.

As he struggled to pull away, the thoughts came anyway, fast and confusing. He didn't want to feel this sort of urgency, this need to take her in his arms. But it had been so long since he'd held a woman and his body wanted hers so badly. At the same time, he had to hold himself back. He wasn't free to do what came naturally. He had to remember…

"I'm sorry," she was saying.

He looked down, startled. Her gaze was still troubled.

"I shouldn't have pushed you into that," she said. "I know you didn't want to do it."

His mind was still too thick to process coherent thoughts. Pulling back away from her, he rose on his elbow and watched her for a moment.

"This isn't going to be easy for either of us," he said at last. "What we're planning to do will go against all our basic instincts."

She nodded. "I know."

Rolling over, she sat on the edge of the bed and looked back at him. She was reeling from that kiss, but working hard to keep that information close to the vest. But, oh my! Her lips were still vibrating. She'd never been kissed like that before. In fact, she didn't know it could be that way. And worst of all, she was dying to feel that way again.

Should she tell him? Should she warn him that she might not be able to keep the sort of distance they were planning to maintain in their marriage? Maybe she should let him know. He had a right to that information.

But before she had a chance to say anything more, Rosa called from the stairs, letting them know that lunch was getting cold. They both rose from the bed, pulled their clothing together and started down to the lunchroom. And Callie let that moment slip away.

The lunch was delicious—tortilla soup and taco salad. As they ate, they both seemed to gradually lose the edgy sensitivity they'd picked up on that bed, and before long, they were talking and kidding again, instead of feeling that strange sensual connection.

"So tell me," Callie said as they started on their bowls of ice cream for dessert. "On the level. What is the truth about you?"

"About me?" He shrugged as though it hardly mattered. "Hard to say. It's probably about halfway in between what you were thinking and what I was saying."

"Oh." She thought for a few seconds. "Well, I guess that's helpful. In a way."

"Okay, here's the real truth," he began, waving his spoon at her.

"As opposed to the unreal truth you've been telling me so far?" she teased.

Giving her a superior look, he ignored her comment and went on.

"Unfortunately it's a very boring story. I had good parents, a great sister, friends and extended family. I did well in school, but I wasn't the best. I got into a good college and did well there. I met a wonderful girl…."

His voice suddenly seemed to fail him. He'd meant to go on and tell her about Jan, she was sure, but right now, he just couldn't do it.

"Anyway, just a normal American upbringing," he said instead, avoiding her gaze as he put his napkin on the table.

"Sure," she said, trying to sound casual after an awkward moment of silence. "With a little more money than most, a little more background, a huge Texas ranch and a major business in the family. Let's face it, Grant. You are one of the blessed."

He nodded slowly. "Yes. You're right. I had a lot of advantages. And I'm grateful." His voice got rougher as he added, "But I'd give it all up if I could change a few things."

With a nod to her, he rose and walked out of the room, leaving it at that.

Callie looked around the room and wondered how often Jan had been here with him. It was obvious he was feeling the emptiness she'd left behind right now—that he was fighting off heartbreak. She wished she knew how to help him, but she was afraid that was a wound that just wasn't going to heal.

Could she live with that? She was going to have to. Either that, or back out of this project. Because Jan was going to be the third member of their marriage, from what she could see. And she couldn't say he hadn't warned her.

The next day, Callie took her lunch hour to go to see her mother-in-law from her first marriage. Marge Stevens lived in a twilight doze most of the time, but she always brightened when she realized it was Callie leaning down to give her a kiss on her withered cheek. Thanks to Grant, she was in a better nursing home situation now, being cared for every minute by loving attendants.

Still, Callie thought how lucky Grant's grandfather was to still be well enough to be living at home, even if he wasn't very mobile any longer. It was just too bad he couldn't see the wedding he was so interested in having take place.

And then, she had an idea. She stopped by Grant's office when she got back to work.

"Grant, I know your grandfather can't come into town for our wedding. But listen. Why don't we take it to him? Why don't we have the justice come out to the ranch? Would he do that?"

Grant thought it was a great idea and she could see that he appreciated her thinking of his grandfather that way. She had a warm glow for the rest of the afternoon.

But in the end, it turned out she should have left well enough alone. The plan had been to have a quiet, private wedding in the justice's chambers with two witnesses. That was it, just a quick transaction, shake hands and off everyone would go. Instead, now that they were having the wedding at the ranch, everything was turned on its head.

She couldn't blame anybody but herself. It had been her idea. But once the setting changed, things started spiraling out of control, and before she knew it, she was being asked what sort of wedding cake she wanted and did she want to have finger food or a sit-down dinner, and did she mind if the cousins from Redmond came? They would stay quiet and in the background, but they were older and had loved Grant as though he were a child of their own and would be so hurt if they found out they hadn't been included.

So suddenly they were having the wedding of the year, out in ranch country at any rate. When everyone you met was just so excited about the wedding, how could you keep them away?

"I don't even have a decent dress to wear," Callie fretted as the whole thing loomed like a curse just a day away. "I mean, if we were really doing this right, I would have a hair appointment and a dress and veil and all the other things a bride expects to have. And here I am, going into a big wedding with little wedding outfits and preparations."

"I thought that was what you wanted," Tina said.

"Sometimes I want dumb things," she said, frowning her frustration. "I'm getting a very bad feeling about this. Is someone trying to tell me something? Is this a sign that I'm not prepared for this marriage? That I'm doing something recklessly without considering all the ramifications?"

"Oh, calm down," Tina said, trying to reassure her. "You've just got the jitters. Everything will be fine tomorrow. You'll see."

Callie tried to calm down. She took a long shower. She washed her hair. She packed a case of things she was planning to take out to the ranch to use in the wedding. Then she repacked the case she'd prepared to take to Grant's apartment after the wedding. Then she repacked it again. Then she put a new shade of polish on her toenails and redid her fingernails.

But the whole time, all she could think about was Grant. How could she marry a man who was still in love with his first wife?

She was getting married for the second time. Was this her second big mistake? She'd married Ralph, her first husband, because he and his mother had been good to her when she was desperate and she was grateful. And now—had she fallen into the same trap again? She was marrying Grant because he promised to take care of all her problems and make life smooth and easy for her. How was that so different from the reasons she'd used to talk herself into marrying Ralph, another man she didn't love?

Why couldn't she seem to learn from her mistakes? Was she one of these people who kept falling into the same pattern again and again and ruined their lives?

"It's different this time," she whispered to herself.

Yeah. Right. That was what those sorts of people always said, wasn't it?

"No, really. It's different. Because this time, I understand what I'm getting into. I'm not expecting marriage to make everything perfect."

Perfect? This might not even end up normally average, forget perfect.

She went back over all the steps in her head, reminding herself of how this was a business deal first and foremost. That they were both in this for something other than the usual love thing. That they both had to keep cool, calm and collected if this was going to work for them.

No emotions. At least, not so anyone would notice.

But she just wasn't sure if that was going to work in the long run. In fact, she was afraid she already liked

Grant a little too much. Should she tell him? If not, could she keep a secret like that for the rest of her life?

This was agony. Maybe they should just forget the whole thing. Maybe she ought to call him and…

It was late when Grant picked up the phone. He heard Tina's voice on the other end.

"You'd better get over here fast," she said.

He tensed. "What's wrong?"

"We've got a bad case of cold feet developing. You might want to come over and try to nip it in the bud."

Funny, but he'd been expecting this. In fact, he'd faced a bit of the old frigid feet thing himself, wondering how he could possibly be contemplating doing something so contrived and difficult to bring off.

"If you still want to marry this woman tomorrow," Tina was saying, "you'd better come and make your case."

"Again?"

"Again."

He sighed. But what the hell—maybe trying to convince her would firm up the crumbling edges of his own confidence.

"Okay," Tina was saying. "I'm going to take Molly and go grocery shopping. You will have about an hour and a half before I get back. Put it to good use."

Good old Tina. He'd gotten to know her better over the past week and understood why she and Callie were so close. He was glad she was on his side. If she were working against him, he wouldn't have a chance.

He was at the apartment in twenty minutes. Callie was home and she let him in, looking curious but not particularly surprised to see him.

"Tina called you, right?"

"She said your resolution was wilting. I came over to give it life support."

She gave him a tragic look, turned and led the way to the couch, where she flopped down, pulling her legs up under her. He sat down in a chair facing her and spent a moment enjoying the way the lamplight played with her golden hair.

"You're not going to desert me, are you?" he asked her softly.

She met his gaze and held it for a long moment before she slowly shook her head. "I don't think so," she said doubtfully.

He could have asked for a little more positive spin on that less-than-ringing endorsement. But at least she wasn't calling him names and throwing things.

"Tell me, Callie. What is it that's making you feel uncertain tonight?"

She closed her eyes, took a deep breath and opened them again.

"Oh, I don't know. This whole thing. I mean, this started out being a small business deal. Remember that? Now we're stuck with this gigantic wedding with all sorts of people coming, lots who I don't even know. This wasn't supposed to happen. It's all gotten out of hand."

"No, it hasn't," he said, leaning forward with his

elbows on his knees, all calm male confidence and optimism. "Callie, the wedding as a party means nothing. Officially joining our lives in the pursuit of a baby—that's what's important. All the rest is frills." He shrugged. "If you want, we'll cancel it and go back to our original plan."

She stared at him. "We can't do that."

"Why not?"

She bit her lip. "Everybody's so excited about it."

"Great." He smiled at her. "Let them have the party without us. We don't have to go."

She smiled, thinking of it. Most of them wouldn't notice the bride and groom were missing until halfway through the day. She could imagine the scene.

"Really?"

"Sure. It doesn't bother me."

She laughed softly, looking at him. Why was he being so nice and understanding?

Because he doesn't want to lose his chance at having his baby. Well, yes. That was true. Still, she liked that he didn't just come in shouting like some men she'd known.

"But it's not just the wedding is it?" he said.

Her smile faded. "No, not really. It's this whole strange situation we've gotten ourselves into. I'm not sure we're doing the right thing."

He nodded. "Is it your first husband? Do you feel as though you're betraying him in some way?" This was a scenario he knew only too well, so it was the first thing that came to mind.

"What?" She looked surprised at the suggestion. Betray Ralph? Hardly. "Oh, no. Not at all."

He was glad it wasn't that. Still, maybe there were deeper emotions here than she even realized herself. When you came right down to it, he didn't know much about the man she'd married before. And what he did know was baffling, to say the least.

"Why don't you tell me about him?"

"Ralph?" She wrinkled her nose. "Now?"

"Sure. We've got to do it sometime. Why don't we get it out of the way now? Tell me why you married Ralph."

She looked down at her hands, folded in her lap. Taking a breath deep into her lungs, she held it for a moment, let it out and looked up at Grant, smiling.

"Okay."

She settled back into the couch. "I told you that I spent many of my teenage years in a group home. You had to leave when you turned eighteen. Ready or not, out you went."

He nodded, his blue eyes dark in the shadows.

"Tina is a year younger than I am and she stayed on. But I had to go. I had to find a place for myself in the world. They gave us classes and counseling and all that, but you get such outlandish expectations when you're young. I thought I could do anything."

She smiled, remembering. "I was going to get a fabulous job and start college and find a boyfriend. It was all going to be wonderful. And when reality slapped me in the face and I couldn't get a job that would pay enough to let me rent a decent place and still have money left over for food, I felt very lost and cheated for a time. I really struggled."

It had been harder than she could express to him, harder than she would want to express to anyone. But it had helped make her into who she was today, she had to admit.

"And then, I saw an ad in the paper for an older woman who needed a paid companion. The job didn't pay much but it came with room and board and would give me time to start taking college classes."

She paused, smiling as she remembered. "Marge Stevens was…is…a wonderful person. She became a second mother to me in many ways. Without her, I don't know what would have happened to me.

"Ralph was her son. He was in his thirties at the time. A lot older than I was. A pleasant, good-looking man. He traveled a lot, but came home at least once a month to visit with his mother. She adored him. He seemed to adore me. He helped me and taught me a lot. One thing led to another, and before I knew it, I'd agreed to marry him."

"Just like that?"

She nodded, suppressing a smile. *Yes, Grant, just like that. Just the way I'm jumping into marrying you, too. See what an idiot I am? I just keep doing it.*

Sighing, she went on aloud. "They'd both been so good to me and they both wanted me to do it so badly. I sort of felt like I owed them. If it hadn't been for Marge, I would never have been able to get through as much college as I did. She helped me a lot. And at the same time, Ralph seemed very ardent and I thought maybe this was love, for me, too."

"Naive," he muttered.

She leaned forward earnestly. "Listen, try to understand. Ralph was pretty much the first man who'd been good to me. My experience with men over the first decades of my life hadn't been real positive. First there were my mother's boyfriends who came and went and treated her horribly when they weren't trying to hit on her little girl behind her back."

She paused for a moment, swallowing hard. She'd never hinted at that before to anyone but Tina, and now here she'd casually told Grant. She looked at his eyes, but she didn't see condemnation. Squaring her shoulders, she went on.

"Then there were the administrators of the group home. One man in particular enjoyed making sure we understood how worthless we were and how much we owed to him and his staff for all we got. And finally, the few guys I dated in college all turned out to be jerks. So when Ralph treated me as an equal, as someone worth talking to, I was just so happy to find a man like that, it helped to win me over."

His eyes flashed and she wasn't sure if it was with anger or something else.

"And you regretted it?" he asked, his voice rough.

"Oh, yes. I definitely regretted it. Not that Ralph ever did anything horrible to me. Not physically. But once we were married, that sweet, considerate man turned into a control freak suspicious of everything I did and everyone I talked to. He couldn't let me go to the grocery store alone. He was sure I was seeing someone behind his back. It was crazy."

"Hmm. What did he do for a living?"

"He was a sort of freelance photojournalist. Every now and then he actually sold a picture. But mostly, he lived off his mother's tiny nest egg and her social security."

"Great guy."

She bit her lip. Funny, but she had an impulse to defend Ralph. He wasn't much, but he'd been hers for a time. Still, she resisted it.

"He drank too much, of course, and finally he got drunk and fell in the street and hit his head just wrong. He was dead in three days."

She reached into her pocket for a band and pulled her hair into a ponytail, tying it back. "It was sad, especially for Marge. But we never had a real marriage."

He nodded, glad they had done this. He thought he'd found out what he needed to know—that she didn't have any deep emotional ties to the man. They could pretty much close that chapter of her life.

But that left what he knew was unspoken between them—the real concern. How was this going to work with him still attached to Jan? Was he going to be able to give Callie what she needed when he was still held hostage to the past?

And what about Callie—could she ever give up on

finding real love herself? Was it all worth it? Seemingly she'd made that decision and decided it was worth it. Was she regretting it? He didn't really think so. Worried, maybe, but not regretting it. He hoped she would feel free to tell him what she was thinking.

"Let's promise one thing to each other right now," he said. "We'll always be honest with each other. We can't deal with a problem if we don't know what it is."

She nodded. She agreed. Sure, she would try to be honest. Later.

He wanted to fix things, make everything okay. But if she started being honest right now, she would have to tell him, "Grant, I'm scared to marry you because I'm so afraid I'm going to fall in love with you, and I know your heart is unavailable." How was he going to fix that?

She couldn't be that honest because she was in too deep. And she couldn't pull away now.

"Don't worry," she said aloud to him instead. "I'm going to marry you tomorrow. There are just a few emotional hurdles I have to leap over first. I'll get there."

He nodded, looking troubled. "Get some sleep. I'll pick you up early tomorrow and we'll head out to the ranch."

"Okay."

He looked at her for a long moment, then turned away. "Good night," he said.

"Good night," she echoed, feeling a bit abandoned.

He reached the door and paused, then looked back at her. She was standing under the light in the entryway. She'd tied her hair back but strands were escaping all around her face, making her look like an angel, all aglow. His heart caught in his throat.

One stride and he was back, taking her into his arms, taking her mouth, taking her breath away. He hadn't meant to do it. He knew he shouldn't do it. But for this one moment, he had to do it.

He filled her mouth and took her sweetness as though he'd been starving for it. Her response was without indecision, so clear and pure and full of affection, it made him tremble.

Pulling her body close, into the curve of his chest, of his hips, he knew she must feel how he wanted her. He needed her to feel it. She had to know he wasn't going to hesitate tomorrow night. He ached to take her body the way he'd taken her mouth. He was more than ready—all flesh and blood and urgency.

Wasn't that the point of all this?

Pulling away, he took her face between his hands and looked deeply into her warm dark eyes.

"Thank you, Callie," he said in a low, hoarse voice. "You make my dreams come true."

Turning, he went quickly into the night.

CHAPTER SEVEN

THE ranch was completely decorated for a wedding. *Her* wedding. Callie was astounded.

"I can't believe it. Look at this place!"

Hanging baskets dripping with flowers hung all along the overhang. Someone had put up a tiny picket fence along the walkway to the house and planted vines with white flowers to wind through the slats. Roses were everywhere—in planters, in bowls, in cones set at the corners.

And inside, the decor was even more elaborate.

"Rosa, everything is so beautiful!" Callie cried as the housekeeper let them in.

"Of course," Rosa said, shrugging. "It's a wedding."

Gena came up from behind her and swept Callie away. "Come on up to my room. I've got something to show you."

Callie followed her up the stairs, lugging her overnight case filled with the white suit and accessories she'd brought along. One step into the room and she knew she was probably not going to use it after all. There, on a dressmaker's model, was the most gorgeous white lace and satin gown she'd ever seen.

She gasped. "Oh, it's beautiful!" She got close but didn't dare touch it. "Where did it come from?"

Gena smiled. "It's mine."

Turning, she stared at the woman. "You were married?"

"Almost. The wedding didn't quite come off like I planned." Reaching out, she pulled at the waist. Callie noted a sad look in her eyes, but Gena pushed that away with a sigh and turned back to smile at her. "It'll be a little big for you, but we've got a lady here on the housekeeping staff who's quite a seamstress. She's coming up to take a few tucks, so put it on and we'll see how we're doing."

The next hour was filled with talking and trying on and sewing, and Callie had to admit, she was so relieved. She was actually going to get to wear a wedding dress. Now things were beginning to fall into place and feel right again.

In fact, she got so comfortable, she felt at ease asking Gena a question.

"Tell me about Grant's wife," she said, turning in her chair. Gena was working on Callie's hair, making ringlets to frame her face and weaving tiny seed pearls everywhere.

"His *first* wife, you mean?" Gena corrected with a smile. She thought for a moment before going on. "Jan was like a hummingbird, small and beautiful and always on the move. She was a firecracker of a person, full of opinions and new causes and things that she was driven to get done. She and Grant met in college. They got married right after he graduated."

Callie nodded, glad to have some picture in her mind where there'd been only questions so far.

"So their child wasn't born until quite a while after they married."

"Right." Gena glanced at her, hesitated, then went on. "I don't think Jan actually wanted children. She was too busy. But she finally gave in and did her duty."

Gena frowned thoughtfully, not noticing that Callie was startled by what she'd just said. After all, the Grant she knew was all about having children. That must have created problems of a sort. Unless Grant's need for babies only cropped up afterward.

"They had their ups and downs, but Grant adored her. He was devastated when she was killed in the accident. And losing Lisa, his beloved baby, almost destroyed him. It was months before he could even talk about it. I really thought he would never marry again. It was too deep a wound." She shook her head, pressing her lips together as she thought about it.

"You know, for a long time, he couldn't look at a picture of either one of them. I finally convinced him he had to put a picture up in his office. But you notice where he put it—high up behind his desk at an angle, a place he never looks."

"Then why put it up at all?"

"As a tribute. I went in with him the day he put it up.

I told him he couldn't pretend they had never existed. They deserve more. And he agreed."

Callie shook her head, feeling so sorry for Grant she was afraid her eyes would fill with tears. And with the makeup she and Gena had just put on, that would be a disaster.

"What do you think about what we're doing, Gena?"

She was silent for a moment.

"I'll be honest, Callie. I wasn't for this at the first. But now that I've gotten to know you a little bit, I've changed my mind."

Callie smiled at the woman who would soon be her sister-in-law. "I'm glad. I only hope you're right."

Grant was pacing the floor. Things had definitely gotten out of hand and that meant he wasn't happy. He was a man who liked to have control of every situation he put himself in.

"Why the hell should I put on this monkey suit?" he demanded from Will, who was lounging on the bed and laughing at his friend's hissy fit.

"Because you're going to give that little gal a proper wedding, that's why."

He rounded on his friend, his hands balled into fists. "Says who?"

Will grinned. "Says your sister, Gena."

"Oh."

His older sister was the one person in the world he did take orders from. He ran a hand through his hair distractedly. Maybe he and Callie should reconsider his idea of skipping out on the party and leaving it to the people who wanted it.

"Listen, it wasn't supposed to be this kind of wedding."

"Everybody knows that. Never mind. Go with the flow."

"Going with the flow usually ends up getting you drowned," Grant muttered.

"Not this time. We're going to be there to hold your head above water. That's what this is all about—family and community support."

Grant grimaced. Will was right. And that was exactly why he and Callie were stuck with this thing. They couldn't disappoint their loved ones.

"Never thought I'd see you so nervous," Will commented dryly.

Grant shot him a look. "I'm not nervous."

"The hell you aren't." Will rose from his lounging position and began to unbutton his shirt. "Time to put on my own monkey suit, I guess. Since I'm being forced to stand up for you, seein' as how nobody else will do it. As if I didn't have better things to do with my morning."

"Exactly my point," Grant muttered, preparing to dress for the wedding.

"At least we don't have to get our hair done," Will joked. "Though the way you've been torturing yours, someone better attack it with a comb."

"You come near me with hairdresser intentions and the wedding's off," Grant responded sharply.

Will shrugged good-naturedly. "Never mind. I always did think the windblown look suited you just fine."

Grant held up his hand, listening. Someone was playing the piano downstairs. "They brought in a piano player?"

Will nodded. "And some lady's going to sing, too, from what I hear."

Grant groaned. "This is like a real wedding."

His friend clapped him on the shoulder. "That's the point, big boy. You get the picture. This *is* a real wedding."

But Grant was looking right through him, his mind in turmoil. Somehow this made everything different. How could this be a mere business deal when you added piano players and orange blossoms? How had everything careened so quickly out of control? Callie had been right the night before. This was all a bit too much. But it was obviously too late to change things now.

Coming down the stairs a few minutes later, Grant saw Tina arriving. He'd sent a car for her and was glad to see she'd made it. And then he saw her little girl coming in behind her—the little girl who looked so much like his Lisa that he looked twice to make sure it wasn't her. He had to reach out and take hold of the banister for a moment.

Why was she here? Why would someone bring a little girl like that to a wedding?

He knew it was irrational, but he couldn't help his reaction. When he saw the child, he reacted in an emotional way he couldn't seem to control. The pain swept over him again, intense and almost unendurable. He couldn't have a little girl who looked like Lisa watching as he married Callie. He was usually a logical, unemotional guy, but something about that just struck him as wrong.

He searched for Rosa and pointed out Tina's child. "Could someone watch her during the wedding?" he asked. "Maybe take her up to the old playroom?"

"Of course," Rosa said with a smile. "Such a pretty little girl."

Gena had come up behind him. "What are you doing?" she asked as Rosa hurried off.

Grant avoided her gaze with a guilty maneuver. "Uh, that's Tina's little girl. I thought she would be happier playing away from the wedding."

Gena frowned. "Did Tina ask you to do that?"

"No, but..." He swallowed hard and turned to look his sister in the face. "Look at her. She looks exactly like Lisa. Don't you see? I can't have her here during the wedding. I just can't."

Frowning, Gena stared at the little girl then turned back. "Grant, I don't see..." But he was already heading back up the stairs and he ignored her comment.

There was no way he could explain. Every time he looked at Molly, he saw Lisa and he felt his own little girl looking at him with a sad reproach he just couldn't face. That was all there was to it. And there wasn't much he could do to change that.

Finally it was time. The backyard had been set up with chairs leaving an aisle down the middle. He walked down that aisle behind Will and they took their positions. The place was packed and he had another qualm, hoping Callie didn't feel intimidated.

"What did you do, take an ad out in the local paper?" Will muttered to him out of the corner of his mouth, looking around at the crowd.

"Not me," Grant murmured back. "You can't pin this one on me."

He looked at his grandfather, sitting in the front seat. The old man gave him a smile that helped make up for a lot of this. At least Grant Carver IV was happy.

The pianist struck up "Here Comes the Bride" and Tina came out, looking pleased as punch, and then Callie, looking so beautiful, he could hardly breathe for a moment.

A wave of relief swept over him. She was smiling at him, looking joyful. It was going to be all right. They would get through this and then, tonight, they were going to begin the task of making a beautiful baby together. He was looking forward to that a lot more than he'd expected to. In fact, almost too much.

He settled down and greeted his bride as she reached him.

"Hi," she whispered.

"Hi, gorgeous," he whispered back.

"Let's get married," she said, and he grinned.

"Let's do it."

Magic. That was the only word she could think of for today. Pure, shimmering, golden magic. She'd thought she'd feel awkward with a room full of people she'd never met before. The only people who were really there for her were Tina and Molly and Grant and his sister. But that seemed to be enough, because everyone else acted as though they'd known her since she'd toddled out into the world. She was the center of attention and praise and questions—she'd never felt so in demand before in her life.

Everyone was so happy for her and for Grant, thinking they were on their way to a lifetime of blissful happiness. At first she felt a little strange about pretending this was a normal marriage and not a business deal. She had to admit they'd put on the trappings of a real love match, so why would anyone think any different? But there was no way to explain. No one would understand.

And anyway, she wasn't much different from the others—even she was beginning to feel like this was a love match. Whenever she looked at Grant she couldn't help but react to how handsome he looked in a tuxedo. She felt a quiver inside. Was this the way love began?

That's not love, you ninny! That is just pure anticipation of your wedding night, that's what that is.

Maybe. There was no denying her heart skipped a beat every time she thought of it. So what? It was exciting and it was wonderful and she could hardly wait to be alone with him. She was on pins and needles, but in a good way. A very good way.

And then, Tina had caught the bouquet and the champagne punch bowl had been drained and the finger sandwiches had all been devoured and cake had been smashed into faces and icing licked off fingers and it was time for them to go.

They joined hands and thanked everyone for coming. People were laughing and calling out good wishes. She'd heard someone had tied things to the back of Grant's car. She saw someone passing out little bags of rice.

This was crazy. It was a real wedding. She'd never thought it would happen to her. She turned to look up into Grant's handsome face.

"One kiss," he whispered. "And we're out of here."

She nodded happily. He bent and touched his lips to hers. She sighed. Magic.

And then it all fell to pieces, like a glass vase smashed by a rock.

Someone shouted. A buzz went through the assembly. Callie turned, confused. What was going on?

"Call 911," someone shouted. "Quick. It's Tina."

"Tina?"

Callie was pushing her way through the crowd, her heart in her throat. By the time she got to her friend, Tina was sitting up, supported by someone who was holding a cup of water to her lips.

"I'm okay," she said, trying to smile at Callie. "I'm just…" Her voice faded and she slumped forward.

She wasn't okay at all. That much was obvious. Callie was frantic until the paramedics arrived to take her to the hospital.

"I have to go with her," she told Grant. "I'm so sorry, I…"

He nodded. "Of course. Go."

"I'll call you from the hospital."

"Fine."

He watched her climb into the back of the ambulance in her wedding gown and he knew his wedding night was a lost cause. But that didn't matter. Tina's welfare was all important now. That, and…

"Where's the little girl?" he asked Gena. "I hope she didn't see any of that."

"No. She's asleep on my bed."

Grant nodded and took in a deep breath. "I guess we'd better look into some sort of child care for her."

"Later," Gena said, putting a hand on his arm. "She can stay with me for now."

"Are you sure?"

"Oh, yes. She's adorable. I'll take care of her until we hear more about Tina."

He nodded, looking broodingly at the road that led away from the ranch, the road Callie had disappeared down, and wondering how long it would be before he had her in his arms again.

It had been a week since his wedding, but he didn't have a wife yet. Tina was home from the hospital but things didn't look good. Callie had been staying at the apartment and spending most of her time at the hospital or taking care of Molly. And Grant was on his own.

So here he sat in his darkened apartment, a glass of bourbon and water in his hand, mulling over where things stood. He'd married Callie, but he hadn't made her truly his wife, and he was about to go out of his mind with gloom over it.

He'd seen her every day. He'd gone over and done what he could for Tina and given support to Callie. He'd hired a service of rotating nurses and child-care professionals to help out at the apartment once Tina was back from the hospital. This was a very trying time for all of them.

Callie had decided to stay at the apartment herself for the short-term, and he'd agreed. Even with a nanny hired, he knew she felt someone should be with Molly to keep her from sensing how scary things really were. He wanted Callie home, but he hadn't pushed. He'd had to bite his tongue a number of times to keep from saying what he felt. But he'd held it back.

What was happening to Tina was tragic and heart-breaking. The cancer she'd been battling over the last year had returned with a vengeance. Chemotherapy and radiation were being considered. Callie had thrown herself into the role of support for her friend and he could understand that. Callie's compassionate side was one of the factors that made her such a quality person.

And she was. The better he got to know her, the more impressed he was with the woman he'd chosen to be the mother of his future children. She was great.

And at the same time, she was so much the opposite of his first wife. Jan had been all fire and passion, dancing and laughter, sharp anger and sweet atonement. She'd kept him on his toes. He'd loved her with a passion just as deep and bright, and he missed her so much he avoided thinking about her.

Just because she'd been such a presence in his life, he'd known he needed someone completely different, someone who wasn't like Jan at all. And Callie was that person. Where Jan ran on impulse, Callie was planned. She used logic and kept her distance until she was sure of what she was doing. He was learning to appreciate those qualities more and more.

Now she was coming home tomorrow. And in some ways, he was more worried about that than anything. A bad pattern had been set by their being apart all this time. That pattern had to be broken. He wasn't sure how and he didn't want to come off like a caveman; he only knew something had to give.

He had a strange feeling in the pit of his stomach. Once she came back if she still had that lost, haunted look in her eyes, chances were good she wasn't going to be in the mood for babymaking. He'd promised he wouldn't push her into anything until she was ready. Circumstances were conspiring to keep that from happening. She was going to need something to pull her out of her current sad reality. Something new. Something to jolt her world and make her see the sunshine.

And, what the hell, something to make her see *him* again.

He frowned, turning the glass in his hand, thinking

over options. He had to do something, no matter what it was. What was the point of having a lot of money if you didn't use it?

An idea came to him, full of possibilities. Narrowing his gaze, he thought over all the options hard and fast. Yes. It was a good idea. In fact, it was a fantastic idea.

He picked up the telephone and punched in the number of the local airport. He was going to order himself up a honeymoon.

CHAPTER EIGHT

CALLIE had barely walked in the door when Grant was hustling her back out it again. In minutes, he had her ensconced in his car and they were sailing along the highway toward the airport.

"Where are we going?" she asked, looking out the window at the passing scene. He'd astonished her and she realized she was glad. With so much sadness in her life right now, she needed a respite. She'd spent so many nights lying awake in anger at what was happening to Tina. She'd spent hours crying in the shower, away from Molly. Grief was exhausting. She needed a break.

"It's a surprise."

She frowned. "But I didn't pack anything. Are we staying overnight?"

He smiled mysteriously and refused to answer.

"You see, this is the problem with surprises," she fretted, only half teasing. "Women need to prepare for these things. We need time to decide what to wear."

"I'll keep that in mind for next time," he said smoothly, ignoring her mock glare.

He could have told her not to worry. It had already been taken care of. He'd called the personal shopper at the island resort where they were staying. He'd given her a few sizes and colors to work with and if she did her job well, a whole weekend wardrobe should be waiting for Callie in their room.

They landed on Santa Talia, a little-known island in the Caribbean. The air felt like liquid silk and smelled like plumeria blossoms. The locals had borrowed a tradition from the Hawaiians and happily piled flower leis around both their necks, until they were swimming in perfume and petals.

The resort consisted of bungalows spread out across rolling greenery and centered around a main building that provided the lobby, dining room and shops. Callie exclaimed over the perfectly furnished room and then gasped when she found the closet full of clothes that were just her size.

"I feel like Cinderella," she told him, happily flinging clothes on the bed to look at them.

"Just call me the Handsome Prince," he teased. "But hang on to those glass slippers."

She laughed but when he caught her eye, she blushed. She knew why they were here. She could feel his growing excitement. She was ready, but completely panicked at the same time.

The last week had been draining and the sadness and

anger over what was happening to Tina still filled her with an uncontrollable need to do something, anything, to feel like she was helping. So it had taken a lot for her to leave the scene, and when she'd first realized they were flying off somewhere for the weekend, she'd silently rebelled for a moment or two.

But she realized she owed Grant something, too. And if a few hours away from Texas would help him, maybe they were just what she needed as well.

"Let's go for a walk on the beach," he suggested.

"Okay."

The sun was setting. They hadn't eaten but neither one of them was hungry. They strolled down the white sand, letting the water lap at their toes, then climbed on some rocks. Grant caught hold of her when she lost her footing. He held her against him for a beat longer than necessary. She could feel his pulse, sense his desire. And for a moment, she could hardly breathe.

They had a sumptuous dinner served in their room but she could hardly eat a bite. A bottle of champagne was provided and they drank a toast.

"To honeymoons," Grant said, lifting his glass until the tiny bubbles sparkled in the lamplight.

"To honeymoons," she agreed, smiling into his eyes.

They went for another walk along the sand. The sky was inky and the moon was a silver ship riding the clouds above them. Moonlight shimmered on the water. The refuge of their room looked inviting as they returned. And Grant very deliberately closed the door.

Cupping her face with his hands, he bent slowly toward her and touched her lips with his.

"I promised you we wouldn't do this until you're ready," he said softly. "Are you ready?"

She nodded, her throat too thick for speech. Her heart was like a caged bird fighting against the bars. She'd never been so scared and so thrilled, all at once. She wasn't sure she was going to live through this. But she was ready.

He muttered something against her lips, but she wasn't sure what it was, and then he was parting them with his tongue. She accepted him into her mouth, at first hesitant, and then greedily. He tasted so good and felt amazing. Raising her arms to circle his neck, she arched into his muscular body, wanting to feel her breasts hard against his chest.

Music was playing somewhere nearby. The sound of the waves on the beach mixed with the tune and made an island symphony. The air was soft, his hands were just rough enough to tantalize, and a fire was beginning to smolder inside her in places she didn't know could burn.

His hands slid down her sides and then the simple dress she'd worn was in a puddle on the floor. She heard someone moan and realized the sound had come from her own mouth. She was going to make love and be made love to for the first time in her life. That was just awesome. A landmark. A red-letter day.

Would she be glad or sorry when it was over? She didn't know. She only knew it had to be done. And now her body was reaffirming that very mandate. She was melting and yet floating at the same time. She didn't feel normal at all, and she loved it. As she pressed her mouth to his neck and kissed him with her tongue, she knew she could get addicted to this feeling. And then, suddenly, she felt an urgency building inside her, a need so intense, she cried out in surprise.

"Just a moment, Callie," he whispered huskily against her throat. "Don't worry. We'll get there."

As he picked her up to carry her to the bed, she knew she was sinking into passion as though it were a very thick and very soft pillow. And passion was a destination she never wanted to leave again.

Sometime later, they lay together, spent for the moment, catching breaths. A whole new world of sensation had opened up for Callie, but there was more. A whole new world of closeness and affection had opened up as well. She knew what it was to have a man. Did she also know what it was to love?

She would have said yes to that question just moments before. Now that the air was cooling her skin, she wasn't so sure anymore.

"Cooler heads prevail," she murmured groggily.

"What's that?" he asked, raising his head and looking at her with a slight smile.

"Nothing. I'm just enjoying the moment," she said, smiling at him. She reached a lazy hand up to touch the skin of his wonderful chest. "I feel so…so good."

"I'm glad." He looked at her warmly, and then almost imperceptibly, his gaze cooled. He looked away. "I hope that did us some good," he said crisply, sounding like things were all business again. "We'll have to keep trying until…"

She closed her eyes, appalled, and drew back her hand. Here she'd been thinking love and he'd revealed he had a calculator where his heart should be. For just a moment, she understood the old saying that hatred is the closest thing to love.

Oh, Grant, don't ruin this.

He leaned over her and began dropping small kisses around her navel. To her shock, her hunger was back so strongly, it was as though it hadn't been satisfied just moments before.

So this was the way it was going to be. Alternating joy and chagrin. Well, if that was her destiny, bring it on. She had to admit, she rather liked it.

By the time their honeymoon ended, they'd had two days of mostly bliss. Callie didn't think she'd ever been so happy in her life. She was an old hand at making love now. She knew the ropes. A lady with experience. That made her laugh at herself, but it was true. They'd made love three times that first night and countless times since. And each time she felt she learned a little more about this man she'd married.

For the short time they were together on the island, they developed a closeness that amazed her. He'd been so warm and loving, she felt as though she could say anything to him, and ask anything of him. Well, almost anything. As long as it had nothing to do with his first wife and child.

And now they were going home. Already missing the place, she looked about to make sure they had picked everything up before leaving.

"Have you had a good time?" Grant asked, smiling at her.

"Oh, it's been like heaven here," she said.

"Heaven I'm not so sure about," he responded with a grin. "But I do agree it's about the best place on our earth." He looked at his watch. "We all packed and ready to go?"

"I think so."

"We've got about twelve minutes before the car arrives to take us to the airport." He looked at her speculatively. "Twelve whole minutes," he said softly.

She started to smile, eyes sparkling. "Twelve whole minutes, huh?"

He nodded, one eyebrow quirked in question. "What do you think?"

She shrugged, feeling an unfamiliar sense of wicked delight. "Why not?"

Laughing, they began a race to see who would be first getting rid of the clothes they'd just put on. In half a moment, they were back on the bed, tumbling together, hot skin and willing flesh, a heady recipe for ecstasy.

Callie marveled later, when she was remembering this crazy, wonderful event, that her response had become so quick and ready in such a short time. She was very much afraid that it was mostly due to the fact that she loved the man. And, almost as important, she loved his lovemaking.

They were back and it was like stepping out of a beautiful fantasyland into the cold, hard reality of everyday life. Things that had seemed so easy on Santa Talia suddenly seemed impossible to achieve.

It had been late in the evening when they'd driven in from the airport. Callie had gone straight to the kitchen to begin to find her way around and get used to the place. She'd come over a couple of times in the days before the wedding, fixing up the spare bedroom into a retreat of her own and moving some of her things in. He'd wondered why she felt she needed her own space at the time, but he hadn't said a thing. He wasn't sure, really, how he was going to feel when the time came.

She made them both some hot chocolate and they sat at the kitchen table and sipped, talking softly about their weekend. They had both been yawning and he was thinking it was time to go to bed when she'd rinsed out their cups, turned to smile at him. "Well, good night," she said.

And off she went down the hall before he realized what was happening, straight into the spare bedroom. The door closed with a crisp finality. And he was still sitting at the table with his mouth hanging open.

He supposed she was just as tired as he was, but

still… He hadn't realized she was going to value her privacy quite so completely and now he was feeling a bit disgruntled—even a little confused. He'd looked forward to having Callie in his bed, to holding her close in the night. He hadn't had that warm companionship for so long, not since…

Well, Jan of course. Not since Jan.

Funny that he hadn't realized where that thought was going until it got there. Usually Jan was right up-front, foremost in his consciousness. But never mind, he was just tired. This had nothing to do with Callie and the fact that they had made love. Not at all.

His instinct was to go straight to her and bang on the door, asking her just what the hell she thought she was doing. But he controlled the impulse. He'd vowed to treat her more calmly than he used to treat Jan. Give her some space. Let things develop naturally.

Still, he hoped he wasn't going to have to point out to her that one weekend in the Caribbean wasn't necessarily going to be enough to start a long line of descendants hatching. It might take a bit more work. In fact, it was going to take more no matter what.

Callie was leaning against the bedroom door with her eyes closed, listening intently. She'd taken that long, lonely walk down the hall, waiting to hear his voice calling her back, losing hope with every step.

Why didn't he call her? Why didn't he laugh and say, "No, darling, I want you in my bed—all night long."

But he never said a word. She supposed he didn't want her to try to take Jan's place in his bed, so she wasn't going to try to push her way in. She knew that in his mind, Jan was his real wife. Callie was his business partner in this baby-making enterprise. She wouldn't encroach. She wouldn't try to take any more of him than she was due. But it was going to be a cold, lonely night with only memories of Santa Talia to warm her.

Tina was worse. The doctors had decided her cancer was inoperable. Her outlook was not good and that cast a pall over everything.

Callie threw herself back into caretaking with a vengeance. Though she insisted on working a full day at the office, she vowed to spend every moment she could with Tina and Molly, trying to help smooth the transition for them both. The golden idyllic space and time on Santa Talia very quickly began to seem like a dream that had taken place far, far away in a past that was receding.

At dinner that night, Grant was edgy, and she wasn't exactly calm herself. They both knew a moment of truth was coming.

Grant had worked late at the office and Callie had spent a couple of hours with Tina and Molly, after which she'd picked up a nice chicken dinner at the deli. She was arranging it on plates while Grant put together a salad and hunted for dressing in the refrigerator.

They ate slowly, talking about a project the company

was bidding on, avoiding the tragic topic of Tina and what could be done. At one point, Callie yawned.

"You're working too hard," Grant told her. "And you're not getting enough sleep."

"You're right," she admitted. "But I just have so much I need to get done."

"You know, you could leave work early so you'd have more time with Tina," he said a bit gruffly.

She hesitated. "I've thought about that, but it wouldn't really be fair to my co-workers."

He frowned at her. "Callie, this is a special case and it's only temporary. Take the time off. Tina needs you."

She smiled at him, appreciating his thoughtfulness, though she knew full well the unspoken motive had something to do with the fact that he didn't want her to neglect *him,* either. But that was all right. She could understand that.

"Actually Molly needs me most," she said, and his eyes darkened. He looked away as he always did when Molly was the subject. That bothered her, but she didn't have a chance to ask him about it as he was already talking about changes he was making at the office, and about how he was going to have a few extended business trips coming up.

They cleared away the dishes and sat, drinking coffee and talking for a half hour. Callie was beginning to wonder how they were going to manage bedtime tonight, when Grant took the bull by the horns and did it his way.

"Callie," he said, looking at her forthrightly. "Don't you think we ought to get back to work?"

She was startled for a moment. She'd just risen, thinking to go to the sink to rinse out her cup, but she turned back to face him. "You mean…?"

"Yes," he said, rising himself and looking down at her. "That's what I mean."

She searched his eyes. "Are you sure?"

"About what?"

She took a deep breath. "I didn't know if you really wanted me to."

"Callie, look at me. I want you. Don't ever doubt it. I should have a sign painted on my forehead, I Want Callie."

She smiled, wondering how he could say that. "Are you sure?"

"I'm sure."

She shrugged, putting down her cup. "Well, okay then. My bedroom or yours?"

He'd had enough of this. Growling, he picked her up and slung her over his shoulder.

"I'll show you where you belong," he said.

She shrieked and laughed as he carried her into his room and dropped her in the middle of his bed. She was still laughing as he slipped off her blouse and pushed aside her bra. But when his lips touched the pink tip of her breast all laughter faded away and she melted into the passionate woman she'd learned how to be on a Caribbean island.

An hour later, with the lights off and the house

buttoned down for the night, Grant felt calm and fulfilled for the first time that day. He liked the smell of her hair and the feel of her soft skin. He loved to feel her legs wrap around his hips and to feel her fingers dig into his shoulder. He was crazy about the way she cried out when it got really good and he was addicted to the way he felt when their time together came to its high point.

For just a moment the traitorous thought came into his head—Jan never cared all that much for lovemaking. Callie seemed to thrive on it. But he banished that thought quickly. No comparisons. It wasn't right and it wasn't fair.

Still, he felt fulfilled and satisfied, like a lazy cat in the sun, just being with Callie. After they made love, he thought it was so full and sweet and solid that she wouldn't possibly want to leave him. And then he felt her slip out of the bed and pull on her robe. He lay very still with his eyes closed as she walked quietly across the hallway—away from him.

Why didn't she want to stay with him? Her absence left a big, cold, empty place in his bed. It was something he was going to have to do something about.

Lately nights were good, Callie had to admit.

Days were bad. Being cheerful for Tina was getting more and more difficult. She was on pain medication around the clock now and usually asleep. A hospice nurse came by twice a day, and of course, there was the nursing service Grant had hired for her.

Molly had a nanny twenty-four hours a day, but she didn't understand why her mommy was always in bed. Callie tried to be there as often as she could to keep things as normal as possible for the child. That was what was most important.

It was impossible for a child so young to understand what was happening, but she had to sense that something sad was going on. Callie hated that, knowing it must be scary for her. She understood feeling scared of things you were too young to fully comprehend. She'd spent her own childhood often frightened of her mother's drunk boyfriends. She didn't want Molly to have those kinds of memories. At all costs, she had to be protected.

There was one puzzle that still bothered her. Grant had been so generous, hiring the nurse and the nanny and coming by to see Tina every few days. So why did he act so strangely around Molly? He always avoided her. And the sad thing was, the girl was fascinated by him. She lit up like a Christmas tree every time she caught sight of him. It was a nagging problem that didn't show any signs of getting better.

Finally one day she brought it up to his sister.

"Gena, what is it? Why doesn't Grant like Molly?"

Gena had looked pained. She'd dropped by to see her brother, but he was working very late, so she'd stayed to have a chat with Callie instead.

"Is he still acting that way?"

"Yes. He avoids her like the plague."

She nodded, pursing her lips. "He should have talked to you about this himself, but since he hasn't, I'll tell you. He thinks that Molly looks just like his daughter, Lisa."

Callie frowned, trying to think back and picture the photograph he had in his office. "Well, they both have dark hair and dark eyes, but other than that…" She shrugged.

"Exactly. They don't look alike at all. I don't know how he got it in his brain, but now he can't seem to shake it loose. He fixates on it. And that makes it impossible for him to accept her."

"But he has to accept her." She looked at Gena helplessly. "She's going to be mine. For keeps."

Gena's eyes widened. "You mean to tell me you plan to adopt her once Tina is gone?"

Callie nodded, feeling a bit lost. "I promised Tina. And even if I hadn't…"

Gena nodded. "Sure, I understand." With a sigh, she threw her arms around Callie and hugged her tight. "Oh boy," she said. "I'm afraid you and Grant are in for one rocky ride."

"If only I could think of some way to make him look at Molly differently."

Gena drew back and searched her face. "Don't you get it? It has very little to do with Molly. It's all about him. He's feeling guilty. He can't shake the fact that he should have been home more and taken a more active part in his daughter's life. All this moping about is because he can't expunge his sense of guilt."

Callie shook her head. This was the first she'd heard of anything like this. "What are you talking about?"

Gena shook her head. "Grant was the typical workaholic. He lived for business. And Jan wasn't any better. She was so busy with her activities and her girlfriends. The two of them had a nanny for Lisa. There were times when they would work all day, then meet for dinner out, then get home too late to see Lisa that day. Believe me, that wasn't unusual. They were the ultimate yuppie couple, living the modern life and treating their daughter like a pet."

Callie was shocked. Somehow she couldn't imagine Grant letting that happen, no matter how crazy he was about his wife. "So you're saying Grant feels guilty about neglecting Lisa, so he wants to neglect Molly?"

"Now that's putting a bit of spin on it." Gena made a face. "I don't think Grant is actually all that complicated. No, but I'm saying he does feel guilty. He's haunted by this vision of Lisa watching him, crying, wanting more attention, and him just taking off for work instead of giving it to her."

Callie nodded, finally feeling she was getting the picture. It did fit, now that she thought about it. And at some point, when she felt comfortable enough to do it, she was going to bring it up to him and challenge him to change his ways. Just not right now.

Grant seemed to have a strange way of dealing with his grief. Besides the way he acted with Molly, there was the fact that there were no pictures of his first family here in his apartment. She'd searched every room. There wasn't a sign that he'd ever been married before and had a child. And yet, Jan's presence hung over the place and haunted the hallways. She wondered if she would ever get used to that.

But all in all, her relationship with Grant was good and just seemed to get better and better. She enjoyed her work. It was odd having Grant as a boss when she also had his ring on her hand. She knew everyone else was gossiping about it behind her back. She didn't mind. If it gave them entertainment, let them speculate. She was just concentrating on doing a good job and doing the best she could for Tina and Molly at the same time. And, of course, getting pregnant.

Was that ever going to happen? It had been over a month now and still nothing. She was beginning to worry. What if their happy ending was out to lunch?

"Don't worry," Gena told her. "Just relax and let nature take its course. You're not a teenager, you know. Your body is used to its barren state. It's going to have to jog itself into a new mode of being and that might take it a little time. It could happen at any moment now."

Gena was prophetic—and Callie was pregnant, and probably had been when they were talking about it. The little stick in the pregnancy test told the tale.

But by the time she'd done the test, she'd known for over a week. Her swollen breasts had given her the first clue. And then it was as though she could feel her body adjusting to the presence of new, growing life inside her. She felt as though her pelvic bones were loosening, getting ready to accommodate seven or eight pounds of bouncing baby boy or girl. Her skin felt more sensitive. And her stomach felt queasy.

It was all very exciting and wonderful and she wished she could share it with Grant. But she didn't want to tell him just yet. Despite the fact that this was exactly what he was waiting for, she didn't know how he would react. After all, if she told him she was pregnant, would he withdraw? Would his work become more important than she was? And most of all, would he quit wanting to make love with her?

She didn't want that. It made her face burn to admit it, but she loved how he loved her. His rough hands on her soft skin, the feel of his hard, exciting body, the thrust, the cry, the almost animal-like intensity of the need for him, the incredible climax, and then it all dissolved into a tangle of arms and legs and hot, sweet skin and she could close her eyes and rest on his chest and pretend that he loved her. That time of the night was the best time for her. She'd never known this kind of body hunger could even exist. She didn't want it to end.

She kept remembering what he'd said that first time in Santa Talia.

I hope that did us some good... We'll have to keep trying...

She knew him so much better now and she could tell that he had a sort of affection of some kind for her. And she thought it was pretty obvious he liked making love. But if he had this guilt thing going about Lisa, might he not have something similar about Jan? What if he decided he couldn't justify making love with someone who wasn't Jan now that there was no need for it?

That night, lying with him in his bed, she knew she wasn't being fair to him. She listened to his even breathing. He was a good man. He deserved to know. It was only right she should tell him. She would do it the next night, she decided, as she slipped out of his bed and made her way back to her own room.

That put her on pins and needles for most of the day. She got home a little early and fixed a special dinner and set the table with candlelight. And then she waited.

When he finally came in, he barely looked at her and was clearly distracted.

"I've got a business trip," he told her. "Sorry it's so sudden. I've got to go to Madrid. Negotiations on the property acquisitions are falling apart and I've got to go see if I can put Humpty Dumpty together again. I may be gone for more than two weeks."

"What?"

"I'm sorry, Callie. I know it's a bad time. But there's no choice. I have to go."

Reaching out, he drew her close and kissed her lips. That almost made up for the news he'd just given her, because he never made spontaneous gestures of affection like that. She was thrilled and happy for the rest of the evening.

But she didn't tell him her own news. She decided that would have to wait until he was back from Europe. Knowing that the child he yearned for was actually on the way might make it that much harder for him to leave, and this trip was obviously important to him.

No, she would wait. She held her secret close inside and enjoyed thinking about how happy he was going to be when she finally told him.

CHAPTER NINE

TINA died peacefully early on a Monday morning. Callie was by her side. She didn't cry. She had already cried buckets over the last few weeks and she had to maintain a cheerful front for Molly.

Luckily Molly didn't notice that much was different. She hadn't seen her mother much except for quick visits to the hospital for weeks and then asleep from the doorway once she was home. She was getting used to life with Callie and Nadine, the nanny Grant had hired, filling the caretaking slots. So it didn't seem odd to her when she and Callie packed up all her things to move her to the penthouse. It was just another adventure.

The funeral was on Thursday. It was sparsely attended. Tina didn't have a wide circle of friends. Gena came and Callie appreciated that. Grant tried to make it, taking a midnight flight from Madrid, but his plane was delayed and he only arrived for the tail end of the service. Callie took one look at him coming in through the arched doorway and all the emotion she'd held so tightly controlled let go as though a dam had been broken. She dissolved into tears and he reached her quickly, taking her into his arms and holding her tightly against his chest, rocking her and murmuring comfort. She couldn't seem to stop crying but she loved the way he held her.

She regained control as they drove back to his apartment. By the time they were at the front door, she was herself again, quietly telling Grant about how the last few days had gone. He listened sympathetically as he pushed the button to open the door. They both entered, lingering in the entryway, and suddenly a youthful screech filled the air as Molly came hurtling toward them on her little chubby legs.

"What the…?"

Grant turned toward Callie, astounded.

Callie caught Molly up in her arms and hugged her tightly. She'd agonized over whether or not to take her to the funeral, but in the end, she'd decided not to. She was just too young to deal with whatever hints she might have picked up on as to what the ceremony was about. So she'd left her at home with Nadine.

"Hello, pumpkin," she said to her now. "Were you a good girl while we were gone?"

"She was just fine," Nadine said, walking toward them with her awkward walk and warm, generous manner. "Did you have a good trip, Mr. Carver?"

Grant was still in shock from finding Molly ensconced in his home. Callie saw it in his face and bit her lip, wishing she'd warned him. But it was too late now.

He muttered something in response to the nanny, but his gaze was on Callie, and she could see that he wanted answers. She was about to hand Molly back when the little girl lunged toward Grant.

"Da Da!" she cried, using the name she'd been using for him from the first. Her face was filled with delight and her little arms stretched toward him.

It took both Callie and Nadine wrestling with the child to get her back under control and out of the room. When Callie came back, Grant was waiting for her, his eyes ice-cold.

"What is Molly doing here?" he asked softly.

Callie sighed. She felt as though she were wilting. After the funeral and everything else from the week, she didn't have much in reserve for arguing. Turning, she looked him straight in the face.

"I was hoping I would come up with a good way to tell you about this, but I just haven't had the time to think about it. I'm just going to give you the facts."

"That would be best."

Callie reached out to steady herself against the high back of a chair. "She's here. She's going to stay with us from now on."

He looked as though he'd been shot.

"Grant, I know how you react to her but I'm sure that will fade quickly if you just let it..."

"No." He was shaking his head emphatically. "No, it's impossible."

She turned her head, avoiding his eyes.

"Callie, it's impossible. I can't have her here. I just can't do it."

She took a deep breath. "Grant, I really think you should try to get over that."

"Get over it?" He stared at her. "How do you get over having your life torn apart? How do you get over losing a child?"

She turned back to face him. "But, Grant, this is another child. A child who needs us. Wouldn't redeeming the life of another child make up at least in part for what was lost?"

His face was cold and his jaw looked like granite. "No."

"I know it was awful. It's still awful." She was pleading now. "But life goes on and you can't take it out on a baby."

He frowned as though he couldn't believe she could be saying these things. "I'm not taking anything out on a baby. I'm just telling you what I can't do. And I can't live with the situation you suggest. I just can't." He sighed impatiently. "Surely Tina has some family somewhere who can take the baby."

She shook her head, fighting the awful feeling of dread that was building in her.

"Oh, come on, Callie. Everyone's got someone."

"I don't. Except you."

She said the last two words so softly he might not have heard. He certainly didn't react.

"And you want me to believe Tina didn't, either?" he said levelly. "She couldn't have been completely alone in the world."

"Well, she does have a stepmother somewhere. But she hated her. Called her evil. I know they haven't spoken in years."

"Still, if she's family…"

She met his gaze with her chin high. "The woman let Tina be sent to foster care rather than take care of her after her father died. Why would she want to take Tina's baby in?"

She saw the hope fade in his eyes, but then he had an idea.

"Then how about some nice young couple looking to adopt? She's a beautiful little girl. She wouldn't have any trouble finding someone who wanted her."

Callie's jaw stuck out even further. "She already has found someone. Me."

"Oh, Callie." He shook his head in disbelief.

She was fighting tears now, but she was determined not to let them show. "Grant, this is Molly we're talking about. My Molly."

"*Your* Molly?"

"Yes." She nodded. "Tina did some paperwork and got me named as legal guardian a week ago. I'm going to adopt her."

His eyes were flat and cold. "Why didn't you tell me?"

She shook her head. "You weren't here."

He stared at her. There was no give in his face, no sign that he might relent. Her heart was breaking.

"I hate to put it this way, Grant, but my responsibility to Molly goes back further than my commitment to you. I can't abandon her. I won't."

He stared at her, hardly able to believe this was the same loving woman he'd become so accustomed to these last few weeks. Where had this steely determination come from?

"There's no one else to take her," she was saying insistently. Her emotions were starting to show. Her voice was rising. "If this means it's over between you and me, that's the way it will have to be, because there is no way I can do that to this child."

Looking at her, he saw the tragedy in her eyes and he realized what she was asking. Could he give her up? Why not? He could find another woman, couldn't he? It couldn't be that hard.

And suddenly, it struck him like a knife in the chest. He couldn't do it. He was so attached to her now, he couldn't imagine life without her. He had to have her nearby. His breath was coming faster than normal and he realized that the threat of Callie leaving scared the hell out of him. He couldn't lose her. He would do just about anything to keep her. But could he do this?

Blinking rapidly, he tried to shift gears, tried to rethink things. Molly was a sweet little girl. It wasn't her fault she affected him the way she did. Maybe… But no. Just thinking about it made him start to sweat. He couldn't do it.

Surely there was someone out there in the world who could take her. Surely there was an aunt, a grandmother, someone. All they had to do was find that person. He had a very good detective agency he used at times for the company. He would call them in the morning. Surely they could find someone.

In the meantime, maybe he could deal with this new situation. He would have to. He couldn't let Callie go. That was not an option.

But the words were difficult to speak.

"We could try it for a while, I suppose," he said, his voice rough as sandpaper. Looking at the hopeful light in her eyes, he wanted to take her in his arms and hold her tightly to him. "We'll see how it goes."

He could see the relief in her face and it warmed him.

"So you want me to stay," she said.

He grimaced. "Of course I want you to stay," he said roughly, trying to control the emotion in his voice.

She sighed and let herself begin to relax. "Well, that's good. Because…because I really should be here right after Christmas." She tried to smile but she knew she looked like she was about to cry. "That's when our baby is going to be born."

"What?" He felt the room spin. It was his turn to reach for support. "You're pregnant?"

She nodded, tears welling in her eyes as she smiled up at him. "Yes."

"Callie." He pulled her close and rained kisses on her face. "Oh, Callie. I'm the happiest man in the world."

And for the moment, he actually meant it.

An almost comfortable routine grew up around their busy days. Callie and Grant ate breakfast together in the mornings, then Grant left for the office and Callie fed Molly and played with her until it was time for her to go to work. She took care of errands and shopping late in the afternoon. Then she went straight home to take care of Molly for the rest of the day into the evening. Grant usually didn't come home until after Molly's bedtime. It was best that way, she supposed.

Still, the situation wasn't ideal and Callie wished Grant would make an effort to get to know Molly better. But she wasn't in the position to be choosy right now. So she let it go for the present.

Her fear that Grant might not feel the need to pay much attention to her once she was pregnant, as though that project had been completed and it was time to move on, proved unjustified. Most of the time their relationship could have passed for a love-match to any casual observer—especially in the lovemaking department. Contrary to her fears, there had been no slacking off in that area. In fact, Grant seemed to relish her changing body, and she relished his interest.

Her pregnancy was progressing normally. Grant insisted on going with her to her first doctor's appointment. The doctor pronounced her in great shape and

Grant talked vitamins and danger signs he'd read about in the waiting room all the way home.

That meant he was home earlier than usual—early enough to witness Molly eating her dinner. The little girl was in her high chair and Callie had turned to the sink to wash off a toy when Grant walked into the room.

"Look at this mess!"

She whirled to see what was going on. "What are you shouting about?"

"There's food all over the white rug." He pointed down. "Look, it's ruined."

She looked at the fancy and probably very expensive carpet and then she looked at Molly. Molly was grinning happily. As Callie watched, she picked up a handful of mashed potatoes and threw it at Grant. The little splat landed on the side of his nose. Molly gurgled happily. Callie could almost hear her saying, "Touchdown!"

Grant turned toward Callie with a see-what-she-did look on his face.

And Callie responded cheerfully with, "Okay. That does it. We're getting rid of the white rug."

Grant looked confused as he wiped mashed potatoes from his face. "What?"

She shrugged. "The white rug has to go. Do you think Molly is the only baby who's going to throw food all over it? White rugs are not compatible with happy babies."

"But..."

"You just wait." She pointed to her still-tiny tummy. "This guy is going to tear this place apart."

He looked a bit nonplussed.

"We're going to have to baby-proof all the rooms," she said.

"Baby-proof my apartment?"

"Didn't you do that for…?"

She stopped. She'd almost said Lisa's name. That was against the unspoken rules. She saw something flicker in his eyes.

But at the same time, she was having second thoughts. This was all wrong. They couldn't dance around this issue the rest of their lives. Lisa had been a real person and deserved to be spoken about like a real person. The way he was treating her, she wasn't real anymore—she was a museum relic wrapped in protective gauze and kept from human view. He must have memories of her that he cherished. Wouldn't it be better if it was possible for him to bring them back out and honor them?

"I'm sure you did a lot of child-proofing once Lisa began to toddle around the room," she said deliberately.

He looked up at her, startled. It was probably the first time he'd ever heard his baby's name out of her mouth. He stared at her for a long moment, then, without saying a word, he turned and left the room.

Well, it looked like that had been a big mistake. But what else could she do? And something had to be done.

She got a red lollipop for Molly. She'd brought over Tina's store of them and put them in a drawer in the kitchen. She still didn't really approve of Molly having them, but she was willing to let her for a while. She had so many new things to learn and new rules to follow. She liked the idea of giving her as many things from her life with Tina as she could, at least for the time being.

But she also had to work on this fixation of Grant's. The next night, she tried a new method.

She and Grant were sitting on the couch, talking quietly just before bed. Suddenly she brought up something she knew he was going to resist.

"I think we should put up a picture of Jan and Lisa."

He froze, staring at her. "What are you talking about?"

"Grant, they were a huge part of your life. You can't block that out and pretend it never happened."

"I don't." His voice sounded like gravel on glass. "Believe me. I think of them every hour of every day."

"Yes, but you think of them in a horrible way. You think of their deaths and how miserable you are without them. You should think about the good times. Maybe if we put up pictures…"

He was shaking his head. "You don't understand at all."

She ignored that. "Let's let the rest of our little family know who they were and that they are still important."

He was scowling blackly. "They're only important to me."

"No. You're wrong. They are a part of who you are. And that's important to me."

He scoffed. "Should we put up a picture of Ralph, too?"

She shook her head. "No. Ralph wasn't really important to anyone but his mother." She smiled, thinking of it. "Funny, but I think his mother was always more important to me than he was."

Which reminded her, a visit to Marge was overdue. It had been two weeks since she'd gone by to see her mother-in-law. It was time to go and tell her about the pregnancy—even though she probably wouldn't understand.

Grant hadn't agreed to let her put up the pictures she wanted to display. She would work on it. Eventually she was sure he would give in. After all, it was to his benefit that he do so. But for tonight, she'd at least pushed a hint of a nose under the tent. And now it was time to start anticipating bedtime—her favorite time of day.

The next night, she had a new angle.

"Could we get a better scanner for the computer?" she asked him. "The one we have here is pretty flaky and I've seen new models that do a much better job on photos."

"What are you scanning?"

"I found a cupboard full of pictures of…of Jan and Lisa. I want to copy them so that…"

"What?" He stared as though he thought she'd gone crazy.

"For scrapbook pages. Have you seen the sort of scrapbooking that everyone is doing these days? That's what I want to do. I want to make a scrapbook filled with the story of your life with your first family. Because the history needs to be preserved and told and not let to drift away."

He didn't look pleased, but he didn't comment, and the next night, she found a new scanner in the entryway.

She fixed up the little office off the kitchen as a scrapbooking room. She had pictures on bulletin boards all around as she tried to work out how she wanted to do her pages and develop a timeline. She started it as a duty but she quickly learned to love doing it. Every evening she tried to go in and spend some time working on her project. On at least two occasions, Grant came to the door and looked in. He didn't say anything. But the second time he stayed, watching her work for a good ten minutes before he turned away.

The next day, she took one of the best pictures she'd found—a studio photo of Jan and Lisa—and had it framed, then put it up in the hallway. When Grant came home that night it was the first thing he saw.

"What the hell is that?" he demanded.

"I think you can see what it is." She tried to remain calm but her heart was beating like a drum.

He turned to glare at her. "If I wanted a picture like that up I'd have put it up," he said.

"This isn't for you, necessarily," she said stoutly. "It's for me. And for the baby that's coming. You don't have to walk by this part of the hallway if you can't stand it. You can walk the other way."

He gazed down at her with his brow furled. "Callie, what the hell are you trying to do?"

"I think you have to try to normalize your feelings. You can't let wounds fester forever."

He slapped the wall with his open hand and barked,

"What right do you have to decide how my wounds should heal?"

She drew breath deep into her lungs and faced him bravely. "For myself, none at all. But I do have a right for our baby."

He stared at her for a long moment, but he shook his head. "No," he said. "Maybe you can make that argument after the baby comes. But you can't make it now." Reaching out, he took down the picture. "Sorry, Callie," he said coolly. "No can do."

He walked off with the picture, but she noticed that he was looking at it. So she'd lost this round. But every time he was forced to talk about his first family, or look at pictures of them, she felt it moved him more toward accepting the past. And maybe she was just kidding herself, but she felt she was making progress. At least she hoped so.

CHAPTER TEN

CALLIE was clearing away the dishes from dinner a few nights later. Grant helped her, then dropped down onto the couch to read the paper. Out of the corner of her eye, Callie could see Molly, who was supposed to be in bed, wending her way into the room, hugging the shadows as though she knew she wasn't really welcome.

Callie turned to get rid of the glasses she was putting away before she could intercept Molly. But the little girl was too fast for her, and by the time she'd turned back, Molly was already at Grant's knee, tugging on his slacks with one sticky hand and holding out a half-eaten red lollipop with the other.

"Da Da!" she cried.

The look on Grant's face would have been comical if the whole situation wasn't so sad.

"Take it," Callie urged softly. "Grant, take it!"

Very reluctantly, he did, grasping the sloppy-looking candy between his thumb and forefinger. "Callie, what the hell am I supposed to do with this?" he growled.

She swept the baby up in her arms and squeezed her tightly. "Grant says 'thank you', Molly. He loves that lollipop." Giving her a loud, wet smack on the cheek, she hurried her back to the nanny's care.

When she got back, he was washing his hands in the sink.

"You do realize she was offering you her most prized possession," she noted dryly. "I guess I'm going to have to teach her that you can't buy love."

"Callie…"

She saw the tortured look in his eyes and regretted her words. "I'm sorry. But she's just a child and she wants you to like her."

"I like her," he said, though his tone was forced. "It's not her fault that she reminds me so much of…"

"Of Lisa," Callie said. She was making a point of talking about them now. "I know. And I know you're trying to be kind to her. You're really making an effort."

"But you want me to love her like she was my own," he said. "And, Callie, that's just not going to happen."

Maybe not. Maybe it was hopeless. And maybe there would come a time when she had to decide who needed her more: Molly or Grant. She only hoped it never came to that, because she wasn't sure which way she would go.

Something woke Grant up the next morning—a movement on the bed beside him. His heart leaped. Had Callie come back to him on her own? He turned and met a pair of dark, laughing eyes, and then a little chubby fist hit him in the cheek and Molly giggled.

"Da Da!"

He jerked back.

"Callie!" he called.

Molly began to bounce on the bed, laughing uproariously.

He turned back to look at her, frowning fiercely. But as he watched, his frown faded. She did look cute. If only he could look at her once and not see Lisa's reproachful face.

"There you are, you rascal," Callie said, coming in and standing at the edge of the bed. "Are you torturing Grant again?"

Molly giggled and bounced out of reach.

"I'll get her out of here," Callie said, reaching for the moving target.

But Grant was smiling at her. "Why don't you come join us instead?" he suggested as he pulled her down on top of him.

"Grant!" She laughed as she slid over to his side. "What are you doing?"

"Enjoying you," he murmured, looking sensual.

"Oh my," she said. "I didn't realize it was open house today."

"I wish I could wake up this way every morning," he said, touching her cheek with his forefinger.

He barely got the words out when Molly dove between them, chattering happily as though she thought she should be part of the conversation.

His head jerked back in surprise and Callie pushed up on her elbow, preparing to make Molly move.

But Grant had calmed himself. "Let her stay," he said. "It's okay."

Callie had to work hard to keep from choking aloud. A happy bubble was rising in her chest.

"She's just being a little dickens this morning," Callie said lovingly. "Nadine tells me that she had to spend half the day yesterday racing around stuffing things back into drawers after Molly emptied them out."

"So she's already getting into the drawers," Grant said. He remembered when Lisa had been at that stage. As he thought of it and pictured Lisa, he steeled himself and waited for the pain to come. But there was nothing. After a moment, he began to wonder why.

They cuddled in the bed for another five minutes and then it was time to get up. But the warm feeling stayed with him all the rest of the day.

Callie was sure they were making progress, but one big hurdle still remained. Gena had said he was racked with guilt. If that was true, surely it would do him good to get it out in the open and talk about it. Did she have the nerve to bring it up?

One night about a week later, he was packing for another business trip. It seemed like a good time. She waited for him to come out of his room, and she told him she wanted to talk about something. He sat down with her on the couch and she launched into it.

He listened to her version of Gena's theory about his feeling guilty because he didn't pay as much attention to Lisa when she was alive as he should have and didn't say a word. Instead he got up and poured himself a drink and went to sit on the balcony, away from her.

She was pretty sure he was furious with her. And why not? Did she really have a right to push him on this?

But an hour later, when he came in, he pulled her into his arms and buried his face in her hair.

"That last day," he said, his voice a bit hoarse, "it was obvious Lisa was coming down with something in the morning. I had a meeting. Jan had a presentation she was giving at Junior League. Neither one of us paid much attention to Lisa. We thought we were so damn busy with such important things."

His voice broke and it was a moment before he could go on.

"The nanny tried to call us all day, but my cell phone wasn't working right and Jan didn't pick up because she was in a meeting hall until late in the afternoon. When she finally got home, Lisa was burning up and the nanny was hysterical. She tried to call me, but the cell still wasn't working and my secretary was out for the afternoon. So she packed Lisa into the car and went racing off to the hospital. She ran a red light. And got hit. She lived another twenty-four hours, but Lisa was killed in the original impact."

"Oh, Grant. Oh, I'm so sorry."

He pulled away and just shook his head.

"But it wasn't your fault. How could you…?"

"Don't patronize me, Callie," he said harshly. "Of course it was my fault. If I'd been a proper father and husband, the accident would never have happened. Of course it was my fault. And I'll pay all the days of my life."

She refused to be cowed by his anger at himself. Following him into his room, she shut the door and made him face her. "You listen to me, Grant Carver," she said sternly. "You are a wonderful, caring man. You may have been careless in the past, but you're older now, more mature. You won't let family needs slide ever again."

"How do you know? What makes you so sure?"

"I know you. I've seen you in action. And most of all…" She walked into his arms. "I love you."

His face registered shock. He hadn't expected that. She was playing against the rules again, coloring outside the lines. He didn't have an answer, but she didn't care. Stepping forward, she rose on her toes and put her arms around his neck.

"Make love to me, Grant," she whispered. "If you can't love me, at least make love to me. That's all you ever promised, and I'm holding you to it."

"I will, Callie," he agreed, cupping her cheek in his hand. "If you promise to stay with me all night. Can you do that?"

She looked up at him, surprised. "Of course. Are you sure you want me to? I thought…well, I know you still consider Jan your real wife and I thought…"

"Oh, Callie." He crushed her in his embrace. "*You're*

my wife. Don't you ever doubt it. I've been aching to have you where I can hold you all night long."

Tears welled in Callie's eyes. "Grant," she whispered. "I'd be honored to share your bed."

He pulled her down onto the velvet comforter and she knew she had a home there at last.

Grant sat down in the plane, ready for his flight to San Francisco, and stared at his briefcase. He had put a large manila envelope inside. Though he hadn't opened the envelope yet, he knew what it contained. The detectives he'd hired were finally giving him a report on all Molly's living relatives. This was what he'd been waiting for. He planned to peruse the document while in his hotel room, but he wasn't looking forward to it.

He had enough to think about for now. For the entire flight, he agonized over all his missteps and misstatements in his recent relationships. He wondered how Callie had put up with him all this time. She was wonderful and he was so lucky to have found her.

When he got to the hotel, he put his bag on the bed, worked the lock and snapped open the case. He began to pull clothes out and very quickly, he noticed something strange. Someone had added something to the clothes he'd packed. The more he dug, the more he found. Red lollipops were stuffed in every crevice of his suitcase. It looked as though a lollipop-loving squirrel had been at work.

And then the coup de grace. The fine wool suit-coat he was planning to wear to a very important meeting had a half-eaten lollipop stuck to the lapel. Stickiness courtesy, he was sure, of little Molly.

He stared at it for a long, long moment. He waited for the anger to explode in his chest and build in his head. But it didn't happen. Instead he started to laugh.

"Molly, Molly," he said, shaking his head. "Oh, Molly."

He laughed until tears filled his eyes.

That night he had a dream and the little dark-haired girl whose face swam into the picture was Molly, not Lisa. And she was smiling.

He woke up and lay staring at the ceiling, thinking. He was on edge, restless. He wanted something. He was aching for someone now, and it wasn't Jan. It was Callie.

Callie. Beautiful, sexy, sensible Callie. What a fool he'd been not to notice.

Rolling out of bed, he went into the bathroom and took a long hot shower, thinking things through. When he came out, he was decided.

He was going home.

The first thing he did was to pull the manila envelope out of his briefcase and tear it to shreds without opening it. Then he called the office where the meeting was to be held and canceled. He lugged his suitcase, lollipops and all, down to the lobby and called for reservations on the next available plane. He was going home to the woman that he loved—and the little girl who thought she could buy love with lollipops.

When he walked into his penthouse apartment, Molly was the first to see him.

"Da Da!" she cried, racing to him.

Pulling the little girl up into his arms, he hugged her. “Thank you for all those lollipops, Molly,” he said. “That was a big surprise.”

She giggled and was suddenly shy. He hugged her close and kissed her cheek just as Callie walked into the room.

“Grant!” she cried, her face filled with candid joy. “What are you doing here?”

He put Molly down gently and she ran off. Turning to Callie, he shook his head, looking her over from top to toe.

“What’s wrong?” she asked, suddenly anxious. “Did I do something?”

“You sure did,” he claimed, a slow smile growing on his handsome face. “You made a family for me, Callie. And I didn’t even have the intelligence to notice.”

She smiled. “Oh, is that all?”

“No. There’s something else.”

He took her in his arms, looking down with all his love filling his gaze. “You made me love you.”

Callie’s tiny gasp gave him shivers. “Do you really mean that?” she asked, her dark eyes luminous, “or are you just singing a song?”

“Both,” he said. “Will you marry me, Callie?”

“I already did, silly.”

“I know. But I just wanted to ask you again.”

“Okay. I’ll marry you anytime, Grant. Anytime at all.”

“Good. Because time is the greatest gift. And I promise, my time will always be yours.”

EPILOGUE

MOLLY loved it at the ranch.

She loved the dogs and the horses and the cows. She loved to make the chickens run. She loved finding where the cat had hidden to have her kittens. She loved all the nice people who seemed to love her right back.

But she was sort of scared of Granpa. He sat upstairs in that big chair and growled at her, all his whiskers quivering. Mommy said he was laughing, but it didn't sound like laughing to Molly. He was like the bear in the book Daddy read to her. Scary. And she had to walk past that room to get to the room where the baby was.

The baby!

She knew she was supposed to love the baby, but she wasn't sure yet. She tried to talk to him but he didn't talk much. Not like Molly. Molly was a big girl now. Next week she would be two and she was going to have a big birthday party.

She had been living at the ranch ever since the baby was born with her mommy and daddy—she used to call them Callie and Grant, but those names were too hard to say. Anyway, she liked calling them Mommy and Daddy better.

"Good baby, good baby," she said, patting him on the stomach.

"Don't pat too hard, honey," Mommy said, pulling her hand back.

Molly felt hurt. She wasn't patting too hard. She didn't want to hurt the baby.

"We have to be extra special careful of the baby," Mommy told her, giving her a hug at the same time. "Babies are easy to break. They can get hurt so easily—things we don't even think of can hurt them. So we have to touch very softly."

She nodded. She understood. Babies were precious and special. But she looked up quickly at Callie's face. Did her mommy love the baby better than her?

She didn't have time to find out because Daddy swooped her up in his arms and gave her little baby kisses on the top of her head.

"G'illa, g'illa!" she cried.

"You want gorilla kisses?" he said, laughing at her. "Okay, here goes."

He planted a few loud, rumbling, smacking kisses on her cheeks and her neck and she shrieked with happiness.

"Shh, the baby," Mommy said, and Daddy put her down.

Molly frowned. People said that all the time. "Don't wake the baby, don't wake the baby." The baby was always asleep. What fun was that? Maybe he didn't even know about fun stuff yet.

Daddy was kissing Mommy. Mommy was kissing him back and that made Molly feel warm and happy.

Daddy seemed to feel the same way, because he said, "I never knew a man could be this happy. I bless the day you tried to kill me with your orchid pot."

Mommy laughed and said, "Me, too. Since that day we've gained a marriage, a daughter and now a son."

"Grant Carver the Seventh," Grant said with satisfaction, looking down at the baby. "We done good."

Mommy and Daddy were happy. That was good. She had a vague sense of missing someone. Mommy told her all the time about Tina, who was her first mommy. Tina went to heaven because God needed her up there. But she would see Tina again someday. She loved Tina, too. She remembered her a little bit and Mommy always showed her pictures.

Molly was getting bored. She thought she heard the cat meow, so she slipped out of the room and headed toward the landing.

She held her breath as she started across the open doorway to where Granpa was sleeping in his chair. But then she saw something. She stopped. There, on a shelf right beside him, was a box with a red lollipop sticking out of it.

Her little heart jumped. She remembered red lollipops. She used to love red lollipops, but Mommy said they weren't good for her. She hadn't had a red lollipop for a long time. And now, there was one right there next to Granpa.

But he was scary. What if he woke up? What if he reached out and grabbed her and growled? Her heart was beating very fast. She crept into the room and reached out. There. The lollipop was in her hand. It was different from the ones she used to have, but…

"What have you got there, young'un?"

She gasped and started to run, her heart in her throat. She couldn't stop. If she stopped, he would take it away from her, and she needed it. Running down the hall, she came to the baby's room and dashed inside. Mommy and Daddy were gone, but the baby was awake.

She pulled on the paper around the candy. It came off easily. Then she climbed up on the chair next to the cradle and leaned down. He had big blue eyes and he stared at her very hard.

"Here, baby," she whispered to him. "Here. Eat."

Suddenly someone was yelling. She jerked back, startled. The maid named Ana was calling out and people were running toward the room.

Ana pulled the lollipop from her hand. "No!" she cried. "You can't give that to the baby. No!"

Molly was scared. She wasn't bad. Didn't they understand? She wanted to give the baby something fun. She wanted to give him the thing she had always loved best. But the faces seemed angry.

Then Daddy was there and he pulled her up into

his arms. "You and your red lollipops," he said, holding her close.

"Don't yell at her," Mommy was saying. "She was doing it out of love."

"You can't do it, though," Daddy told her, being very serious. "You can't give things like that to the baby. He's not ready."

Tears were popping out and running down her fat cheeks and her lower lip was trembling.

"You love the baby, don't you?" Daddy said.

Did she? She looked down at where he was watching. And suddenly, she saw something in his big blue eyes. He was her brother. He was hers. Maybe she did love him. She nodded and gave a big sniff.

"Of course you do."

"Tell you what," Mommy said, tousling her hair. "You wait just a second. I have an idea." She reached in and rummaged in the big bag of baby care items she took with her everywhere these days.

"Here." She pulled out a bright red pacifier and showed it to Molly. "What do you think? Do you want to be the one to give it to him when he's ready?"

Molly's eyes lit up and she nodded, smiling through her tears.

"Only when I say it's a good time, okay? But you will be the keeper of the red pacifier. I'm going to trust you."

"And you know what?" Daddy said. "Next week at your birthday party, you're going to have all the red lollipops you can handle. Okay?"

Molly nodded again and threw her little arms around his neck. She was a big girl now. She was learning lots of things. And that was good, because that little baby was going to have a lot to learn from his big sister and she wanted to be ready.

"We love you, Molly," Daddy said.

She nodded. She knew that. She loved them, too.

Even the baby.

* * * * *

THE MARRIAGE SOLUTION

BY
BRENDA HARLEN

Brenda Harlen grew up in a small town surrounded by books and imaginary friends. Although she always dreamed of being a writer, she chose to follow a more traditional career path first. After two years of practicing as an attorney (including an appearance in front of the Supreme Court of Canada), she gave up her "real" job to be a mum and to try her hand at writing books. Three years, five manuscripts and another baby later, she sold her first book—an RWA Golden Heart Winner—to Mills & Boon.

Brenda lives in Southern Ontario with her real-life husband/hero, two heroes-in-training and two neurotic dogs. She is still surrounded by books ("too many books," according to her children) and imaginary friends, but she also enjoys communicating with "real" people. Readers can contact Brenda by email at brendaharlen@yahoo.com.

For Neill, the man I love
and who also happens to be my best friend.
And for Jamie, with thanks.

Chapter One

Craig Richmond tapped his foot impatiently as he waited for the door to open. He knew Tess was home—he'd called first to make sure, determined that her campaign of avoidance was about to come to an end. He wasn't going to let their fifteen-year friendship fall apart just because they'd made the mistake of sleeping together.

Not that *he* thought it was a mistake. More like a long-denied fantasy finally realized. But Tess obviously regretted making love with him. And while he was disappointed that there wouldn't be a repeat performance of their one night together, he wasn't going to abandon everything they meant to one another because of it. Tonight they were going to talk about what happened and find a way to move past it.

At last the door opened and she was there.

He drank in the sight of her, from the dark, slightly

tousled hair, wide eyes the color of a clear summer sky and temptingly full lips, moving lower, lingering a moment in appreciation of her feminine curves before following the endless length of shapely legs.

He'd been angry that she was ignoring his calls, hurt that she was shutting him out, but mostly he'd been lonely without his best friend. He'd missed her smile and her laughter, her warmth and compassion. He'd missed talking to her and just being with her. And because he'd missed her friendship so much, he was determined to ignore the desire that stirred whenever he was with her—as he'd ignored it for so many years already.

He met her gaze, saw the confusion and awkwardness he felt reflected in her eyes and forced a smile. "Hi."

"Hi," she replied to his greeting.

He waited for her to step back and invite him inside, but she remained on the threshold, barring his entry.

He shifted the takeout bag he carried from one hand to the other. "Can I come in?"

She hesitated a moment before she responded, "I told you on the phone that this isn't really a good time."

"There hasn't been a good time for the past several weeks," he pointed out. "And I'm not leaving until we've had a chance to talk. So we can talk here, in the hallway, or you can invite me in to share my Pad Thai."

"I'm not very hungry." But she finally stepped away from the door and let him in.

Craig went directly to the kitchen, as comfortable in her apartment as he was in his own, and took two plates from the cupboard. Tess hovered uncertainly behind him as he divided up the noodles. He glanced back at her, noted the pallor of her cheeks and the dark smudges under her eyes that had escaped his initial scrutiny. He wondered if memories of their lovemaking had been keeping her awake at night, too, and derived a certain amount of satisfaction from that thought.

"Let's eat," he said, carrying the plates to the table.

She sat across from him, eyed the meal warily.

He frowned at her obvious lack of interest, but determinedly dug into his food. Several minutes passed in silence while he ate and Tess poked at her noodles. Then he heard her fork clatter against the plate. He looked over and saw that her cheeks weren't just pale now, they were tinged with green.

"Tess—"

Before he could say anything else, she shoved back her chair and raced down the hall. He heard the slam of the bathroom door and the muted, yet unmistakable sound, of retching.

He pushed his own plate away, his own stomach feeling a little unsettled now, too. Maybe Tess had a touch of the flu that was going around.

Or maybe there was another explanation for both her physical symptoms and her determination to avoid him since the night they'd had sex and the condom broke. Maybe she was pregnant.

Tess Lucas stared at the pink cardboard box in Craig's hand and felt her cheeks flush the same color. Last night, he'd shown up at her apartment with dinner. Today, it was a pregnancy test.

She closed her eyes, as if that would make the box—and the possibility—go away.

She'd been feeling tired and nauseous for a couple

of weeks now, but had assumed she had probably caught some virus. And the tenderness in her breasts was likely an indication that she was about to get her period. Because she *was* going to get her period—any day now, she was sure. Then she could stop worrying about the possible repercussions of faulty latex.

Unfortunately, when she opened her eyes again the box—and Craig—were still there.

She took the package from his outstretched hand and moved into the living room, dropping it on the coffee table before sinking into her favorite overstuffed chair. Craig followed her into the room but remained standing.

"That isn't quite what I expected you to do with it," he said dryly.

"What did you expect?"

"That you'd be as anxious as I am to know the truth."

"The truth is that it's been a long week and I don't have the energy to jump to conclusions like you're doing." She'd been trying for casual, but the strain in her voice was obvious to her own ears.

"I'm not jumping to any conclusions yet," he responded in a tone that was infinitely patient and reasonable.

Of course, Craig was always patient and reasonable, calm and unflappable. It was one of reasons he was such an effective vice president at Richmond Pharmaceuticals, the family-owned company he would run someday.

Tess couldn't even fake that kind of control. She couldn't pretend that the possibility of pregnancy didn't terrify her. She wanted children—someday. But not now and not like this. She felt her stomach rising again and drew in a deep breath, trying to will the nausea away.

"Please, Tess. Take the test."

"Why are you doing this?" she asked wearily.

"Because I think it would be better to know for sure than to sit around worrying about it," he told her.

"Well, I don't." She didn't care if she sounded unreasonable to him. She didn't want to know the truth; she didn't want to think about how completely and irrevocably a baby would change her life.

"You need to find out," he said gently. "So that you can consider your options."

"I'm twenty-nine years old—I know what my options are. And *if* I'm pregnant, I'll have the baby." Although she strongly believed that a woman had the right to make her own decisions about her body, she had no doubt what hers would be.

Craig nodded toward the table, to the pregnancy test she'd tossed aside. "Why don't you take the test, then we'll know?"

As much as she hated to admit it, she knew he was right. He usually was. She grabbed the box and took it to the bathroom.

Her heart was pounding, her head was spinning and she felt as though she was going to throw up. Again.

She closed the door behind her and pried open the end of the box with trembling fingers. The contents spilled out onto the counter: one page of instructions and a foil-wrapped plastic stick. It certainly looked harmless enough, not like something that had the power to change her whole life.

And, of course, it didn't. Her life—or at least her relationship with Craig—had been changed by her own actions.

The attraction had been there from the beginning—

at least on Tess's part. A shy teenager, she'd developed an almost painful crush on him. But she'd kept her adolescent dreams locked deep inside and they'd become friends. Now almost fifteen years of friendship were in jeopardy because of one night of insanity.

Not that everything had changed in that one night. There had been subtle shifts in their relationship over the years—casual flirtations and occasional tensions. But they'd mostly managed to ignore those undercurrents for the sake of their friendship. Until the night they'd made love.

She'd hoped they might somehow manage to get past what had happened, but she wasn't optimistic. Not when the mere sight of his mouth brought back memories of his lips moving over her body and the most casual touch reminded her of his hands caressing her bare skin. How could they possibly resume any kind of platonic relationship when she couldn't forget that she'd been naked with him—and couldn't stop wanting to get naked with him again?

But right now the awkwardness between them was the least of her worries. More important, was deciding what she was going to do about her future. Because she didn't need the test to tell her the truth she'd been trying so hard to deny, that she'd known deep inside for almost two weeks now. And the truth was that the tiny being she carried in her womb—Craig's baby—had already taken firm hold of her heart.

But he would want the proof, so she peed on the stick and waited. And while she waited, her mind wandered and worried.

She didn't know what his thoughts and plans were

with respect to having a family—except that he'd recently broken up with the latest in a seemingly unending string of girlfriends because she'd been hinting about the future and he wasn't ready to commit to anything further than a week away. And while Tess had always dreamed of having children one day, she'd also hoped to have a husband—someone with whom to share the joys and responsibilities of raising children. After finding her fiancé in their bed with his ex-wife, she accepted that that was another dream that wouldn't be a reality. She would have this baby on her own and make whatever adjustments were necessary to her life to be the best single mother she could be.

She stared at her watch as the final seconds ticked away.

Then she took a deep breath, wiped her hands down the front of her skirt and picked up the plastic stick. According to the instructions, if there was only one line in the window, she wasn't pregnant; if there were two lines, she was.

She turned the stick over.

One.

Two.

Her knees suddenly buckled and she sank down onto the edge of the bathtub.

She was going to have a baby.

She was overwhelmed.

Terrified.

And just a little bit excited.

A baby.

Tess didn't know whether to laugh or cry, but she knew that nothing in her life would ever be the same.

* * *

How long did the damn test take?

It was the question that dogged his heels as Craig paced across the tile floor of Tess's kitchen.

There had been a whole shelf of pregnancy tests in the pharmacy and he'd read the directions on every single one, wanting to make an informed choice, to make this difficult process a little easier for both of them. As if anything could. But he was certain he'd at least picked the box that promised the quickest response.

Who knew that two minutes could seem like an eternity?

Or maybe Tess was still balking at taking the test. Maybe she wasn't ready to face the results.

He couldn't blame her for being scared. Since he'd first acknowledged the possibility that she might be pregnant with his child twenty-four hours earlier, he'd felt as though there was a vice gripping his chest—an increasing pressure that stole his breath at unexpected moments.

After the end of his brief and regrettable engagement more than a year and a half earlier, he'd been careful not to make any promises or commitments to the women he dated. He'd certainly never contemplated fathering a child with any of them. A baby was the ultimate responsibility—a lifelong commitment—and one that he had no intention of taking on. Ever.

He refused to bring an unwanted child into the world—refused to give any woman that kind of weapon to wield against him in battles about custody and access and child support. No way. He knew only too well what it was like to *be* that weapon and he'd decided the only way to ensure the same thing would never happen to any child of his own was to never have children.

So he'd always been careful about birth control, determined to protect any woman he was with as much as himself. And while he was aware that no method of contraception was one hundred percent effective, he'd never before had a condom break.

The fact that it had happened with Tess both relieved and frustrated him. He knew she didn't sleep around, so the only potential repercussion to worry about was pregnancy. But that was a huge worry, not just because he wasn't ready—and might never be ready—to be a father, but because he hated to think how an unplanned pregnancy would affect Tess's life. She was his friend, his confidante—the one woman who meant more to him than any other—and he'd failed to take care of her.

He winced at the selfishness of his own actions. He'd known immediately that something had happened, but he didn't pull out. It felt too good to be inside her, deep in the warm heat of her body. And then her legs had wrapped around him, her fingernails had dug into his shoulders and he'd been helpless to do anything but follow the urging of his body and drive them both to the finish.

He shoved his hands into his pockets as he continued to pace. The last thing he needed to be thinking about right now was making love with Tess, but as hard as he tried, he couldn't seem to banish the memories. And if he couldn't think about that night without guilt and remorse, he also couldn't forget how perfect everything had been up to that moment when he'd realized the condom had broke. He couldn't sleep without dreaming of her and then he'd wake and ache with desires.

He'd known having sex with her would change their friendship and he'd expected a certain amount of awkwardness. But he hadn't expected that he wouldn't be able to look at her without wanting to get her into his bed again.

He forced the tempting picture from his mind and glanced at his watch.

She *must* have finished the test by now.

The sound of her shoes clicking softly on the tile seconds before she stepped into view confirmed that she had.

Her eyes were wide, her cheeks white, her lips pressed tightly together.

Despite her obvious distress, he felt some of the pressure inside his chest ease. Maybe it was strange, but he'd found the not knowing worse than the truth. Now, at least they could face their future.

"We're going to have a baby," he said.

She nodded slowly.

He wanted to take her in his arms, to reassure her that they were in this together. But he suspected that she wouldn't appreciate the overture, especially since it was his desire to comfort her that had led to another kind of desire and landed them in this current predicament.

She moved past him into the kitchen and he caught a whiff of her scent, something subtly fruity and distinctly Tess. He felt the stir of desire again, immediately followed by a stab of guilt at the realization he was lusting after his best friend—the woman who was pregnant with his child.

She opened the fridge and pulled out a can of ginger ale. "Do you want one?"

"Sure," he agreed.

She passed him the can and took another out for herself, popped the top. Her hands, he noted, weren't quite steady and her complexion had taken on the slightly green tinge he recognized from last night's incident with the Pad Thai.

"Are you going to be sick?" he asked.

"I hope not." She took a long swallow of her soda. "But someone needs to fix this baby's internal clock because my supposed 'morning' sickness usually seems to strike in the evening."

"Has it been very bad?" he asked, both curious and concerned.

She shook her head. "I can't complain. I remember my sister was sick all day during the first few months of her pregnancy with Becca."

"I'm sorry, Tess."

"About what—the nausea or my pregnancy?"

"Both," he admitted.

"Don't be," she said. "Even though this wasn't planned, I want this baby."

"What can I do?"

Her smile was wry. "You've already done your part."

"As I recall, we did that part together."

"You're right." She dropped her gaze as her cheeks colored. While Tess had always been frustrated by her blushing, he'd always been fascinated by it. She was a smart, savvy professional woman, and yet the pinking of her cheeks hinted at an innocence that was surprisingly arousing and incredibly tempting.

"And we'll do the rest together," he said. "I'm not going to leave you to deal with this on your own."

"I am on my own and I can manage this pregnancy on my own."

He should have guessed that was how she'd approach this. Strong, capable, independent Tess—she didn't need anyone or anything. As she was constantly reminding him whenever he made the mistake of offering to help. Her independence was one of the things he admired about her even when it frustrated the hell out of him.

But this time, he wouldn't let her cut him out of the equation. It was, after all, his baby she was carrying and he was determined to find a solution that would work for all of them. "We could get married."

Tess stared at him, clearly stunned by his suggestion.

Okay, he was a little surprised, too. He didn't know where those words had come from, had no clue that such an idea would pop out of his mouth. But now that it had, he realized it was, in some ways, a logical response to the situation. A baby deserved to be loved and cared for by both parents, and marrying Tess would ensure that they'd both be involved in their child's life.

Since his close call with Lana, the mere thought of committing himself to any one woman for the rest of his life was enough to make him break out in hives. Yet here he was not just thinking it but saying it. Out loud.

He tugged at his tie, swallowed.

Tess seemed to recover from her shock first, because she laughed.

He frowned.

"I'm almost tempted to say 'yes'," she told him. "Just to see if your face could possibly get any whiter."

"Instinctive reaction to the M-word," he admitted.

She smiled gently. "I know."

"That's no reason to laugh off the suggestion." And now that he'd spoken the word out loud—without choking on it—he found the idea taking root in his mind.

"You're kidding, right?"

"We're going to have a baby. Why shouldn't we get married?"

"Is that a question or a proposal?" she asked. "Because if it's a question, I can give you a thousand reasons why we shouldn't get married. And if it's a proposal, the answer's no."

"A thousand reasons?" he challenged, both relieved and annoyed by her automatic refusal.

"Starting with the fact that you don't want to get married," she reminded him.

She was right. He could hardly deny it now when he'd told her exactly that when he'd broken up with Lana and repeated it numerous times since then.

The truth was, he loved women—blondes, brunettes, redheads. He loved the way they looked and the way they moved, their scents and their softness. He loved everything about them, but he'd never fallen *in* love with any of them.

Tess believed the scars from his mother's abandonment prevented him from opening his heart, and maybe there was something to that. When Charlene Richmond walked out of her husband's home she'd abandoned not just her marriage but her children. One day she was there and the next she was gone, and he'd been devastated.

She came back a few months later, claiming to want the sons she'd left behind, but Craig had already learned not to trust too easily or love too deeply.

"Maybe I've changed my mind about marriage," he said to Tess now.

She shook her head. "I need you to be my friend more than I need a husband, Craig."

"I am your friend." He took her hands in his, linked their fingers together. "That doesn't mean I can't be more."

"Anything more will only complicate the situation."

"It seems to me the situation is already complicated."

She unlaced their hands and stepped away from him.

"You could at least give it some consideration," he said.

"No," she said again.

"You're being unreasonable, Tess."

She didn't think so. Unreasonable had been going home with Craig, kissing him, touching him, falling into bed with him. Now she was facing the consequences of those impulsive actions and she was determined to do so rationally and reasonably. She'd expected that he, of all people, would appreciate a logical approach to the situation. "I don't expect anything from you, Craig."

"Why the hell not?" he demanded.

She blinked at the anger in his tone. "Because…I'm not going to hold you responsible for something that was my fault."

"Do I have to remind you again that we made this baby together?"

"You know what I mean," she said, ignoring the heat that infused her cheeks. She certainly didn't need him to remind her of the night they'd made love—the night their baby had been conceived.

"No, I don't."

She sighed. "We both know that what happened that night only happened because you were feeling sorry for me."

He placed a finger under her chin, forced her to look at him. "Do you actually believe that?"

Uh-oh. This was dangerous. The simple touch set every nerve ending in her body on full alert and the way he was looking at her now had her hormones rocketing.

She'd often thought a woman would have to be blind not to notice his obvious good looks, and Tess's almost perfect vision allowed her to fully appreciate the sun-kissed golden highlights in his dark blond hair, the deep brown eyes fringed with gloriously long lashes, the wide, full mouth that quirked easily into a grin, and the strong, square chin that held just the hint of a dimple. Then there was the body: six feet four inches of lean, solid and dangerously sexy male.

She'd known Craig since she was in junior high—he'd been in high school, an assistant coach of her baseball team and a basketball player himself. His wiry body had filled out since then. His shoulders were broader now, his muscles firmer.

But Craig Richmond was a lot more than a terrific face and gorgeous body. There was an aura about him, a confidence bordering on arrogance and the sheer force of his personality drew her even as her common sense warned her to stay far away. And now, just the touch of his hand on her chin was enough to send her pulse racing.

She knew he was waiting for an answer, but she couldn't even remember the question. God help her, he'd simply touched her and her mind had gone blank.

"Do you really think I made love to you out of pity?" he asked.

She swallowed, her throat suddenly dry. "Didn't you?"

He smiled, a slow, sexy curving of his lips that caused her heart to trip over itself. "No."

The single word skimmed over her like a caress—teasing, tempting. She forced herself to pull away from him. She couldn't afford to let her hormones overrule her common sense, not again.

"We made love that night because it was what we both wanted," he reminded her.

She closed her eyes, trying to shut out the all too vivid memories. She didn't want to remember how incredible it had been, the way she'd responded to Craig's kisses, his touch. The way their bodies had come together, naturally, instinctively, as if they'd been made for each other. Even as she'd moved beneath him, she'd been painfully aware that no one had ever made her feel the way he did, and she knew that no one else ever would. Because no one else knew her like Craig did, no one understood her as he did. And the realization terrified her.

"I threw myself at you," Tess said miserably. "I was feeling rejected and alone. I needed someone that night and you were there."

His eyes narrowed. "Don't pretend it wasn't personal, because I don't believe that for a minute. The attraction has been building for a long time—since the kiss we shared under the mistletoe last Christmas, if not longer."

"That kiss didn't mean anything," she lied.

He propped a hip against the counter and quirked a brow. "Wanna try it now—so I can prove you wrong?"

"No," she responded quickly.

His lips curved.

She crossed the room, needing to put some distance

between them. This trek down memory lane wasn't doing any good and it certainly wasn't helping to solve her current dilemma.

"Friendship and chemistry are both solid foundations for a relationship," he said. "And if we got married, our baby would have a real family."

He almost sounded like he meant it—as if he *wanted* to marry her and be a father to their child. And though she wished, more than anything, that she could give her baby a family, she couldn't do it like this. Marrying Craig for all the wrong reasons wouldn't be right for any of them.

"It's the twenty-first century," she reminded him. "Our child won't be ostracized by society because his parents never married."

She couldn't believe they were even having this conversation. All this talk about marriage and family from a man who wouldn't date any woman for more than a month in case she got ideas about commitment, was making her head spin. Obviously her pregnancy had shaken both of them.

"Can we both just take a step back?" she suggested. "Let the reality sink in before we make any definite plans for the future?"

For a moment she thought he was going to refuse, but then he asked, "How far back?"

"I don't know. I know there are a lot of decisions to be made, but I need time." She looked up at him, silently pleading with him to understand. "I don't want to screw this up. I don't want to ruin our baby's life by making bad choices."

"You won't."

"How do you know?" she asked, her words less of a challenge than a plea for reassurance. "How am I supposed to know what's the right thing to do?"

"We'll figure it out together."

"I wasn't sure—after that night…"

"What?" he prompted gently.

She just shook her head.

"Why are you so determined to forget how spectacular we were together that night?"

She looked away from the heat in his eyes and tried to ignore the answering warmth that spread through her body. Spectacular didn't begin to describe the night she'd spent in his arms. "Because remembering won't do us any good."

"Don't you think physical compatibility is important in a marriage?"

"I think you should have your head examined."

"Why won't you at least consider it?" he challenged.

"Because I still have a dress hanging in my closet as a memento of the last man who promised to love me forever."

She saw the shadows pass over his face, like clouds blocking out the sun. "I won't make you any promises I can't keep," he said. "But I will take care of you and our baby and I will be faithful."

She felt as if her heart was breaking—not just because she wanted more than he was offering, but because he believed he wasn't capable of giving more. She had faith in the healing power of love, but Craig's statement proved that the scars left by his mother's abandonment still hadn't healed and she had to wonder if they ever would. And she refused to set herself up for heartbreak by marrying someone who couldn't love her.

"We made this baby together," he continued when she didn't respond. "And we should share that responsibility. Not just for the next eight months, but forever."

Then he kissed her lightly on the cheek and walked out.

Chapter Two

Two weeks later, after the shock had worn off and he'd had time to think, Craig kept circling back to the same place. Maybe marriage and a baby weren't a lifelong dream of his, but he owed it to Tess—and their baby—to do the right thing. And as much as he racked his brain for another solution, he'd started to believe that marriage was the best one.

He wanted his baby to have a father and he wanted to help Tess, and marrying her would accomplish both of those objectives.

Which is exactly what he told her when he stopped by her office Friday afternoon.

"We should get married."

Tess turned around so quickly when he spoke that she knocked her coffee mug, spilling its contents all over the papers spread out on her desk. She swore under her breath as she moved her equipment out of the way of the spreading puddle.

As Craig hurried to the small kitchen to find a roll of paper towels, he realized he probably shouldn't have blurted it out the way he had.

His mother often teased that he had a way with words and a natural charm that could persuade anyone to do what he wanted. He'd thought Tess would appreciate a straightforward approach. The silence that stretched between them as they worked to clean up her desk caused him to question that assumption.

She didn't say anything at all until her wastebasket was filled with wet towels and illegible pages and the remaining papers had been spread out to dry.

"In the future, you might want to open a conversation with 'hello'," she suggested.

"Sorry," he said. Then he smiled. "Hello, Tess."

"Hello, Craig," she responded politely.

He dropped into the chair beside her desk. "Now that we've dealt with the social niceties, can we get to the reason I'm here?"

"Please," she agreed. "I'd like to know what's behind the sudden change in your attitude about marriage."

"The baby," he admitted. "Our baby needs a father."

She was quiet for a moment, considering his statement, then she nodded. "I don't disagree," she said. "But do you really want to be the baby's father—or do you just want to do what you've convinced yourself is the right thing?"

"I want to be a father." Parenthood wasn't something he'd ever looked forward to in the abstract sense, but now, knowing his best friend was pregnant with his child, he found it was true.

"I'm a little surprised," she admitted. "But I'm also relieved. I think our child will benefit from having both of his parents involved in his life."

"His?" he wondered aloud.

She shrugged. "I don't know yet, of course. But it doesn't seem right to refer to the baby as 'it'."

He could see her point and while he hadn't given much thought to the gender of their child, he found he liked the idea of having a son. A little boy who might grow up to take his place in the business Craig's grandfather had founded. Of course, a girl could do the same thing. And when he thought about it, he found himself intrigued by the idea of a daughter—a little angel who looked just like her mother.

"Whether the baby's a boy or a girl," he said. "I don't just want to be involved, I want to be there for him, or her, every day. I've been thinking about this since you took that test—I've hardly been able to think about anything else—and I really believe marriage is the perfect solution."

"I didn't ask you for a solution," she said.

He took a deep breath, tried to figure out what he'd said or done to put her back up. Because it was obvious to him now that her back was up about something.

"I'm only trying to help," he said.

"Just like you were helping when you took me home that night?"

She winced, and he knew she regretted the words as soon as she'd spoken, but that couldn't erase them. Nor could it alter the truth in them. She blamed him, as he blamed himself.

"I'm sorry," she said. "That was out of line."

"No," he denied. "You have every right to be mad at me. If I'd been thinking about what you needed instead of what I wanted, I would have just been your friend that night."

She managed a weak smile. "I think I was pretty clear on what I needed."

Yeah, she had been. But he should have looked beyond the invitation in her eyes, beyond the softness of her lips and the yield of her warm curves. Except that having Tess in his arms had been a dream come true and he hadn't wanted to let her go.

Her smile faded as she folded her hands on her desk and faced him solemnly. "I'm not angry with you," she said. "But maybe you should be angry with me."

"Why?"

"Because—" she hesitated, her teeth sinking into her bottom lip. "Because I'm not sure I didn't get pregnant on purpose."

He frowned. "What are you talking about?"

She looked down at the fingers laced together in front of her and took a deep breath. "You know how much I've always wanted a family of my own," she began. "Especially since my mom died. When I broke off my engagement to Roger, that dream seemed to slip away from me and that hurt more than anything else."

She swallowed. "I didn't set out to get pregnant. At least, I don't think I did. But I wonder if, subconsciously—"

"Tess," he interrupted gently. "The condom broke. It had nothing to do with your conscious or subconscious desire for a family."

She dropped her gaze again. "The condom broke because it was more than a year past its expiration date."

He stared at her, stunned, as the events of that night replayed in his mind.

He mentally fast-forwarded through all the hot, sweaty stuff to the relevant moment when he'd realized they were in the guest room and his condoms were across the hall in his bedroom. He'd intended to go to his room to get them, but Tess had surprised him by admitting there were some in her purse. Since her purse was on the dresser beside the bed—a helluva lot closer than the night table in his bedroom, which was at least thirty feet away—they'd used the ones in her purse.

The out-of-date condoms.

"I didn't know it at the time," she said quickly. "I didn't know until I checked the box when I got home."

"Why didn't you check the box before you bought them?"

Her cheeks colored. "I did. But I bought them a couple of years ago—when Roger and I first started dating. But he always took care of protection and I never really thought about it afterward."

"You've been carrying those condoms in your purse for two years?" he asked incredulously.

She shook her head. "I only opened the box a couple of months ago when I decided that I was going to prove to myself that I was over Roger. But I didn't have any need for them…until that night."

"Not until that night, huh?" He couldn't fight the smile that tugged at his lips.

Tess eyed him warily. "You're not mad?"

Maybe he should be angry, at least annoyed. But he

knew Tess, and he knew, despite her own concerns to the contrary, that she would never have gotten pregnant on purpose.

"Do you believe in fate?" he asked.

Her expression grew more wary. "I'm not sure."

"I'm not sure, either," he admitted. "But I can't help thinking that fate has been sticking her nose into things since you broke mine."

"That wasn't fate," she scoffed. "That was *you* staring at Barb MacIntyre instead of paying attention to the baseball game."

His smile widened. "I was fifteen and Barb MacIntyre had breasts."

Tess shook her head, but she was smiling now, too. "You should have been paying attention to the skinny kid with the bat."

"I'd never known a girl who could smack a line drive like that," he told her, wincing a little at the memory. But he'd sure as hell paid attention after that. Not just because he'd been impressed by Tess's athletic abilities, but because something in her wide blue eyes had tugged at him when she stood over him—as he'd lain bleeding all over the dirt at third base—and asked if he was going to die, too.

Several weeks later, he'd learned that was the same day she'd buried her mother—and been taken directly from the funeral to her new foster home. She was a fourteen-year-old orphan with more guts and attitude than he'd ever seen, but he recognized that the stubborn tilt of her chin and the angry glint in her eyes only masked the pain she carried inside. And he knew—even then—that she would wreak havoc on his life.

What he didn't know and couldn't have guessed, was that she'd also become the best friend he'd ever had.

He rubbed a finger over the bump on the bridge of his nose.

Tess's eyes followed the motion and the corners of her mouth twitched as she tried, not entirely successfully, to hold back a smile.

"You're not still mad about that, are you?" she teased.

He shook his head. "That broken nose was one of the best things that ever happened to me. I didn't think so at the time, of course," he confessed. "But in retrospect, I can appreciate that it's the reason we became friends."

"What does any of that have to do with now?"

"I think in another fifteen years we'll look back on this and realize your pregnancy was the best thing that could have happened."

"I already know it is," she confessed softly.

"Then why is it so hard for you to imagine that us getting married could be another one of those things?"

He didn't quite manage to disguise the impatience in his voice, and Tess sighed.

"It's not that I can't imagine it," she admitted.

In fact, it was almost too easy to picture herself married to Craig, sharing the joys and responsibilities of parenthood with him, building the family she'd always wanted with him.

But although her heart yearned for the whole fairytale package, she knew it could never exist outside of her dreams. Because he wasn't her Prince Charming and her pregnancy wasn't something they'd planned for or dreamed about together. As far as she knew, Craig didn't even want kids—it was just his deeply-ingrained sense of responsibility that refused to let him walk away from their baby.

"Then what is it?" he demanded.

She didn't know what to say, how to explain the battle that had been waging inside her since she'd seen those two lines on the stick. She could do what was easy—or she could do what was right. And she really wanted to do what was right.

The buzz of the intercom saved her from answering, at least for now.

"Carl's on line three," Elaine, the receptionist, announced.

Carl Bloom was one of the owners of SB Graphics and, therefore, one of Tess's bosses. Which meant she needed to get Craig out of her office and her mind back on the job.

"Thanks," Tess replied. Then to Craig, she said, "I have to take this call."

"I can wait," he said.

"I'd rather you didn't. This is probably going to take a while and I have a meeting with Owen Sanderson—" Carl's business partner and her other boss "—later this afternoon that I still need to prepare for."

"We need to finish this conversation," he said.

"I know," she agreed. "But not now."

"Then come to my place tonight for dinner."

She stared at the blinking light on her phone as she considered his invitation, the light flashing like a neon "danger" sign inside her head. But what was the danger in sharing a meal with a friend?

"Okay," she agreed. "I'll see you later for dinner."

"Seven o'clock," Craig said as he rose from his chair.

"I've got steaks we can barbecue—red meat has lots of iron, it'll be good for both you and the baby."

She shook her head as he walked out the door.

When she'd first suspected she might be pregnant, she'd worried about telling Craig. She'd tried to anticipate his reaction and had guessed that he would either balk at the idea of being a father and slowly but inexorably distance himself from her and the child she carried, or he would resign himself to the consequences of their actions and fulfill his responsibilities with respect to child support and weekly visitation. She hadn't expected him to embrace the idea of parenthood.

Then again, the idea might be easier for him to embrace than the reality. Once their child was born, he might change his mind about what he wanted.

Or he might not, she admitted on a sigh. And that was an even greater concern for Tess, because she'd never known Craig to give up on something he really wanted.

She pushed these disquieting thoughts aside and reached for the phone to talk to her boss.

The software program Tess was revising was being especially stubborn, and the last couple hours of fighting with it had caused her hands to cramp from too much keyboarding. She raised her arms over her head to stretch out the tight muscles and glanced at the clock above her desk, surprised to note that it was already quarter to seven. She was supposed to be at Craig's for dinner in fifteen minutes.

She saved the program, then shut down her computer and called to let him know she'd be there soon.

Making a quick trip to the ladies room, she wasn't surprised to find that all her coworkers had gone and the outer office was empty and dark. When she'd first graduated from DeVry University, she'd accepted a position at a huge software company in Arizona. She'd enjoyed her work there, but the hours had been long, her bosses demanding. She'd come back to Pinehurst even knowing that her chances of landing a job as a programmer were less than slim because she'd wanted to have a life outside of her work and because she'd wanted to be closer to her stepsister's family and Craig. She'd been thrilled—and very lucky—to find SB Graphics.

SBG was a digital animation software company which had been started almost twenty years earlier by Owen Sanderson and Carl Bloom, both MIT graduates. Although the partners had talked about moving the business to Los Angeles, they'd come to realize they could compete with the big corporations on the west coast from their location in Pinehurst.

They were both family men who not only appreciated that their employees had lives outside of the job but insisted upon it. In fact, when Deanna, one of the team leaders, had given birth to her first child last year, the bosses had encouraged her to take whatever time she needed at home with her baby. Then, when she'd made the decision to come back, they'd let her work from home or bring the baby into the office as required when day care was a problem.

Tess hadn't thought about it much at the time, but now that she was expecting a child of her own, it was a huge relief to know that her employers understood and were sympathetic to the demands of parenthood. She could only hope that the father-to-be would be as considerate and accommodating of her needs.

We should get married.

As if the words hadn't been surprising enough, the conviction with which he'd spoken them had completely unsettled her. She knew, probably better than anyone, how unyielding Craig could be once he'd made up his mind about something. For some reason, he'd decided marriage was what he wanted. Now she was going to have to convince him there were other alternatives.

She ran a brush through her hair then slipped into her blazer. Maybe if she looked like a together, professional woman she would feel like a together, professional woman when she and Craig discussed their baby's future. Maybe he would actually listen to her when she offered a more suitable—more reasonable—solution.

She sighed as she zipped her purse. Yeah, and maybe she'd go to bed tonight and wake up to find it was the day after her canceled wedding and she was alone in Craig's guest room because nothing had happened between them the night before. Except that she wouldn't really wish that night away even if she could. She might not be looking forward to doing battle with Craig about what was best for their baby, but she wanted this baby. More than anything, she wanted this baby because it meant she would never be alone again.

Her stomach growled, loudly protesting that it had been ignored since it rejected the chicken salad sandwich she'd had for lunch several hours earlier. As she made her way down the hall, her mouth watering in anticipation of the juicy steak Craig had promised her, she noticed the light on in Owen's office.

She knocked before peeking around the partially open door. "I was just on my— Oh," she halted her explanation when she realized Owen wasn't behind his desk and another man was in his office. "I'm sorry. I thought you were Mr. Sanderson."

"Jared McCabe," he said, rising to his feet and offering his hand.

"Tess Lucas," she told him, moving forward to take it and wondering, as she did so, why his name sounded familiar to her.

His gaze narrowed speculatively. "You were the team leader on version four of DirectorPlus."

DP4 was an easy-to-use software interface utilized by animation directors to control background characters in movies and video games. She nodded in response to his statement even as she wondered how he knew she'd worked on the project—and why she couldn't make such an easy connection with his name.

"It's a terrific program," he said.

"Are you a customer of SB Graphics?"

He smiled. "Potentially."

"Then you'll be interested to know that version five is going to be even better," she promised him.

"I'm counting on it."

His comment struck her as strange but before she could ask what he meant, Owen stepped into the room.

"Jared, I found—" He stopped in mid-sentence, obviously surprised to see her. "Tess, I didn't realize you were still here."

"I was just on my way out and saw your light on," she said, suddenly feeling uneasy.

"Tess is always the first one in and the last to leave,"

Owen told Jared. "And not just a dedicated worker but an incredibly talented one."

While Tess appreciated the words of praise, she couldn't help but wonder why her boss thought Jared McCabe would care about her work habits. But now wasn't the time for her to ask that question, so she only said, "I didn't mean to interrupt." Then, to Jared, "It was nice meeting you, Mr. McCabe."

He smiled again. "It was my pleasure, Ms. Lucas."

"Enjoy your weekend," Owen said.

Tess nodded, her mind swirling with questions about the mysterious Mr. McCabe. Then she thought about her upcoming dinner with Craig and remembered she had bigger issues to worry about.

Chapter Three

It was after seven-thirty by the time Tess pulled into the visitor parking lot of Craig's building but she stayed in her car a few more minutes, psyching herself for the next round with him. She hated the awkwardness between them—hated feeling edgy, irritable, confused. But she knew that wasn't likely to change until they'd come to an agreement about her pregnancy and his role in their baby's life.

She also knew that if she was to have any chance of talking Craig out of this crazy marriage idea, she would have to stay calm and focused. She could admit that marriage was an option, but she needed to convince him that there were compelling reasons to disregard that option.

Friendship and chemistry are both solid foundations for a relationship.

She shook her head trying to block out the echo of his words in her mind.

And if we got married, our baby would have a family.

A family was the one thing she'd always wanted and the greatest gift she knew she could give to her child. And Craig knew her well enough to know it was the most tempting thing he could offer.

But if she gave in to temptation, what would it cost? What would a marriage of convenience do to their friendship? How could she risk the solid relationship they had for the illusion of something more?

Tess pushed aside the questions along with her trepidation as she climbed out of the car. She'd asked him to be her friend—she needed to remember that he was the best friend she had and not do anything to screw that up.

She greeted the doorman by name as she made her through the lobby. Nigel responded with a smile and a wave, reaching for the phone to call Craig's apartment and let him know she was on her way up.

Craig opened the door just as she stepped off the elevator.

"Sorry, I'm later than I expected to be," she said. "I got caught up with Owen as I was on my way out." She considered mentioning the odd encounter with the stranger but decided that could wait until later.

"Not a problem," he said. "I'm a little behind schedule myself because of an impromptu visit from my mother."

"I'm sorry I missed her," Tess said, kicking off her shoes inside the entrance before following him into the kitchen.

"No, you're not."

She frowned.

"Long story," he said. "And right now I'm going to put the grill on so we can eat soon."

"Can I help you with anything?" she asked.

"You can throw the salad together if you want." He gestured to the ingredients on the counter.

"Okay." She washed the lettuce and began tearing it into pieces. She'd really hoped that having dinner with Craig tonight would be a step toward getting their relationship back on track, toward the resumption of their friendship. But she couldn't deny that being alone with him here—for the first time since the night their baby had been conceived—filled her with foreboding.

Truthfully, she was more afraid of her own reactions to him than anything he might say or do. Ever since the night they'd spent together, every little touch sent tingles of awareness through her veins. Even the briefest contact taunted her with the recollection of how it felt to *really* be touched by him.

She forced the memories aside and began slicing the cucumber with a vengeance. Craig came into the kitchen, picked up the plate of steaks. As he moved past her, she caught the scent of his aftershave. Once familiar and comforting, it was suddenly new and arousing. She brought the knife down hard, as if the action could sever her wayward thoughts—and cut her finger instead.

"Damn!" She stuck her finger in her mouth to staunch the flow of blood.

He set the plate back on the counter with a clatter. "Are you all right?"

He grabbed her wrist, his fingers strong and firm as he tugged her hand away from her mouth. With his other hand, he turned on the faucet and shoved her finger under the stream of cool water.

"I'm fine," she said, her voice strangely breathy. He was standing close, so close she could feel the heat emanating from his body. Too close.

He moved her hand out of the water to inspect the cut. It was still bleeding, but it wasn't very deep.

"Keep it under the water," he said. "I'll get a Band-Aid."

She did as he requested, too shaken to do anything else.

Craig was her best friend—she shouldn't be indulging in sexual daydreams with him cast in the starring role. But maybe the erotic images that haunted her were a result of the hormonal changes of pregnancy. Yes, that made sense. Once she had this baby, her relationship with Craig would settle back to normal. The next eight months might be a challenge, but she was confident she could get through them knowing that this fierce attraction was a temporary phenomenon.

Craig returned with a tube of antibacterial ointment and a Band-Aid, and she breathed in his scent again. He tore a paper towel off the roll and carefully dried her hand. Her finger, almost numb from the cold water, was infused with heat by the simple touch. Damn, it was going to be a long eight months.

"Okay?" he asked.

She nodded, then glanced up. And saw the awareness she felt reflected in the depths of his brown eyes. If this attraction was a temporary phenomenon, apparently it was affecting him, too.

But then he tore his gaze away from her to pick up the tube of cream and she managed to breathe again. His motions were brisk, efficient and so completely impersonal Tess wondered if she'd imagined the sizzle in the air between them.

He wrapped the Band-Aid around her finger. "There you go."

She swallowed. "Th-thank you."

"I'm going to put the steaks on." His smile seemed strained. "Try not to cut off any appendages while I'm gone."

Craig flipped the meat on the grill, listened to the sizzle and pop as the marinade dripped onto the hot coals. It reminded him of the heat that had flared between him and Tess when he'd touched her. He'd tried to keep the contact casual, impersonal, but the skin of her hand was soft in his and the scent of her hair tantalized his senses. And as he'd leaned over her by the sink administering first aid to her bleeding finger, he couldn't help but notice how the soft fabric of her blouse molded to the curve of her breasts. And he couldn't help but remember how those breasts had filled his palms, how she'd moaned in pleasure as he'd caressed them, with his hands, with his lips.

He breathed deeply of the cool night air as he willed the haunting images away. Tess would hardly be impressed if she knew about his prurient fantasies.

He was supposed to be her friend—and he had been, for fifteen years. There had been times in recent years that he'd wondered whether there could be anything more between them, but he'd always discarded the thought. He valued her friendship and he didn't want to do anything to risk it. No matter how many times he'd wondered what it would be like to touch her, to kiss her, and not like a friend.

Now he knew—and he knew that being friends wasn't enough anymore.

It was a huge leap from one night together to marriage, and he knew it wasn't a commitment he'd be considering now except for the fact of Tess's pregnancy. But instead of feeling trapped by the circumstances, he felt as if he'd been given an incredible opportunity. If only he could find a way to convince Tess of that fact.

He kept the conversation light and casual during dinner, and she finally seemed to relax a little. At least until he inadvertently brushed his knee against her thigh under the table. Then she jerked away as if he'd stabbed her with his steak knife, and he accepted that easing the tension between them wasn't going to be that simple.

"I've got Chunky Monkey for dessert," he said.

She loaded the dishwasher while he scooped her favorite ice cream into bowls. When he was finished, he decided that it was time to get to the purpose of her visit.

"You know that I wanted you to come over tonight so we could finish talking about my proposal."

Tess took the bowl he handed to her, passed him a spoon she'd taken out of the cutlery drawer. "I don't recall hearing an actual proposal."

Craig followed her to the table, enjoying the gentle sway of her hips as she moved. Then her response registered and he frowned. "What do you mean?"

She dipped her spoon into the ice cream. "You didn't ask me to marry you. You said we should get married."

He watched her lips close around the spoon, heard her soft hum of pleasure as she tasted the ice cream. He shoved a spoonful into his own mouth, hoping that the cold substance would help alleviate the heat raging through his system. It didn't work.

"I asked," he said.

"No, you didn't. You never ask," she continued. "You just assume you'll get what you want."

"I do not," he protested indignantly.

"Yes, you do. Because nobody ever says no to Craig Richmond."

As he scooped up some more ice cream, he realized she might be right. As Vice President in charge of Research and Development at Richmond Pharmaceuticals, he held a position of power and he knew how to wield that power effectively, but he'd never realized that his professional demeanor carried over to his private life.

Was that why she'd turned him down, because he hadn't asked?

He swallowed another mouthful of ice cream. "All right. Tess, will you marry me?"

She smiled but shook her head. "No."

"No?" So much for her theory that no one ever said no to him.

"I didn't refuse your so-called proposal because it wasn't in the form of a question," she told him. "I refused because my pregnancy isn't a good enough reason for us to get married."

Tess swirled her spoon in her ice cream, then licked the back of it. And he nearly groaned aloud at the erotic images the action evoked.

"I would never deny you access to our child," she said, drawing his attention back to the topic of conversation. "And I'm not going to marry a man I don't love and who doesn't love me just so my child will have a family when we can accomplish the same thing by sharing custody."

"I don't want to be a weekend dad." He couldn't stand the thought of his child being shuffled between households, never feeling as if he truly had a home, somewhere that he belonged. He didn't want his child to grow up thinking his father didn't want to be part of his life. He scrubbed a hand through his hair. "Why can't you accept that this is important to me?"

"Why can't you accept that I don't want to get married?"

"Because you were addressing wedding invitations not six months ago," he pointed out.

"That was different," she told him.

"Because you thought you were in love with Roger?"

"Maybe I was wrong about him, but that doesn't mean I'm willing to give up my dreams and settle for a loveless marriage."

He pushed his empty bowl aside. "Did you ever tell your fiancé that you spent four years of your life in foster care?"

She frowned. "What does that have to do with anything?"

"It doesn't change the fact that he was cheating scum and he didn't deserve you," he told her. "But I have to wonder if the relationship wasn't doomed anyway because you didn't let him see who you really are."

"Four years in foster care didn't make me who I am."

"A friend once told me that everything we experience in life—the good and the bad—helps to make us the people we are."

She shrugged, unable to argue against her own words. "Do you have a point?"

"Did he know about the foster homes?" he asked again. "Did he know how your mother died? How completely alone you felt when you realized her death made you an orphan? Did he know how much you looked forward to the monthly visits you were allowed with your stepsister, because she was the only family you had left?" He shook his head, then answered his own questions. "Of course he didn't know because you never told him."

"I didn't think it was relevant," she said.

"Or maybe you're more wary of commitment than I am. You say you're holding out for love, but maybe that's just an excuse to be alone because you're too afraid of being hurt again to let anyone get that close."

"I didn't know you got a psych degree along with your MBA."

The dripping sarcasm in her voice proved that he'd made his point. He only regretted that he'd hurt her in the process.

"I don't need a pysch degree because I know you," he reminded her gently.

She sighed. "Okay. Maybe you're right. Maybe I'm as much a coward as you are a commitment-phobe. Which suggests to me that a marriage between us would be doomed from the start."

"Except that we're also both stubborn and determined," he reminded her. "If we wanted to, we could make it work."

She set the spoon down, looked up at him and he saw the conviction in her deep blue eyes. "I remember what kind of marriage my parents had, how much they loved each other. I was only eight when my dad died but I remember how happy they were together.

"When my mother married Ken, I knew right away it was different. She was on her own with me, he was on his own with Laurie. They married to give us—me and Laurie—a family, but neither of them was ever really happy."

"That doesn't mean we couldn't be," he persisted.

"If I get married, I want it to be because someone wants to be with *me*, not because I'm carrying his child."

"I do want to be with you, Tess. I want us both to be there for our baby. I don't know how this love thing works. I'm not even sure I believe it exists—not love of the happily-ever-after variety, anyway. But I want this baby to know he has two parents who will always be there for him, and the best way to ensure that is by getting married."

She placed a hand over her chest. "I think that's the most romantic proposal I've heard yet."

He felt the frustration building inside him. "Is that what you want—romance?" he demanded. "Would it make a difference if I filled the room with flowers and soft music and candlelight?"

"No," she said again and shook her head. "Nothing is going to make a difference because we both know it would be worse for our child to live in a loveless home than to have two parents who never married."

"We could make a marriage work, Tess."

"Do you really want to take that chance? Do you want our child to find himself in the middle of a custody battle if it doesn't?"

"No, I don't," he admitted, understanding that she

was only thinking about what he and his brother had gone through. "But that wouldn't happen because we would always do what was best for our child."

"That's why I want to work out the details of custody and access now."

"I don't want access," he said stubbornly. "I want my child to know he's an important part of my life every day, not just on alternate weekends."

"Is this about Charlene walking out on you?"

She never referred to the woman who'd given birth to him as his mother, because she felt—as he did—that Grace, his father's second wife, was more of a mother to him than Charlene had ever been.

"This is about you and me and our baby," he insisted.

But Tess—being Tess—didn't accept his denial. She reached across the table and laid her hand on top of his.

"Charlene couldn't handle the responsibility of having children," she said. "But you've made it clear that you want to be a part of our baby's life, and I would never stand in the way of that."

He turned his hand over, laced his fingers with hers. Her hand was so small inside his and yet he drew comfort and strength from her presence, gained a measure of peace from her understanding. She knew him better than anyone, she understood his hopes and fears and she was always there for him. It was the kind of unconditional acceptance he'd never been sure of with any other woman, and yet another reason he believed they would make a marriage work.

But she was holding out for love, and as much as he cared about her, that wasn't something he could give her. If he could love anyone, he wanted to believe it would be Tess. But he didn't have it in him. And he wouldn't lie to her—he wouldn't use the words she wanted to hear to get what he wanted. Or maybe he just knew better than to even try because Tess would see right through him.

She gave his hand a reassuring squeeze. "You're going to be a wonderful daddy, Craig."

"Don't you mean part-time daddy?" He hated to think about missing a single day of his child's life. He'd been five years old when his parents split up, but he remembered the feeling of loss, the sense of rejection when his mother walked out on them.

It had been months later before Charlene Richmond had decided she wanted to share custody of her children—or maybe she finally realized that by having them live with her part-time, she could get significant financial support from her husband. And the next few years had been a constant shuffle from one house to the other for Craig and his brother, Gage, the only consistent presence in their life being the nanny their father had hired and who accompanied them from place to place. Because as much as Charlene claimed she wanted to spend time with her sons, she was content to let the nanny deal with their day-to-day needs and, in fact, rarely interacted with them during their visits.

Then, one day when they showed up, she just wasn't there. All she'd left was a note saying that she was getting married and moving out of the country and was, therefore, relinquishing full custody to the boys' father.

At first, Craig had been relieved—the fighting would finally stop and he and Gage would finally be able to settle in one place. But the relief had soon been replaced by a niggling fear that his father might decide to go away, too. That no one loved him enough to stand by him.

He wouldn't let his child feel the same way.

As much as Tess understood Craig's reasons for wanting to get married, she wasn't willing to sacrifice what was left of their friendship and give up her own dreams for a marriage of convenience she believed was destined to fail.

But when he looked at her as he was looking at her now, with such intensity and determination, she could feel her resolve weakening. Then he stroked his thumb over her skin and she felt a frisson of awareness skate up her arm and warmth spread through her body.

She tried to pull her hand away, knowing that if she had any hopes of maintaining a clear perspective on things, she couldn't allow him to touch her. But Craig held firm.

"I've tried not to pressure you—"

She almost laughed at the absurdity of the statement as she felt the pressure closing in on her from all sides.

"—but you can't keep your pregnancy a secret forever. Let's go away somewhere and get married before the speculation begins."

And despite all her reasoning and common sense she actually found herself tempted by the idea. Because the thought of having this baby on her own, of being—if not solely, at least primarily—responsible for its happiness and well-being, terrified her. But she'd never been the type to balk at a challenge or take the easy way out and she wasn't going to do so now just because she was scared.

She carefully withdrew her hand from his grasp. "I can't marry you, Craig."

"Think about this logically," he said. "We've known each other for years. What we have between us—friendship, trust, respect—they're more important than love. And more enduring. There's no reason for a marriage between us not to work."

She didn't buy his argument. Yes, friendship, trust and respect were important, but she wouldn't enter into a marriage without love. "Look at your parents. Your dad and Grace," she amended. "It's obvious to anyone who sees them together that they love one another. Do you really want to settle for less than that?"

"I would never think of marrying you as settling," he said.

He sounded so sincere and was looking at her with such earnestness in his dark eyes that Tess almost believed him. In her heart, she wanted to believe him. But her disastrous experience with Roger had made her wary. And while she'd known Craig a lot longer than she'd known Roger, so much had changed between them in the last few weeks that she wasn't sure she really knew him at all anymore.

At work she was a confident, competent professional but that was because she'd spent years studying manuals and mastering computer code. There was no such training to succeed at relationships and she felt at a distinct disadvantage when it came to the games that men and women played.

Craig, on the other hand, had dated more women than she could count—beautiful, sophisticated women. He would never be happy with someone like her and she'd be deluding herself if she believed otherwise for a single moment.

Tess sighed and pushed away from the table. She crossed over to the window, looked out at the brilliant array of stars scattered across the sky. No, there was no way she could marry Craig.

"You might not think of it that way now," she said. "But you'd eventually start to resent me, and the baby, for putting you in this position."

And for Tess, the thought of losing Craig's friendship and support was far worse than the prospect of raising a child on her own.

He didn't say anything for a minute and she let herself hope he was actually considering what she'd said. She didn't hear him leave the table, wasn't aware that he was behind her until he put his hands on her shoulders and gently turned her around to face him.

She met his gaze evenly, almost defiantly. She knew him well enough to know that he wasn't easily dissuaded from something he wanted, but she could be equally stubborn. And there was no way she was going to further jeopardize their friendship by marrying him. Her mom and Ken had been friends before they married and they'd had nothing left when their marriage had fallen apart. Tess refused to let that happen. Craig could use whatever arguments he wanted, she wasn't going to change her mind.

But his response wasn't at all what she expected. He didn't argue or plead or use any of the other tactics she was confident she could handle. Instead, he lowered his head and he kissed her.

At first, she was too stunned to react. And then, as

his lips continued to move over hers, soft but firm, strong yet coaxing, she simply melted.

He slid his fingers into her hair and tipped her head back to deepen the kiss. She opened for him willingly, all thoughts of resistance gone. Whether it was the pregnancy hormones running rampant through her system or her new awareness of Craig as a man, she had no desire to be anywhere but in his arms.

She shivered as his fingers massaged her scalp, moaned as his tongue tangled with hers. Somewhere, in the back recesses of her mind, she knew she should end this kiss. She shouldn't allow this to happen but she was powerless to stop the desire that flowed hot and thick through her system. She wanted this—she wanted Craig—more than she'd ever thought possible.

He stroked his hands down her back, tugged the blouse from the waistband of her slacks, and she trembled with anticipation. Then his hands were on her skin and she could no longer think. She could only feel and she loved the way it felt to be touched by him, to touch him. She ran her hands up his chest, found the buttons at the front of his shirt and quickly worked them free.

He slid an arm behind her knees and scooped her up, cradling her against his chest as his lips continued their sensual assault. She'd never been swept off her feet before—literally or figuratively—and if she let herself think about it she might worry that Craig was her first on both counts and that it felt so completely right.

He carried her into the living room, laid her down gently on the soft leather sofa and levered himself down beside her. Their bodies were aligned, their legs entwined, on the narrow couch. She could feel the evidence of his arousal against her belly and wriggled her hips to position him between her thighs.

Her blouse was undone now, too, and he slid the garment over her shoulders, letting it drop to the ground. Then he shifted their bodies so that she was lying beneath him and dipped his head to nuzzle her throat, the scrape of his jaw against her tender skin sending deliciously erotic tingles through her body.

His lips moved lower, caressing the swell of her breasts above the lacy cups of her bra. She felt her nipples tighten, the heat spread through her body. As if in response to an unspoken request, he flicked his tongue over the aching peak, then closed his teeth over the thin fabric. Tess gasped and thrust her hips upward. Impatiently Craig pushed the strap off her shoulder and took her nipple in his mouth. He manipulated the peak, tasting, teasing, then he suckled hard on the breast, thrusting it against the roof of his mouth with his tongue. She bit down on her lip to keep from crying out as she rocked her hips against him, aching for the fulfillment of his lovemaking.

"Let me make love with you, Tess."

His words paralleled her thoughts, proving they were—if at odds over everything else—at least in synch in their desire for one another.

She gripped his shoulders with trembling hands. "Yes."

He undid the button of her slacks, slid the zipper down. His fingers found the wet heat inside her and she almost flew apart right then.

"Let me remind you how good we are together," he whispered the words against her lips as his hands continued to tease and torment her. "Let me show you how wonderful it would be to make love every night if we got married."

It took a minute for his words to penetrate through the fog that surrounded Tess's brain. When they did, the heat flowing through her veins suddenly chilled.

"What…" She had to pause for breath, forced herself to ignore the traitorous demands of her body that insisted his words didn't matter. "What did you say?"

He leaned forward again and brushed his lips against hers, softly coaxing. "I said I want to make love with you."

She wanted to melt against him, to lean into the kiss, to go back to where she'd been before she'd heard the words that had doused her own desire more effectively than an icy rain. "Why?"

He smiled, that slow, sexy smile that made her insides all trembly and weak. "I thought that was obvious."

"Is it?" She felt her cheeks flush but wouldn't allow herself to be distracted by his easy charm. Not again.

Instead, she pushed herself up and scrambled off of the couch. She found her discarded top and shoved her arms through the sleeves, turning her back on him to fasten the buttons and zip up her slacks. It wasn't about modesty so much as hiding the hurt she was afraid he'd see in her eyes when she spoke her next words. "Or was this part of your plan to convince me to marry you?"

She heard him sigh. "I didn't plan this at all, Tess, things just got out of control. But to be perfectly honest, I think the attraction between us is further proof that our marriage would succeed."

She turned back to him, confident that any residual hurt would be shrouded by the anger that was beginning to boil inside her. "We should get married because we're good in bed together?"

He stood up and took a step toward her. "We're a lot better than good, but that's only one factor."

"That's what this was to you?" She impatiently brushed away the tears that spilled onto her cheeks. "A factor?"

"Of course not," he denied.

But she knew him well enough to recognize the guilt that flickered in his eyes. Tess straightened her shirt.

"Go to hell, and take your proposal with you."

Chapter Four

Tess wasn't really surprised that she didn't hear from Craig through the following week, but she was sorry. He'd been the one person she'd always felt she could count on and she'd screwed it up by, well, screwing him. It was crude but true. Have sex with a guy once and it changed *everything.* And now, when she needed his support more than ever, he was conspicuously absent from her life.

More than a month had passed since she'd taken the home pregnancy test and though she'd scheduled her first prenatal appointment, she still didn't know what was the best thing to do for her baby. What she did know was that she'd drive herself insane if she continued to stare at the same four walls inside her apartment. So Saturday morning, with no destination in mind, she climbed in her Saturn coupe and drove. When she found herself in the west end of town, she decided to drop in on her sister.

Technically, Laurie was Tess's stepsister but neither of them had any biological siblings and the relationship they'd developed over the years was as strong as any made by blood. Although the marriage between their respective parents hadn't worked out, the girls had stayed in touch after the divorce. Laurie was the only other person Tess could imagine confiding in about her current situation, and right now she desperately needed to confide in someone.

"It's not even 10:00 a.m.," Laurie complained as she pulled open the front door.

Tess held up the tray of coffee and the box of doughnuts. "I brought breakfast."

Laurie stepped away from the door and Tess followed her into the kitchen. She set the doughnuts and coffee on the table, then scooped ten-week-old Devin out of his infant carrier. She always loved spending time with her sister's kids, had always dreamed of having a baby of her own someday. Now that day was on the horizon.

"I can't believe how much he's grown." Her voice was filled with awe as she stared at the chubby infant cradled in her arms.

Laurie smiled. "He's gained five pounds already."

"Is that normal?" she asked, struck once again by how little she knew about babies, how much she needed to learn.

"The doctor likes to see newborns gain at least a pound a month, so he's a little ahead of schedule."

She brushed a kiss on the soft, downy head, breathed in his soft, baby scent. "Already an overachiever, aren't you?"

The baby, of course, didn't respond.

But then his big sister wandered into the kitchen.

"Juice, mommy." Two-year-old Becca waved a plastic cup at her mother.

"Please," Laurie told her, taking the cup.

Becca shook her head no. "Ap-ple."

Tess smiled as the child's mother shook her head.

"She doesn't quite understand 'please' and 'thank you' yet," Laurie explained as she took the juice from the refrigerator and refilled the cup. Becca took the cup back to the living room where she'd been playing with the building blocks scattered across the carpet.

"What does Becca think of her little brother?" Tess asked.

"It varies from day to day, although usually she just ignores him. Once he's big enough to actually play with, I suspect that will change." Laurie sat down on the other side of the table and took one of the paper cups from the tray. She removed the lid and smiled as she inhaled deeply. "Cappuccino. I guess I'll have to forgive you for arriving before noon."

"I am sorry for dropping by without calling first," she apologized. "But I really need to talk to you about something."

Her sister waved off the apology. "You know you're always welcome—and I'm always starved for adult conversation."

Tess managed a smile as she stroked a hand lightly over Devin's soft, downy head. He'd already settled against her breast and was sleeping soundly. In less than eight months, she'd be able to cradle her own baby this way. The realization filled her with a strange sort of longing and almost none of the panic she'd learned to expect since her pregnancy was confirmed. "Where's Dave?"

"Grocery shopping." Laurie passed the other cup of coffee to her. "He won't be back for at least half an hour. Now stop procrastinating and tell me what's up."

"I'm pregnant."

Her sister choked on a mouthful of coffee, sputtered. "Pregnant?"

Tess nodded.

Laurie considered the revelation for a long moment before she said, "I didn't realize you'd been dating anyone...since Roger."

"I wasn't. I'm not." She felt her cheeks burn. "It's Craig's baby."

"Craig Richmond?"

"Yeah."

Laurie took a cautious sip of her cappuccino. "Well, this is an interesting development."

"*Interesting* is one word for it," Tess agreed dryly. "*Insanity* is another."

"And I thought you were insane for not going after him years ago," her sister teased.

Tess frowned; Laurie grinned.

"So what was the cause of this insanity?" she asked, reaching into the box for a chocolate doughnut.

"The wedding that didn't happen." Tess bit into her jelly-filled and chewed as she considered how to explain something she wasn't entirely sure she understood herself. "I thought Roger was the one," she said softly. "I thought I'd finally met the man with whom I'd spend the rest of my life. That we'd get married and have children and—well, you know that story."

"Actually, I never understood what you saw in that guy," Laurie said.

"I thought you liked him."

Her sister shrugged. "I wanted *you* to be happy."

She sighed. "Instead, on the night that should have been my wedding night, I ended up at a bar having a few drinks." She looked away, embarrassed by the recklessness of her behavior. "And then a good-looking guy sat beside me at the bar and asked me to dance and I was feeling lonely enough to accept his invitation."

"And?"

"And we danced." She took another bite of her doughnut. "And he was starting to hint that he wanted to do a whole lot more when Craig came into the bar. He told me later that he saw my car in the parking lot and was worried about me. My fault, I guess, for picking a bar on his side of town." And she wondered now whether that had been mere coincidence or a subconscious choice. "Anyway, he took me home."

"I can't believe Craig would take advantage of you in that situation," she said indignantly.

"He wouldn't. He didn't. He only wanted to take me home." Devin stirred in his sleep, and Tess gently rubbed his back until he settled again. "But I didn't want to go home. I didn't want to be alone."

"So he took you back to his place," Laurie guessed.

"He held me while I cried." She picked up her coffee again. "And then he kissed me."

Laurie waited, obviously expecting more of an explanation, but Tess had no intention of traveling any farther down memory lane. Not when the events of that night still haunted her dreams.

"Kissing doesn't make babies," Laurie said at last.

Tess managed a smile. "No, but since you've had two of your own, I didn't figure you needed a complete play-by-play."

"Not all the details—but I get the feeling you're holding something back."

She sighed a little wistfully. "Just that it was the single most incredible experience of my life. Never in a million years would I have imagined that sex could be so…so…everything."

"It is when it's with the right person," her sister agreed.

"He's not the right person," Tess denied. "Not for me."

"Why not?"

"Because we're friends."

"Obviously a little more than friends," Laurie commented.

Tess ignored the sarcasm and concentrated on finishing her doughnut.

"What did Craig say about the baby?"

She wiped the powdered sugar off her fingers with a paper napkin. "He offered to marry me."

Her sister smiled. "When's the wedding?"

Tess scowled. "What makes you think I'd say yes?"

"Because you'd have to be crazy not to. He's a wonderful man—gorgeous and sexy, smart and rich. You've had phenomenal sex together and he's your best friend. Most marriages don't start out with so much going for them."

"But he only offered to marry me because I'm pregnant."

"Which shows that he's also responsible and honorable."

"I *can't* marry him," Tess insisted.

"Why not?"

"Because I recently escaped one near-matrimonial disaster and am not particularly anxious to rush into another."

"What makes you think that marriage to Craig would be a disaster?"

"Because he doesn't deserve to be trapped into a marriage he doesn't really want and because I don't need a husband to have this baby."

Devin stirred again and brought his fist to his mouth to suck on it.

"Maybe you don't need a husband," Laurie admitted after a long pause. "But having grown up without a father yourself, don't you want one for your child?"

She sighed; her sister always knew what buttons to push. "Of course I *want* my baby to have a father. But wanting and having aren't always the same thing. And I don't ever want Craig to resent this baby or to hate me because he was trapped into marriage."

"Honey, Craig is not the type of man to be trapped into anything. If he didn't want to marry you, he wouldn't have offered."

"I'm not sure he wants to marry me," Tess said. "He wants to be a father."

"He doesn't have to marry you to be a father to his child."

Which was exactly the point Tess had tried to make to him.

"Maybe his reasons for wanting to marry you go deeper than you know," Laurie suggested.

Tess shook her head. "No, he was very clear on why he wants to get married."

"Oh." Her sister was obviously disappointed. "What are you going to do?"

"I'm going to have this baby, on my own and I'm going to hope that Craig and I can salvage our friendship."

"Are you sure that's what you want?"

Tess wasn't sure about anything anymore—except that it was nearly impossible to think about Craig as a friend when she could still remember how it felt to have her naked body joined with his, when she yearned to experience that sense of closeness and completion again. But no matter how compelling the physical attraction was, she knew marriage wasn't the answer. Although it might solve some of her immediate problems, it wasn't a viable long-term solution.

"At this point, I think it's the best I can hope for," she said.

"Do you want to know what I think?" Laurie asked.

"Probably not," she admitted, "but you might as well tell me anyway."

"I think you're afraid you could fall in love with him."

"If I was going to fall in love with Craig, it wouldn't have taken fifteen years to happen," she pointed out.

"There's no statute of limitations on love."

She shook her head.

"Now that I think about it," her sister continued, "it makes perfect sense. You've always dated men who let you set the boundaries of the relationship and you never let any of them get close enough to touch your heart. I used to worry that you were afraid to fall in love—because of the mess your mom and my dad made of their marriage. But now I wonder if you maintained that emotional distance because you were already in love with Craig."

"I loved Roger," Tess said.

"You *wanted* to be in love with Roger," Laurie said. "Because you didn't want to admit your feelings for Craig."

"I'm *not* in love with Craig."

"You're not the type of person to act on impulse," her sister pointed out. "But somehow you ended up in bed with Craig and I don't think that ever would have happened unless you harbored some pretty strong feelings for the guy. And if that's true, marrying him wouldn't be such a bad thing."

"I thought you'd be on my side," Tess said peevishly.

"I am on your side," her sister promised her. "I just want you to be happy."

She remained silent, willing her to let the subject drop. But Laurie wasn't going to do so without one last remark. "I think you could be happy with Craig—if you give yourself a chance."

Tess was grateful when her niece's chants of "Da-dee" interrupted their conversation.

"Da-dee, Da-dee." Becca repeated, racing toward the door as a key turned in the lock.

Tess watched as her brother-in-law, in a smooth and obviously well-practiced move, shifted the grocery bags he carried to one hand and scooped the child up in his free arm as he stepped through the door.

Dave kissed his daughter's cheek loudly. "How's my girl?"

At the sound of his father's voice, Devin's eyes

opened wide and he tried to twist his head around. Tess turned the baby in her arms so that he could see the father he obviously adored as much as his sister did.

She remembered the excitement she'd always felt when her father came home at the end of the day: the comforting feel of his strong hugs, the familiar scent of his spicy cologne. Along with the warmth of the memory came a pang of guilt. Did she have the right to deprive her baby of the same thing?

She forced the question—and the doubts—from her mind as Dave set Becca back on her feet and carried the groceries into the kitchen. The kiss he gave his wife was long and lingering. Tess looked away, her heart sighing. It was obvious that Laurie and Dave were very much in love and very happy together, and Tess was genuinely happy for them—if just a little bit envious.

This was what she wanted: a husband who loved her, a family they could raise together. But the fairy tale was out of her reach. Reality was an unplanned pregnancy and a proposed marriage of convenience from her best friend.

After Tess had stormed out of his apartment the previous Friday night, Craig knew she'd need some time and distance to cool off. Because he'd recognized that she was truly ticked—Tess using any kind of swear word was a clear indication of that—he'd given her a full week. But he didn't want to let it go much longer than that without making things right between them again.

He wanted to get back to the place where he could call her at any time of the day just to say hi or stop by her apartment on a whim just because he wanted to see her. He hadn't truly understood how much he looked forward to talking to her and seeing her until he'd forced himself to take a step back and found that she was his first thought every morning and the last before he went to bed at night.

He'd spent the better part of the week considering how to approach her and had at last come up with a plan. Unfortunately, when he finally went over to her apartment Saturday morning to implement it, Tess wasn't home.

But Craig wasn't going to give up that easily.

It was almost noon when she returned and found him waiting in her living room.

"How did you get in here?" she demanded.

"I used the key you gave me."

Her gaze narrowed. "The key I gave to you in case of an *emergency*?"

"I thought it was an emergency," he told her. "I tried calling all morning and you never answered."

"Obviously I wasn't here."

"Well, I didn't know that until I came over," he pointed out. "Because usually you have your cell phone when you're out and you weren't answering that, either."

"I forgot to turn it on when I went out," she admitted.

"A few things on your mind?"

She ignored the jibe. "So you came over here and let yourself in—"

"I knocked first," he felt compelled to interrupt in his own defense. He could tell that she was annoyed with him and getting more annoyed by the minute, and he was worried he wouldn't get a chance to apologize before she kicked him out.

"Okay," she conceded. "You knocked and then you let yourself in. But why—when you realized I wasn't here and there wasn't any kind of emergency—didn't you leave?"

"Because I'd already ordered the flowers and thought someone should be here to accept delivery."

She looked around, as if only now noticing the bouquets of roses that he'd set around the room. There were vases of red and pink and white and yellow and peach and lavender and something the florist called bicolor roses. He'd ordered a dozen of every color, hoping the extravagant display would soften Tess's heart toward him.

"I told you I didn't want flowers," she said. "And filling my apartment with them isn't going to change my mind."

But she didn't sound quite so annoyed anymore, and she picked up the vase of white roses to sniff the fragrant blooms.

"These aren't a lead-in to another marriage proposal, they're an apology."

Her lips curved slightly as she glanced around at the colorful display. "You must be very sorry."

"Sorrier than you can know."

She touched the petal of one of the purple flowers. "I have to admit, I like this kind of apology. But I'd also like to know what you're apologizing for."

"I'm not sorry I kissed you," he admitted. "I'm not sorry we almost made love—well, actually I *am* sorry it was only an almost. But I'm mostly sorry that you thought I was trying to manipulate you."

"Weren't you?"

He couldn't help but smile. "Sometimes you give me too much credit, Tess. The truth is, what happened wasn't a planned seduction but simple runaway lust."

"Really?"

She seemed relieved to know that he couldn't contain his desire for her, which was ironic because the same realization completely unnerved him.

"Really," he assured her. And he'd figured that if he couldn't be alone with Tess without wanting his hands on her, he'd just make sure they weren't alone together. Or he'd keep a ten-foot distance between them at all times.

"Then I guess I do forgive you."

"Thank you."

She smiled. "Thank you for the flowers, even if they were an unnecessarily extravagant gesture."

He exhaled a silent sigh, certain they'd taken the first step toward reestablishing the camaraderie that had meant so much to him over the years and hoping that his next words wouldn't undo the progress they'd made.

"I still think we should get married, but obviously we don't agree on that, so I'd like us to at least work together to do what's best for the baby."

"I'd like that, too," she said.

"And I thought that going to a movie tonight would be a step in the right direction. There's a new James Bond film playing downtown."

Tess hesitated, although she wasn't sure why. She was a huge James Bond fan and she and Craig had gone to the movies together plenty of times before. But there was something about his deliberate casualness and apparent acquiescence that sent up warning flags in her mind.

"Do you already have plans?" he asked when she didn't immediately respond.

"No," she admitted.

"It's just a movie," he said in a matter-of-fact tone she knew was meant to be reassuring.

But she knew Craig too well to trust that his motives were as simple as he claimed. "Just a movie?"

"And maybe a bite to eat after," he added.

She hesitated another moment before giving in—because she really did want to see the movie. "Okay."

He smiled. "Great. I've got some errands to run this afternoon, but I'll come back to pick you up around seven."

"Or I could meet you at the theater," she suggested.

"I'll pick you up," he said again. "It's more appropriate for a first date."

"It's not a date," she said.

His smile only widened. "I know it's a little unorthodox, considering that you're already pregnant with my baby, but I thought we should have a few dates before we discuss marriage."

And which confirmed what she'd feared—Craig had not given up.

"I thought you agreed that marriage was out—that we were going to work together to do what's best for the baby."

"No," he denied. "I only agreed that we *dis*agreed about marriage and this is what's best for our baby."

"Maybe this isn't such a good idea."

"I'll see you at seven," he said, already on his way to the door.

"I think we need to talk about this some more."

"We can talk tonight."

"Wait, Craig—"

Her entreaty was cut off by the click of the door closing behind him.

Tess huffed out an exasperated breath, wondering what exactly she'd agreed to.

Chapter Five

A ten-foot distance, Craig decided later, wasn't a realistic option when a man was trying to court a woman. And the simple act of sharing popcorn with Tess was wreaking havoc on his self-control.

In the darkness of the theater, their attention occupied by the action on the screen, he reached into the bag and his knuckles brushed hers. He felt her hand pull away from the casual contact, sensed the stiffening in her shoulders. He withdrew his hand, munched on the popcorn. Her scent continued to tease his nostrils. So simple, so Tess and so utterly seductive.

He shifted uncomfortably in his seat and tried to focus on the movie. But all he could think about was the woman beside him. How she'd responded to his touch; how she'd opened up to him—not just her body, but her heart; and the feeling that he'd found a part of heaven when he'd buried himself inside her.

No, there was no way they could ever go back to being just friends again. It wasn't enough anymore.

But how was he ever going to convince Tess?

And why was it so critical that he do so?

He'd thought long and hard about the situation—he'd barely been able to think of anything else since he learned that she was going to have his baby. And he'd given serious consideration to her suggestion of shared custody. But in the end, he couldn't accept it. It wasn't what he wanted for their child and it wasn't what he wanted for him and Tess.

He wanted to be with her, to raise their child with her. He believed they could do it—build a life together, be happy together. He knew that she deserved more than a marriage based on friendship and parental responsibilities, but the reality was that she guarded her emotions as closely as he did.

They were both private people who didn't open up easily to others. And yet, they'd become the best of friends, sharing hopes and fears with one another that they'd never share with anyone else. He had no secrets from Tess. She knew him better than anyone—and she loved him anyway. As he loved her.

Okay, so maybe it wasn't the romantic kind of love Tess was looking for. But it was a comforting and comfortable feeling—because he knew that she was the one person who would always stand by him. And he would do the same for her.

The rustles and murmurs of people beginning to shuffle out of the theater distracted him from his thoughts. He looked up and frowned as he noticed the credits scrolling upward on the screen. He hadn't even realized the movie had ended, although he didn't doubt that James Bond had blown away the bad guys and got the girl. He always did.

Tess enjoyed the movie and she enjoyed being with Craig in the casual, relaxed atmosphere of the theater. She'd missed this—the comfortable friendship they'd shared for so many years—so much that she almost wished there was a way to go back to the time when they'd been just friends. But she wouldn't wish her baby away and she knew that things had started to change between them long before she woke up in his bed, anyway.

She pushed those thoughts and questions out of her mind and concentrated on the screen, but she jolted when his thigh pressed against hers, felt her pulse race in response to the casual brush of his fingertips if they met hers inside the bag of popcorn. By the time the picture of the embracing couple faded to black, Tess felt hot and tingly all over.

She'd seen dozens of movies with Craig over the years, maybe hundreds, and never before had her body been so attuned to every move of his. She was acting like a high school girl on a first date and she mentally damned him for putting that idea in her head. Except that she'd been fairly innocent in high school and had never imagined taking advantage of the darkened theater to straddle her date and have her way with him. She might be appalled that she was entertaining such thoughts now but she couldn't deny them.

But this is Craig, her conscience scolded. *Your best friend, the father of your baby.*

Okay, maybe she should try to forget the father of her baby part because her body was all too aware of how *that* had happened—and more than willing to do it again. Or maybe her body was responding so acutely to his because of the pregnancy. Yes, that made sense. She remembered reading somewhere that it wasn't unusual to experience an increase in sexual desire during pregnancy.

Obviously that's what she was feeling—it really had nothing to do with Craig specifically and everything to do with the hormonal changes in her body. Everything would go back to normal after the baby was born. All she had to do was stay out of Craig's bed—and keep him out of hers—in the interim.

Which was why she accepted his invitation to go for pizza after the movie was over—because she needed some time to cool off before he took her home and she dragged him inside with her and locked the door.

"Why is it that women can't resist James Bond?" Craig asked her as they were sharing a large pepperoni and three-cheese pizza at Marco's.

Tess smiled. "Because he's handsome, adventurous and daring."

"He's also reckless, ruthless and unfaithful."

"True," she admitted. "But he always saves the world."

"If I saved the world, would you marry me?"

She should have known better than to let her guard down, that Craig would eventually find a way to circle back to his own agenda. "James Bond never wants to marry the girl," she pointed out to him.

"You're avoiding my question."

"If the world needed to be saved, I'd rather do it myself than rely on someone else to do it for me."

"What if you couldn't do it yourself?" he asked, selecting another slice of pizza.

"Are we still talking about saving the world or raising a baby?"

"I don't doubt you're capable of raising this baby on your own," he said. "I just wish you'd consider how much easier it would be for both of us if we shared the day-to-day responsibilities."

"I have considered it," she told him.

He looked up, obviously surprised by the admission.

"And I'll admit there are reasons I might consider marriage in these circumstances."

"Such as?" he prompted.

She unzipped her purse and pulled out a folded sheet of paper.

He stared at her. "You made a list?"

"I figured you'd want reasons and I wanted to make sure I'd considered all the pros and cons."

He took the page from her hand, unfolded it. "There are a lot more pros than cons," he noted with approval.

"Not every factor carries the same weight."

"Hmm." He scanned her notes, his lips curving. "You think I'm smart, fun and great in bed."

She snatched back the list and pointed to what she'd written in the other column. "I also noted that you have one enormous, intractable flaw."

"Not just good but great, huh?" His smile widened.

She huffed out an impatient breath. "Yes, okay, the sex was phenomenal. Now that we've stoked your ego, can we focus on what's relevant?"

"I think sexual attraction and physical compatibility are very relevant."

"So you've said before," she told him. "And so is your inability to commit to an adult relationship."

"Just because I've chosen not to make a commitment doesn't mean I'm not capable of commitment."

She nodded. "You're right. I almost forgot that you were engaged once. And that lasted what—all of three months?"

"You were engaged once, too," he reminded her.

"Yes, but I didn't just change my mind."

"I didn't change mine, either," he said. "I just realized that I'd let Lana steamroll me into an engagement I didn't want and I wasn't going to let her steamroll me into a marriage."

"Because you couldn't make a commitment."

"Because I didn't want to make a commitment to her."

"Your relationship with Lana ended two years ago and you haven't had a relationship that's lasted longer than a few weeks since then."

"That's not true," he said. "I dated Michelle Gable for almost four months."

Tess snorted. "She was the travel writer, wasn't she?"

"So?"

"So she was out of the country for at least half of that time."

"Okay," he relented. "Maybe I haven't wanted to make a commitment to anyone before. But I want to, now. I want to be with you, Tess, to be there for our children."

"*Child*," she corrected automatically. "Singular."

He looked at her with wide-eyed innocence. "Didn't I ever tell you that twins run in my family? On both sides."

"That's not funny."

"It's true." He held up his hand as if swearing an oath. "My maternal grandfather had a twin brother and my cousins, Kevin and Kayla, on my father's side are twins."

She wasn't sure she believed him. And even if he was telling the truth that didn't mean she would have twins.

But the mere possibility threw her. What if she was pregnant with twins? Two babies would mean twice as many feedings, twice as many dirty diapers, twice as much laundry. How would she handle all of that on her own?

She drew in a deep breath as she battled against the rising panic. She wasn't going to worry about something over which she had no control. Not yet, anyway. And not when she suspected that Craig was trying to make her panic—and run to him for help.

She gestured to the last slice on the tray and casually asked, "Do you want to finish that?"

"You go ahead," he said. "You might actually be eating for three these days."

Tess ignored him and bit into the pizza.

Grace Richmond inhaled the pungent aromas of garlic and oregano, her mouth already watering in anticipation of the spicy Italian sausage pizza she and Allan always shared when they came to Marco's. Saturday night was their usual date night. No matter how busy things were at the office for Allan or how involved Grace might be in whatever charitable committee she was currently assisting, they looked forward to spending this one evening together.

Today they'd gone to a pottery show at the local art gallery, then wandered through some of the downtown shops before taking in a movie at the Odyssey Theater. Allan had made reservations at their favorite French restaurant, but after the movie Grace hadn't been in the mood for a fancy meal and had suggested they stop by Marco's for a quick bite.

Allan had shaken his head in mock dismay that she would turn down five-star cuisine for pizza, but had graciously given in to her request. In all the years they'd been together, he'd given her everything she'd ever wanted and so much more than she'd ever dreamed of and her greatest wish was that both of their sons would find special women who could do the same for them.

Right now Gage wasn't anywhere near ready to settle down and though Craig hadn't shown any inclination to get serious with anyone since his broken engagement with Lana, she sensed that he needed the stability of a relationship. She worried that if he didn't find balance in his life soon, he would become too career-focused and settled in his ways to ever find a woman willing to put up with him.

As she glanced around the restaurant searching for a vacant table with thoughts of her eldest stepson on her mind, she saw him. At first she assumed it was just someone who looked like him, that she'd conjured his image because she'd been thinking of him. But then she recognized Tess sitting across from him.

She didn't think anything of it at first—after all, Craig and Tess had been friends for a long time—and she was actually going to suggest to Allan that they join the younger couple. Then she saw Craig reach across the table and touch Tess's hand, and Tess looked up at him and the sizzle in the air was almost tangible.

Grace took a mental step back, then a physical step. She didn't know what, if anything, was going on between Craig and Tess, but she didn't want to interfere, even inadvertently.

She squeezed Allan's hand as the hostess finally started toward them. "Let's go somewhere else to eat."

He turned and frowned at her. "I thought you wanted pizza."

"I changed my mind," she said.

He looked at her strangely.

She couldn't blame him and she couldn't explain why they needed to leave, she only knew that they did.

"I'd just rather go somewhere else. Or maybe we could pick something up on the way home." She leaned closer and dropped her voice so that no one would overhear. "Maybe something that can be heated up later."

She loved that he immediately understood what she was offering. She loved even more that after so many years together, his eyes still darkened at the thought of making love with her.

"Suddenly I'm not in the mood for pizza, either," he said, and led her back outside.

Tess was fixing glitches in a new software program Tuesday morning and wishing she could so easily fix the glitches in her life.

You could be happy with Craig.

Her sister's words echoed in her mind as they'd been

doing for the past three days and they tugged at her because she suspected that they were true.

She could be happy with Craig. As he'd pointed out when he first proposed the idea of marriage, they'd been friends for a long time and they shared common interests. But would that be enough to sustain a long-term relationship? Could she give up on her dream of falling in love and being loved in return? Could she fall in love with Craig? Or was she, as Laurie suspected, already in love with him?

She punched at the keyboard, reconfiguring the program, her fingers moving automatically as her mind continued on its wayward path.

She knew that Craig would be a wonderful father and that their child would benefit from having him around full-time. He'd probably be a great husband, too. Craig excelled at everything he did.

And he was offering her everything that she'd ever wanted: not just a baby, but a father for her child and a husband—a family. He would probably even complete the picture by finding a house with a white picket fence and a puppy to romp in the backyard. Yes, she could definitely be happy with that. It was the kind of life she'd been dreaming about since she was a little girl.

The tougher question was: could Craig be happy?

And it was her inability to answer that question with any degree of certainty that continued to hold her back.

When the phone rang on her desk, she reached eagerly for the receiver, grateful for the interruption of these disquieting thoughts.

"Hey, Tess."

She felt her pulse leap in recognition as Craig spoke. It had been like this since the night they'd made love—her body betraying her every attempt to restore the normalcy of their relationship.

"What's up?" Despite the racing of her own heart, she managed to speak casually.

"Is this a bad time?" he asked.

"I am in the middle of something," she said, although for the life of her she couldn't remember what it was. Something about the sound of his voice stirred up the unforgettable memory of its soft whisper against her ear as they'd made love and banished everything else from her mind. Yeah, sleeping with the man who was her best friend had been a very big mistake.

"Then I won't keep you," he promised. "I was just calling to see if you were free for dinner tonight."

"Actually, I'm not," she said. "I took a couple of hours off this afternoon to run some errands and need to stay late to catch up."

"You still have to eat," he reminded her.

"I'll pick up something on my way home."

"What time will that be?"

"I don't know."

His voice dropped. "I'd really like to see you tonight."

"I'm not going to marry you, Craig."

"So you keep saying." She could almost hear the smile in his voice. "I'd still like to see you tonight."

She didn't allow herself to hesitate; she couldn't afford to waver. "No."

"Are you afraid you might change your mind?"

"No," she said again, although they both knew she was lying.

"How about tomorrow, then?"

She sighed, uncertain how long she could hold out against his persistence. "Maybe."

Tess should have known that Craig wouldn't be appeased with a *maybe* and that he wouldn't wait until the next day. It was about six-thirty when he showed up at the office carrying a large paper bag and two crystal wineglasses.

"Since you couldn't go to dinner, I brought dinner to you," Craig told her, already unpacking the contents of the paper bag.

She wanted to send him away, to insist that she had work to do. But her stomach growled loudly as the scents of tangy tomato sauce and sweet basil tickled her nostrils.

"Chicken parm and spaghetti." He opened the lid and set the container in front of her.

How was she supposed to hold out against a man who knew all her weaknesses? It wasn't fair. She pushed aside her notes and picked up a plastic fork.

"I was going to get something to eat on the way home," she reminded him.

"I just wanted to make sure you had a proper meal."

Of course—this wasn't really about her, it was Craig's way of making sure she was taking care of the baby. Her suspicions were confirmed when he reached into the bag and pulled out a carton of milk. He filled the two wineglasses, handed one across the desk to her.

"I thought white was appropriate, since we're having white meat," he explained. "This is a domestic vintage, light-bodied, fresh, pleasing to the palate with a lingering finish."

As much as she wanted to resent his heavy-handed manner, she was helpless to resist his charm.

Craig held up his glass, tapped the rim against hers. "To date number two."

"This isn't a date," Tess said.

Craig merely smiled and sipped his milk.

"I'm not dating you," she insisted.

His smile widened. "I think two dates could be called dating."

"Saturday night wasn't a date, either."

"Oh." His brow furrowed as he considered her statement. "But we went to a movie together…shared popcorn…and a kiss good-night."

"That wasn't a kiss," she said, dismissing the moment when they'd stood outside her door and he'd brushed his lips against her cheek.

She'd been surprised when he'd parked instead of dropping her off at the front door as he would have done in the past. And with every step they'd taken up to her apartment, her anticipation had mounted so that by the time they reached her door her pulse was racing and her skin was flushed—and not from the physical exertion of walking the three flights of stairs.

She'd wanted him to kiss her, but she couldn't help remembering what had happened the last time, how quickly a kiss had turned into so much more. And though her body ached with wanting the so much more, she knew she couldn't fall into bed with Craig again with everything still unresolved between them.

As it turned out, she'd fallen into bed alone and had

lain awake late into the night, thinking about that kiss—the sizzle of awareness, the breathless anticipation and the undeniable disappointment when his lips brushed against her cheek. It was just like so many kisses they'd shared before—gentle and fleeting, over before it had begun without any hint of wanting something more.

"It was so a kiss," he said, managing to sound insulted that she'd implied otherwise.

"Not a date kiss."

He glanced up as he twirled his fork in the pasta, frowning with what was obviously feigned confusion. "What's the criteria for a date kiss?"

She shook her head, realizing too late the dangers of engaging in this type of conversation with a man who could heat her blood with a look, send her hormones rocketing with a casual touch and—God help her—make all of her reservations melt with a simple kiss.

"Come on, Tess. Help me out here."

As if he needed any help. The man had probably been on more dates in the past six months than she'd experienced in her lifetime. Besides which, she knew from firsthand experience that he didn't need any advice or guidance in the kissing department.

"I hate to think that I left you—" he paused, as if searching for the right word "—dissatisfied."

"I wasn't. You didn't." She shoved a forkful of pasta in her mouth and willed the heat to fade from her cheeks.

"I could try again," he suggested.

"Not necessary," she said. "Because that night was *not* a date. This is *not* a date. I'm *not* dating you and I'm *definitely not* going to marry you."

"I'm pretty sure it was a date," he said, pointedly ignoring the rest of her protest.

"We've been going to the movies together for years," she reminded him.

He tilted his head, considering. "If we've been dating for years, it shouldn't surprise you that I want to marry you."

She wouldn't let herself smile. She wouldn't admit that his charm and perseverance were effectively chipping away at her resistance. She had to stay strong—or at least fake it.

She sliced through the chicken breast with a plastic knife as she debated telling him about the two appointments she'd had today: one with Dr. Bowen, an OB-GYN, another with Jessica Armstrong, an attorney.

Since she was hungry and didn't want to fight with Craig anymore before she'd eaten her dinner she decided to tell him about her visit to Dr. Bowen first.

"I had a prenatal checkup today," she told him.

"How was it?"

"Good. It was just a routine first appointment. She put me on prenatal vitamins, told me to eat healthy and exercise and scheduled me for a follow-up next month."

"Can I come?"

"If you want," she agreed.

"I do."

Tess exhaled. Okay, maybe they *could* do this. As long as they could avoid the issues of marriage and sex, maybe they could just be two friends who were having a baby together.

The thought eased some of the pressure that had been building up inside her and they finished their meals in comfortable silence. She decided, in the interest of keeping the peace, that she would save telling him about the lawyer until another day.

When they were finished eating Craig emptied the last of the milk into Tess's glass. She'd already had two glasses, but she dutifully downed the third knowing it was good for the baby and would make him happy. And she was grateful they seemed to have taken a step toward resuming the easy camaraderie they'd once shared.

As she finished the milk, Craig gathered up the take-out containers, stuffed them back into the paper bag.

"Thanks for dinner," she said.

He smiled. "My pleasure."

She turned her attention back to the papers that were on her desk, waiting for him to leave. She reread the same paragraph three times before she gave in and glanced up at Craig, still standing beside her. "I thought you were going."

"I'm waiting for my good-night kiss," he said.

"You're going to be waiting a while."

"Come on, Tess. You can show me a proper date kiss."

"This wasn't a date," she reminded him.

"You know, it would help repair my sorely damaged ego if you at least pretended to be interested," Craig said.

"I don't think I've damaged your ego," Tess said dryly. "I don't think it's possible. Your ego's as rock-hard as your head."

"Ouch. Now that did hurt."

Tess laughed. "Go home, Craig."

He grinned at her and bent to touch his lips to her forehead. "Good night, Tess."

* * *

It was Thursday and Tess was becoming increasingly discouraged by her inability to track down either Owen or Carl. Every time she tried to catch one of them, he was on the phone or in a meeting or out of the office. And now, the receptionist told her, they were both out of town.

While Tess was frustrated by this latest obstacle, she was more unnerved when Elaine revealed where they'd gone: San Diego. Because she'd finally got around to doing some Internet research on Jared McCabe and learned why his name had been familiar to her. He was the President and CEO of GigaPix, a company she'd applied to right out of college, and a competitor of SBG.

While Tess wanted to talk to Owen and Carl before assuming the worst, she couldn't help but think the future of SBG was in question—and her job along with it.

This thought was weighing heavily on her mind when she got home from work that night. She kicked off her shoes inside the door and shuffled through the mail that she'd picked up downstairs. Telephone bill, credit card application, advertisement from a local pizza place and an envelope embossed with the names Huntington & Whitmore, Attorneys at Law and a return address in New York City.

Tess put the other mail aside and frowned at the letter from the lawyer. Not her lawyer, but a firm from the big city.

Craig's lawyer?

Her stomach plummeted at the thought as she slid a shaking finger beneath the edge of the flap and tore it open.

Re: 40 Centennial Drive

Her anxiety gave way to confusion and she quickly scanned the contents of the letter.

Her apartment building was being sold and this was her notice to vacate by the end of October. She reread it three more times before the reality sank in. Now she was pregnant and unmarried, potentially unemployed and soon-to-be homeless.

Then Tess did something she hardly ever did—she sat down and cried.

Chapter Six

Craig was at Tess's apartment less than thirty minutes after they got off the phone.

"What are you doing here?" she asked when she answered the door.

"You sounded like you could use a friend," he said, and he held up the pint of ice cream in his hand. "So I brought two of them—Ben and Jerry."

She managed a wan smile and stepped away from the door so he could enter. "You know me so well."

"Well enough to know that everything's not always fine just because you say it is." He went straight to the kitchen, found a spoon in the drawer and handed it to her along with one of the pints.

"I was overreacting," she said, prying the lid off the ice cream.

"You don't usually overreact."

"I try not to. I guess I was just feeling a little out of sorts when I got home and then I found the letter."

Craig followed her into the living room, took the envelope she handed to him. He read the contents while she dug into the ice cream.

When he was finished, he sat beside her on the sofa. "I'm sorry, Tess. I know how much you love this place."

"It's just an apartment," she said. "Logically, I know that. But I've lived here since I moved back to Pinehurst. I know the neighborhood and the neighbors. I have a second bedroom that I was planning on making into a nursery."

"So you'll move to a new neighborhood and meet new neighbors," he said gently.

"I know." She offered him a spoonful of ice cream, which he declined with a shake of his head. "It's just one more thing that I wasn't prepared to deal with right now."

"You don't have to deal with it right now," he told her. "You have a couple of months to decide what you want to do, to make a list of desirable locations and the best schools and nearby parks."

"You're never going to forget that list, are you?" She shoved another spoonful of Chunky Monkey into her mouth.

He grinned. "Probably not."

"I like to know that I'm making the right decision for the right reasons," she admitted.

"That's why I know you'll figure this out," he said.

She sighed. "How is it that you always know exactly what to say to make me feel better?"

"It's a gift."

"It is." She put the lid back on the container and took

the leftover ice cream to the freezer. When she came back, she sat down next to him again. "And as much as I appreciate the ice cream, I'm even more grateful for your friendship."

He tucked his arm around her shoulders, drew her close. "I'll always be there for you, Tess."

She snuggled against him, laid her head on his chest. "I'm so afraid of losing you," she admitted softly.

"That's never going to happen," he said, then added, teasingly, "Of course, if you really wanted to be sure not to lose me, you could marry me."

She sighed, a release of breath that seemed to come from deep within. "I don't know why I thought we might actually have a whole conversation without the M-word."

"Wishful thinking," he told her, his hand moving in gentle circles over her back.

"Apparently." She stifled a yawn.

"I just want to make sure you don't forget my offer."

"I don't think that's likely."

"I could have it written into our vows that there would always be Chunky Monkey in the freezer," he offered.

"Tempting," she said. "But no."

He could feel the tension slowly seeping out of her as he continued to rub her back. And though his body was painfully aware of the softness of her curves nestled against him, he found himself enjoying the quiet comfort of the moment. There had been so much dissension between them lately, but he was glad that he could be here for her now.

After only a few minutes, Tess was asleep.

He wasn't surprised that she was tired. She was always on the go, always rushing from one thing to the next. She didn't seem to realize how much energy she was using just growing their baby inside her.

He knew, because he'd been doing a lot of reading on the subject. He'd bought a couple of books and had done some research online. It was amazing what could be found on the Internet—although he could gladly have done without the live birth videos he'd found himself watching. At first he'd been fascinated by the process, captivated by the miracle of birth. Until he'd superimposed Tess's image over the panting and obviously pained woman. Then, he'd been terrified.

He knew childbirth was a natural process, that women had been having babies for thousands of years—and most of those without the aid of modern technology. But even today, there could be complications and the thought of anything happening to Tess terrified him.

Of course, there was no going back now.

All he could do was stay by her side. Even if she wouldn't marry him—and he hadn't entirely given up on that idea yet—he would be with her through every step of this pregnancy, through labor and childbirth. And for the eighteen years after that, if she would let him.

Laurie responded to Tess's knock on the door Saturday morning with Devin propped on her hip and the shoulder of her blouse stained with spit-up milk. Her hair was mussed as though she'd repeatedly run her fingers through it—or had tried to pull it out by the roots—and her eyes filled with weary desperation.

The joys of motherhood, Tess thought.

But her sister managed a smile and held out the baby. "Can you take him while I get Becca ready?"

"Sure." Tess dropped her purse by her shoes and took Devin in her arms. "Is everything okay?"

Laurie nodded. "The kids are just fussing because they miss their daddy. Becca usually loves her swimming lessons but today she's parked in front of the television and refusing to get dressed and Devin hasn't let me put him down all morning."

"How long has Dave been gone?"

"Since Wednesday." There was a world of suffering in her response. "But he's coming home tomorrow."

She ducked into the living room and turned off the television. Becca howled in protest.

"You can't go swimming in your pajamas," Laurie told her daughter.

"Don't wanna go swimming." Becca crossed her arms over her chest and stuck out her bottom lip.

"If you don't go swimming, you won't get to see Kelly and Rachel."

"Don't wanna go swimming," Becca repeated.

Laurie sighed and rolled her eyes at Tess. "I'm just going to change my shirt, then I'll see if I can wrestle little miss pouty into her bathing suit."

Fifteen minutes later, Laurie had her daughter by the hand and was ready to head out the door. "He should be okay until I get back, but there's a bottle of expressed milk in the fridge if he starts to fuss. And drops," she pointed to a vial on the counter "to give him after his bottle. He's got a touch of colic and the medication seems to help."

"Colic?" Tess was sure she'd heard of it, but she had no idea what it was.

Laurie nodded. "It's basically gas. I give him some

drops when he nurses but he still cries all the time. The doctor said there's nothing really I can do and it's okay to just let him cry—but I can't stand to hear him so upset."

"Gotta go swimming, Mommy." Becca tugged impatiently on her mother's hand.

"Are you sure you're going to be okay?" Laurie asked her.

"I'll be fine." She ushered her sister out the door. "You just worry about Becca's swimming lessons."

"We'll be back in a couple of hours."

"Go."

Tess shut the door and smiled at her nephew. "Well, it looks like it's just you and me, kid."

Devin's answering smile wobbled, his lower lip jutted out and his eyes suddenly filled with tears.

An hour and a half later, Tess wondered why she'd ever thought she was cut out to be a mother. She'd fed Devin half his bottle and given him drops. She'd changed him, rocked him, paced with him and he still continued to fret and whimper. By the time Laurie and Becca returned, Tess was almost ready to sit down and cry right along with him.

"What's the matter, little guy?" Laurie passed off a takeout bag to Tess in exchange for the baby. Almost immediately, Devin's sobs subsided into soft hiccupping sounds. He rubbed his face against his mother's shirt, stuffed his thumb into his mouth and closed his eyes.

"Did he give you a hard time?" Laurie asked, rubbing her hand in circles against his back.

"Let's just say I now know what the expression 'trial by fire' really means."

"I'm sorry."

Tess shrugged. "I just felt so helpless. Nothing I did seemed to soothe him." She looked at him now, peaceful and content in his mother's arms. "I guess he just wanted his mommy."

"He has those moods," Laurie admitted. "And sometimes even mommy can't help."

"What do you do then?"

"Pass him off to Daddy. Devin likes to move around, so Dave usually takes turns walking the floor with him."

Which wouldn't be an option for Tess without a husband.

"Do you ever just let him cry?" she asked.

"I've tried," Laurie admitted. "But then Becca wakes up and I've got two cranky kids on my hands."

Tess peeked at the now sleeping baby and wondered how it was that such a tiny person had so much control over the adults in his life.

"Can you get Becca into her booster seat while I put Devin down for a nap?" Laurie asked.

Tess managed that task more easily and handed her niece the bag with the child's meal in it.

Becca reached inside eagerly. "Toy." She pulled out her French fries, then the cheeseburger and then frowned into the empty bag. "Toy," she said again.

"You can have your toy after you eat your lunch," Laurie said as she came back into the kitchen. "It's the only way I can get her to eat sometimes," she confided.

"How did you learn all this stuff?" Tess asked. "Is there a Parenting 101 course?"

Her sister laughed. "You'll learn quickly enough when you have your own."

But Tess wasn't so sure. And after the difficult morning she'd spent with Devin she was even less convinced that she had what it took to raise a baby alone. So why was she determined to do this on her own when Craig was so obviously willing to share the responsibility?

"Tess?"

She glanced up, startled. "Sorry?"

"I just asked if you wanted some ketchup for your fries."

"No, thanks."

"Ket-chup, ket-chup," Becca demanded.

"Okay, honey." Laurie got up to get the ketchup and squirted a drop on her daughter's hamburger wrapper. "Are you okay?" she asked Tess.

She smiled. "How could you tell I was having a panic attack?"

"Because I've been there. Although I have to admit, I don't think I would ever have considered doing it on my own."

"You think I'm crazy, don't you?"

"Certifiable," Laurie agreed.

"I just don't want to screw this up."

"This?" Laurie asked. "The baby—or your relationship with Craig?"

She popped a French fry in her mouth. "Both."

"Is he still pressuring you about marriage?"

"Not directly."

"What does that mean?"

She felt herself blushing. "He's decided to court me."

"Oh, Tess. That is so sweet."

"It's so annoying," Tess told her. "Every time I turn around, he's there. Taking me to dinner, sending me flowers, bringing me ice cream, calling just to say hi, taking me to dinner. He feeds me a lot."

Her sister laughed.

"All done," Becca said, holding up her empty hands.

Laurie used a napkin to remove the last traces of ketchup from her daughter's fingers and face then pulled a plastic wrapped toy out of her pocket.

"Toy?" Becca said.

"Yes, toy."

"Mommy, open."

"Okay, honey." Laurie tore open the plastic, removed the miniature blue dog.

"Doggie," Becca said, dancing away happily with her new toy.

"It sounds like he's making a real effort," Laurie said. "How is it that you're still resisting him?"

"It's not easy," she admitted. And it wasn't. Craig had been so wonderfully attentive and supportive and she knew he'd be a great father.

"Then what's holding you back?" her sister asked.

Tess sighed. "I'm not sure I even know anymore."

Two months after he'd first proposed and despite repeated rejections of numerous subsequent proposals, Craig was still trying to figure out a way to convince Tess to marry him.

He refused to be frustrated by her refusals. He truly believed that marriage was the best solution to their situation and he was confident that Tess would realize it, too. Probably. Maybe. Eventually.

But it wasn't in his nature to sit back and wait for something he wanted, and he'd never wanted anything as much as he wanted to give his baby a family. Maybe he was old-fashioned. Maybe his image of family—a mother and father married to one another, raising their children together—wasn't the norm anymore. But it was what he'd longed for desperately growing up and it was what he wanted for his child.

He didn't ever want his son or daughter to have to answer the kinds of questions he'd been subjected to. Children weren't deliberately cruel, just innately curious, and he'd soon grown accustomed to inquiries about the mother who wasn't around. And he'd learned to feign indifference, refusing to let anyone see how much it hurt that his mother had walked out—that she hadn't cared about him enough to take him with her.

Not that he'd wanted to go, but why didn't she want to take him? He sometimes imagined that the letter she'd supposedly left was a forgery, that she'd really been kidnapped, torn out of his life against his will. Or that she'd gone willingly but only because she'd been suffering from some horrible illness and chosen to disappear from his life so he wouldn't have to watch her die. But despite the elaborate fantasies woven in his child's mind, his heart had always known the truth—she just didn't want to stay, she didn't want to be his mother, she didn't love him enough.

Tess's pregnancy might have been an accident, but it wasn't a mistake. Although he might not have planned on becoming a father at this point in his life, he wasn't going to shirk his duties or responsibilities. Yeah, there had been a moment—even several moments—of sheer panic and terror when he'd first faced the possibility that Tess could be pregnant with his child. But along with the acceptance had come an increasing sense of awe and anticipation and the startling realization that he loved this baby already. And he wouldn't give his child cause to doubt it.

Unfortunately, he was going to need something more than his own conviction and determination to sway Tess toward marriage. But what?

He picked up his beer and took a long swallow from the bottle, certain that if he thought long and hard enough, the answer to that question would come.

There wasn't anyone he knew as well as he knew Tess and he was sure there wasn't anyone who knew her as well as he did. Her favorite color was yellow, her lucky number twenty-two and she was addicted to home renovation and decorating shows. Her CD collection contained everything from opera to Ozzy; she read Patricia Cornwell novels and loved Disney movies. She enjoyed skiing but didn't know how to skate, adored dogs and was allergic to cats. She liked green apples and red grapes, drank her coffee black and ate her eggs scrambled. She was obsessive about punctuality and completely devoted to her family. He knew all this and more, but he didn't know how to convince her that a marriage between them would work.

He'd considered, but immediately rejected, the strategies he might use with any other woman. Tess wasn't the type to fall for any kind of grand romantic gesture and he knew that whisking her away for a weekend in Paris would more likely lead to apprehension than acquiescence.

"I didn't expect to be swept off my feet," she'd told him when he'd expressed doubts about her engagement to Roger. *"I don't* want *to be swept off my feet."*

He frowned, remembering their conversation, searching within it for a key to unlocking the barriers she'd put between them.

"What do you want?"

"I want to be with someone who wants to be with me. To share a home with him, raise a family together."

He scowled as he tipped his bottle to his lips again. He'd been sorry, for Tess's sake, that things hadn't worked out the way she'd hoped with Roger. But he'd also been relieved. He'd never thought the man was good enough for her and Roger's infidelity only proved how unworthy—and stupid—he was.

As Craig pushed himself off of the couch to head to the kitchen for another beer, he banged his shin on the corner of the glass coffee table. Damn, that thing was dangerous. Too dangerous to keep with a child toddling around.

Not that the baby would be toddling for quite some time, but his throbbing leg was a painful reminder that he'd need to do some serious childproofing of his home before that eventuality. Except that when he tried to picture a baby crawling on the antique Persian carpet, the image wouldn't come.

He twisted the cap off another bottle as he mentally rearranged furniture to make room for a crib and play-pen and all the other paraphernalia that went along with a baby and he realized that it just couldn't be done. His condo simply wasn't big enough for him and Tess and their child.

Okay, maybe he was jumping ahead a little, putting Tess into the picture, too, but he couldn't imagine making a home for their baby that didn't have her in it.

Because she was the mother of his child, he assured himself. Not for any other reason.

Except whenever he thought of Tess now, it wasn't always about the baby growing inside her womb. In fact, the image that most often came to mind was of Tess in his bed, naked and soft, her hair spread out on his pillow, her lips—swollen from his kisses—curved with satisfaction. It was the same picture that haunted his dreams and he would wake up yearning, reaching for her.

They'd been friends for fifteen years. Good friends. Best friends. And in all those years, he'd never considered breaching the boundaries of that relationship. Okay, maybe that wasn't entirely true. There was that one time—he'd just come home after his first year of college—when he'd realized the skinny awkward girl he'd said goodbye to in September had suddenly blossomed into a woman—a beautiful, desirable woman. But he'd ignored the immediate stir of interest, reminding himself that she was Tess—just Tess. His friend, his confidante.

Now suddenly, the woman who'd been "just Tess" for so many years was so much more. Except that she was brandishing their friendship like a shield against the possibility of any deeper relationship, and he was faced with the formidable task of having to convince her the status quo wasn't enough anymore.

But as he sat down to nurse his beer and his shin, he thought he might finally have an idea about how he might do just that.

Tess left for the office even earlier than usual Monday morning. She didn't know if Owen and Carl were back from their trip yet, but if they were, she was determined to catch them before anyone else showed up at work.

As it turned out, they were both waiting in her office when she walked in.

"Good morning," she said, forcing a nonchalance she didn't feel.

"Good morning," they both echoed her greeting.

She set her cup of coffee carefully on her desk and sank into her chair. "What's going on with GigaPix?" she asked.

"I told you she suspected there would be changes coming," Owen told his partner.

Tess tried to take comfort in his use of the word *changes* rather than *unemployment.*

"I hope you haven't been worrying yourself about this," he said to Tess.

"I'd rather plan than worry," she said, although she'd been doing a lot of the latter anyway. And though her pregnancy and the uncertainty of her relationship with Craig were the foremost concerns in her mind, the possibility of losing her job was a very close second.

She loved her job as an animation software programmer and though she was confident she would find other work to ensure she was taking home a paycheck, she knew there wouldn't be the same kind of opportunities she'd had at SBG because there weren't any other software companies in Pinehurst.

"That's good," Carl said. "Because no final decision has been made as of yet."

"But you're thinking of selling out to GigaPix," she guessed.

He nodded. "Jared has big plans for our programs

and with a staff twice the size of ours, I have no doubt he can implement them. But he's also agreed, for the sake of continuity and as a gesture of goodwill, to hire some of our programmers to continue working with the SBG programs. You're one of the programmers that we've recommended and Jared has agreed that he'd like to make you an offer."

The fear that had been building inside, verging on panic, finally started to dissipate.

Carl smiled. "You look a little surprised."

"I am," she said. "More than a little. When I saw both of you in here, I thought you were going to tell me that I was losing my job."

"On the contrary, if everything works out, this will be a heck of a promotion for you, Tess."

She wasn't just relieved, she was elated. A promotion was more than recognition of the work she'd done, it was an acknowledgment that she was capable of so much more. "When will you know for sure?"

"It will probably take a few more weeks to get all the details worked out," Owen said. "Once everything is ready to go, Jared will come back to speak with you himself, but we wanted to give you a heads-up."

"Thank you," she said. "Both of you, for recommending me."

"No thanks required," Carl told her.

"You've earned this," Owen added. "And you deserve it."

She wanted to laugh and shout and jump in the air, but she managed to limit herself to a smile as the two men rose to their feet.

"Just one question," Owen said, pausing at the

door. "How did you make the connection between Jared and GigaPix?"

"His name triggered something," she admitted. "So I did an Internet search and found out who he was. I actually applied for a job at GigaPix when I was finishing up at DeVry, thinking that I'd like to live in California, but I got an offer in Arizona first, then I came back here."

Owen smiled. "Looks like you'll get that chance to work at GigaPix and live in California after all."

She kept the smile on her face until her bosses had left her office, then buried her face in her hands as excitement and despair battled inside her.

California.

She'd assumed—wrongly, it turned out—that she would continue to work here. It hadn't occurred to her that Jared would move SBG across the country. Of course it made sense that he would, she just hadn't thought that far ahead. And it was still a tremendous opportunity for her, she knew it was. The Golden State. Her dream job.

There was just one problem: it would take her almost three thousand miles away from her baby's father.

Chapter Seven

Tess felt a quick surge of apprehension when she pulled into the parking lot of her apartment building and recognized Craig's Lexus in one of the visitor spaces. He was waiting on the front step for her this time and smiled when he saw her coming up the walk. He didn't wait for her to approach him, but met her halfway, taking her arm and steering her back toward the parking lot again.

"Craig, I'm just getting home. What are you doing?"

"There's somewhere I want to take you."

"Can't it wait?"

"Actually no, it can't."

She heard the excitement in his voice and decided she didn't want to dim his enthusiasm with talk of moving across the country. So she followed him back to his car, settled herself in the passenger seat.

She didn't ask where they were going but watched

the scenery outside her window and noted that they were moving north, in the direction that Craig lived. But when he drove past the exit for his condominium complex, she was baffled. Even more so when he turned into a long drive that led toward a two-story saltbox style home.

"Do you know the people who live here?" she asked cautiously.

"No," he said.

He pulled up alongside a red minivan that was already parked in the driveway. "Good, Tina's already here."

"Who's Tina?"

"The real estate agent."

He went around to open her door, but she remained immobile, not even unclipping her seat belt.

"What are we doing here, Craig?"

"Looking at the house."

"Why?"

"Because you have to move out of your apartment soon and there isn't enough room for you and me and the baby in mine."

She glanced wistfully at the house, then shook her head. "You know I can't afford to buy a house. Especially not a house like this." Especially not now.

She'd spent the first couple of years after college paying back her student loans. The savings and investments she'd so carefully compiled over the last few years might have made a nice little down-payment, but not on a house like this. And not when she would be moving to another state when GigaPix took over SBG. Because she knew that moving to San Diego was the logical thing to do, even if she wished, for personal reasons, that it wasn't a move she had to make right now. But it was the best thing for her career. Sure, she could probably find another job in Pinehurst, but nothing comparable to the position at SBG. And if she was going to support her baby, she needed to work.

Craig reached across to unfasten the belt for her. "There's no harm in taking a look."

"I just think it's a waste of time—yours, mine and the real estate agent's," she said, but she finally climbed out of the car.

"I'm glad to see you were running a little behind schedule, too," Tina called out the apology as she was unbuckling her baby from the back seat. "My usual after-hours sitter is sick and my husband was stuck in a late meeting at the office, so I had to bring Chloe for the tour."

"Not a problem," Craig told her, easily lifting baby Chloe from her mother's arms. "A beautiful woman—no matter how young—is always welcome."

Tina laughed. "That's the one thing I remembered about you, Craig—always a charmer." She hefted the diaper bag and briefcase onto her shoulder, then turned to offer her hand. "You must be Tess."

Tess shook her hand. "It's nice to meet you."

"I'm glad you were able to make it this afternoon," Tina said, already moving up the flagstone walk toward the front door. "This property was only listed two days ago, but there have been at least half a dozen couples to look at it already and I received a page while I was on my way here that there's an offer expected to come in on it tonight."

"That's fast," Craig commented.

Tina shrugged as she inserted a key into the lock. "Everything moves fast in this neighborhood."

Tess followed Craig, who still had Chloe in his arms, more fascinated by the comfort he displayed with the baby than by the gleaming hardwood floors and wide center staircase.

"We'll start the tour in the master suite," Tina said, leading the way.

It didn't take Tess long to realize why she'd started there. The room had a two-sided fireplace that divided the sleeping area from a sitting area, French doors that led to a private balcony and an ensuite bathroom with a separate shower and soaker tub and a skylight overhead.

"What do you think?" Craig asked.

"I think this room is almost bigger than my whole apartment."

"Probably," he admitted. "But what I really like is that there's enough room in the sitting area for a crib and change table and rocking chair."

Looking at Craig, standing in the center of the room with the baby tucked comfortably against his shoulder, Tess could picture it, too. It was almost too easy to imagine living in this house with him, sharing this room—and a bed—with him, raising their child together. She turned away, ignoring the ache that pierced deep into her heart, and followed Tina into the next room.

There were five other bedrooms and three more bathrooms on the upper level, then a den, formal living room, huge family room, another bathroom, dining room and kitchen on the main level. The kitchen was a dream: maple cabinets, granite countertops and a huge island. Not that she was much of a cook—but she could still recognize and appreciate the potential. There were French doors off the eating area to a large patio that overlooked the spacious backyard. And in the backyard was a covered sandbox and a wooden climber/swing set.

Craig came to stand behind her, looking over her shoulder into the yard. "You like it?"

She turned around, saw Chloe was patting Craig's cheeks with her dimpled fists, clearly infatuated with the man who was carrying her in his strong arms.

"What's not to like? It's beautiful."

"It would be a great place to raise a child," he said.

Chloe clapped her hands together, signaling her agreement.

Tess smiled. "It would, but it's practically sold already. And even if it wasn't, it's way beyond my means. Heck, it's probably even beyond my dreams."

"It's not," he told her. "We could—"

"No." She interrupted quickly, before he could finish making the offer, before she could be tempted by it.

And she would be tempted, because she'd known from the moment she stepped inside the front door that she wanted this house. She wanted her baby to have a home with a yard and a swing set.

"Think about it, Tess. It could be ours. Yours and mine and our baby's."

She could only shake her head as she swallowed around the lump in her throat. She had to tell Craig that SBG was being sold, that she would soon be moving to California. But not here—not with the real estate agent hovering in the background—and not now.

Soon, she promised herself. Just not yet.

It was Friday and Craig was spending the night with a cold beer and ESPN. He'd declined an invitation from his brother to join Gage and some friends for drinks at Maxie's, a local drinking establishment that was popular for its selection of martinis and two-story dance floor. Although he wouldn't have minded spending time with Gage, he'd grown weary of the bar scene a long time ago. And Maxie's had never been one of his favorite places—even less so since the debacle with his ex-fiancée.

Lana had worked in marketing at Richmond Pharmaceuticals, although he'd never been introduced to her before the night they'd crossed paths at Maxie's. His eyes had met hers across the bar and she'd smiled and started toward him. He found out later that she'd known exactly who he was before she ever came over to introduce herself.

They were engaged less than a year later and then Lana pressed for a short engagement insisting that she was eager to become Mrs. Craig Richmond and start their life together. It hadn't taken him long to realize that she was even more eager to start spending his money.

She'd asked for a temporary leave of absence from work so she could concentrate on planning their wedding, which included trips to New York City with her girlfriends to look for the perfect bridal gown, to search out the best master pastry chef to design their wedding cake, to find the most exclusive florist to import and arrange their flowers.

Craig had been startled by the cost of everything but he knew the wedding was important to Lana and he wanted her to be happy. It was a few months before their planned nuptials that he happened to come home early one day and overhear his fiancée admitting to her maid of honor that she had no intention of returning to her job in marketing. "I'll hardly need a paycheck from Richmond Pharmaceuticals when I'll have access to the entire Richmond fortune," she'd said matter-of-factly.

Craig had confronted her later that night, advising her not to waste the postage sending out invitations because there wasn't going to be a wedding. She'd sent them anyway, certain she could manipulate him into following through. He'd responded by personally calling each of the three hundred invited guests to advise that the wedding was off.

When her tears and pleas were similarly unsuccessful in changing his mind, she'd actually threatened to sue him for breach of promise. He'd dared her to try. She'd found someone richer—and more gullible—instead.

But that near miss had reminded Craig of the lessons he should have learned when his mother walked out of his life: when a woman said she loved him, his heart was going to take a beating. In his experience, women used emotions to camouflage their real motivations, and he'd been careful since his broken engagement to keep his relationships with women brief and uncomplicated. He made no promises and asked for none in return.

Until he'd proposed to Tess. But that was different. She was his friend—they liked and respected one another and wouldn't confuse their relationship with unwanted emotions.

Of course, he had yet to convince her to marry him.

Over the past several weeks, he'd managed to see her almost every day—either by stopping by her office or showing up at her apartment. If he didn't see her, he'd at least talk to her on the phone. He sent her flowers once a week and various other gifts: a new book by her favorite author, a cheesecake from her favorite bakery, a CD by her favorite jazz musician, an orange ceramic hippopotamus toothbrush holder because it was tacky and he knew she'd love it. Nothing too extravagant or pricey—just little tokens to let her know that he was thinking about her.

He took her to the theater, the flea market, a dog show. And although she was still insisting that she didn't want to marry him, he thought her protests were less adamant than they'd been at first and he was optimistic that eventually he would wear her down. Hopefully before their baby was born.

He glanced at the clock, considered calling her. But it was almost ten and when he'd spoken to her earlier that day, she'd told him that she was tired and planning an early night. When the phone beside him rang, he wondered if it might be Tess. But it was Nigel, the nighttime doorman, telling him that his brother was on his way up.

"I thought you were going to be at Maxie's tonight," he said, when he opened the door to let Gage into his condo.

"I was." Gage helped himself to a beer from the fridge, twisted the cap off, then dropped onto the sofa beside his brother and propped his feet up on the coffee table. "Then Debby showed up."

Craig picked up the remote and lowered the volume on the ball game. "Debby? The love of your life? The one who was going to ruin you for all other women?"

"Yeah, well, she tried," Gage muttered.

"What happened?"

"She started hinting—and none too subtly, either—that she expected a ring on her finger for our one-year anniversary."

"When would that be?" Craig asked, trying to remember when his brother had first mentioned the woman's name. It seemed to him it had only been a few months earlier.

"Valentine's Day," Gage said. "Six months from now."

Craig chuckled at the bafflement in his brother's voice.

Gage took a long pull from his bottle. "I'm twenty-seven years old. I have no interest in tying myself down to one woman at this point in my life—no matter how spectacular the sex is."

"Too much information."

His brother just grinned. "Speaking of information, there was another reason I wanted to stop by tonight."

"You mean there's a purpose to this visit other than to hide out where your girlfriend can't find you?"

"Yes," Gage said. "And it concerns your girlfriend."

Craig didn't know what to say. He knew Gage couldn't be talking about Tess—he couldn't know about the recent developments in their relationship—could he? And since Craig hadn't been dating anyone else in recent months, he was truly baffled by his brother's statement.

"Or rather, your ex-girlfriend," Gage said, which didn't clarify his statement for Craig at all.

"Karen?" he asked.

"Lana."

He found it a little disconcerting that his brother would bring up her name when she'd so recently been in his own thoughts. "What about her?" he asked.

"She was at Maxie's tonight."

That was even more surprising because he'd heard that she'd moved to Texas with her billionaire husband, Preston Sinclair.

"Dancing up a storm in a tight little dress that showed her God-given assets to full advantage."

"Not God-given," Craig told him.

"Well, you would know." His brother sighed with obvious disappointment. "And I should have guessed that they were too perfect to be real."

Just like the rest of her, Craig thought, but kept the comment to himself. Instead, he said, "And you should have realized Preston Sinclair wouldn't appreciate the way you were ogling his wife."

"Ex-wife," Gage said.

"They're divorced already?"

His brother nodded. "And Lana was making it clear to anyone and everyone that she's a single woman again."

Craig picked up his bottle, took a long swallow as he considered this revelation. He thought he should feel something but he really didn't care. Whatever feelings he'd had for Lana had been put to rest a long time ago.

"She made a point of talking to me," Gage continued. "Asking about you. I told her you were seeing somebody."

His brother was full of surprises tonight, although this was one Craig was grateful to hear. "Thanks."

Gage shrugged. "Hey, for all I know, you are seeing somebody. Just because your brother is always the last to know what's going on in your life..."

He ignored the not-so-subtle question along with any inclination to confide in his brother. Until he and

Tess figured out what they were going to do, he thought it was best to keep the news of her pregnancy quiet.

"If I ever feel the need to spill the details of my personal life, I'll let you know," he said instead.

"You'd have to actually have a personal life first," Gage pointed out.

Craig got up to get another couple of beers from the fridge.

"Does this mean you'll let me crash in your guest room tonight?" his brother asked, accepting one of the bottles.

"You can't hide out here forever," he said. "But for tonight—sure."

Craig wasn't surprised that Tess didn't respond immediately to his knock on the door Sunday morning. She'd always been a pretty sound sleeper and he knew she didn't believe in rising early on weekends, so he knocked harder and waited. He knew she was home because her car was in the parking lot downstairs and he'd just raised his hand to knock a third time when the door was pulled open.

"Are you trying to wake my neighbors, too?" she asked moodily.

Craig smiled and stepped past her into the apartment. "No, just you." He touched his lips to her cheek. "Good morning."

She raised a hand and pushed her tousled hair away from her face. Her eyes were still heavy-lidded from sleep, her face bare of makeup and her torso clad in an oversized, wrinkled T-shirt. She looked deliciously rumpled and incredibly tempting.

He'd always thought she was beautiful, just as he'd

always thought it was ridiculous to describe pregnant women as glowing. But there really was something different about her now, an indescribable something that simply took his breath away. And while there wasn't any obvious evidence of their baby growing inside her yet, he could already imagine how she would look when her belly was round with his child, and the mental image stirred within him both pride and possessiveness.

"What's so good about it?" she mumbled.

"You get to spend it with me," he told her.

She yawned. "Is there a second prize?"

"No." He turned to the kitchen. "Why don't you go get dressed while I make myself some coffee?"

"Because I didn't plan on getting dressed today," she said belligerently. "I want to stay in bed all day."

He grinned. "That sounds even better than what I had planned."

"Are you always this funny first thing in the morning?"

"Are you always this grumpy first thing in the morning?" he countered.

"Yes."

He measured coffee grounds into a paper filter. "If that's true, maybe I should rethink this whole marriage idea."

"You should definitely rethink it," she told him. "Because I am *not* going to marry you."

"You know, you don't sound quite as adamant as you did a couple weeks ago."

"I just need coffee. I can't argue coherently when my brain isn't even functioning."

She sat down at the table to wait for the coffee. As

she crossed one leg over the other, he couldn't help but notice that the oversized T-shirt she wore barely covered the tops of her thighs, displaying her long, slender legs to advantage. It was an effort to look away, to turn his attention to the cupboard where the mugs were located.

"Have you been cutting down on your caffeine intake?"

She glared at him. "I have one cup of coffee in the morning. The doctor has assured me that it won't harm the baby."

He poured coffee into a mug, added a generous amount of milk and passed it across the table to her.

"I take it black."

He grinned. "I know. The milk is for the baby."

"Has anyone ever told you that you're pushy and obnoxious?"

"Frequently," he admitted.

She sipped her coffee, grimaced.

"Do you want me to make breakfast or do you want to grab something to eat on the way?"

"On the way where?" she asked, her voice tinged with suspicion.

"It's a surprise."

"I've had enough surprises in my life lately."

"Well, today there's one more. Go get dressed."

Tess set her chin stubbornly. "I'm not going anywhere."

He sipped from his own mug. "I'd suggest you go and put some clothes on."

"Or what?"

The challenge in her voice was almost too much to resist. "Or I'll carry you to your bedroom and dress you myself." He allowed his eyes to skim over her boldly. "Or maybe just undress you. The choice is yours."

Her eyes dropped and she gulped down the rest of her coffee. "I'll get dressed."

He nodded. "Good idea."

Tess was stubbornly silent throughout most of the drive. It didn't take her long to figure out they were headed into New York City, but she didn't suspect why until she saw the approach for the George Washington Bridge. When she did, she was helpless to prevent the smile that curved her lips.

"We're going to Yankee Stadium?"

Craig chuckled and nodded.

"Why are you laughing?" she asked suspiciously.

"Because most of the women I know have a weakness for flowers or jewelry. Your weakness is baseball."

She shrugged. "It's just a different kind of diamond."

And it *was* her weakness, Tess admitted to herself as Craig sat back down beside her with the hot dogs he'd purchased at the refreshment stand. She loved the whole atmosphere of the ballpark: the bodies crammed shoulder-to-shoulder in the stands. Men, women and children, their faces glowing with excitement as the action played out on the field below. She breathed deeply, inhaling the scents of roasted peanuts and spilled beer, dry dust and fresh sweat.

"Are you having fun?" Craig asked, handing her a hot dog generously doctored with ketchup and mustard.

There was no way she could deny it, especially when her Yankees were winning.

"Yes, I am." She took a bite of her hot dog.

He grinned and handed her a napkin. "Good."

The crack of a bat echoed through the stadium and

the crowd rose as one to watch the ball soar high over the right field fence.

"Another two runs for the Yankees," Tess said proudly.

She was enjoying herself, more than she'd expected. She hadn't had many opportunities to relax lately and that Craig had not only known she needed such a diversion but provided it, reminded Tess how well he could read her. And how nice it was to have someone in her life that she could count on.

She took another bite of her hot dog as a voice inside her head nagged to remind her that he could be a permanent part of her life—her husband and a father to their baby.

Except that she didn't want to marry a man who didn't love her, who would never love her. And the one thing she knew about Craig was that he'd closed off his heart to the kind of happily-ever-after love she dreamed of sharing with a man someday. Just because she'd screwed up with Roger didn't mean she'd given up hope of finding the kind of once-in-a-lifetime love her parents had shared.

But maybe she needed to rethink her dreams now that she had a baby on the way. Maybe it was selfish to want more than what he was offering. Maybe she was being unrealistic in wanting the man she loved to love her back.

Her breath caught in her throat as panic ballooned inside her. Oh, no. No way. She nixed that thought immediately.

She was *not* in love with Craig!

He was her friend—her best friend. Other than Laurie, he was the only person in her life that she could really count on. Falling in love with him would be crazy.

She swallowed the last bite of hot dog, felt it slide

like lead into her stomach as she tried to reassure herself that she wasn't in love with her best friend. She was simply overreacting to the situation, dealing with the hormonal overload from her pregnancy. Yes, that made sense. Certainly more sense than that she'd fallen in love with her best friend.

What was love anyway?

She'd thought she'd been in love with Roger, but obviously she'd been wrong. She cared about Craig, that was only natural given their history and yes, she'd even go so far to say she loved him—as a friend. But anything more than that wasn't possible.

There should be some kind of test for love—a questionnaire, maybe. No less than three questions and if you didn't answer all questions positively, you weren't in love.

Question number one: Do you think of him at all hours of the day, even when your mind should be occupied with other tasks?

Question number two: Do you miss him when you're not with him and look forward to the next time you'll see him again?

Question number three: Can you imagine yourself spending the rest of your life with this person?

Tess mentally reviewed the list of questions and her answers. Yes…yes…and…yes.

Oh, God—she *was* in love with Craig.

"Tess?"

She glanced up, saw the concern in his dark brown eyes, in the crease between his brows.

"Sorry?"

"I asked if you wanted another hot dog."

She shook her head. "No. Thank you."

The crease between his brows deepened. "Are you okay? You seemed to go pale all of a sudden."

"I'm okay."

"Are you sure? Maybe it's the sun. Are you too hot?"

"I'm fine," she snapped.

"Okay." He still looked unconvinced but he let it drop.

Fine, she mocked herself.

How could she be fine when she'd just realized she was in love with her best friend?

Oh, she'd really made a mess of things now. She felt like she was standing at the plate, watching the balls scream past in quick succession before she even had a chance to swing the bat.

She'd had sex with Craig: strike one.

She was pregnant: strike two.

She'd fallen in love: strike three.

She was out.

Out of her mind—in love with her best friend.

Now what was she going to do?

Well, the one thing she was not going to do was tell Craig she'd made the colossal mistake of falling in love with him.

Because she knew how he'd react: he'd be shocked, then panicked, then he'd withdraw from her. Maybe not immediately and probably not obviously, but inevitably—because Craig didn't do messy emotions.

She'd been worried about how the revelation of her pregnancy would affect their friendship but that was nothing compared to *this.* Craig didn't trust love and he wouldn't trust her feelings if she was foolish enough to admit to them. He wouldn't believe she wasn't using the words for some ulterior purpose. Because he didn't believe that anyone ever had or could love him unconditionally.

Tess knew otherwise, of course. His father—although often preoccupied with the business—had always been there for Craig. And Grace—Allan's second wife—had fallen in love with both of her stepchildren as quickly as she'd fallen for her husband. But it was the withdrawal of affection from his natural mother that had left such deep wounds, and though Tess wanted to believe her love might be enough to heal them, she couldn't be certain. And she wasn't ready to face yet another rejection.

No, the one thing she knew for certain was that she wasn't going to tell Craig about her newly discovered feelings.

The whole office was buzzing with the news that SBG was being bought out by GigaPix and speculation was rampant about the fate of SBG's employees. As Tess strode briskly down the hall toward the conference room for her meeting with Jared McCabe, she was grateful the moment of truth, at least for her, had finally arrived. She wiped her damp palms down the front of her skirt before knocking on the door.

"Come in."

Tess did so, entering the room to face Jared McCabe across the wide polished table. He offered his hand, as he had the first time they met, then gestured for her to be seated.

"As of October first, SBG will become a subsidiary company of GigaPix Corporation and its operations will move to the corporate headquarters in

California. I'd like you to come to San Diego to be part of the GigaPix team." Then he opened one of the folders that were lined up in front of him and outlined the terms of his offer, including a salary that almost made her eyes pop out.

She should have been reaching for a pen, asking where to sign the contract of employment. Instead, she said, "It's a generous offer."

Jared closed the folder, his eyes narrowing speculatively on her.

She swallowed. "And I'm grateful for it. But..."

He waited silently.

She swallowed again, not quite believing the words that were coming out of her mouth. But she'd lain awake through most of the night thinking about so many things: her career, her pregnancy and overriding all else, the realization that she'd fallen in love with her baby's father. And she'd finally understood why she'd been unable to tell Craig about her intention to move to California—because she'd never really intended to go.

Sure, she'd entertained the idea, maybe even dreamed about the possibilities. But the reality was, she couldn't move three thousand miles away from her best friend, the father of her child, the man she loved.

"But I can't move to San Diego," she finished.

Now that Tess had made the decision to stay in Pinehurst, she was scrambling. She had until October thirtieth to find a new apartment but only until the first—less than two months away—to get a new job.

She was poring over the classified section of the newspaper when Craig stopped by her apartment Saturday morning with croissants and cappuccino. He took a seat across from her at the table completely covered with newspapers and watched her work.

She tried not to let his scrutiny distract her as she circled the apartment ads that sounded promising, then looked up the locations in her map book. She had a notepad beside her, where she was jotting down the addresses and making notes about the proximity to schools, parks and recreation centers.

She was waiting for him to make a crack about her "list" but he only said, "You're overthinking this, Tess. Just check out the places that sound good and go with what you like."

"I'm not overthinking it," she denied. "I'm trying to save myself time running around to places that are unsuitable."

He picked up one of the newspaper pages she'd scanned and set aside. "Here's one," he said, and began to read. "Rooms available for rent in a privately owned home overlooking green space in desirable Woodland Park neighborhood. Private bath and kitchen, huge backyard, plenty of parking."

"Let me see that." She grabbed the paper from his hand, frowning as she looked for—and failed to find—the listing. "You made that up."

"Well, I didn't want to actually advertise it in the paper. Imagine what kind of crazies might respond."

She pushed a hand through her hair. "Craig, I'm serious about this. I need to find a place so I can get settled in and ready for the baby."

"I'm serious, too. I want you to move in with me."

"But you don't have..." Her eyes widened. "Oh, my god—you bought the house?"

"Well, I've signed the papers," he said. "The deal doesn't officially close until next week."

She shook her head. "You're crazy."

"Actually, Tina assured me it was a wise investment."

"Is that why you bought it?"

"No," he admitted. "I bought it because I could picture our child sleeping in the nursery and playing in the backyard and then I couldn't imagine anyone else living there."

She felt her throat tighten with unexpected emotion.

"What do you think?" he asked. "Want to move in with me?"

She should say no firmly and finally. This idea was almost as crazy as marriage and yet she couldn't help but be tempted.

"There are plenty of bedrooms to choose from," he reminded her. "And then we could both be there full-time for our baby."

"Living together doesn't seem that different than getting married," she protested.

"I'm still open to marriage," he told her. "But I thought I should put this out there as an alternative."

No way. If she said yes to his offer she'd be as crazy as he was. But she did need somewhere to live and she did want her baby to have a father.

And she wanted to be with Craig.

She took a deep breath. "Okay."

"Okay?" He stared at her, clearly taken aback by

her sudden capitulation. “Is that an okay—you’ll move in with me?”

She shook her head. “No, it’s an okay—I’ll marry you.”

Chapter Eight

They were the words Craig had started to despair of ever hearing her speak. That she'd said them now left him completely speechless. At least for a moment.

"You really want to get married?" he asked cautiously, when he'd finally found his voice.

"Sure."

It wasn't quite the definitive response he would have liked, but it was an improvement on no. Still, he had to ask, "Why?"

"Do you want me to make a list of all the reasons I've changed my mind?"

"You mean you haven't already?"

"No." Her fingers curled around the pad of paper in her hand, gripping it so tightly her knuckles turned white. "It was an impulse—and one I'm already starting to question."

"Don't," he said quickly. "I don't know what caused this sudden change of heart but I really believe this is the right decision. I'm glad we're finally on the same page about what we want."

Tess didn't meet his gaze but stared instead at the list clutched in her hand.

"We are on the same page about what we want, aren't we?" he asked.

"I want my baby to have a family," she agreed, finally looking up at him. "And I can't think of anyone who would make a better father than you."

Her confidence bolstered his doubts and her willingness to take this leap of faith strengthened his determination to ensure she would never regret it. "Thank you."

He reached across the table to uncurl her fingers from the paper and link them with his own. "How soon do you think you can get away for a wedding and honeymoon?"

She seemed startled by his question. "You don't waste any time, do you?"

"Now that we've made the decision, I don't see any point in waiting."

"You're right," she agreed. "But a honeymoon isn't necessary. This isn't—"

He touched a finger to her lips, halting her protest. "Make no mistake about it, Tess, what I want is a real marriage and what I'm asking of you is a real commitment."

She swallowed. "I thought…"

"What did you think?"

"I thought you just wanted both of us to be there for our baby—to live separate lives under the same roof."

"Where would you ever get that idea?"

"From you," she said. "Not ten minutes ago. When you asked me to move in with you, you said there were a lot of bedrooms…"

"That was before you agreed to marry me," he pointed out.

She chewed on her bottom lip. "What exactly do you mean by a real marriage?"

He smiled. "I'm sure you can guess."

"You mean…one bedroom."

"I'm hoping," he admitted. "But that decision is yours."

"Oh." She exhaled and it sounded almost like a sigh of relief.

The unenthusiastic response immediately deflated his hopes. "Apparently you had a different idea."

"It's just that you haven't seemed…interested…in me. Lately."

He was stunned. "Why would you think that?"

"Well—" her cheeks flushed prettily "—you haven't even kissed me in weeks."

He hadn't done so deliberately, because he hadn't wanted to pressure her. But damn, it had been hard to keep his hands off her. "Not for lack of wanting," he assured her.

"Oh."

But he could tell by the furrow in her brow that she still didn't get it. And he knew he had to tell her the whole truth so that wherever they decided to go from here, that decision wouldn't be based on any kind of miscommunication.

"I haven't kissed you, Tess, partly because I didn't want you to accuse me of trying to seduce you into marriage, but mostly because I was afraid that if I started, I wouldn't want to stop."

"Oh," she said again, then, more softly, "I wouldn't want you to stop, either."

It took all of his willpower not to pull her into his arms and test her statement right then. But from the moment he'd found out she was pregnant, he'd tried to think about what was best for Tess and his baby rather than his own wants. And that meant getting married before they did anything else.

He took a step back, away from temptation. "Let's go shopping."

Tess stared at the dazzling collection of diamond engagement rings displayed on the burgundy velvet cloth. She felt completely overwhelmed—not just by the selection of rings but by everything that had happened in the past hour since she'd agreed to marry Craig. She was still trying to wrap her head around that impulsive decision and he was already planning the wedding.

Maybe she should be grateful—obviously someone had to take care of the details. But she hadn't thought beyond the moment and she didn't seem capable of making any more decisions right now. She couldn't even decide on a ring and they'd been in the jewelry store for at least thirty minutes already, tucked into a private office with Brian Shaw, manager of The Diamond Jubilee.

Craig laid his hand on her shoulder. "What do you think?"

She thought she was going to go blind if she kept staring at these rocks. "A simple gold band would be fine."

She saw a muscle in his jaw flex then relax. He turned to the jeweler. "Could we have a minute, Mr. Shaw?"

"Of course, Mr. Richmond."

He didn't say anything else until they heard the soft click of the door behind Mr. Shaw as he left the room. When he spoke, his voice was gentle, almost concerned. "I know this isn't going to be the wedding you always dreamed about, Tess, but I want to make it special for you."

"I just don't want you to feel obligated—"

"Tess," he interrupted.

She glanced up, hoping he wouldn't see the combination of excitement and uncertainty she felt reflected in her eyes. Desperately hoping he wouldn't suspect the unacknowledged and ever-growing feelings in her heart.

"I'm *very* happy you agreed to marry me," he said. "And I'd like to buy you an engagement ring as a token of my appreciation and affection. Do you have any objection to that?"

"No," she said, because any other response would sound ridiculous. And she didn't object, but she was disappointed. She wanted to be marrying Craig not just because she was pregnant with his child, but because he loved her as much as she loved him. "I'm sorry—I guess I'm just feeling a little overwhelmed because everything is happening so fast."

He smiled. "Maybe I don't want to give you a chance to change your mind."

She turned sideways in her chair so she could see his face. "What if you change yours?"

"After weeks of campaigning for you to marry me, why would I change my mind now?"

"Because now you know it's really going to happen—

we're going to get married and have a baby together and you're going to be stuck with both of us for the rest of your life."

"Are you trying to scare me?"

"Maybe."

"Then you'll have to try harder. I've thought about this from every angle, considered every alternative. The truth is, you're the only woman I can imagine spending the rest of my life with."

It wasn't a declaration of love, but it was an affirmation of his commitment to her and Tess knew she would have to be satisfied with that—at least for now. If he cared about her enough to marry her, she wanted to believe that someday he might fall in love with her, too.

In the meantime, he was anxious to put a ring on her finger and though Tess wanted to accommodate him, the vast selection of diamonds simply overwhelmed her.

He gestured to the collection spread out before them. "Is there anything you like?"

She looked them over again, hoping that something would catch her eye, but none did.

"They're all spectacular," she said, "but they're…"

Craig smiled when she paused. "What are you trying not to say? Gaudy? Tacky? Ostentatious?"

She still hesitated, thinking that any of those descriptions would fit. "They're just not me," she said at last.

He selected a ring at random—an enormous heart-shaped solitaire on a braided gold band—and slid it onto her finger. The diamond overwhelmed her slender hand so much that even Craig shook his head. He tried another ring—a pear-shaped diamond that weighed a ton—or at least several carats. "What do you think?"

She looked at him and raised her brows. "I wouldn't be able to go out in public without worrying that I'd be mugged."

He chuckled softly. "Okay, maybe we need to look at something different."

A brisk knock preceded Mr. Shaw's return a few minutes later. "Have we made any progress?" he asked.

Craig shook his head. "I think we're looking for something out of the ordinary."

"And a little more subtle," Tess added.

"A colored stone, perhaps?" Mr. Shaw asked. "We have a fabulous selection of Colombian emeralds and Indian sapphires."

Craig looked at Tess. She shrugged.

"Let's take a look at the sapphires," Craig suggested.

"I'll be right back," the manager promised, bundling up the unwanted diamonds before disappearing again.

"Why a sapphire?" Tess asked, hoping that he would give her a response that was more unique than some cheesy reference to the color of her eyes.

"Because it was believed by ancient civilizations that the world rested on top of a sapphire and that the color of the sky was a reflection of the stone." He picked up her hand, laced their fingers together. "You're giving me everything I want, Tess. In return, I want to give you the world."

From any other man, the explanation might have sounded scripted, but he spoke as if the words were really coming from his heart and she couldn't help but be touched by his sincerity.

Then she caught the twinkle in his eye just before he added, "And because a sapphire will match your eyes."

He grinned when she tugged her hand out of his grasp.

Before she could respond, Mr. Shaw returned, this time with a smaller, but still impressive, collection of rings that he laid out carefully on the velvet cloth.

Tess surveyed the selection, her gaze lingering on a modest square-cut sapphire flanked by graduated baguette diamonds. It was different and stunning, and obviously Craig thought so, too, because he immediately reached for it.

"Do you like it?" he asked Tess, watching closely as if to gauge her reaction.

"It's beautiful."

He smiled, apparently pleased that they'd finally found something they both liked. He took her hand and slid the circle of gold onto the third finger. It fit as if it had been made for her.

"That one's a Diamond Jubilee original. Designed by my daughter," Brian Shaw said proudly. "It's an eighteen-karat gold band with a one-carat Kashmir sapphire and six of the highest quality baguette diamonds."

"Is there a wedding band that goes with this?" Craig asked.

"No," the manager admitted. "But we can design one to match if you like."

"It will have to be ready by the middle of the week," he said.

"Of course, Mr. Richmond."

His response made Tess wonder, once again, if anyone actually succeeded in saying no to Craig. Lord knows she'd tried—she'd told him over and over again that she wasn't going to marry him. And now she was wearing his engagement ring on her finger.

Craig reached for Tess's hand as they left the jewelry store, rubbed his thumb over the ring on her finger. It was a symbol—solid, tangible proof that she would soon be his wife. He waited for the wave of terror to hit, was prepared to battle back the fear. He wasn't going to screw this up. He'd made a promise to Tess and he intended to keep it.

But as his finger stroked over the smooth band, he felt none of the expected panic. What he felt instead was satisfaction, happiness even. He frowned. Their marriage was a means to an end—his way of ensuring his place in his child's life. So why was he suddenly beginning to think that it could be so much more? Why was he thinking about the benefits of having Tess as his wife instead of just the mother of his child?

He continued to ponder these questions as they walked back to his car. "Did you want to grab a bite for dinner before I take you home?" he asked.

"Just because I'm pregnant doesn't mean you always have to be feeding me," she told him.

"Actually, my offer had nothing to do with your pregnancy and everything to do with the fact that I'm hungry and I thought you might be, too."

"I guess I am," she admitted.

"Are you in the mood for anything in particular?"

"Honey garlic chicken wings."

"Really?" He was surprised—Tess wasn't usually a big fan of chicken wings.

She shrugged "I seem to be having some unusual cravings lately."

"Like what?"

"Dill pickle potato chips. Coconut shrimp. Caesar salad."

"At the same time?"

She laughed. "No. Not so far, anyway."

"But tonight you want honey garlic chicken wings?"

"Yes."

"Okay, then, chicken wings it is."

They picked up a double order of honey garlic wings, fried rice and egg rolls and took it back to her apartment. Tess dug into the food with surprising appetite and no indication that she was still suffering from the nausea she'd complained about only a few weeks earlier.

"Have you had any more morning sickness?" he asked.

She gave a slight shake of her head as she licked sticky sauce from her fingers and he found his gaze riveted to the actions of her tongue, forgetting his own question until she responded, "The nausea seemed to pass after the first six weeks. Now the only problem I seem to have is controlling my appetite. I've already gained back the few pounds I lost in those early weeks and another four."

He let his eyes skim over her still slender form. He'd always thought she was a little too thin and though he really couldn't tell that she'd added a few pounds, he thought she looked great. Healthy. Glowing. And all the other clichés about pregnant women. "The extra pounds look good on you."

She dipped her egg roll into the plum sauce. "Let's see if you still think so in another six months."

"Let's see how much you really eat," he teased. "I need to know if I can afford to feed you for the next six months."

"Actually, that is something we should discuss."

He spooned some more rice onto his plate. "I was kidding, Tess."

"I know," she said. "But I don't expect you to be financially responsible for me."

"What does that mean?"

"I want to pay my own expenses."

He sighed wearily. "Tess, you're going to be my wife. For better or for worse; for richer or for poorer. I'm not going to start divvying up the household bills."

"Then I can buy the groceries."

"That's not necessary," he protested.

"Yes, it is. I need to make some kind of contribution."

"Fine," he relented, because he knew it was important to her even if he didn't really understand why. "You can buy the groceries."

"Thank you."

"Do you want to do the cooking, too?" he asked.

She dragged a chicken wing through the sauce in the bottom of the container. "Do you want to live on meat loaf and peanut butter sandwiches?"

"No," he admitted. "But I probably could live on your oatmeal chocolate chip cookies."

She smiled. "Cookies I can do."

He studied her thoughtfully. "How is it that someone who can bake like you do—" and she did make the best cakes and cookies and all other kinds of desserts "—can't master a simple pot roast?"

"Have you ever made a pot roast?" she challenged.

"No."

"Then how can you say it's simple?"

Okay, she had a point there. "You're going to insist on sharing kitchen duties, aren't you?"

"Unless you want to take on all the responsibility yourself," she told him.

"You know I'm not a great cook, either."

"But you're good with a barbecue."

"Maybe I should hire a housekeeper—someone who can appreciate the great kitchen we're going to have."

"Or maybe we should learn to cook."

"Hiring a housekeeper would be easier," he pointed out, as he started clearing their dishes from the table. "Someone to cook *and* clean."

And he would do it, Tess realized. Because he could afford it and it would make their life easier. But she didn't intend to take advantage of his offer.

"If you do the cooking, I'll do the cleanup," she said, trying to take the plates from him so she could load the dishwasher.

He nudged her gently aside and completed the task on his own. "I don't mind the cleanup and you shouldn't be putting your pretty hands in dishwater."

"Pretty hands?" she asked skeptically.

"Very pretty," he said, linking them with his own. "Especially now that you've got my ring on your finger—proof that you're going to marry me."

"You know the old saying—be careful what you wish for?"

He smiled. "I'm not worried."

But she was. She didn't usually make decisions impulsively—especially not decisions of this magnitude. True, she'd spent a lot of time over the past couple of weeks thinking about Craig's proposal and the reasons to accept or refuse. But she'd remained firm in her belief that marriage would be a mistake—until she realized she'd fallen in love with him, then all common sense had apparently deserted her. Or maybe she'd fallen in love because all common sense had already deserted her—it was the only explanation she could think of for loving a man who'd made it clear he didn't want any emotional entanglements.

"Maybe you should be worried," she said. "I know you didn't flinch at the four pounds but I'm going to gain at least twenty more over the next six months."

"Uh-huh." He reached out and laid a hand on the tiny bulge of her tummy. "I can't wait for your belly to grow round, for everyone to know it's my baby you're carrying."

His touch was gentle, his smile almost reverent and in that moment Tess knew that if she hadn't already been in love with him, she would have fallen right then.

"You really are looking forward to being a daddy, aren't you?"

"The idea threw me for a loop at first," he admitted. "But yeah, I'm excited about having a baby with you and very glad that you finally agreed to marry me."

She was excited, too. And apprehensive. Because as much as she wanted to marry him and give their baby a family—she was worried that she would end up wanting more from their marriage than he could give her.

He took her hand again, held it up to gaze at the ring she was wearing. "You know, this makes it official."

She nodded.

"Which means that you have no reason to question my motives when I do this."

Then he kissed her.

And it was a real kiss this time. Lips on lips, soft yet firm but all too brief. His eyes stayed open, watching her as he kissed her again, lingering just a little longer this time.

She leaned forward, sliding her arms around his neck and instinctively pressing her body closer to his. Craig didn't need any more of an invitation.

His mouth covered hers again, his tongue gliding over the seam of her lips, dipping inside when they parted on a sigh of longing and her brain shut down completely.

She couldn't think, she couldn't reason, she could only feel. She felt her heart hammering against her ribs, her blood pulsing through her veins and the ground shifting beneath her feet.

He didn't try to deepen the kiss. He didn't touch her at all except with his lips. And never had she been so completely devastated by a kiss. She wasn't inexperienced, but she'd never experienced anything like this. She'd been kissed passionately, angrily, lustfully, but never so…tenderly. And it was his infinite patience and tenderness that arrowed straight to her heart.

When he finally eased his lips from hers, she was breathless and aching with wanting. And she knew that if he asked to stay she wouldn't say no because she wanted nothing more than to make love with the man she loved.

But he didn't ask.

He only said, "Good night, Tess." And then he walked out the door.

* * *

Craig wasn't sure how his parents would react to the news of his upcoming marriage but he did know that he couldn't imagine such a momentous event taking place without his family being present. So after confirming all the other details he made his way to his father's office.

He timed it so he'd arrive when Lorraine, his father's secretary, would be at lunch. That way, there wouldn't be any witnesses if his father started screaming. Not that his father ever really yelled but Craig had never dropped this kind of news in his lap before so he was prepared for almost anything.

Anything except finding his mother in a passionate lip-lock with his father when he walked through the door.

He immediately looked away, startled—though more pleased than embarrassed—to witness his parents kissing.

It amazed him that even after twenty years of marriage, they were still so obviously in love with one another. It was what he'd once wanted, too—an enduring connection with someone, a sense of belonging to that other person, a forever kind of love. But the closest he'd ever come to that feeling of unconditional acceptance was his friendship with Tess and that bolstered his conviction that their marriage, even though not based on love, would succeed.

"Sorry," he apologized quickly. "Your door was open."

"That's okay," Grace said, stepping out of her husband's arms. "I was just on my way out."

"Actually, I'd like you to stay for a few minutes, please. There's something I wanted to talk to both of you about."

"What's on your mind?" Allan asked.

Craig couldn't think of a way to ease into the topic, so he simply said, "Tess and I are getting married."

He noted the obvious surprise on both of their faces. Then his father frowned, his mother smiled.

"This is…unexpected," Allan said at last.

"The wedding's on Saturday at the Coral Beach Resort in Christ Church, Barbados. I know it's short notice, but I'd like you to be there if you can."

"Short notice?" Allan sputtered. "A month is short notice. This is less than a week and—"

"Of course we'll be there," Grace interrupted, laying her hand on her husband's arm.

His father closed his mouth, but the frown remained.

"Thank you," Craig said to his mother, already moving back toward the door. "Tess and I will be leaving on Friday and staying for a week, but you can make whatever arrangements suit you best."

"I'll call the airline today," she promised him.

He nodded. "I've got to get back to the lab."

And he backtracked out of his dad's office before they could inundate him with the questions he knew had to be racing through their minds.

Chapter Nine

Tess stood on the edge of the patio, waiting for her cue to head down the stone path toward the flower-covered archway on the beach where her groom was waiting. Only eight days had passed since she'd accepted Craig's proposal and today she would become his wife.

One hand clutched the bouquet of fresh, tropical flowers in her hands, crushing the delicate stems. The other pressed to her quivering stomach, willing her nerves to settle.

She caught a glimpse of her reflection in the window of the gift shop and almost didn't recognize the woman who looked back at her. Craig's preparations for the wedding had included The Ultimate Indulgence Package at the hotel spa and she'd spent the morning being scrubbed and buffed and polished, her hair swept into some fancy do on top of her head, her makeup artfully applied. He'd taken care of everything—all she had to do was walk down the aisle.

Her pulse began to race as the first notes of "The Wedding March" sounded. She'd never heard a calypso version of the song before, but it seemed appropriate for an island wedding.

Taking a deep breath, she put one foot in front of the other.

Since she was a young girl, she'd dreamed—as every young girl does—of getting married one day. But even in her wildest fantasies she'd never imagined that she'd find herself with a man like Craig Richmond. He was a real-life Prince Charming: kind, compassionate, giving—not to mention devastatingly gorgeous and sexy as sin. And he was going to be her husband.

And though she knew that he was only marrying her because of the baby, she really did love him and secretly vowed that she would do whatever she could to make him happy.

She turned the corner and saw Craig standing in front of a decorative arch set up under the palm trees on the beach. He was formally dressed in a dark suit and tie that had to be uncomfortable in the ninety-degree heat, but he looked cool and composed and so incredibly handsome her breath caught.

His eyes met hers and he smiled.

Only then did she realize that he wasn't alone. The minister was there, of course, but so was Craig's brother, Gage, and Grace and Allan. And on the other side of the minister stood Laurie and Becca, both holding smaller bouquets of flowers similar to her own.

Her eyes blurred with tears and her steps faltered, until

Craig stepped forward and held out his hand. And the last traces of nerves settled as she placed her hand in his.

She had little recollection of the actual ceremony. It all seemed to happen so fast and then the minister was pronouncing them husband and wife and inviting Craig to kiss the bride.

She expected a perfunctory wedding kiss. But when he lowered his head and brushed his mouth over hers, there was nothing casual or cursory about it and she felt her lips tremble in response. He lingered, drawing out the moment without deepening the kiss, and she tasted warmth and tenderness, heat and passion and so much more.

They had dinner with their families on a private terrace of the dining room and later, when they returned to their room, a bottle of chilled champagne and two crystal flute glasses awaited them along with a note of congratulations from the management and staff of the hotel.

"The honeymoon package," Craig explained.

"They think about everything, don't they?" She set the card back onto the table, suddenly nervous.

"You could give me a little credit for finding the hotel," Craig said.

"You're a brilliant man, Mr. Richmond."

"Don't you forget it, Mrs. Richmond." And then he winced. "I'm sorry. I didn't ask if you wanted to take my name, I just—"

"It's okay," she interrupted. "I like the sound of Tess Richmond. And it makes sense to have the same name my child will have."

He picked up the bottle of bubbly, studied the label. "I should call down to the desk to see if they have any nonalcoholic champagne."

"Don't worry about it," she said. "I don't need any champagne." The formalities of the wedding now over, she couldn't wait for Craig to take her in his arms again. Every nerve ending in her body hummed with the anticipation of being kissed until the world began to tilt.

He set down the bottle, then his eyes shifted and locked with hers. The intensity in his gaze stole the air from her lungs, made her head spin.

This is it, she thought. Now he would kiss her again.

Instead, he took a step in retreat. "I forgot to confirm our brunch reservations at the dining room."

And then, before she had a chance to respond, he was gone.

Tess sat on the edge of the bed and closed her eyes against the tears of confusion and frustration.

Dammit, he was the one who'd wanted this marriage. She hadn't asked him for anything, but he'd convinced her that they should be together, that they could be the family their baby deserved. And before the ink was even dry on their marriage certificate, he'd hightailed it out the door.

She swiped impatiently at the tears that slipped quietly down her cheeks and stood up to unfasten the zipper at the back of her dress.

Of all the ways she'd imagined spending her wedding night, this was not one of them. He'd promised to be right back, but she knew there was no sense in waiting up. He wouldn't come back until he was sure she was asleep. She didn't know where he'd gone—to the bar? The beach? The airport? It didn't really matter where he was. What mattered was that he wasn't with her.

He'd married her so that their child would have a stable home with two parents who loved him and he'd got what he wanted. The parents loving one another didn't come into play in his scenario.

But Tess did love him. She couldn't make him believe it or understand it any more than she could stop loving him. She could only hope that, over time, he might learn to love her, too. But that wasn't likely to happen if he couldn't even stand to be in the same room with her on their wedding night.

She wanted to stuff her dress into the garbage but reason won out over frustration and she hung it carefully in the closet instead. Then she stripped off her undergarments and opened the top drawer of the dresser rummaging inside for her nightgown. She heard the crinkle of tissue and pulled out the package Laurie had given to her before she left.

She unwrapped the tissue, examined the delicate silk and lace garment more suited to seduction than sleeping. Obviously, her sister hadn't planned for Tess to be alone on her wedding night, either. She hesitated, then impulsively slipped the nightgown over her head, the soft fabric sliding over her body like a caress, cool against her heated skin.

She took her time brushing her teeth, sat for a while in bed reading a novel, hoping that Craig would return even while she knew he wouldn't. After a long while, she finally gave up waiting and tried to sleep.

Craig cursed himself as he walked alone on the beach. He had to be a complete idiot to be out here on his wedding night, on his own, while his bride was in their honeymoon cottage getting ready for bed.

For weeks he'd been trying to deny the attraction between himself and Tess, focusing his efforts on courting her and trying not to think about the night they'd made love. His proposal might have originally been motivated by a desire to give his baby a family, but now that they were married he found himself wanting more. And right now, what he wanted was Tess in his bed.

He glanced back at the light visible in the bedroom and wished he could be in there with her now, holding her, touching her, loving her. But he couldn't forget her hesitation when he'd told her he wanted a real marriage. She'd seemed not only surprised but reluctant and it was that reluctance that gave him pause. Because no matter how much his body ached for the woman who was now his wife, she was still his friend and he didn't want to risk causing further damage to their relationship by pushing the boundaries she'd established.

She'd agreed to marry him so that their baby could have a full-time father, which was exactly what he'd wanted. Their marriage was a means to an end, a necessary step to guarantee his involvement in his child's life. He'd gotten exactly what he wanted.

So why did he feel so dissatisfied? Why did Tess's acquiescence suddenly bother him so much?

He picked up a round stone and tossed it toward the ocean. The pebble disappeared into the darkness, then plopped softly into the water.

He wanted to marry her, now he was married to her. So, why wasn't he happy?

Because he wanted *more.*

He wanted it all.

He almost laughed out loud at the ridiculously vague notion, made even more ridiculous by the realization that he already had it all. He had a challenging and rewarding career, a beautiful home in the suburbs, a child on the way. What else was there?

Love.

He ignored the soft taunt from his subconscious as he hurled another stone into the water.

He didn't believe in love or want any part of it. Love was a fickle and transient emotion, a weapon yielded to hurt and manipulate. No, he wasn't looking for love.

He wasn't looking for anything more than what he'd got by marrying Tess—a partnership with the mother of his child in a relationship unclouded by messy emotions.

Had Tess not heard the click of the door as it latched, she would still have known the exact moment Craig returned to the cottage. Over the past twenty-four hours, she'd become achingly aware of his presence and of his absence. She kept her eyes closed, waiting, wondering.

If he believed her to be asleep, would he crawl into bed beside her? If he did, she could just happen to roll over, to snuggle close against him.

She held her breath, hoped he couldn't hear the thunderous pounding of her heart over the hum of the air-conditioning unit. She sensed his hesitation, then let out a slow, frustrated breath as she heard his footsteps on the tile floor and the slide of the patio doors as he exited onto the deck.

Why did she care, anyway? Why was she so obsessed with a man who obviously didn't want to be with her?

Because he was her husband, dammit, and she loved him.

She opened her eyes, stared unseeing at the ceiling in the darkness.

Craig was the one who'd wanted this marriage. He'd all but forced her to walk down the aisle and now that his ring was firmly on her finger he thought he could ignore her. Tess felt the slow surge of anger. She was not going to let him ignore her.

She sat up in bed and swung her feet onto the floor. Striding purposefully across the room, she hesitated only briefly before sliding open the patio door and stepping out onto the deck.

Craig was seated on one of the padded chairs, his feet propped onto a stool. His eyes were closed, but she sensed the tension in his body.

"Craig?"

His eyes flew open and his head turned. "I thought you were asleep."

"I was waiting for you," she said softly.

She moved forward into the moonlight, heard his sharp intake of breath and fought back a smile. It sounded like Craig was impressed with the silk-and-lace peignoir that Laurie had given to her.

"Why?" he asked, his voice sounding a little strained.

She perched on the edge of the stool. One of the straps slid off her shoulder as she leaned forward, exposing the top curve of her breast. "I wanted to make sure you confirmed our reservations."

His gaze dipped to her cleavage. "Oh—yes."

She nodded. "Good."

"You should…uh…get some sleep."

"I'm not very tired."

"Oh. Okay."

He was flustered. It took a minute for the realization to sink in, but when it did, it helped ease some of the tension she was feeling.

Tess stretched her legs out in front of her, allowed her knee to brush against his as she extended it and he practically leapt out of his chair. He crossed to the edge of the deck, clamped his hands down on the railing.

She sighed. "You promised me this wouldn't happen."

"What are you talking about?"

"You said if we got married, I wouldn't ever lose you," she reminded him. "But ever since the night we slept together, there's been a distance between us that I don't know how to bridge and it just seems to be growing wider. Now I've got your ring on my finger, but you seem farther away from me than ever before." She felt her throat tighten and looked away so he wouldn't see the tears that blurred her eyes. "And I don't know what to do or how to fix us."

He moved back to where she was sitting, then held out his hand and drew her to her feet. "Things have changed," he agreed. "But I don't think there's anything that needs to be done or anything wrong that needs to be fixed."

"You can't tell me you're happy with the way things are between us right now."

His smile was wry. "No," he admitted.

"Then tell me what you want."

"You."

Her heart stuttered.

"If you want the truth—there it is," he told her. "It's not easy going back to being just friends after what happened. I can't be in the same room with you without thinking about that night. Without wanting you. It's a constant battle to keep my hands off of you."

Her earlier anger and frustration were forgotten as she tipped her head back to look at him. "I haven't asked you to keep your hands off of me."

"No, but I know your body's going through a lot of changes and—"

"And I want your hands on me."

"Oh, God, Tess."

She felt his grasp tighten on her fingers. "The day I agreed to marry you, you said that you wanted a real marriage," she reminded him. "Well, that's what I want, too. And I want it to start tonight."

His fingers were still laced with hers but he made no move toward her, and Tess knew he was making sure this was her decision. Her knees were trembling so badly she wondered that she was able to stand but she managed to raise herself onto her toes and touch her lips to his.

His body remained stiff, immobile but his lips molded to hers as he kissed her back. The nerves in her stomach dissolved, replaced by something stronger, fiercer, undeniable. She slid her hands up his chest, clasped them behind his head as she pressed her body against his. She heard him groan deep in his throat before he grasped her wrists in his hands and pulled away from her. He held her at arm's length, his breathing labored, his eyes dark with desire.

"Are you sure?" he asked hoarsely.

Tess smiled, no longer plagued by any doubts. "I want to make love with my husband." She wanted to show him, in actions if not in words, how much she loved him.

He released her hands and very gently cupped her face in his palms. He stroked his thumbs over her cheeks, the simple gesture surprisingly sensual. Then he slid his hands into her hair, tipping her head back so he could settle his lips over hers. His kiss was so soft, so tender, she felt as though her heart would melt.

She lost herself in his kiss, her earlier tears of disappointment and frustration forgotten. This was what she wanted, what she needed. She opened up her heart and her soul and she gave him everything that she had. Everything that she was.

He kissed her cheeks, her eyelids. "God, Tess, I want you so badly. But I didn't want to rush you."

At any other time, she might have taken exception to the fact that he'd been making decisions for her. Right now, however, she didn't care about anything but the passion that flared between them like a three-alarm blaze.

"Stop talking and kiss me again."

He did, covering her mouth at the same time that he lifted her around the waist and carried her back inside. He set her back on her feet beside the bed, but continued to ravish her mouth with hot, hungry kisses. His hands skimmed over her hips down to the hem of the silky nightgown, then beneath it. She heard her own sigh of satisfaction as his hands met the bare skin of her thighs. It seemed like an eternity since she'd felt his hands on her, since she'd had her hands on him.

She reached for the buttons of his shirt, fumbling in

her haste. His fingers circled her wrists, pulled her hands back down to her sides.

"I'm trying to take my time here," he whispered against her lips. "I want to enjoy touching you for a while."

"I want to touch you, too."

"Later," he promised, and released her hands to tug her nightgown over her head. He eased her back onto the bed and lowered himself beside her.

His hands moved to her breasts and she gasped as he brushed his thumbs over the already taut nipples, the contact sending ripples of pleasure through her body.

"They're heavier," he noted. "And fuller."

She nodded, surprised that he was aware of the subtle changes to her body.

"Are they more sensitive?" he asked, lowering his head to flick his tongue over one distended nipple.

She gasped again, arched instinctively toward him.

He raised his head to look at her and grinned. "I take it that's a yes?"

"Yes," she agreed breathlessly.

His tongue swirled around the peak, then his lips closed over it and Tess felt the heat begin to build inside her. He taunted her breast with his tongue, his teeth, until she was panting.

"I think the next few months are going to be a lot of fun." He lifted his head only long enough to murmur those words, then turned his attention to her other breast.

Tess moaned and writhed beneath him.

"Oh, yeah, this is going to be fun."

She grasped his shoulders, digging her nails into the firm muscles as she tried to maintain some equilibrium as the world spun around her. She'd never felt so close to losing complete control just by having her breasts massaged. Then again, she'd never felt anything before like she felt with Craig. Every touch, every kiss, left her breathless, eager for more.

"Craig…please…"

He skimmed his hands over her body, slowly, his fingertips barely making contact with her skin, yet she burned everywhere he touched and her breath quickened in response to the teasing caresses.

Desperate to feel the warmth of his skin under her hands, she tugged at the front of his shirt, mindless of the buttons that flew as she tore it open.

Craig chuckled against her mouth. "That was a good shirt."

"It was in the way." She pushed the shirt off his shoulders, ran her hands down the smooth planes of his chest. She found the buckle of his belt, worked it free. He kissed her hard on the mouth, then rolled away from her and off the bed to shed the rest of his clothes. She hadn't realized she'd been holding her breath until he lay down again beside her, his flesh bare and hot against hers, and she was able to breathe again.

The hard muscles of his chest brushed the tips of her nipples and caused twin arrows of heat to spread from the point of contact to the throbbing warmth between her thighs. She thrust her hips toward him, wordlessly seeking the fulfillment only he could give her. But he held back, teasing her with featherlight caresses, soft kisses.

"Not yet," he whispered the words against her lips. "I've only just begun."

And he continued his exquisite torture, relentlessly

driving her higher and higher. She was quivering beneath him, her body strung tight as a bow. Sensation upon sensation seemed to assault her from every direction as he continued to stroke her body with his hands, his lips, his tongue. Desire such as she'd never experienced slammed into her with the force of a freight train.

She fisted her hands in the sheet as his hand skimmed over the curve of her belly and found the tangle of curls between her thighs. He slid a finger inside the slick, wet heat. She shuddered and screamed out his name as the intimate intrusion pushed her over the edge.

Then he raised himself over her, pressing her into the mattress with his body. She welcomed his weight, parted her thighs to urge him closer.

"I've never wanted anyone the way I want you, Tess."

He buried himself inside her in one sure stroke. Tess gasped and clutched his shoulders, her nails biting into his flesh. She'd forgotten how big he was, how completely he filled her, fulfilled her. He began to move inside her, slow, steady strokes that seemed to touch her very soul. As she lifted her hips in response to the rhythm he'd set, she felt herself climbing again, soaring.

This time, when the spasms rocked her body, he went with her.

Chapter Ten

"I'm crushing you," Craig said, murmuring the words into her hair. He knew he should roll off of her, but right now he couldn't even move. It was a wonder he could even speak, his climax had so completely drained him.

Was it the anticipation, he wondered, that had made their lovemaking so phenomenal?

Or was it Tess?

"I'm okay," she told him, her fingertips tracing lazily down his back. "Better than okay."

He managed to lift his head enough to look at her. "Better than okay?"

Her eyes were closed, but her lips curved. "Much better."

"How much better?"

Her lashes fluttered, revealing beautiful blue eyes

still dark with passion. "Do you want a number on a scale of one to ten?"

"Of course not."

Her eyes drifted shut again.

"Maybe."

She chuckled softly. "Twelve."

He was grateful her eyes were closed, so she couldn't see him grinning like an idiot. He was relieved to know that the most incredible, mind-numbing sexual experience of his life hadn't been a disappointment for Tess.

Twelve, she'd said.

Well, weeks of wanting her, dreaming about her, had eroded his self-control. He was willing to bet he could do better next time.

He tipped his head to kiss her, skimmed a hand over her breast. She murmured and wriggled beneath him, the movement eliciting an immediate response from his own body. He deepened the kiss.

Oh, yeah, he'd do much better this time.

When Tess awoke the following morning, she didn't have the usual impulse to get up and get moving. No, she felt far too content this morning to want to be anywhere other than exactly where she was: snuggled under the sheets in Craig's arms. Craig Richmond—her oldest and dearest friend and now her husband.

If she allowed herself to think about it, she might still worry that marrying Craig was an impulse she'd eventually regret. But it was hard to believe that when her skin still tingled from his touch, when her body was molded to the warmth of his own. Sometime over the past few weeks she'd managed to convince herself that the out-of-control passion she'd experienced that first night had been an anomaly. Or that the memories had been distorted by her imagination and her newly-discovered feelings for him. But last night had proven her wrong.

They'd barely spoken to one another throughout their lovemaking marathon, communicating their wants and needs with their bodies rather than words. Every stroke of his fingertips, every touch of her lips, every brush of their flesh, carried a message of want, of need. Time and time again, passion had flared between them, burning higher and brighter and stronger until it consumed them both. And then they'd finally slept, their heads side by side on one pillow, their limbs still entwined.

With Craig, she really felt as though she were making love and not just having sex. The depth of his passion overwhelmed her; the power of her response stunned her. She had never experienced anything like it with anyone else and she knew she never would. Because she knew now that the reason she responded to Craig so completely, the reason he'd been able to touch a part inside her that no one else had ever come close to finding, was because she loved him.

And she was scared. How much longer could she keep up the charade of their marriage without revealing her feelings for him? She'd always thought that sex and love were separate entities, but now she knew differently. Making love with Craig was more than the physical union of two bodies, it was an experience that touched the very center of her soul. She was so afraid he would realize that when she shared her body, she was sharing her heart. And yet, she could no more withhold herself than she could withhold her love.

"I can almost hear you thinking." His words, murmured so close to her ear, startled her.

"I thought you were sleeping."

"I was, but I'm awake now." He skimmed a hand down her side, over the slope of her hip, down her thigh.

She leaned her head back against his chest, savored being in the warmth of his embrace. But she knew that although she'd fallen head over heels for Craig, he'd only married her because of the baby. She wanted their marriage to work, but more than anything she wanted him to be happy.

He turned her in his arms, brushed a light kiss against her lips.

Tess pulled back. "If at any time you change your mind, if you decide this isn't what you want, will you tell me?"

He smoothed the line above her brow with his finger. "Haven't we already had this discussion?"

"Just promise me that you'll let me know if you don't want to stay married."

"I've had lots of time to think about this—too much time. I'm not going to change my mind." He kissed her again, lingered. "When we exchanged those vows, I meant every word. I've made a promise to you, Tess. To you and our baby. And I will be there for you, forever."

She wanted to believe him. But in those vows he'd also promised to love her and although she knew Craig cared about her, he wasn't in love with her. And that was the only thing that was missing. If Craig loved her, if this was a real marriage—based on shared hopes and dreams instead of an inopportune pregnancy—she'd be the happiest woman alive.

Still, she was happy. And relieved. She knew that

Craig would stand by her and that he'd be a father to their baby. It would have to be enough. She had no right to ask for, or expect, anything more.

"And I'm not going to let you change your mind, either," Craig said. "I will do everything I can to make our marriage work, to make you happy."

"I am happy," she told him.

"Good." He sat up abruptly. "By the way, I have something for you."

"What?"

"A wedding gift." He threw off the covers and swung his legs over the side of the bed. Unconcerned about his nakedness, he crossed the room and pulled something out of the front pocket of his suitcase.

"You already gave me the best gift," she told him, "bringing my sister and her family here for the wedding."

"Then I'm hoping this will be a second-best gift." He climbed back onto the bed and handed her a large envelope.

She turned it over and tore open the flap, her brow creased in concentration as she examined the official-looking document.

It was a property deed, transferring one-half ownership of the house he'd bought to her. Tess stared at the paper for the longest time, not certain what she should do or say. No one had ever given her a house—or anything remotely like it—before.

"I don't know what to say," she admitted at last. "I never expected… I mean…it's *your* house."

"It's *our* house now," he said.

"But you bought it. I can't—"

"Yes, you can. I bought it for us—for our family."

"But…"

He tugged the deed out of her hand and tossed it aside. "It's done, forget about it."

She scowled. "Will you let me say one thing?"

He hesitated. "All right."

"Thank you." She was still uncomfortable with the enormity of the gesture, but she understood that sharing his home was Craig's way of showing that he wanted her and the baby with him and she couldn't reject such generosity.

"You're welcome."

"I didn't get you anything," Tess said. Everything had happened so fast, she'd never even had a chance to think about a wedding gift for Craig.

"You've given me far more than you realize." He splayed his palm over the gentle curve of her belly. "Although it's still hard to believe there's a baby growing inside you."

She put her hand over his. "He's still really tiny."

"How tiny?"

"About two-and-a-half inches."

"Wow." He rubbed his hand in gentle circles. "Does he look like a baby?"

"I don't know. I'll get to see him when I have the ultrasound in a couple more months."

"Why are you having an ultrasound? Is everything all right? Are you feeling okay?"

The immediate concern in his voice made her smile. "I'm fine, the baby's fine. It's a routine procedure, just to check on the baby's development."

"Oh." He exhaled audibly. Then asked, "Can I come with you?"

Tess smiled. "If you'd like."

"Yeah, I would. I want to be there with you, every step of the way."

And he would, she knew, because that was the type of man he was. He would be there for her and he would love their child. He just wouldn't love her.

Craig kissed her lightly. "What has you looking so sad all of a sudden?"

She forced another smile. "I'm not sad, I was just thinking."

"About what?"

"How very lucky our baby is going to be."

The six days they spent on the island after their wedding were so idyllic that Tess hadn't wanted to leave. They'd taken various tours around the island—a cigar factory, a rum distillery, an historic plantation house. They'd enjoyed a five-hour catamaran cruise that included snorkeling and swimming with turtles. They'd walked into Bridgetown and picked up some touristy souvenirs. It had truly been a magical trip and she couldn't remember any time in her life when she'd ever been happier.

The plane touched down on the runway and she felt a pang of regret that the honeymoon was now officially over. It was now time to get back to reality, to face the world and the inevitable questions and speculation about their hasty marriage—not that people would be speculating for too long before her pregnancy became obvious—and remember that Craig had only married her to give their baby a family.

The thought shouldn't have hurt as much as it did.

After all, Craig never made any promises of love. Nor had she for that matter. At least, not out loud. They'd both been concentrating on practical considerations when they'd decided to marry.

But when she'd promised to love, honor and cherish him, she'd meant every single word. She would never have been able to recite those vows otherwise. And they'd been so close over the past few days, she'd started to hope that his feelings for her might be growing as well. But maybe it was nothing more than the newly-discovered passion between them—and how long could she expect that to last when her pregnancy started to show?

She listened to the announcement on the speaker asking all passengers to remain seated with their belts fastened.

"What are you thinking about?" Craig asked.

"That a week has never gone by so quickly."

"I know what you mean." He brushed a strand of hair away from her face, stroked a finger along the edge of her jaw. "We had a good time, didn't we?"

She nodded.

"You know," he said, "this plane refuels and goes back."

She had to admit there was a part of her that wished they could have stayed in their enchanting paradise a little longer. Maybe even forever. But as tempting as the idea was, it was unrealistic. "We had to come back sometime."

There was a ding as the seat-belt light went out and people began to scramble out of their seats, digging through overhead bins for their carry-on luggage. Tess unbuckled her belt.

"You're worried, aren't you?" Craig asked.

She wasn't surprised that he sensed the reason for her melancholy. "Everything will be different here. People are bound to talk about the hastiness of our marriage and it won't be long before they know why we got married."

"And that bothers you?"

"Of course, it does. I don't want anyone thinking that I tricked you into this marriage, that I'm taking advantage of you."

"No one who knows me would believe that," Craig said dryly, reaching into the overhead compartment for their bags.

"Maybe," Tess acknowledged. But she knew there would be plenty who thought so just the same.

When they got home from the airport, Craig carried their bags into the house after giving firm instructions to Tess to wait outside.

He came back a few minutes later, swept her into his arms and carried her over the threshold. He set her back on her feet in the foyer and placed a soft kiss on her lips. "Welcome home, Tess."

And with those words, her tension eased.

She followed him upstairs, carrying only her shoulder bag as Craig insisted the luggage was heavy. Too weary to argue, she let the comment pass. His protective attitude would likely get worse as her pregnancy progressed and she decided that she'd better learn to pick her battles. And really, she didn't mind letting a man carry her suitcase.

She paused in the doorway of the master bedroom. She'd been in here before, when he'd first brought her to see the house but the room had been freshly painted since then and his furniture moved in.

"What are you smirking about?" Craig asked, setting their suitcases down on the far side of the room.

"I'd been thinking that I was sorry our honeymoon was over," she admitted. "And then I got a look at your bed."

He raised his eyebrows.

"It's as big as the one we had in Barbados."

"All the better to ravish you in," he said, sweeping her into his arms and rolling with her on top of the plaid comforter.

She giggled as he nuzzled her neck, biting playfully on her nape. "And do you intend to ravish me?" she asked breathlessly.

His hands were already working the buttons on her blouse. "Oh, yeah."

She sighed as his hands skimmed over her bare skin. She knew she could always rely on Craig to keep his promises.

Craig was indulging in a second cup of coffee and scanning the newspaper as he waited for Tess to finish in the bathroom. He'd been tempted to join her in the shower, but the couple of times they'd tried that the cleansing ritual had rapidly turned into foreplay. Not that he had any complaints, but Tess had firmly banned him from the bathroom this morning so they wouldn't be late for Becca's birthday party.

Three weeks had passed since they'd been pronounced husband and wife and he found that he'd adapted easily to this marriage thing. In fact, he was quite enjoying being married to Tess, waking up with her every morning, spending hours making love with her. She was the most incredibly passionate woman he'd ever known and the woman he really believed he could be happy with for the rest of his life.

For the baby's sake, of course.

Because that was what their marriage was about—giving their child a family. The fact that he and Tess were so obviously compatible was a nice bonus but he wasn't going to complicate their relationship by imagining that his feelings for Tess were growing. No, it was sex, it was simple. And he intended to keep it that way.

He heard the shower shut off and contemplated going upstairs to help Tess towel off. But as he set the newspaper aside to do just that, the phone rang. He was hanging up when Tess walked into the room, fully dressed, a few minutes later.

"What is that in your shampoo?" he asked, sniffing her hair as she moved past him to turn on the kettle.

"What do you mean?"

"The scent," he said impatiently. "What is it?"

She found a cup and plopped a tea bag into it. "Apples, I think. Why?"

He'd thought that's what it was—he'd just never expected to find the fragrance of fruit so arousing. "It's sexy."

"Sexy?" She glanced up, her eyebrows raised in disbelief. "My shampoo?"

"You have no idea how many nights I used to lie awake, unable to get the scent of your shampoo out of my mind."

"Really?" She was clearly intrigued by this revelation.

"Really." He stepped behind her, inhaling deeply as he dipped his head to nuzzle her throat. It was, he'd quickly learned, one of her most erogenous zones and the quick shiver that ran through her body proved it.

"Craig," she said warningly.

"Hmm?" He slid his arms around her, tucking her back against his front.

"We have to go shopping this morning to get a birthday present for my niece."

"I know." He reluctantly stepped away as Tess reached for the now boiling kettle.

"And then we have dinner at your parents' house later."

"Yeah—Mom just called to remind me."

"Are we going to tell them about the baby tonight?"

"We probably shouldn't wait too much longer," he said. "But I don't know if tonight is too soon. My dad was shocked enough by the news we were getting married—finding out he's going to be a grandfather so soon might give him heart failure."

She sipped at the herbal tea he'd been encouraging her to drink instead of coffee, made a face.

She claimed it tasted like flowers but she tolerated it anyway. At least when he was around. She still snuck coffee when she didn't think he was looking, so, unbeknownst to her, he'd replaced his regular grind with decaf. He missed the caffeine jolt himself but figured it was a small sacrifice to make for the health of their baby.

"Craig?"

"Hmm…" he said, unable to remember what they'd been talking about.

Tess shook her head. "I think the lack of caffeine is hindering your brain function."

He frowned and stared into his cup. "How did you know about the coffee?"

"It tastes like decaf," she told him. "As for sharing the news of my pregnancy, I don't think we'll be able to wait too much longer—not at the rate this baby seems to be growing."

He sipped his coffee, secretly acknowledging that she was right about the taste. "Yes, well, I think there's something I should tell you in that regard."

"About the baby, or the coffee?"

"The baby," he clarified.

She looked at him suspiciously. "What?"

He refilled his mug. "Big babies seem to run in my family."

"Big?" Tess echoed. "How big?" She took another sip of her tea.

"My brother was a little over nine pounds." He shot her a look of apology. "I was almost ten."

She choked, coughed. "Ten pounds? Why didn't you tell me this before?"

"It's not as if we could do anything about it," he pointed out reasonably.

"But *ten* pounds?" She was clearly stunned. "Well, it would explain why none of my clothes are fitting anymore."

"It might also explain why my mother left," he joked.

She didn't laugh.

"It's hard not to think about her, isn't it?" she asked gently. "Now that you're going to have a child of your own."

He didn't like to admit it, but he knew he couldn't hide the truth from her. "It scares me sometimes, to think that I could walk out on my child like she did."

"You couldn't," she assured him. "You wouldn't

have fought so hard to be part of your baby's life if you had any doubts."

"But there was a time—at least I think there was—when she wanted me and Gage, too."

Tess pushed away from the table to stand behind his chair, wrapped her arms around his shoulders. "She made the biggest mistake of her life when she walked out on you," she said. "You're smarter than that."

"Do you really think so?"

"Yes, I do."

He turned his head to look at her. "Do you know what I think?"

"What?"

He pulled her onto his lap. "I think that marrying you was the smartest thing I ever did."

Tess stayed late at the office on Friday, surfing the Net for job postings. There were plenty of employers looking for software programmers, just none in the immediate vicinity of Pinehurst or even within a reasonable commuting distance. But there were some IT support positions available so she printed copies of those that sounded interesting.

She hadn't had a chance to update her résumé yet, unwilling to use the computer at home because she hadn't yet told Craig about the fate of SBG. She was going to, of course, but she wanted to have another job lined up first. She didn't want him to feel compelled to find something for her at Richmond.

She wouldn't trade on their relationship for a job when she was a recent college graduate looking for work and she especially wouldn't do so now that they were husband

and wife. But with only a few weeks left until the transition took place she was quickly running out of time.

And running behind schedule she noticed when she glanced at the clock.

She grabbed the pages from the printer and tucked them into her purse on her way out of the office. A week, she promised herself. If she hadn't resolved her job situation in a week she'd tell him anyway rather than run the risk of him finding out from someone else.

She made a quick stop on the way home to pick up Chinese food because it was her night to cook and she hadn't taken anything out of the freezer for dinner. Of course, Craig would tease her that she'd purposely forgotten—and maybe she had. But she'd had other things on her mind before she'd left for work that morning. Most notably the fact that, after a three-day conference in Boston, her husband was finally going to be home tonight.

She was just unpacking dinner when he got in. He dropped his briefcase on the floor and pulled her into his arms.

"Isn't a dutiful wife supposed to be waiting at the door when her husband gets home?" he teased when he finally ended the kiss so they could both catch their breath.

"I'm kind of new at this wife thing," she reminded him.

"Did you miss me?" he asked, his hands moving down the front of her sweater, deftly unfastening buttons along the way.

"Stop that," she protested, swatting at his hands in order to avoid answering his question. Because she'd missed him more than she wanted to admit. "I'm trying to be a good wife by getting your dinner on the table."

"I've been waiting—" he glanced at his watch "—sixty-three hours to get my hands on you."

She couldn't help but smile, because sixty-three hours was exactly right by her calculations, too. "I thought you'd be hungry," she told him.

"I am," he assured her, and kissed her again.

She sighed into his mouth, her tongue meeting and mating with his.

His hands slid down her back, over the curve of her buttocks, pulling her tight against him. She was suddenly conscious of the slight bulge of her tummy and worried that her growing belly would diminish his ardor. But there was no hint of disinterest in the way he was touching her and her concerns melted away in the heat of their passion.

She reached between their bodies to tug at the button of his pants, push the zipper down. Then she slid her hand inside his boxers and wrapped her fingers around the solid length of him. A groan rumbled deep in his throat as he pushed up her skirt and quickly discarded her panties.

He lifted her off her feet, bracing her against the granite countertop. It was cold and hard, but she didn't care. She was focused on the heat of his skin and the glorious strength of his body as she wrapped her legs around his hips. She cried out as he plunged into her and her head fell back, her fingers gripping his shoulders, as the first waves of pleasure swamped her.

She'd never known such unbridled passion—hadn't thought she was capable of acting so outrageously. They hadn't even bothered to remove their clothes—other than what was absolutely necessary to enable them to complete the act. It was all so primitive, almost violent. And so incredibly erotic.

He dipped his head, his teeth scraping over the lace-covered peak of her breast, and she gasped. Then his lips closed around the aching nub, suckling wetly through the fabric, until she felt her core shatter into a billion kaleidoscopic pieces.

And still he continued the delicious torment—his mouth, his hands and his deep steady thrusts driving her again and again to the edge—and beyond.

Relentlessly, mindlessly, gloriously beyond.

She didn't know how long they stayed there, bodies locked together, braced against the counter. She vaguely wondered if she should be shocked by what had just happened, but she was too satisfied to feel anything but blissfully content.

"God, Tess, no one has ever made me lose control like you do." He sounded bewildered, almost angry, but his hands were gentle as he eased her feet back to the ground.

"Should I apologize?" she asked, when she was finally able to speak.

He smiled, somewhat ruefully. "No. It's just that..." He stepped away to fasten his pants, shook his head. "This wasn't what I wanted."

She frowned as she buttoned her sweater. "I thought it was what we both wanted."

"I was thinking about making love with you the whole way home," he admitted. "But I didn't expect it to happen like this. I should have been able to control my desire, to be careful with you—to at least wait until we were in the bedroom."

He shook his head again. "I missed you so much, Tess. I was only gone three days and I missed you."

A tiny spark of hope flickered in Tess's heart. Was it possible, she wondered, that Craig was starting to have feelings for her? That she was more to him than the mother of his child?

She cupped his face in her hands, kissed him gently. "I missed you, too."

"Yeah?" He seemed pleased by the thought.

"Yeah."

"I don't understand what's happening," he said, sounding bewildered again. "This was supposed to be simple. We got married to give our baby a family, to give him a secure and stable home. This—" he gestured vaguely. "You—me. I don't understand why it seems so complicated all of a sudden."

The tiny spark flared a little brighter.

"I thought it was just that I've gotten used to having you around, but it's more than that. Dammit, Tess, I need you." He turned away from her, scrubbed his hands through his hair. His next words were barely a whisper. "I've never needed anyone before."

She hated the anguish she heard in his voice, hated that he was fighting so hard against the feelings he had for her and secretly thrilled to realize that he *did* have feelings for her.

Maybe the fairy tale wasn't so far beyond her reach, after all.

Chapter Eleven

The food at Marco's was always fabulous, the portions generous and the service prompt. Tess pushed aside her plate and sighed in contentment at the end of another sinfully indulgent meal.

"Okay, now you can tell me the truth," Craig said. "Were you really craving spinach-and-ricotta ravioli or did you just want to get out of cooking tonight?"

"Does it matter?" she asked. "I'm sure you enjoyed your chicken marsala more than you would have meat loaf."

"I can't disagree with that, although you do make a great meat loaf."

"I make a passable meatloaf," she corrected. "We both know I'm not very creative in the kitchen."

"As I remember, you were very creative in the kitchen Friday night."

Tess hoped the candlelight concealed her flaming cheeks. "I was referring to cooking."

He smiled. "Are you blushing, Tess?"

Obviously the light wasn't dim enough. "No, I'm not blushing." She felt her cheeks burn even hotter. She was twenty-nine years old, it was ridiculous to be blushing. "It's warm in here."

He continued to smile, clearly not accepting her explanation for a moment.

"Did you remember that I have a doctor's appointment tomorrow?" she asked in a blatant attempt to change the subject.

He nodded. "It's on my calendar at work."

"Were you planning to come?"

"Definitely," he said. "We should be able to hear our baby's heartbeat this time."

She'd thought his interest in her pregnancy might wane after a few weeks but he was constantly surprising her with information or questions about the baby growing inside her.

"Have you been reading pregnancy books again?" she asked.

"Internet research," he corrected.

"Have you been researching baby names, too?"

He'd started tossing out name suggestions a couple of days earlier, mostly outrageous and ridiculous suggestions that she didn't take seriously except as a reminder that they did need to choose some possible names for their baby.

"I've come up with a few more names," he admitted.

"Such as?"

"Esmeralda."

Tess made a face.

"Jasmine."

She shook her head.

"Ariel."

"Can you try to be serious about this?"

"I'm trying," he said. "But what if we pick a name, say Sarah, and she doesn't look anything like a Sarah?"

"What, exactly, does a Sarah look like?" she countered.

He scowled. "You know what I mean. You might think you have the perfect name picked out and then find it doesn't suit the baby once she's born."

"You're right," she agreed. "After all, Sarah would be as completely inappropriate as Esmeralda, Jasmine or Ariel for a boy."

"You really think it's going to be a boy?"

"I think we should pick out a boy's name and a girl's name," she said.

"In case we have twins?"

She glared at him across the table. "We are *not* having twins."

"You don't want more than one baby?" he asked.

"I want to have one at a time."

"Then we only need one name," he pointed out reasonably.

She was helpless to prevent the smile that curved her lips. He was so often difficult, occasionally infuriating and somehow always irresistibly charming.

Her smile froze when she recognized the woman approaching their table. It was Lana—Craig's former fiancée—and she looked absolutely stunning in a pink spandex dress that showed off her flawless figure.

Even before Tess got pregnant, she wouldn't have had the confidence to wear such a revealing outfit. Nor, she was forced to admit, would it have looked half as good on her. And now—well, she wasn't quite into maternity clothes yet, but she was wearing only the loosest-fitting pieces in her wardrobe. Tonight she had on a long tunic-style top over a wraparound skirt that mostly disguised the slight curve of her belly.

"Mr. and Mrs. Richmond," Lana greeted them in a falsely sweet tone. "How are the happy newlyweds?"

"We're fine, thanks." Craig's tone was clipped, cool—clearly signaling that he was less than pleased by the interruption.

Lana tossed her immaculate blond hair over her shoulder, unaffected by the lack of warmth in his response. "I almost didn't believe it when I heard the rumor you'd married," she went on, her gaze moving from Craig to Tess, then dropping pointedly to Tess's belly. "Then I heard that you were going to be a daddy—and suddenly it made sense."

"Lana…" There was an unmistakable note of warning in Craig's voice.

She laughed softly, derisively. "Come on, Craig. Are you really going to tell me that you didn't marry her because she was pregnant?" There was a nasty edge to the question, a malicious challenge in her tone.

"Why Tess and I got married is none of your business," he said tightly.

Tess had thought she was prepared for the snide remarks that would follow the disclosure of her pregnancy, but this encounter proved that she hadn't been prepared at all. Not for someone like Lana. And not for

Craig's response to undermine all of her hopes for their relationship.

She knew when they got married that he'd only wanted to secure his place in their child's life, but over the past several weeks she'd allowed herself to hope that things had changed. That he was starting to love her, too. Obviously she'd been wrong.

"But it is my business," Lana retorted. "After all, you put a ring on my finger once, too."

"You put the ring on your own finger," Craig said. "All I had to do was pay for it."

Lana's cheeks flushed, with embarrassment or anger, Tess wasn't sure, as she turned from her former fiancé to his new wife.

"I really do want to congratulate you," she said to Tess. "If I'd known that getting knocked up was the key to holding on to a man like Craig, I might have done it myself." Her gaze drifted downward again, then she shrugged. "I imagine it's a comfort to know you'll at least have your baby when he grows bored with you."

Then, with a satisfied smile, she turned and sauntered away.

Craig reached across the table to take her hand. "Please don't let her get to you," he said.

"You've dated a lot of women over the years. Something like this was bound to happen sooner or later." Tess strove to keep her tone light, to hide her hurt as she disentangled her hand from his. "And I can understand that she would be upset about your marriage when it wasn't so long ago that you were engaged to her."

"It was almost two years ago," he said. "And she's been married *and* divorced since then."

"But she obviously loved you at one time and you must have loved her."

"I'm not sure love had anything to do with it. Love was only a tool Lana used to get what she wanted."

Tess flinched at the bitterness in his tone. Whatever feelings he'd had for his ex, there was no denying how much she'd hurt him.

"That's no reason to give up on love," she said gently.

He just shook his head. "I'm sorry about Lana. She's obviously still angry with me and you just got caught in the crossfire."

She wanted to believe him, but she had to ask, "How long do you think it will be until you grow bored with me?"

"I won't," he promised. "You're it for me—my best friend, my wife and the mother of my child and that's all I need."

Tess let it go. She knew she had no right to ask for anything more.

Craig was doing something he rarely did—playing hooky from work. But he didn't feel too guilty about it because his boss was playing hooky, too. Actually, they were spending the afternoon playing golf because beating up on a dimpled white ball was one of his father's favorite ways of clearing the mind and the Pinehurst Golf Club was his venue of choice when he wanted to talk to either of his sons.

When Craig had agreed to this game, he'd wondered about the real purpose behind the invitation. But having played through sixteen holes without any business issues or family matters being dropped into the conversation, Craig began to suspect that maybe his dad had really just wanted to play golf.

Now they were on the green at the par-four seventeenth. Rather Allan was on the green, having driven his second shot from the fairway to drop about twelve feet from the flag. Craig had needed a third shot to chip his ball onto the green but was still only on the edge of it.

About thirty feet to the hole, he guessed, as he pulled his putter out of his bag. A difficult but not impossible shot.

His dad removed the flag and stepped out of the way.

Craig didn't worry too much about sinking his putt, he just wanted to move his ball closer to the hole so he was even more surprised than his father when the ball actually rolled straight into the cup.

"Nice shot," Allan said.

"Lucky shot," he corrected.

His dad shook his head as he crouched down to study the slope of the green. "You're on your game today."

"I'm still two strokes behind you."

Allan glanced up at him and grinned. "Usually it's about five."

Craig acknowledged the point with a nod as his father lined up his shot.

He tapped it gently. It rolled toward the hole, circled the lip then dropped in.

"Now I'm three back," Craig said, noting the scores on the card.

His dad retrieved the balls from the cup, tossed Craig's to him.

"I have to admit," Allan said, "I was a little concerned when you showed up at my office the day you told me you were getting married. But I have no doubts anymore that it was the right decision for you. You seem happier and more relaxed than I can ever remember you being."

Craig fell into step beside him as they crossed over the wooden bridge to the eighteenth tee. "I am happy," he admitted. "Tess fits into my life, so much that I already can't imagine being without her."

Allan smiled. "You know your mother's feeling pretty smug about this whole thing."

"Why's that?" Craig took his driver out of his bag and a tee out of his pocket.

"Because she told me more than ten years ago that you'd end up with Tess."

"You're kidding."

His father shook his head. "You'd just come home after your first year of college and you looked at her as if you were seeing her for the first time."

Craig remembered the moment—the realization that the tomboy friend he'd said goodbye to in September had somehow turned into an attractive woman in the eight months he'd been gone. It had been a surprise and a temptation.

But Tess had given no indication that her feelings had changed, so he'd kept his own under wraps and they'd fallen back into their usual routines. And that had been that—until the night he'd slept with her.

He pushed the memory of that night out of his mind to focus on the ball in front of him. He set his feet, drew back his club and connected.

"Nice." His dad watched the ball soar through the air

and drop into the middle of the fairway, leaving Craig in good position to birdie the hole. "And then you went and got engaged to Lana and Grace laid awake at night worried you were going to spend the rest of your life with the wrong woman."

"She never said anything about that to me."

"Of course not," Allan agreed. "You were thirty years old—old enough to make your own choices—and your own mistakes."

Craig remained silent while his father set up to tee off. He didn't want to talk about Lana, but he couldn't dismiss the comments she'd made at the restaurant only two days earlier.

He didn't believe she'd heard about Tess's pregnancy—more likely she'd only been speculating as to the reason for his marriage because of the quickness of it. But he hadn't been able to deny it, not when Tess was starting to show and the pregnancy would be readily obvious to everyone in a couple of months and he knew he needed to tell his parents before they heard it from someone else.

He heard the whoosh of air, the thunk of the club face against the ball, then watched the white sphere rise high and higher against the blue sky before dropping on the fairway—about ten yards behind Craig's ball. Ordinarily that would be enough for him to make some teasing comment about his father's game slipping but there was something else on his mind.

"Dad…"

"Hmm?" Alan dropped his club into his bag and started walking up the fairway.

Craig fell into step beside him again trying to find the

right words to tell his father about the baby. In the end, he figured straightforward was best. "Tess is pregnant."

His dad surprised him by nodding. "I sort of figured that when you were in such a hurry to get married."

"I should have told you then," Craig admitted. "But I knew you'd be disappointed."

"Actually, I'm kind of intrigued by the idea of being a grandfather. And your mother is over the moon."

"I think I knew you'd be pleased about that but I was worried that you'd be disappointed in me."

"Why?" Allan pulled his seven-iron out of his bag and set up beside his ball.

"Because we had the talk about safe sex and contraception."

"Sometimes all the precautions in the world can't overcome the whims of fate." His second shot landed just short of the green.

"I just wanted you to know that I wasn't careless," Craig told him. "I wouldn't be—especially not with Tess."

"I don't need the details," his dad told him.

Craig managed a smile as he carried his eight iron over to his ball. "I wasn't going to share them."

"Good." Allan was silent while Craig took his shot, nodding when it landed on the green.

Then he surprised the hell out of his son by saying, "Grace was pregnant when we got married. We were planning to get married, anyway, but we moved up the schedule when we found out she was expecting. She lost the baby a few weeks later."

Craig grabbed his bag and scrambled after his father. When he caught up and found his voice all he could think to say was, "I had no idea."

Allan shrugged. "You and Gage were both kids—it wasn't the kind of information we would have shared with you then."

"I always wondered why you never had any more kids."

"We wanted to and we kept trying for a while. But Grace had three more miscarriages during the first five years of our marriage. And I finally had a vasectomy," his dad admitted, "because I couldn't bear to go through it all over again—the excitement, the hope, the devastation. I always worried that it was harder for Grace because she had no children of her own. She would have been a great mother."

"She *is* a great mother," Craig said.

His father smiled. "You're right. She is."

They played out the hole—this time Craig earned the birdie, Allan the par, which meant that father still finished two strokes ahead of son.

"That means you're buying the beer," Allan reminded him as they made their way toward the clubhouse.

"Good thing it's a payday," Craig joked. Then, more seriously, "I never thought about the possibility that Tess could lose this baby. I don't know what we'd do if she did."

"I didn't tell you about the miscarriages to make you worry. I only wanted you to realize that things don't always work out the way we plan. And as difficult as it was for both of us to deal with each loss we always knew we had each other. When you hit the rough spots in your marriage—and believe me, no matter how rosy everything seems right now, there will be rough spots—just remember that you love her."

Craig didn't correct his father's assumption, he

didn't tell him that the subject of marriage would never have come up except that Tess got pregnant. Because he believed that the reasons for their marriage didn't matter so long as they were both committed to making it work and didn't try to complicate their relationship with unwanted emotions.

He tucked his sunglasses into his pocket as he followed his father into the clubhouse. They'd just been seated and ordered their drinks when his dad raised his arm, waving to someone across the room.

Craig glanced over his shoulder to see one of Tess's bosses, Owen Sanderson, and his wife, Peggy, making their way toward them.

"Why don't you join us?" Allan invited. "Craig's buying today."

"Old man beat you again, huh?" Peggy teased, as Owen pulled back one of the vacant chairs at their table for her.

"He always does," Craig agreed easily.

"Well, today drinks are on us," Owen insisted. "To celebrate your recent marriage and my impending retirement."

Tess was already home when Craig got back after the round of golf with his father, standing in front of the stove cooking dinner.

It was a picture most men would envy: a beautiful woman—his wife—greeting him with a smile and a ready meal at the end of the day. He knew that he could go to her, put his arms around her and she would tip her head back to meet his lips with her own. Then they would turn off the stove and go upstairs and on the way, he'd be thanking his lucky stars that he'd managed to convince this incredible woman to marry him.

Even now, knowing what he did, he couldn't stop himself from wanting her. And so he stayed where he was in the doorway to the kitchen.

She smiled when she saw him standing there. "Laurie put together a binder of simple recipes she promised that even I couldn't screw up, so I thought I'd try cooking something other than meat loaf tonight."

Putting a lid over the pan she started toward him, the easy smile still on her face. "How was your game?"

It would be easy to fall into the routine, to pretend nothing had changed. But he couldn't ignore the sense of betrayal that ate away inside him. He couldn't believe that the woman he trusted more than any other had lied to him.

"When did you know that SB Graphics was selling out to GigaPix?" he asked.

Her steps faltered, her smile faded. "How did you find out?"

"I ran into Owen Sanderson and his wife at the golf course."

She winced, confirming the guilt he'd wanted her to be able to deny.

"They'd just booked an Alaskan cruise to celebrate his retirement."

"Peggy suffered a minor stroke last year—I know it scared Owen and made him decide to slow down and spend more time with her."

"When did you know?" he asked again.

She moved back to the stove, turned the chicken. "The beginning of August."

More than a month ago—and she hadn't told him.

He knew how much she loved her job, how disappointed she must have been to learn that the company was selling out to a competitor and yet she'd never said a single word to him about it.

He took a bottle of water from the fridge, twisted the cap off, took a long swallow. "Was it before or after you agreed to marry me?"

She folded her arms across the chest. "Where are you going with this, Craig?"

"Before or after?" he asked again.

"Before," she admitted.

He nodded then tipped the bottle to his mouth again. Her response confirmed what he'd suspected—what he'd feared.

"Well, that explains why you suddenly did a one-eighty in your attitude about marriage. Within the space of a few weeks you were hit by the realization that you were pregnant, losing your apartment and soon to be unemployed. I can understand that you were feeling desperate." He gripped the bottle so tightly he cracked the plastic. He tossed it into the sink. "Desperate enough to marry me."

Tess stared at him. "You think I married you because I was losing my job?"

"Well, there was never any doubt that I'd be able to support you and the baby, was there?"

Her eyes narrowed, flashed with anger. But her voice, when she spoke, was carefully controlled. "I didn't marry you for your bank account."

"Then why did you marry me?" he demanded.

"Because I'm in love with you, you idiot."

* * *

The only response to Tess's declaration was sudden and complete silence.

Craig stared at her, clearly stunned—and obviously terrified. She should have expected such a reaction. Nothing unnerved him more than talk of messy emotions.

She turned back to the pan on the stove. "I probably should have found a better way to say those words for the first time."

Out of the corner of her eye, she saw him take a step back, a physical retreat that reinforced the emotional withdrawal she'd already glimpsed in his eyes.

"I don't need or want such declarations," he said coolly.

And her heart broke just a little bit more.

She dumped rice into the pot of boiling water, covered it with a lid. "Maybe you don't," she agreed softly. "But maybe I needed to finally tell you how I feel because keeping it bottled up inside certainly hasn't made it go away."

"This wasn't in the plan, Tess."

"Yeah, well, it caught me off guard, too."

He frowned at that.

"Do you think I wanted this? How do you think it makes me feel, being in love with a man who obviously doesn't feel the same way about me?"

"You know I care about you, Tess."

She swallowed around the lump in her throat. "Yes, I do know that."

Neither of them seemed to know what to say after that and a long moment passed before Craig spoke again. "I'm going to check in at the lab."

Tess only nodded.

He walked out.

She stood there for several minutes after he'd gone, trying to understand how the marriage that had started out so promising could, just one month later, already be falling apart.

She should have told him about her job—she knew that. But she'd had valid reasons for keeping the news to herself for the present. At least, they'd seemed valid at the time. Now, obviously, she recognized the mistake in not telling him from the outset.

But how could she have guessed that he would jump to such conclusions? And how could he believe she would marry him for his money—especially when he was the one who had bullied her into this marriage?

Okay, that wasn't a fair statement to make. She'd gone into this marriage with her eyes open accepting the terms he'd offered. It was her own fault for expecting more—for hoping he might one day fall in love with her as she'd fallen in love with him.

It wasn't until she smelled it burning that she remembered she'd left dinner on the stove. She dumped the charred chicken and scorched rice into the sink, thinking that Laurie was wrong.

She had managed to screw this up, too.

Chapter Twelve

It was almost five hours later before Craig came home again.

Tess had put her pajamas on and tried to sleep, but after tossing and turning for longer than she wanted to admit she finally got up to make herself a cup of peppermint tea. She had just settled down at the table with it when he got back.

"I overreacted to the news about your job," he said. "It just caught me off guard, to hear it from Owen rather than you."

"I should have told you," she admitted softly. "But I wanted to have another job lined up first. I didn't want you to think that you had to find something at Richmond for me."

"I've been thinking about that," he admitted. "And I

know it doesn't require a computer science degree, but we have an opening—"

"I'll find another job," she interrupted. "But thank you."

"I'm trying to apologize here, Tess."

"It's really not necessary." She stood up, carried her cup to the sink to dump the tea. "We each had our own reasons for agreeing to this marriage, I shouldn't be surprised that you wondered about mine."

His, on the other hand, had been clear from the outset—to give their baby the stability of a two-parent family, no emotional commitment required or even desired.

She felt his hands on her shoulders and stiffened instinctively. He stilled and she thought for a moment he might pull away. But he slid his hands down her arms and around her, drawing her back against the hard length of his body.

She wanted to stay mad—she was definitely still hurting. But she was scared that if she let this issue come between them, they wouldn't get past it, so she closed her eyes and let herself relax against him.

His hand splayed over the slight bulge of her tummy, rubbed gently. The tenderness of the gesture was at odds with his earlier antagonism—or maybe it wasn't. Because she was finally realizing that his feelings for her were completely separate from his feelings for their baby.

The baby was the reason he'd married her—she wouldn't let herself forget that again. But she couldn't stop loving him just because he refused to love her and she couldn't give up the hope that her love would help him open his heart.

Without giving herself time to think she turned in his arms and lifted her mouth to his.

He might have been caught off guard at first but he quickly overcame his surprise to take control of the kiss. His mouth moved over hers in a slow sensual glide that made everything inside her quiver and melt. Then his tongue dipped inside, stroking hers in a slow, lazy dance of seduction and the heat in her belly spread until her whole body felt as though it was on fire.

He scooped her into his arms and carried her to the bedroom.

Passion flared quickly, burned hotly. Their bodies were attuned to each other now and moved together effortlessly. Her climax came easily, wave after wave rushing over her, sweeping her away on a seemingly endless tide of pleasure that soon carried him along with it.

It was several more minutes before their breathing had leveled and their bodies had cooled. When Craig lifted himself away from her she shivered with the chill, finally accepting that the physical closeness they shared could never compensate for the emotional intimacy she needed.

"Craig…"

He smoothed her hair away from her face, kissed her softly. "Please don't complicate this, Tess."

Maybe she should have let it go, but she couldn't. "Don't you want more?"

"What we have between us is real and good—why can't that be enough?"

"I don't know," she admitted softly. "I only know that it's not."

His eyes were filled with sadness and regret as he

trailed his fingertips down her cheek. "I'm sorry I can't give you what you need."

"So am I," she said softly.

Then she rolled onto her side, turning away from him so he wouldn't see the tears in her eyes.

Tess debated over her decision for several days before she made the call, wanting to make sure she wasn't acting impulsively. If she was going to justify her decision—and she knew she would have to—she needed to know that it was based on logic and reason rather than emotion. It was hard, though, to remove her feelings from the equation when she was still hurt by Craig's accusations and his dismissal of her feelings.

Her conversation with Jared McCabe was brief but when she hung up she was relieved that she'd at least taken a step forward. Now she only had to talk to Craig about her decision.

She knew his department was launching a new drug trial this weekend and he'd left a message on the machine earlier warning that he would be late. She understood that he liked to be on hand to ensure there were no snags early on but she hadn't expected that he would be this late. She wondered if they'd run into some problems—or if he was just avoiding her.

Pushing the thought out of her mind, she got ready for bed. She brushed her teeth and settled in with a book, determined to wait up for him to get home.

She stayed awake until after midnight, then finally fell asleep facing the empty side of the bed.

Craig woke up desperately wanting a shower and coffee, not necessarily in that order. So when he caught a whiff of his favorite French Roast in the air, he followed the scent into the kitchen. His eyes were gritty from lack of sleep, his jaw was in desperate need of a razor and his clothes were rumpled from being slept in.

Tess, on the other hand, looked bright and fresh sitting at the table reading the paper. "I made real coffee this morning—I figured you could use it."

He nodded as he made his way to the cupboard for a mug. "Thanks."

She waited while he filled his mug and took a long sip. It was hot and strong and the jolt of caffeine cleared some of the fog around his brain.

"I didn't hear you come in last night," she said.

There was no censure in her voice, only concern. But he felt the weight of guilt anyway, conscious of the fact that he could have called—should have called. But things had been tense between them since their argument about Tess losing her job and everything that came after and he'd taken the easy way, leaving a message on the machine at home when he knew she was still at work, trusting that she would track him down at the lab if she needed anything.

Because of that guilt, or maybe just because he wanted to make an effort to get their relationship back on track, he carried his mug to the table and sat down across from her.

"It was early this morning," he admitted. "I didn't want to disturb you so I crashed on the sofa."

"Did you run into problems with the trial?"

He nodded. "Some idiot lied on his intake form about

a medication he was taking and within half an hour of dosing, he was vomiting all over the place."

"The drug didn't show up on his prescreen blood work?"

"He wasn't taking it then. Apparently he came down with some kind of bronchial infection last week, went to his doctor to get something for it because he didn't want to be cut from the study.

"We're lucky it was a relatively mild drug interaction but Kaitlyn had to take him to the hospital to be checked out, leaving the rest of us to work on damage control while still trying to keep the study on schedule. Thankfully there were no other complications, at least not while I was still there."

"Sounds like it was a rough night," she said sympathetically.

He nodded again.

"Did you want some breakfast?" she asked. "I've already had mine, but I could—"

"No, thanks," he interrupted, feeling even more guilty that she was being so considerate when his own actions had been so thoughtless. "I'm just going to have another cup of coffee and grab a shower before I head back."

"Oh."

He finished his coffee in one long swallow and stood up to get a refill.

He glanced over at Tess, saw that she was staring at the paper but not reading. There was obviously something on her mind, something he instinctively suspected he didn't want to get into—not in his current sleep-deprived state, anyway—but he felt compelled to ask, "What are you thinking about?"

"I wanted to talk to you," she admitted. "But I didn't want to dump it on you like this."

"What is it?"

"I'm leaving for San Diego tomorrow."

"San Diego? What are you talking about?"

"I've been offered a short-term contract at GigaPix."

He couldn't have been more stunned if she'd stood up on the table and started dancing.

It had been eight days since they'd argued about Tess losing her job and though things had been a little awkward between them since then, he'd honestly thought they would soon be back to the way things used to be. He sure as hell hadn't bargained on something like this.

"You said you loved me."

"My decision to go to San Diego doesn't have anything to do with my feelings for you."

He didn't believe her. "Then why are you doing this? Why now?"

"Because I realized that, despite my qualifications, no one's going to want to hire a woman who will be taking maternity leave in a few months and because Jared needs some help finishing up the program I'd been working on at SBG."

"You don't need to work, Tess. I can afford—"

"No," she interrupted sharply. "It's not about how much you're worth, it's about my self-worth. I won't let you believe that my marriage to you was some kind of retirement plan—"

"I know it wasn't."

She looked at him skeptically. "Do you?"

"Of course. I was just surprised to find out about SBG and I reacted without thinking." He realized it was the closest he'd come to actually apologizing for the accusations he'd made and he could tell by the look on Tess's face that it was too little too late.

"In any event," she continued. "The money Jared is offering will more than compensate for the time I'll need to be off with the baby."

"Don't do this, Tess."

"It's only for six weeks," she said.

Six weeks sounded like forever to him and he was suddenly, desperately afraid that if she left, she would never come back.

"We hit a rough spot, Tess. Every marriage goes through periods of adjustment. How are we going to work through it if you run away?"

"I'm not running," she said. "Although I won't deny that I need some time away and Jared's offer seemed like the perfect opportunity to take it."

He gulped a mouthful of hot coffee, barely felt the burn. "I'm not giving you a divorce."

She seemed genuinely startled by his statement. "I'm not asking for a divorce, I'm only asking for six weeks."

Except she wasn't really asking and they both knew it. She'd made up her mind and he could either acquiesce or argue with her but it wouldn't change her decision.

"You've made the arrangements already," he guessed.

She nodded.

"Then I guess this discussion is over."

Tess didn't ask Craig to take her to the airport and he didn't offer. He didn't want her to go and there was no way in hell he was going to make it easier for her. But when he got up Sunday morning he saw her suitcases standing in the hallway beside the front door, mocking him like twin exclamation marks at the end of a sentence: You blew it!! And he felt a kind of helpless anguish he couldn't ever remember feeling and didn't know what to do about.

He found her in the kitchen, writing a note.

Had she planned on leaving without even saying goodbye to him?

"I was just jotting down the address and phone number of where I'll be staying in San Diego in case you need to reach me," she said. "And there's a copy of my itinerary on the fridge."

He took the sticky note she offered, noted the residential address. "I thought you'd be staying in a hotel."

She shook her head. "I don't even want to imagine what a hotel would cost for six weeks."

"Whose place is this?" he asked.

"Jared's sister's. She's a singer in some country band and is on tour in Europe for a few months so I'm subletting her apartment."

He nodded, as if it was okay. As if the idea of his wife moving halfway across the country to live in a stranger's home was even remotely acceptable to him.

She glanced at her watch. "My cab's going to be here in a few minutes."

He followed her to the living room, where she stood by the window to wait for her ride. He didn't want her going away with so much still unresolved between them. He didn't want her going away at all. But he didn't know what to say—he didn't know if there was anything he could say—to change her mind. "Tess…"

She turned around, one hand holding the edge of the curtain, waiting.

But he seemed at a complete loss for words, and she'd already said everything there was to say.

Then she heard the beep of a horn.

"My ride's here."

"Wait." He took her hands, held on for a long moment.

She waited again, her throat tight and her eyes burning, knowing she was a fool for even letting herself hope he might say the three little words she so desperately wanted to hear.

Despite all the reasons she'd enumerated for accepting the six-week contract in California, she knew that if he said those three words, she'd call Jared McCabe in a heartbeat and cancel her trip.

"Don't go, Tess."

Three words—but not quite the ones she needed.

She drew a deep breath and stepped away. "I have to."

Then, before she could change her mind, she picked up her suitcases and walked out the door.

Craig had barely slept since Tess had been gone.

No matter how many times he changed the sheets, he could still smell her scent on her pillow—a scent that haunted him with memories of all the nights they'd lain there together and taunted him with her absence.

He tried sleeping in one of the spare rooms and even on the sofa, but it didn't make any difference. He wanted to be in his bed with Tess.

There wasn't anywhere he could go in the house without thoughts of her intruding. But it wasn't just in the house, it was everywhere he went. It seemed that not more than an hour passed on any given day without him thinking about her, wondering what she was doing, missing her.

It was strange how easily he'd adapted to her presence and how difficult it was to adapt to her absence.

They spoke on the telephone almost every day but he usually initiated the calls and their conversations were always cordial but short, as if neither of them knew what to say to the other.

So when his brother showed up at the house on Wednesday night in the third week of Tess's absence, Craig was grateful for the distraction.

Until Gage asked, "Where's your wife tonight?"

Craig hadn't told his family about her six-week contract in California because he didn't want to talk about it. As if by not discussing it, he could pretend she wasn't really gone.

"In San Diego," he admitted.

"Business trip?"

"Yeah." It was the simplest, if not the complete, answer.

"Well, at least now I know why you've been so surly," his brother noted. "When's she going to be back?"

"The middle of November."

Gage frowned. "That's a long trip."

Twenty-five more days, Craig knew, though he was hardly going to admit to his brother that he was counting.

But Gage's eyes narrowed thoughtfully. "You're obviously not giving me the whole story."

Craig shrugged, as if his wife's absence was inconsequential. "She was offered a six-week contract at GigaPix and she decided it was too good an opportunity to pass up."

"And you just let her go?" he asked incredulously.

"It wasn't my choice to make."

"Okay, then," Gage allowed. "What did you do to make her want to leave for six weeks?"

"What makes you think I had anything to do with it?" he challenged aware that he sounded just a little defensive.

"The fact that you've barely been married two months and you're here alone and looking miserable."

He sighed. "You're right—I screwed up. I found out that Tess knew she was losing her job before we got engaged and basically accused her of marrying me for my bank account."

"Well, that would do it." Gage shook his head, obviously disgusted by his brother's idiocy. "Where would you ever come up with an idea like that?"

"It's why Lana wanted to marry me."

"You're not seriously comparing Tess to that piranha." His brother sounded as indignant as Tess had been.

"I had a momentary lapse."

"No wonder she's pissed at you."

Craig started to defend his position, then realized there really was no defense. Because he knew Tess and he should have known that she would never use him. Then again, he'd never thought she would leave him after they'd exchanged wedding vows, either. But here he was and she was gone.

She'd said she loved him, yet she'd walked away without so much as a backward glance.

It's only six weeks.

But it was more than that. To Craig, it was further

proof that no one had ever loved him enough to stay. Not his mother or Lana. Not even Tess.

And that realization might have bothered him far more than anything else—if he hadn't learned a long time ago to lock down his emotions.

Tess had been working fourteen hours a day since she got to California, partly because she was anxious to get the DirectorPlus Five program up and running, but mostly because she needed to focus on something other than the mess she'd already made of her marriage. And so, by the end of her third week, only halfway through the term of her contract, she finished upgrading the program.

She didn't tell Jared right away, because she wanted to run it through some test exercises, checking for flaws and gaps before she turned it over. Which was why he found her at her desk Saturday morning when she'd been given explicit instructions to take the weekend off.

"You're going to make me look bad—working longer hours than the boss."

She continued tapping away at the keyboard, her eyes on the screen. "I should have warned you that I can become a little obsessive when I get started on something."

"Aren't pregnant women supposed to rest?"

"I've been sitting in front of a computer, not climbing mountains with a fifty-pound pack on my back."

"I know I should probably be thanking you rather than complaining," Jared said. "But I'm worried that you're pushing yourself too hard."

"I'm not," she said. "And I'm done."

He frowned. "What?"

She turned to look at him and smiled. "I'm done."

As realization dawned, the confusion on his face gave way to sheer delight. "It's really finished?"

"Yep."

"But you're weeks ahead of schedule. My programmers said it would take at least six weeks to get it up and running."

"Your programmers weren't as familiar with the software as I am," she reminded him.

"Can I play with it?" he asked, sounding as excited as a child with a new toy.

Tess laughed and pushed away from the desk so Jared could get to the computer.

Several minutes passed while he put the software through its paces, then he turned back to her. "Wow."

She smiled again. "It's great, isn't it?"

"This calls for a celebration," he decided.

"What did you have in mind?"

"Getting you out of this office, for starters," he said. "Have you seen anything of the city since you arrived?"

"Only what's between here and your sister's apartment," she admitted.

"Then we definitely need to do something about that."

She wasn't sure what he had in mind and was pleasantly surprised when he took her to the zoo.

"This is amazing." Tess stared at the park map in her hand trying to figure out which way to go, what she wanted to see first. "I had no idea it was so big."

"A hundred acres in the middle of the city," Jared told her. "With about four thousand animals here—and more than seven hundred thousand plants."

"I want to see everything," she said.

He laughed. "Well, the zoo closes at five, but we could always come back another day."

"Actually, I've already booked my flight to go home," she told him. "Now that the program's finished, there's no reason for me to stay."

"I guess you're anxious to get back," he said.

She nodded. Though she'd had work to keep her busy through the days, she'd found the nights unbearably lonely. She'd missed Craig—talking with him, laughing with him, even arguing with him. But mostly she missed going to sleep beside him at night and waking with his arms around her in the morning.

Not for the first time, she wondered if she'd taken the coward's way out—jumping at the chance to come to San Diego rather than staying in Pinehurst and fighting it out with Craig. But she'd been so angry he could think—even for a moment—that she'd marry him for his money and she'd been devastated when he'd walked out after the declaration of her true feelings—blatantly rejecting her love.

"Let's start at the Reptile House," Jared suggested, interrupting her wayward thoughts.

Tess shuddered. "Let's not."

"You said you wanted to see everything," he reminded her.

She glanced at the map. "Let's start with the koalas and kangaroos," she said, noting that those exhibit areas were on the opposite side of the park.

"All right," he agreed. "We'll start with the koalas and kangaroos."

They worked their way around the north side of the park and circled back toward the Giant Panda Research

Station, stopping for ice cream after Tess had used almost a whole roll of film taking pictures of Hua Mei and the other black-and-white bears.

She was glad for the rest. Having spent the better part of the last three weeks behind a desk in a climate-controlled office, the muscles in her legs were protesting the vigorous workout and the unaccustomed heat.

Tess finished her double scoop of orange-pineapple sherbet and wiped her fingers on a paper napkin. "Next stop: Polar Bear Plunge."

"Ready when you are," Jared said, offering his hand to help her up from the bench.

She accepted and was glad she had because when she stood up she almost fell down again.

He moved closer, grabbing for her other hand to keep her upright. "What's wrong?"

"I don't know," she said. "I just felt light-headed all of a sudden."

He gently guided her back onto the bench. "Sit for a minute."

"I've been sitting," she reminded him.

"Yeah, but it won't hurt you to sit some more."

So she did and the dizziness passed. Mostly, anyway.

"Okay?" he asked after several minutes.

She nodded.

He helped her to her feet again. "I think we should call it a day."

"But we haven't seen the monkeys," she felt compelled to point out.

"We've seen enough for today."

"Okay," she agreed, because she was ready to go.

Jared cranked up the air conditioning in his car as

they drove out of the parking lot and Tess leaned back and closed her eyes. She wasn't aware that she'd fallen asleep until Jared shook her awake when they arrived at the hospital.

Chapter Thirteen

Tess wanted to be annoyed with Jared for not consulting her before deciding she needed to see a doctor but the truth was, she was glad to be there. Though she didn't want to express her concerns aloud she knew she'd feel a lot better after she'd been checked over and reassured that everything was okay.

Except that when she excused herself to go to the bathroom while waiting for her exam, she found her underpants spotted with bright red blood and knew that everything wasn't going to be okay.

"The problem seems to be a low-lying placenta," Dr. Smye told her, after he'd reviewed the report from her ultrasound.

She swallowed. "What does that mean?"

"What it means for you right now is that you get to spend the night here. The bleeding wasn't heavy and it stopped on its own and that's a good sign. Your baby is measuring right where he should for twenty-two weeks and is active, which is another good sign. But bleeding at any stage is a concern and could be an indication that you'll have trouble maintaining your pregnancy."

She didn't want to ask the question, wasn't sure she wanted to know, but she found herself saying, "What do you mean?"

The doctor looked at her with kindness and compassion in his weary eyes. "It means that you might lose this baby."

And the panic that she'd been trying to hold at bay since she discovered the bleeding suddenly closed in on her from all sides making her eyes sting, her throat burn and her heart ache.

"No." Tess shook her head as she spoke around the tightness in her throat. "I can't lose this baby."

"I can't promise you that you won't," Dr. Smye said.

His tone was somehow both gentle and matter-of-fact, indicating that he'd seen this condition before, spoken these words before. But his experience and expertise didn't reassure Tess because this time it was her baby he was talking about.

"It's simply too early to tell," the doctor continued. "For now, we can only hope that you won't experience any more bleeding and that the placenta will move away from the cervix. But your own doctor will want to monitor that with regular ultrasounds every three to four weeks for the duration of your pregnancy."

Tess silently vowed that she would do everything she could, everything Dr. Bowen told her to do to keep her baby safe.

After the doctor was finished with her, Jared came back into the examining room.

"I called your husband," he told her.

She dropped her head back against the pillows and closed her eyes.

"Don't you think he'd want to know?"

"Of course," she admitted. "But now he'll feel obligated to drop everything and come out here..."

"His flight will be in at eleven," Jared confirmed.

"Was he...was he very angry?"

"Angry?" He frowned. "Why would you think he'd be angry?"

"Aside from the fact that he didn't want me coming out here in the first place?"

Jared hesitated, as if considering his words. "I don't know you all that well and I don't know what the situation is between you and your husband," he said at last. "But I do know that the man I spoke to on the phone was deeply concerned about you, Tess."

"Because of the baby," she said softly. And she was concerned about their baby, too, but she still couldn't help wishing that Craig cared as much about her.

He sat in the chair beside her bed. "Did you marry him because you were pregnant?"

She shook her head. "No, but he only proposed because I was pregnant."

"I wouldn't be so sure of that."

But she was. She'd hoped Craig would grow to love her, but the way he'd reacted when she told him she loved him confirmed that she'd been harboring a futile hope. He didn't now and never would love her.

"He married me to give our baby a family," she admitted. "That's all that matters to Craig."

"Obviously, you have reasons for believing that," Jared said. "But you should know that when I talked to him, he only asked about *you*—he never even mentioned the baby."

Throughout the six-hour flight to San Diego, Craig couldn't stop thinking about Tess. It seemed like the longest flight he'd ever taken. And then the cab ride from the airport to the hospital seemed to take forever all over again.

By the time he arrived at Memorial Hospital in San Diego, almost ten hours had passed since Jared McCabe's phone call. So much could happen in that period of time and his heart was in his throat as he rode the elevator to the fifth floor. And then he had to stop at the nurses' station to find out what room Tess was in because he'd forgot to get that information on the phone.

It was almost midnight by then and he half expected someone would try to turn him away. But whether the nurse read the determination in his face or felt sorry for him because he was so obviously rumpled and weary with exhaustion, she led him to Tess's room.

"She's sleeping now but you can go in to check on her—for your own peace of mind. Then I'd suggest you find a hotel for the night and come back in the morning."

"I want to stay."

She shrugged, clearly not intending to fight him on the issue and pushed open the door for him to enter.

He tiptoed quietly into the room, his steps almost faltering when he saw Tess. She looked so fragile and pale in the narrow hospital bed, her rounded belly covered by a thin sheet, an IV tube in the back of her hand.

In all the years he'd known her, she'd rarely been sick even with something as simple as a common cold. She'd always been healthy and strong, almost invincible. But she looked fragile and vulnerable right now, and he wanted nothing more than to take her in his arms and protect her.

Except that it was his fault she was here. If he hadn't pushed Tess about losing her job at SBG, she never would have come out here to work for Jared and she wouldn't be lying in this hospital bed right now.

He knew he didn't deserve her forgiveness, but as he bent down to touch his lips to her forehead, he silently prayed that she'd give it to him, anyway.

Her eyelids fluttered, then opened slowly. "Craig?"

"Shh," he said softly. "They'll kick me out of here if they find out I woke you."

"I wasn't really sleeping," she admitted.

"You should be," he said.

"So should you. It's—" her eyes darted to the clock on the wall across from her bed "—3:00 a.m. your time."

Your time—as if they were from different worlds. And suddenly he felt the distance of those three time zones like an unbridgeable chasm between them.

No, he refused to believe that the thoughtless words he'd spoken to her more than three weeks ago could create such distance between them. This was Tess—his best friend, his wife, the mother of his child. And he was going to fight to keep her.

He lowered himself into one of the ugly vinyl-covered chairs beside the bed. He reached for her free hand and wasn't surprised to see that his own was shaking. His entire system had been a jumble of quivering nerves since he'd received Jared's telephone call.

He brushed her hair away from her face, noted the dark circles under her eyes, the pallor of her skin. "How are you?"

"I'm okay. A little scared, but okay." She squeezed his hand. "I'm glad you're here."

And those last few words made all the difference to him. Throughout the trip from New York, he'd wondered whether he was doing the right thing, whether Tess would be happy to see him or resent his presence. Now, some of the tightness around his chest finally eased.

"I wasn't sure, after the way things were between us when I left—"

"You said you wanted some time," he reminded her. "I was giving you time."

She nodded, then moved her hand to her tummy.

"What's wrong?" he asked immediately. "Do you need the doctor?"

"No, I'm okay," she said, and guided his hand to the side of her belly.

He immediately felt a series of little vibrations through the taut skin.

"Is that—" he cleared his throat, which suddenly felt tight.

She nodded, her eyes shining with excitement. "That's our baby," she confirmed.

He felt the baby move again.

"The doctor said I could lose the baby," she admitted softly, staring through tear-filled eyes at his hand covering their baby. "I can't let myself even think about it—especially when I feel him moving like this, inside of me and know that he's depending on me…"

It was a possibility he'd forced himself to consider on the long trip west and one he'd been glad not to have to face. At least not yet.

He brushed a tear off her cheek. "You're doing everything you can to take care of our baby, Tess. That's all you can do."

And then, hoping to take some of the sadness from her eyes, he said, "I notice you still seem to be stuck on 'he'."

"Well, the ultrasound technician thought he was a he."

He kept his hand on her belly, savoring the skin-on-skin contact after having been apart from her for so long.

She'd only been gone half of the six weeks she'd intended but he knew—from his conversation with Jared—that she'd finished the program and had intended to come home. He'd learned something else from Jared and he asked her about that now.

"Why didn't you tell me that you'd been offered a permanent position at GigaPix?"

"Because I had no intention of accepting it."

"But why?" That was another question he'd been mulling over since the software company CEO had told him about his initial offer. He knew how much she loved her job and how hard it would be for her to find anything else comparable to what GigaPix could offer her.

"Because I'm having your baby," she reminded him. "And if I moved three thousand miles away, you would hardly ever see him."

"You turned down the job so I could be part of our baby's life?"

"So we could be a family," she said.

He was stunned by the admission and humbled by what she was offering. But mostly he was ashamed that he'd accused her of using him to get what she wanted when she'd been putting his wants ahead of her own all along.

"Is that still what you want?" he asked gently.

He hadn't realized he was holding his breath waiting for her response until he finally released it when she nodded.

"Does that mean you'll come home with me?"

"As soon as they let me out of here," she promised.

Tess and Craig returned from San Diego on Tuesday. Grace managed to hold off until Thursday before stopping by for a visit with her daughter-in-law.

She was surprised, but not displeased, when the door was answered by a woman who introduced herself as Irene Chambers—a retired nurse hired by Mr. Richmond to take care of the house and meals and look after his wife. Grace knew how important this baby was to her son and she was glad to see that he was taking such good care of his wife.

Irene showed Grace into the living room, where Tess was sitting with her feet up flipping through the pages of a parenting magazine, then excused herself to make tea.

Tess immediately closed the book when Grace stepped into the room, her eyes lighting up with pleasure. "This is a wonderful surprise," she said.

"I would have been here sooner," Grace admitted, "but Craig asked me to give you some time to settle in."

"If I was any more settled, I'd be a fixture," Tess told her.

She chuckled as she sat down on the other end of the couch, but with her back against the arm so that she was facing her daughter-in-law. "How are you feeling?"

"Good. I saw Dr. Bowen this morning and the baby—"

"I didn't ask about the baby," Grace interrupted gently. "I asked about you."

"Oh," Tess said.

And she sounded so surprised Grace wondered if she'd lost all sense of herself through the course of her pregnancy and she made a mental note to slap her son for allowing that to happen.

"I'm good," her daughter-in-law responded to the question at last and left it at that.

She sighed. "I love both of my sons, but that doesn't mean I'm blind to their faults. And I know something had to have happened between you and Craig for you to take off for San Diego the way you did."

"A misunderstanding."

"Is that a diplomatic way of saying that he reacted first and asked questions later?"

"It doesn't matter now," Tess said.

"Of course it does," Grace said, even though she appreciated Tess's loyalty to her husband. "I know you're both concerned about the baby, but I can't help feeling there's more going on."

"He wasn't happy about my decision to go to California," Tess admitted.

"Although I'm sure he was somehow instrumental in that decision."

Tess was silent for a moment before she said, "We had an argument about our reasons for getting married, I told him I loved him and he walked out."

"I'm sorry."

"But you're not surprised," her daughter-in-law guessed.

No, Grace wasn't surprised. Disappointed that he was still carrying around such old baggage, but not surprised.

"Craig hasn't had an easy go of it with women and emotions," she explained. "His mother played a lot of head games with both of the boys—giving and withdrawing affection as suited her moods. Gage, thankfully, was too young to really understand it. But Craig tried so hard to please her, with varying results and ultimately she rejected him completely when she chose her new husband over her children.

"Then there was Valerie—remember the girl he dated through his senior year of high school?"

Tess nodded.

"She and Craig had planned to go to the same college, but she decided to go to Notre Dame instead of Princeton. I have no doubt it was the right choice for her and even if she'd gone to Princeton, their high school romance wouldn't have survived the pressures and changes of college life. But Craig took her decision as another personal rejection.

"Then, of course, there was Lana. You know what a number she did on him."

"But he should know me well enough to know that I would never use my feelings against him," Tess protested.

"And yet, didn't you do exactly that?" she asked gently.

Tess looked startled. "What do you mean?"

"You told him you loved him and when he couldn't give the words back to you, you left."

"I didn't do it to hurt him. I did it because I needed something to focus on so *I* would stop hurting."

Grace nodded. "I'm not saying you were wrong to go. I'm only trying to help you understand how it probably looked to Craig."

"I do love him," Tess said. "He makes me angry and frustrated and crazy sometimes, but I love him."

"I know you do," she assured her. "And deep inside, he knows it, too."

Tess's eyes filled with tears and she dropped her gaze. "Do you think..." She hesitated, then shook her head.

But Grace already knew what she was thinking. She heard the question she didn't ask as clearly as if she'd spoken it aloud. "Do I think he could ever love you?"

Tess shook her head again. "It's a crazy thought."

"Oh, Tess. It's not crazy at all." Grace reached over and squeezed her hand gently. "But you're getting hung up on the words, honey. I'm not denying that they're important, but you need to stop listening to what he's not saying and start reading what he does."

Tess looked puzzled.

"Maybe it's a mental block with him, but just because he isn't saying the words doesn't mean he doesn't love you."

The period from Thanksgiving through to Christmas was usually Tess's favorite time of year. She loved to decorate and bake and shop and wrap. This year, however, her activity was severely restricted by doctor's orders and her own concerns about her baby, leaving Tess dependent upon others to assist with the tasks she enjoyed so much.

And despite her concerns, everything got done. Mrs. Chambers had taken care of the baking, although she let Tess sit at the table in the kitchen for a couple of hours each afternoon to help ice the sugar cookies. Grace and Allan and even Gage, had come around to help put up the decorations, wrapping garland around banisters, hanging wreaths and bows, setting Tess's collection of nutcrackers on the mantle of the fireplace. Laurie had taken care of most of her shopping and the wrapping, allowing Tess to write the tags and stick on the bows but nothing more strenuous than that.

But the highlight of the holiday preparations for Tess was when Craig took her to get the tree—just the two of them.

It was a crisp, clear day and the ground was covered in a thin blanket of fresh snow. Because he worried that the ground might be slippery, he kept her hand tucked in the crook of his arm as they slowly made their way up and down the rows of spruce and balsam and pine in search of the perfect specimen. And when they'd found it, he'd settled her down on a nearby stump to watch as he wielded his axe in battle against the blue spruce.

When the tree finally toppled, he turned to her with a look of such triumphant joy in his eyes and a smile of such pure joy on his face that her heart stuttered. She loved his boyish enthusiasm and his ability to find pleasure in the simplest things and she knew that he was going to be a terrific father to their child.

He struggled to get a grip on the trunk, then dragged the tree over to where she was sitting.

"Our first Christmas tree," he'd said proudly.

She smiled and nodded but she couldn't help wondering if their first would also be their last. She knew they both wanted this marriage to work but she also knew that they couldn't go on forever as they'd been going the last several weeks.

The distance between them was her own fault. He hadn't wanted her to go to California, but she'd gone anyway. Her pride had demanded it. There was no way she could stay in Pinehurst, unemployed, after he'd compared her to Lana. She'd needed to go to San Diego to prove that she could still support herself, that she wasn't looking for a free ride. Except that she wasn't capable of supporting herself right now, and though it was by circumstance rather than choice, she wondered if Craig resented her dependence on him.

It took a great deal more wrestling to get the tree strapped onto the top of his car and then unstrapped again and set up in their living room. But once that was all done, he actually let her help decorate it—although he kept a close eye on her to ensure she didn't do too much reaching or bending. And afterward, he popped a bowl of popcorn and they sat together on the sofa, snacking and drinking hot chocolate and watching the lights twinkle.

"What do you think?" he asked.

"It's perfect," she assured him. And though it was a little lopsided and a couple of the branches had broken when Craig maneuvered it into the house, it was perfect to Tess.

The baby kicked hard, demanding she pay attention to him instead of the tree and she smiled as she laid her hand on her belly to assure him that he hadn't been forgotten.

Craig put his hand beside hers and rubbed gently. He'd been touching her belly a lot recently, fascinated by the baby's seemingly constant activity.

"Can you believe that by this time next year he'll be sitting here with us?" he asked.

"By this time next year, he probably won't be doing much sitting at all," Tess said. "He'll be crawling around, trying to pull ornaments off of the tree and tear bows off of presents."

"Now who's been reading up on child care?" he teased.

"Well, I have to do something while I'm under house arrest."

"Bed rest," he corrected mildly.

"Same thing."

"I can understand why you're feeling frustrated."

"I'm not really frustrated," she said. "Because I know I'm doing what's best for the baby. But I am starting to get bored. It seems that all I do is sit around reading or watching reruns of *CSI*."

"Maybe we could find you a hobby."

"I tried knitting," she admitted.

"You knit?" The surprise was evident in his voice.

"No, I don't knit," she said irritably. "I said I *tried*."

He chuckled. "I imagine your attempt lasted all of about three minutes."

"Four," she disputed.

"Well, it won't be too much longer before you'll have our baby to keep you busy."

"I know." And it was that thought which kept her off her feet when she desperately wanted to be doing something. "And your mom and my sister have been stopping by frequently—whether to keep me company or keep an eye on me, I'm not sure, but I appreciate having someone around to talk to."

"Speaking of my mother," he said. "She dropped by this morning with a fresh pine wreath for the front door and some mistletoe."

"Mistletoe?"

He smiled. "Not very subtle, is she?"

Tess couldn't disagree, but she knew that Grace was only trying to nudge her son and his wife closer together and she was touched—if a little embarrassed—by the gesture.

"What did you do with it?" she asked.

"I hung it up in the hall, where she'll be sure to see it the next time she visits."

She nodded.

"I thought about putting it over the couch," he said. "But then I decided that would be too obvious and I shouldn't need a leaf hanging overhead as an excuse to kiss my wife."

Tess didn't know what to say.

Was he suggesting that he did want to kiss her?

He hadn't done so in so long, she thought he'd lost complete interest. But the way he was looking at her now—as he hadn't looked at her in a very long time—made her feel all warm and tingly inside.

He brushed his thumb across her bottom lip in a slow, sensual motion. "Do I need an excuse?"

She swallowed. "Do you want to kiss me?"

"More than you can imagine," he said.

And then he *was* kissing her.

Tess's eyes drifted closed as his mouth moved over hers in a patiently masterful dance of seduction.

In everything else he did, he was decisive and purposeful—moving forward without hesitation. But when he kissed her, it was as if everything else faded away and they had all the time in the world.

He deepened the kiss slowly, gradually, as if giving her time to decide that this was what she wanted. It was definitely what she wanted.

His tongue glided over the seam of her lips, and she opened to welcome him. He dipped inside, teasing her with gentle strokes of his tongue. Oh, yeah, she wanted this. It seemed like forever since he'd kissed her like this and she only wanted it to go on forever.

She wished she could get closer to him; she wanted to feel the hard length of his body against her. But the mound of her belly made that impossible.

Then the baby kicked—hard.

She felt Craig's smile against her mouth, but still he kept kissing her, his hands moving down to her waist—or what had once been her waist—to caress the roundness of her belly. The baby kicked again, although less forcefully this time, then settled.

When he finally eased his lips from hers, she was breathless and dizzy—and she was pleased to note that he looked a little dazed himself.

He might have stopped kissing her, but he was still holding her in his arms, and for the first time since she'd returned from San Diego, she finally felt as though she was home.

"I've missed you so much, Tess."

She knew exactly what he meant, because although they'd been living together, even sharing the same bed, there had been a distance between them—the distance of suspicion and hurt that had driven a wedge between them since before she left for California. A distance that she knew they'd finally started to bridge.

"I've missed you, too," she admitted.

Maybe he wouldn't ever say the words she wanted to hear. Maybe he wouldn't ever love her the way she loved him. But she knew that he cared about her and was committed to their marriage and their family and that was enough for a fresh start.

Something changed between them after that kiss.

Craig wasn't sure exactly what or why, but he was grateful to see that some of the shadows had cleared from Tess's beautiful blue eyes. She smiled more frequently and laughed more easily and they grew closer and closer with each day that passed.

They had a wonderful Christmas together and spent time with each of their families over the holidays. They stayed at home on New Year's, sipping non-alcoholic champagne as they watched the celebration from Times Square on TV.

At her first check-up of the new year, Dr. Bowen confirmed that because the placenta was still covering the cervix, Tess would have to deliver the baby by caesarean section. She also ordered weekly ultrasounds to monitor the baby's development and ensure the procedure could be scheduled before Tess went into labor on her own.

Craig and Tess immediately began making serious

preparations for their baby's arrival. Because the doctor had ordered Tess to stay off of her feet, Craig got her a wheelchair so he could take her around to shop for furniture and little outfits and the million other things their baby would need. He brought home paint samples so they could pick the color for the nursery and he let her watch while he painted and set everything up. They had a lot of fun preparing for their baby's arrival, but more than that, they seemed to have rediscovered the joy of spending time with one another and simply being together. They no longer slept on opposite sides of the bed, but cuddled close together in the middle—or as close as they could get these days.

Craig had so much to be grateful for and so much more to look forward to and he was happier than he could ever remember being.

But did he love her?

That was the question that would often spring to mind when he found himself lying awake beside her in the night just watching her sleep.

He wanted to say that he did. He wanted to give her the words that he knew she wanted to hear. But as strong as his feelings for her were, he just didn't know. His affection for her was real and his commitment to their family unshakeable, and that—at least for him—as enough.

It was after midnight when Tess awoke, feeling achy and even more uncomfortable than usual. The baby was restless, too, kicking up a storm inside her belly.

She was still more than a month away from her actual due date, although at her doctor's appointment earlier that day, Dr. Bowen had scheduled her C-section for two days' time. She'd thought Tess could probably go another week to ten days further into her pregnancy with little risk but wanted to err on the side of caution. Tess was relieved she wouldn't have to carry so much extra weight around for very much longer. She imagined the baby would be relieved, too, to be released from his confinement. No doubt that's why he'd been so restless lately—there wasn't much room for him to move around in there anymore.

She felt a twinge in her lower back and rolled onto her other side hoping a change of position would ease the ache. The baby twisted around again, too, and now he was pressing directly on her bladder.

Tess got up to make a trip to the bathroom, then went downstairs to get a drink, frowning as the ache in her back seemed to worsen. She'd had cramps in her legs all day, too. Probably the strain from carrying the extra twenty pounds around. Or maybe she was stiff from lack of exercise. The further along she'd progressed in her pregnancy, the more the doctor—and Craig—had restricted her activities.

After about half an hour of walking, she thought the pain had started to ease. Or maybe she was just feeling too weak and weary to continue pacing the floors. Whatever the reason, she finally made her way back up to the bedroom, crawled under the covers and drifted into a restless sleep.

It was several hours later before she woke up again, gasping at the pain that ripped through her belly like a jagged knife.

* * *

When Craig returned to the bedroom after his morning shower, his initial surprise at finding his wife sitting up in bed was immediately superseded by deep, bone-chilling fear. It wasn't just that she was awake so early, it was the way her hands were fisted in the sheets, her brow crinkled in pain and the slow, shallow breaths that seemed to require all of her concentration.

"Tess?"

She turned her head, her eyes wide and slightly panicked. "I think…I'm in…labor."

Oh, no. Oh, Christ. Christ no. This was *not* supposed to be happening.

"You're not supposed to go into labor," he reminded her, as if maybe she'd just forgotten and could somehow miraculously put a halt to the process. "You have a C-section scheduled Thursday."

"Yeah, well…I guess we forgot…to tell…the baby," she joked weakly.

He forced away the panic, focused his thoughts. It wasn't going to do Tess any good if he fell apart.

"Okay," he said. "I'm going to help you get dressed, then we're going to call Dr. Bowen to meet us at the hospital."

"Okay," she agreed.

He found a pair of leggings and tunic top then dug through the drawer for a pair of warm socks. Tess's feet were always cold—it was a strange thought to be having in the moment, but maybe his mind needed to focus on something mundane because somehow holding those socks in his hand helped him to concentrate on what needed to be done.

But as he carried the clothes back over to the bed, he couldn't help remembering Doctor Bowen's warning to Tess: "if we let you go into labor on your own, it could be dangerous for both you and the baby."

He closed his eyes and said a quick and silent prayer that they would both be okay. After everything they'd been through already, he had to believe everything would be fine. He just had to get her dressed and to the hospital and then let the doctors take care of her.

He set the clothes on the bed and pulled back the sheets.

That's when he saw the blood.

Chapter Fourteen

After about two seconds' debate, Craig called an ambulance. And as he rode with Tess on the way to the hospital, he was glad he'd done so. He didn't understand all the medical jargon the paramedics tossed back and forth between themselves and over the radio, but he knew when they pulled out of the drive with the lights flashing and sirens screaming that Tess's condition wasn't good.

He held her hand tightly in his own as the medic set up an IV for a Ringers lactose infusion. Craig knew that Tess was in danger of going into shock and if she did—no, he wasn't going to allow himself to consider the possibility.

But she was so pale, and obviously in a lot of pain with the contractions that seemed to come with alarming frequency and increasing intensity.

"She's at thirty-four weeks," Craig told the paramedic. "And scheduled to have a C-section Thursday. Dr. Bowen's her OB-GYN."

"I don't think this baby's going to wait until Thursday," the paramedic responded. Then to his partner, "Tell Memorial to call in Drs. Bowen and Greis to prep for a priority one section."

It probably wasn't an unusual request, but there was something in the other man's tone that alerted Craig. "What's wrong?"

The paramedic gave a slight shake of his head.

"Tell me."

Tess must have picked up on his panic, because she tried to push herself up. "The baby…?" It was all she managed before she collapsed again when another pain seized her.

Craig swallowed hard, squeezed her hand tighter.

"Relax, Mrs. Richmond. You're not going to help your baby by fighting me. Let's just move you over on to your side for a minute." As he spoke, he slid his arms beneath her, helped turn to her gently. "We're going to be at the hospital in a minute and a half."

But a minute and a half, Craig knew, could be too late.

He heard the driver, still patched through to the hospital, relay the information given to him by his partner.

Tachycardia, the paramedic said, which Craig knew was an abnormally rapid beating of the heart. Because they monitored blood pressure and heart rates during their trials in the lab, he knew that anything over one hundred beats per minute at rest was considered fast and Tess's rate was over one hundred and forty. Her blood pressure, on the other hand, was dangerously low because of the bleeding and he knew she was starting to fade.

"Craig." Her voice was growing weaker and her skin alarmingly pale.

"I'm here," he told her.

"Promise me…"

"Anything," he said hoarsely.

"Promise me you'll take care of our baby."

"Always."

Her eyes drifted shut. "If anything happens to me—"

"No," he interrupted, refusing to let her finish the thought. "Nothing's going to happen. Everything's going to be fine."

But she didn't hear him.

She'd already drifted into unconsciousness.

He thought he'd be relieved when they finally got to the hospital. And he was—until they whisked Tess away and directed him to a waiting room.

Dammit, he didn't want to be in a waiting room. He wanted to be with Tess.

But he needed to stay out of the way so the doctors could do their job—so they could save Tess and the baby.

Dr. Bowen had already started the emergency surgery and Dr. Greis—the neonatal trauma specialist—was standing by when a social worker came out to talk to Craig.

"Dr. Bowen is doing everything she can," she'd told him. "But you should know that she might not be able to save both your wife and your baby."

"Save Tess," he'd responded without hesitation.

Because in that moment, he'd finally realized the truth that had eluded him for so long: he loved her.

He knew Tess would be devastated if she lost this baby, and he would, too. But they might be able to have other babies someday, and even if they couldn't, at least they'd have each other.

But the thought of losing Tess—no, he couldn't let that happen.

The social worker had shaken her head sympathetically. "You don't get to choose, Mr. Richmond. If the doctor can get in and get the baby out in time, then his chances are good. But she won't know your wife's chances until the baby is delivered."

And now all Craig could do was wait.

He sank into one of the hard plastic chairs that lined the walls of the dreary room and pressed the heels of his hands to his eyes. She'd lost so much blood. Maybe too much. And if they didn't stop the bleeding, she could die.

She could actually die.

And if he lost her, Craig knew that something inside him would die, too.

He heard footsteps near the door and his head shot up. He blinked away the moisture that blurred his eyes, desperately hoping it was Dr. Bowen coming back or anyone else who could tell him what was going on with Tess.

But it was his mom and dad and though he was disappointed, he was also glad for their presence.

"How is she?" Grace's voice was soft, but he saw the same strain and worry on her face that were etched in his own.

This wasn't easy for any of them. He knew how

much his mother and father cared about Tess, how excited they were about their first grandchild and how scared they must be for both Tess and the baby right now.

Craig could only shake his head helplessly. "I don't know. They took her away as soon as we got here and no one's been able to tell me anything since then." His eyes locked on the double doors that led to the emergency room. "It seems like she's been in there forever."

"We've got some of the best doctors in the country at this hospital," his father said.

"I hate feeling so helpless," Craig admitted. "Knowing that her life is on the line and there's nothing I can do."

"You can pray," Grace said.

And he had been—steadily and fervently—since they'd brought Tess in. Although he'd never been a very religious person, he was begging God now, pleading with Him to save his wife and baby.

"Your brother's on his way," Grace said. "And I called Tess's sister. She's going to come, too, as soon as she can."

"Thank you," Craig said.

"In the meantime, I'm going to go to the chapel. Do you want to come with me?"

He shook his head. "I can't. I need to stay here…in case there's any news."

His mother nodded. "I won't be long."

Allan came back—Craig hadn't even realized he'd gone until he returned—and pressed a cup into Craig's hands.

"Thanks," Craig said automatically, although he made no effort to drink it.

His dad sank into the vacant chair beside him.

"She's strong," Allan said. "And she's worked too hard to do what was right for this baby to give up now."

He was right. Tess was strong. Strong and stubborn and sexy and kind and generous and loving. She was honest and beautiful and real.

And with Tess, Craig had found the fulfillment and contentment that had always seemed unattainable. With Tess, he didn't wonder about what he was missing out on, what was missing from his life because his life was finally complete. Because he'd finally been lucky enough to find a woman who really loved him and whom he could love back.

And he was going to tell her exactly that the first chance he got and every day for the rest of their lives together because he refused to believe that he'd finally found love only to have it taken away from him.

When Tess woke up she was in a hospital bed, Craig sitting in the chair beside her.

She had a moment of confusion, thinking she was still in San Diego, still months away from her due date. Then disjointed memories of the past several hours rushed through her mind and she slowly sorted through them. The contractions. The ambulance. Bits and pieces of conversation nudged at her consciousness. Emergency C-section. Severe blood loss. Shock. Fetal distress.

"The baby?" she asked.

"Right here." Craig shifted closer, and she finally noticed the tiny wrapped bundle cradled in his arms.

"Oh." She exhaled a shaky sigh as more memories

filtered through the haze and she remembered hearing the indignant cries of her baby as they pulled him out of her belly. It was the most beautiful sound she'd ever heard.

Craig laid the baby on the bed beside her. "Five pounds ten ounces, healthy and strong. You did a great job, Tess."

She felt the sting of happy tears as she gazed at her beautiful baby. "Wow."

He smiled. "That was my first reaction, too."

"It seems like we waited for him for so long and now he's finally here."

"Yeah. Except that he's a girl."

"A girl?" she echoed, certain she hadn't heard him correctly.

"They ran out of pink blankets—that's why she's in blue," he explained. "But she's very definitely a girl."

"Oh."

"You're not disappointed, are you?" Craig asked.

"Of course not. I'm just surprised."

"We're going to have to come up with another name," he told her.

They'd chosen Jacob Allan when they'd believed the baby was a boy but had never settled on a girl's name because they hadn't thought they'd need one.

"Grace Catherine Richmond," she said.

Grace for his mother, of course, and Catherine for hers.

She watched surprise flicker over his face, then pleasure. "I think it's perfect."

Tess touched her lips to the soft downy hair at the baby's temple. "Me, too."

"There's something else I need to tell you."

"There's not another baby," she said, remembering all the times he'd teased her about the possibility of twins. "The ultrasound technician might have made a mistake about the baby's gender, but she was very clear that there was only one baby."

"No, there's not another baby," he said, then grinned. "Not yet, anyway."

"Then what is it?"

"I love you, Tess."

She stared at him, certain she couldn't have heard him correctly. "What?"

"I probably should have set the scene," he said, almost to himself. "With flowers, soft music, candlelight. Not mint-green walls and the antiseptic smell of a hospital room. But after everything that's happened today, I didn't want to wait. The most important thing is that we're here together—you and me and our baby girl."

Then he leaned over to kiss her. It was a gentle brush of his lips on hers, fleeting and soft and infinitely sweet.

As much as she enjoyed the kiss, she wanted to hear him say the words again—if he'd, in fact, said them the first time and she wasn't having some kind of drug-induced hallucination.

But as he continued to kiss her, she remembered what Grace had said and she realized her mother-in-law was right. She'd been too hung up on wanting to hear the words that she'd missed seeing the proof of his love in all the little things he said and did. Like right now.

She sighed softly, contentedly as he eased his lips from hers.

"I really do love you, Tess."

And suddenly her heart felt as if it was going to burst right out of her chest.

"I know it took me a while to realize it but it's true and if you'll marry me—I'll spend the rest of my life proving it to you."

It was the longest explanation of his emotions he'd ever given and Craig had never been as nervous as he was in that moment, waiting for Tess to respond to his declaration.

When she finally did speak, it was only to say, "Did you just ask me to marry you?"

"Yes."

"But we're already married."

He should have known she would get caught up in the technicalities.

"I know," he said. "But you were pregnant when I asked you the first dozen times and I know you think that was the only reason I proposed. And maybe at the time it was. But I've been thinking about all the reasons I want you to be my wife now and—" he pulled out a folded page out of his pocket "—I made a list."

"You're kidding?"

"Nope." He unfolded the paper and handed it to her.

He'd written a title at the top: Reasons I Want You to Marry Me. Then there was an itemized list numbered one through twenty-five, each line reading simply "I love you."

She looked at the list, then at him and back at the page again. But she didn't say anything.

"I could have written a hundred pages with the same words," he told her, "and they still wouldn't begin to describe how much I really do love you, Tess. Maybe I'm the world's biggest idiot for taking so long to figure it out but now that I have, I know that I want to spend every day of the rest of my life proving it to you.

"And I want to marry you again—to renew our vows—just because we love each other."

Still she hesitated and he felt his hope begin to fade. Maybe this was a bad idea. Maybe he'd waited too long. Or maybe he was rushing this—considering that she'd just had a baby and was recovering from emergency surgery. Or maybe as he was realizing how much he loved her, she'd realized she didn't love him anymore.

"That is," he said, "if you still love me."

This time when she glanced up from the paper in her hand he saw the depth of emotion in her eyes.

"I didn't choose to fall in love with you," she reminded him. "And I couldn't choose to stop even if I wanted to. But my feelings haven't changed.

"Or maybe they have. Because I love you even more now than I did then. So if you really want to get married again my answer is definitely yes."

"I really want to get married again," he assured her. "Because I've finally realized how lucky I am to have you—and I'm never going to let you go."

Then he cupped her face in his palms and pressed his lips to hers in a kiss filled with hope and love and promises. A kiss that was interrupted by the indignant cry of a newborn baby who wanted her daddy to know he was going to have to share mommy's attention.

Craig reluctantly eased away to look down at their baby girl. "She's probably hungry."

"She must have worked up an appetite—it's hard work being born."

"She certainly didn't do it the easy way," Craig

agreed, watching as Tess unbuttoned her gown to put the baby to her breast.

Gracie rooted around for a moment before she found the nipple, but when she did, she latched right on and began to suckle. It was the most amazing thing Craig had ever seen—his beautiful wife nursing their beautiful daughter.

"I thought it would be harder than that," Tess murmured, stroking a finger gently over the soft, downy hair on top of Gracie's head.

"Some things are just natural," he told her.

And he knew now without a doubt that, for him, loving Tess was one of those things.

Epilogue

Tess lifted the flap of the envelope, pulled out two airline tickets. "What's this?"

"Your anniversary present," Craig said and smiled at her. "Two weeks in Barbados, just me and you."

"What about the kids?"

"Grandma and Grandpa Richmond are looking forward to having their house turned upside down by our rugrats."

"For two whole weeks?" Tess couldn't believe anyone would volunteer for such a momentous undertaking. Gracie was now nine and a half years old, the twins—Eryn and Allie—were almost seven and Lucy had just turned four. Of course, their grandparents thought they were all little angels. Well, two weeks under the same roof would certainly change *that* opinion.

"I thought we deserved to do something special for

our tenth anniversary." He slipped his arms around her waist and drew her closer. "Or is it only our ninth?"

"Both." They had renewed their vows, as Craig had wanted, on the first anniversary of their wedding.

"So, what do you think? Are you ready to ditch our kids for two weeks alone with me?"

After ten years, the passion between them had not dimmed and she was very much looking forward to the opportunity to spend some uninterrupted time with her husband. She tossed the tickets aside to link her hands behind her husband's neck. "Definitely."

"I love you, Tess."

And just like the first time he'd ever said those words to her, her heart expanded with so much joy she thought it might burst. "I love you, too."

"Remember all the sightseeing we did on our first honeymoon?" he asked.

"Yes."

He grinned lasciviously. "Good. Then we don't have to do all of that again."

"So what will we do for two whole weeks?"

"It will be my very great pleasure to show you," he whispered the words against her mouth before deepening the kiss.

She let her eyes drift shut, felt herself drowning in a myriad of sensations. Would she ever get used to the explosive currents that raced through her at his simplest touch?

She didn't think so, but they had the rest of their lives together to find out for sure.

* * * * *